in the arms of saturn

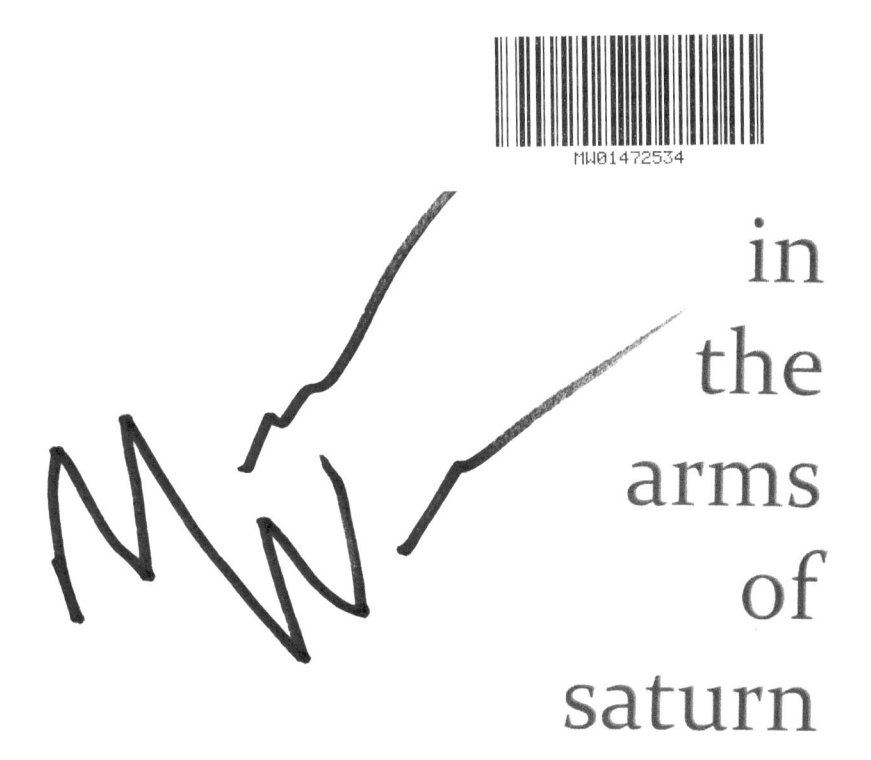

michael wilford

5 BID PRESS

A Five Bid Press Book

In the Arms of Saturn
Copyright 2020 Michael Wilford
Cover Design by 5 Bid Press

All rights reserved.

ISBN: 979-8-698856-83-2

5bidpress.com
theothermichaelwilford.com

For Vickie
as most tend to be

*In memory of the departed.
My chain of souls...*

Ralph Gustavsen - 9/25/1967 - 11/14/2011

Virginia "Nannie" Yorke - 8/16/1917 - 5/31/2012

Richmond "Bumpy" Yorke - 1/16/1935 - 12/1/2016

David Wilford - 8/12/1961 - 9/13/2018

Louise Belanger - 1/9/1936 - 2/24/2019

Brenda Lewis - 11/24/1947 - 9/4/2019

I'll see you again on the other side.

*Special thanks to
Ginny Estes...*

*For helping me get out of my head
when it seemed I wasn't coming out on my own.*

*For lifting me up when I
was insecure about my art.*

*And above all else,
for giving me the most amazing
daughter in the world.*

This is a work of fiction.

It deals with real places, which I've fictionalized to a degree.

It deals with religious subjects, but is intended to be objective.

It deals with real life trauma, born of my mind and forged through personal experience.

There has never been a fire at Portsmouth Naval Shipyard as described in these pages.

Twisted Oak, Maine is the creation of my friend, Earl Yorke.

-MW

"You become. It takes a long time."

Margery Williams Bianco

"I do not fear death. I had been dead for billions and billions of years before I was born, and had not suffered the slightest inconvenience from it."

Mark Twain

"The universe is a big place, perhaps the biggest."

Kurt Vonnegut

wake
up
mark
you're
dead

WAKE UP, MARK. You're dead.

A part of me stirs. My mind feels at once ancient and new as it reaches across the formless black of...

Where am I?

Mark. Follow my voice.

No. This isn't real. I can't identify the woman speaking. Names like Elora, Shannon, Kelly, and Mallory pass through my mind. I know them all intimately... somehow... but here in the darkness, wherever it is that I am, I cannot attach a face to any of them.

But it is, the voice persists, *you've returned to us. It's okay to be confused—*

I'm not dead! I return, anger and frustration distilled suddenly into a hollow tantrum. My voice is swallowed in the crushing silence of this place.

The woman doesn't speak again. After a few moments I stop trying to make sense of the enveloping darkness, I cease trying to find shapes in the murk. Where was I before? What had I been doing? I remember... snow.

No. Not snow.

Blood.

Blood on the pavement. Not mine. No, this is the blood of Nathan Kelson slowly oozing through the macadam of Beech Street, filling every pore in a halo around his head. He looks broken and folded over on his back, an earbud still hooked over one ear, dub-step music pumping so loudly that I can hear it over the shrieking voices in the distance and the sigh of my RAV4 cooling down.

His body convulses, suddenly informing me that he lacks control over himself. All that remains is the soul slowly escaping through his wide, staring eyes, still glistening with the elation of his runner's high. A foot twitches, a newly broken-in Brooks Ghost running shoe upon it. The same brand I use for running.

I step away from the car, unaware that my phone is still in my hand until it begins to vibrate. Lifting it to view at my hip, I send my wife's call to voicemail and lock the handheld before clipping it back to my belt. As the wind gusting over the Piscataqua River bombards me with scents of salt and seaweed, I turn my attention back to the man I'd just struck with my car, suddenly and disturbingly grateful I'd only been reading the text that had distracted me from the road and hadn't been in the process of answering it.

Anxiety swells in my chest, branching out through my body like the spider's web of bloodied cracks in my windshield. Almost against my will, my feet carry me toward the man, stepping around the still expanding puddle of blood. Additional footsteps are heard behind me as rubber soles and bare feet carry concerned witnesses toward the scene where they'll soon glimpse a real-life corpse.

An ambulance siren pierces the mild spring air somewhere far off.

I come to stand over the still trembling, still living body. I gaze down at his face, his eyes anchored upon an unblemished sky as blood runs into his eyebrows and down the bridge of his nose. Some of it pools in his left eye socket, though he doesn't seem aware and does not try to blink it away. Not even reflexively.

A woman approaches behind me, stepping into my peripherals. Her hands press immediately to her face, muffling the inevitable gasp as she beholds the shattered person beneath us. She steps back and away, out of sight, only to be replaced by several more people. The sirens grow louder in the distance, somehow more urgent. They are joined by several others of fluctuating patterns.

I'm going to prison, I think in that nagging voice that always seems to add obvious, crushing commentary during moments like this. Not that I've ever had a moment *quite* like this.

A hand grips my shoulder. A voice asks if I'm all right.

Am I hurt? No. Am I all right? Decidedly not.

I say nothing, my gaze still fixed on those vacant eyes, waiting for them to suddenly lock with mine. But they don't. Instead, I watch as the last ember of consciousness dulls and snuffs itself out, I watch as Nathan Kelson gives up the ghost.

It's another two minutes before the ambulance arrives. I'm frozen over the corpse. I haven't moved, as if moored to it by my own anxiety. As the earsplitting, strobing vehicle screeches onto Beech, my eyes lift for the first time in what feels like hours from the body. The ambulance slows and approaches beneath a canopy of whiffling leaves so dense it casts an unbroken slab of shadow over the street, surrendering to the sun on the corner where I stand. Where I've just taken an innocent life.

All at once the sirens cut out and the ambulance comes to a halting stop feet from the corpse. Such precision leaves me aware on a certain level that these paramedics are veterans. As the doors swing open and their boots clap the pavement, I see their faces through the windows. A man and a woman, the man short and stocky with a block face. Wrestler build. He is clean-shaven, the first creases of old age running across his brow and out from his eye sockets. The lines arch over the dome of his bald head. The woman comes around the passenger side. She is mid-twenties with long, black hair. Her body is slender. *A runner's body*, I think. She dashes ahead of the man, who seems already to know that things are beyond their capabilities.

The paramedics crouch before the body, urging onlookers back as they set their orange cases on the ground, unzipping them. Touch registers at my hip. The woman's hand easing me gently back before returning hastily to her partner. They produce a large plastic bubble, a breathing apparatus with a cup that is pressed around the man's nose and mouth. The woman works this while the man gingerly repositions the body and goes to work searching for a pulse. As they fight the good fight, the other sirens grow louder.

Suddenly a police cruiser, one of the new silver Chargers the Eliot Police replaced their Crown Vics with, turns the corner and roars down the darkened corridor. Seconds later another cruiser, almost identical, only this one belonging to the Kittery PD, turns onto Beech from the opposite direction. The sirens cut out, leaving only the sounds of concerned voices and running engines beneath the loud, urgent medical jargon of the paramedics.

The cruisers make barricades of themselves, blocking both lanes as they maneuver to an idling halt. Somewhere off in the distance the shriek of another siren signals the approach of additional emergency personnel. My gaze falls to the ground as if I might somehow avoid what comes next by acting oblivious. Bloody footprints stamp the pavement. I must have inadvertently backtracked through one of the puddles as the paramedic moved me.

I feel as though I've violated this man further.

A voice, distant and commanding, almost zealous, "I need everyone to move back and away – all the way back down to that row of hedges. Sir, if you can't bring that dog under control—"

Ah, yes, the barking of a dog somewhere in the din.

Voices blend as myriad questions are voiced simultaneously. No answers come, only the repeated directive to back away to the row of hedges.

Polished boots step into my vision. Neatly pressed blue pants, creased perfectly down the middle of each leg. I'm aware suddenly that this will be *my* cop, and I retreat further into myself. A voice comes unintelligible and barely perceptible from somewhere worlds away. It sounds like the voice of a neighbor through a shared wall. The officer finishes speaking and waits for me to respond. He delays only a few seconds before gripping me gently by the biceps, waiting silently until my eyes find his.

"Sir," the officer speaks, I assume repeating his words from before. "Sir is this your vehicle?"

I follow his finger, noting a porcelain hand garnished with freckles, pointed toward my silver RAV. I nod, feeling absent from reality. My eyes find his again. I search his face, also pale, also dabbled with freckles. Red sideburns, little more than stubble, poke out from beneath his navy-blue hat. The lines on his face help me place him in his early fifties.

Nowhere in him do I sense preconceived judgment, unlike the cop still barking at gawkers along the periphery of the scene. My cop seems only to be doing his job.

"How about we walk away from all this...?" the officer says, gesturing toward the corpse as though it's nothing more than a dislodged bumper.

This helps cool the building storm in me, though the fires of anxiety continue to spread through my body. As he leads me behind my car, I think I see his eyes go to the phone clipped to my belt a few times. Paranoia inks into my emotional cocktail.

"Can I get your name?" The officer produces a leather-bound pad from a pocket.

Just like in the movies, I think.

In a weak voice, little more than a whisper, I tell him my name is Mark Wells. I run a hand nervously across my bald, stubbled head, feeling the usual sinking stomach as it reaches the smooth area at the crown. I've been shaving my head scorched-earth style for the better part of a decade.

No man should have to cope with the onset of pattern baldness in his twenties, let alone its lasting effects at age 32.

"Wells..." he chews my name over thoughtfully for a moment. "You aren't one of Eric Wells' boys are you?"

My heart sinks at the thought of my father, lost when I was sixteen in a shop fire at the Shipyard. He'd saved three others before venturing back in, never to reemerge. It's an event that nobody in this town, especially the police and other emergency personnel who'd attended it, seem inclined to forget.

"Yes," I answer simply, unsure what else he wants me to say.

For a moment the cop persona evaporates, the man's eyes glistening as he seems to return to the night of the fire in his mind. "I was there that night. I'm sorry about your dad." He gazes wistfully toward the river before the shriek of a young girl from the sidelines regrounds him. "So... um... what happened here, Mr. Wells?" He's already scrawling, eyes on the pad.

My mouth cracks open. Somehow I manage to say, "I..." before trailing off and surveying the sharp corner at Beech Street where the shadows are chased so abruptly away by the glaring sunlight. For a moment I think of how perfectly arranged everything is, every element, for just this sort of accident.

"If you need a moment..."

"I... I was coming around the corner. The sun was in my eyes. I didn't see the man until it was too late." Most of this is true. The part I don't add is that I had my phone in-hand and was reading a text from an old girlfriend, a woman with whom I'd grudgingly settled for friendship. Elora Kennedy. My lost love. The irony is that she hardly ever texts me out of the blue. It's usually I who initiate contact.

Most often after a few drinks.

"Was the man in the road, on the shoulder?"

"I—I don't..."

The officer pauses with his pen tip millimeters from the pad. Despite his unassuming manner, he seems just now to remember that I've been struggling, understandably, with all of it. Professional indifference is shed for what feels like genuine sympathy, a rare commodity these days. "I know you've just been through a lot. Try to remember best you can. We're just trying to put this together."

I swallow against a lump in my throat, my gaze sweeping over the paramedics who've ceased revival efforts, now tending the body with sullen faces. The woman rounds the ambulance with defeat slogging her steps, shoulders drooped. She returns hugging a white blanket, which she drapes over the corpse while her partner muscles a gurney out of the back of the ambulance.

Looking back to the officer, I draw a long breath, "He was partway into my lane. Not off the road and not in the middle. It's a tough corner, I run it all the time myself. You avoid the loose pavement to keep from rolling an ankle. The sun was in my eyes... I didn't see him."

"Were you speeding?"

I immediately answer no, a little too hastily perhaps, but it's the truth.

Other cruisers roll up, additional men in uniform urging onlookers back to the hedges. My anxiety tightens like a belt across my chest as they begin separating witnesses, I assume to preserve the independence of their statements. Other onlookers are urged to leave the scene. Someone has set up orange cones and strung yellow tape around the roadside. A new cop is walking the scene, photographing the corpse and gored pavement through a long-barreled camera lens.

Radio chatter burps from the walkie-talkie on my officer's belt. He grips the receiver on his shoulder and answers with a string of cryptic code-talk. He backs away, eyes on my license plate, and scrawls additional notes. I wonder why he hasn't done this already. Is he green? He can't be if he was at the fire sixteen years ago.

Lifting his cap and scratching at red stubble on his head, he steps back to me. "I'll need your personal information. Is there anything else you can tell me about this incident?"

He's referring to the event as an incident and not an *accident*. I try to shrug it off, telling myself I'm being paranoid. Nothing about this exchange suggests I'm about to be arrested.

I fill out a statement form, providing my name, address, phone number, email, all the usuals. Beneath the personal information section is an area of about twenty condensed lines. Barely enough space to describe what I'd eaten for lunch, let alone summarize the events that transpired here minutes ago. But I try just the same, summarizing in my own longhand exactly what had happened. I'm careful not use the word *phone*. By the time I finish, Nathan Kelson is on a gurney guided by stone-faced paramedics around the ambulance and over the loose chunks of concrete.

time
is
ours
to
conduct
here

THESE MEMORIES ARE of no consequence here, Mark. You don't need to torment yourself with them.

Memories? I just ran that man down with my car!

Oh really? Though I can't see the owner of the voice, there's a simpering to it that makes me feel like I'm being addressed by a superior.

I need to lawyer up. They'll want my phone records and—

Mark, try to calm down.

How can I calm down? My life is going to be ruined, Kelly is going to leave me – no, no I'll be going to jail!

Hollow laughter is shot into and seized by the echoless ether. Not malicious, nor judgmental… more like the sound of an adult amused over a child's innocent naivete.

Let's try something different, the woman says after she's had her laugh. All at once I feel a warming touch at the bottom of me. It feels like my very soul is set aflame with love. As she speaks again I squint against a blinding light suddenly building around me—

Around us?

Time is ours to conduct here.

I'm in my driveway at home, weeks after the accident. Standing before me is the same cop who'd taken my statements at the scene of Nathan Kelson's untimely end. I've seen him a few times since, during interviews at the Kittery Police Department where the Shipyard fire edged its way into nearly every conversation (always revisited reverently by those whose careers it had apparently defined). During my brief and almost trifling court appearance, I was charged with Involuntary Vehicular Manslaughter. This usually carries a minimum three-year prison sentence, but it became quite clear through further interviews and litigation that my last name and its connection to the worst tragedy in the history of Kittery, Maine, had garnered leniency from the prosecution and judge.

In her odd dissertation, the judge actually referenced the fire.

I ended up paying a sum of $10,000 in damages, which felt paltry, but I wasn't about to insist on a more severe sentence.

"I was still cutting my teeth, just out of the academy when that fire broke out," my auburn-haired cop says, gazing thoughtfully over the neighborhood cul-de-sac where a pair of kids argue over a yellow plastic shovel in a patch of grass. "A lot of people call it Kittery's Nine-Eleven."

I simply nod along with him, anxious to see him and the rest of Kittery PD forever removed from my life. I don't want to talk about the fire, nor do I care what it means to him as a first-responder. All that matters is my father died in that fire running back in for what would have been his fourth life saved. I've shamelessly allowed their sympathies and nostalgia to taint a case that should have landed me behind bars.

The officer seems to extract something from my silence. He looks me up and down appraisingly before tossing a glance back to his cruiser, slanted across my driveway as though he'd lacked the time needed to park properly. His lips purse thoughtfully, bleaching at the edges and rendering them pale as the rest of his porcelain face. He fishes a yellow slip from his breast pocket, a carbon copy of the report he initially took at the scene, I imagine.

"Here," he holds it out to me. The silence between us does its own talking. It says, *This is the end. With this slip of paper your world of hurt goes away.*

I can feel Kelly's eyes on me through the picture window of our gray cape. I feel my wife's hatred, her disappointment at having missed an easy out on our marriage.

My world of hurt isn't going away. It's set to swell.

"Thank you," I say, voice as bland as the dinner that awaits me tonight, assuming Kelly is functional enough to cook. I take the paper and fold it with feigned reverence before sliding it into the pocket of my jeans. "I wish... well, more than anything I wish things had turned out differently."

He takes a tentative step toward me. Emerging in his body language is the sudden impulse to hug me, and I recoil from it in a way that darkens my officer's face. His body grows rigid. He glances longingly at his cruiser for a moment, then back to me. "You did nothing wrong, son." Palpable hesitation now, so strong I can feel it wafting off him, then, "You've been through enough as it is."

There it is, exactly what I could have done without: the firm-ish confirmation that I'd been granted leniency because my father had the good grace to die heroically in a fire.

"Thank you," I croak, saying it once more and silently willing my cop back toward his cruiser. The folded leaf of carbon paper seems to gather weight in my pocket as I watch him backtrack a couple paces.

He hesitates again, something falls off between us, and his face darkens as if crossed by shadow. I'm not sure if he's reading something in me or still sifting back through the night of the fire, the night that defined the careers of him and so many other local cops. Then, all at once, his face clears like chalk scrubbed from a slate. "You take care, Mr. Wells. If you need anything else just give me a call."

And just like that he's gone.

i'm not dead

YOU SEE. EVERYTHING turned out just fine.

You speak like this already happened.

No, it simply is happening. *Time is relative here... relative to the soul conducting its flow.*

That makes no sense.

It would if you'd simply accept that you're dead.

I'm not dead.

For some time there is only crushing, black quiet. Then a face grows within a slowly materializing corona of light, a face I simultaneously love and hate.

Kelly is long past her third glass of wine. The third glass consistently marks a divergence in the mood of my wife of five years. While the first two simply warm up the engine, the third sets the pistons of contempt pumping in her mind, and she almost always seems to seek me out to feed on the scraps of my dignity.

I've counted seven glasses drained out of a box in the fridge since she started at 9am. With the sound of my cop's Charger snarling out of the cul-de-sac, off in search of more Shipyard fires, she turns her hateful gaze upon me as I close the front door.

"So thassit?" she asks, already slurring at three in the afternoon. It's a Friday, so I suppose it's passable. The other days of the week she spends getting hammered are tended by their own excuses, and there are *always* excuses.

She's sprawled on the charcoal upholstery of our sectional couch, gaze shifting constantly to the glass of wine a mere arm's reach away on the coffee table. Her salted blonde hair is a greasy, snarled mess falling over the receding bumps of her breasts. She's been determined to subside on an exclusive diet of alcohol for the last three years, long enough now to have its lasting effects presented. Where once her body was athletic and toned, she's now gaunt, almost *hollowed out* in places. There's little left of the girl I'd met at UNH almost a decade ago.

Kelly sighs, struggling out of her alcoholic laze with just enough effort to snatch the wine glass from the table, spilling runs of topaz-colored liquid down its stem that dabble the hardwood (not to mention the fabric of her sweater). She lets loose a long sigh, into which all of her loathing flows, before tipping the glass to her lips and draining what's left down her throat.

"You're lucky," she says, considering the glass for a moment before heaving herself up and brushing past me toward the kitchen, a scowl of put-out inconvenience on her face. She wishes I'd been put away, removed conveniently from her life so she could avoid the trifling business of divorce.

She vanishes into the kitchen. The sound of the fridge opening and fresh wine bubbling into Kelly's glass registers as I collapse on the couch, unsure what to do with myself. When after a few minutes Kelly fails to return, I assume she's gone upstarts to succumb to the usual late-afternoon pass-out, and fish my phone from my pocket.

Pressing the power button, my lock screen shows a picture of me and Kelly on vacation a few years earlier. We're sitting shaded by a cluster of palm trees in Labadee, Haiti, each lifting umbrella-garnished drinks, beaming at the camera. It's like a portal to a different time. A *happier* time, before it grew obvious we couldn't conceive.

I wonder why I haven't changed the picture to something else. Our cat is pretty damned photogenic.

The thought passes. I slide my thumb across the touch screen and enter my secret code. The text app shows a red notification, a new message from my boss, Tim.

Hope ur holding out ok, bud. Don't worry about things here, we've got the world of computers held at bay until u come back. Let me know if u need anything or want to grab a drink.

I've always enjoyed the pally relationship we have. Though we're separated by more than twenty years in age, in my experience Network Techs are nearly all the same. Regardless of how many years we've been on this earth, we're all fifteen-year-old geeks at heart.

I close the text without answering. As much as I care for Tim and appreciate the gesture, I feel it's best to keep shying away from the outside world to maintain what I hope he perceives as thoughtful isolation. As my text history reappears, my gaze falls upon the text from Elora. The one that I was reading as I took Nathan Kelson's life. I've read over our correspondence at least a dozen times since the accident.

Her: *Hey there, bestie* – I hate it when she draws attention to the fact that we're friends and nothing more – *me and the band have a gig coming up in North Conway the last Thursday of June. It would be great to see you!*

Me: *I'll see what I can do. Weekdays are tough, but I'd love to see you, too!*

I tend to use the word *love* excessively with Elora. I'm not sure if this is a subconscious thing or what. In any event, she either doesn't catch the subtext or ignores it like so many others walking around with men's hearts leashed cruelly behind them.

Her: *Aw, c'mon! Wouldn't it be great to hang out again? I haven't seen you in a while. I'll be staying overnight. The hubby has to work so he'll be staying in Mass. We'd really be able to catch up.*

It's this last part that gets me. I'm not sure if she's a master manipulator or what, but it's clear that she's fishing, and she's using the right bait to hook a pathetically hopeful/hopeless Mark Wells fish. I agree immediately.

After all of this, Elora responds: *Cool. Ttyl.* She knows she has me, and I know on the most horrible, subconscious level that nothing is going to happen. Still, I hope.

This was well over a month ago. Crickets since.

I finish parsing our text history and lock my phone with a sigh. Again I feel the weight of the yellow carbon paper in my pocket.

The crash of a glass shattering somewhere off the kitchen is followed by the skittering of paws across the hardwood. Eventually the cat comes barreling out of the kitchen, running from some unseen accident with Kelly.

Suddenly the years we've logged as husband and wife feel like some unseen accident.

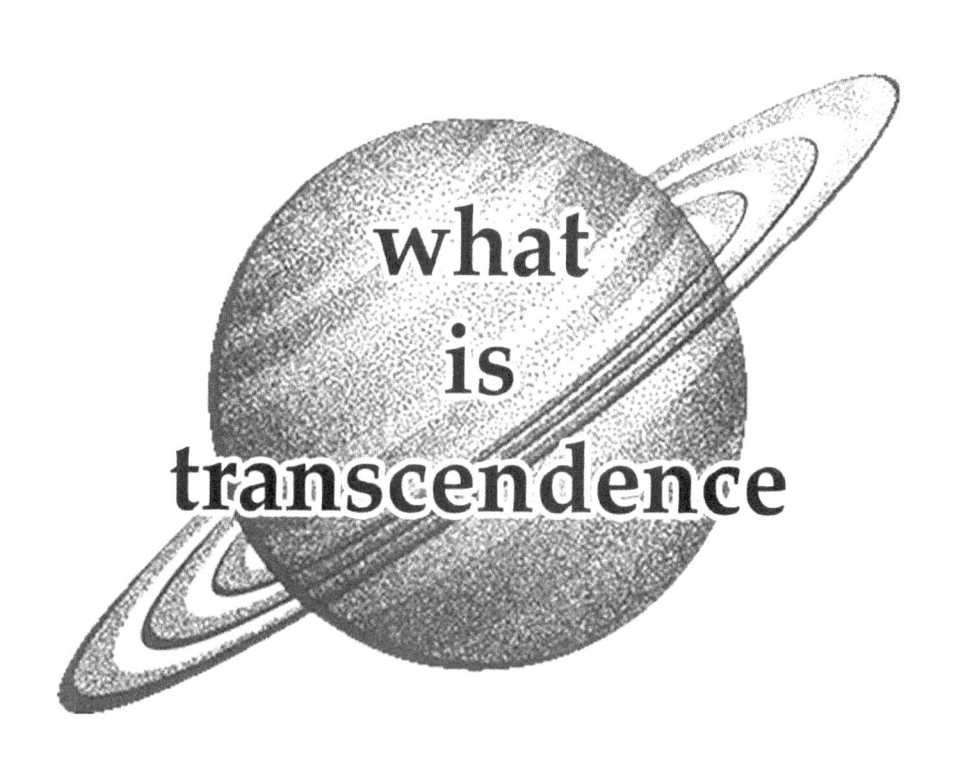

what is transcendence

SHE'S YOUR SOULMATE, Mark. You've no reason to allow the events of your life to affect how you see her here, says the voice.

Elora Kennedy is my soulmate, I return reflexively.

The voice assumes its simpering character again. *Of course she is. As I am. As is your boss Tim for that matter.*

I'm at a loss for words, mostly due to the cumbersome weight of nothingness still pressing down upon me. For the first time since I've woken here, I want to trust the voice.

We meet here, rejoin, and when we're ready we return together to life. The lessons we learn, the consciousness we build as we approach Transcendence… we do it all together.

What is Transcendence?

The voice goes silent, but the silence speaks as though penetrated by unintelligible words, all at once here and nowhere. It says I'm still latched helplessly to my former life.

But I'm not dead.

Kelly passes out early, just as I knew she would. By 7:00 she's rematerialized with no sign of having cleaned up the mystery accident that had disturbed the cat. She's settled into one of the crooks of our sectional, heavy eyelids working against her as some sitcom laugh track blares from the TV. In this moment I can't help picturing her with the baby in which she'd placed the entire stock of our marriage. The baby that would never come from her body. Our marriage was rendered loveless once upon a time in a single visit to the OB/GYN. There the prognosis of a bicornuate uterus hit my wife with the same existential trauma millions of poor souls unable to conceive have endured for centuries, and she was no less crushed.

By 7:30 nearly every part of Kelly is sinking into the couch as she watches the TV with glazed, absent eyes. I can't help picturing her holding our would-be baby, unable to channel the energy to lift her wine glass, let alone keep the infant from being eaten by the couch with her.

My resentment flares. I focus on my breathing, watching her eyelids roll down, only for her to emerge from the fringe of sleep in a panic moments later. It's during her second such awakening that a spark seems to fire in her mind, informing her that her body needs more wine.

She emerges from the sleep that will ultimately claim her for another second, reaching feebly toward the coffee table but struggling to free herself from the groove she's sunken into. After a moment she gives up and falls back into the crook, eyes already closed.

I'm at the opposite end of the couch, tablet in hand, trying to convince myself my stomach isn't too full for a seventh beer. For all the judgement I've laid at Kelly's feet today, I'm determined to pass out as well.

My gaze lifts from the tablet as a gusting crosswind blows through the room from the open window overlooking our fenced-in backyard. It whistles along the eaves while blades of grass, long overdue for a mow, are swept in waves. For a moment I'm lost in thought, noting how the playful wind operates with its own innocent consciousness. I want to join its mischief, an impulse I fail to fully grasp.

Looking back to the tablet, I close my e-reader app and snatch up the TV remote, killing the sitcom laughter. Returning to the tablet, my finger hovers briefly over the Facebook app as my better judgement reminds me that I'm drunk and should avoid social interaction.

Kelly is sawing wood now, no doubt dreaming of a reality where my relationship with a fire that forever shook this town hadn't prevented me from being sent upriver. She's been further swallowed by the sectional, cocooned in her own alcoholic way.

The depression swirls like black ink through the ever-present guilt I carry now. I've escaped jail, yet my life has never felt more dismal, devoid of meaning. Here I am, drunk beside a woman I barely look at anymore, who made no effort to hide her dismay at my striking good luck, if you could call it that. It used to be I drank to celebrate the good times, not to forget the bad. I've fallen so far, and here beside me is the physical revelation of what my life might become if I can't pull myself together.

I tap the Facebook icon as my attention pries itself from Kelly. There are no notifications. No surprise. I tap the messenger icon and scroll through my direct-message feed with Elora. Most of them have started exactly like this, with me feeling drunk and confident, ready to drown her in heavy subtext, hoping she'll come around and realize she's loved me all this time. It's so decidedly *teenage boy*.

I tap the text entry box and the onscreen keyboard pops up. I don't know what I'm going to say, only that it's important I say something. Tonight is the night I spill it all.

Not once do I consider the former win over my own terrible judgement as I form my message: *I'm in love with you. I know you know it.* The words flow into the box without a single typo, and I pause with my index finger over the Enter key. I've entered this arrangement of words hundreds of times, easily. And just as I've done for years and years, I press and hold the Backspace key until the text box is empty.

My news feed is the usual fare: pictures of food, pictures of friends hitting the sauce on their Friday night (not that I judge), and pictures of small children enjoying milestones that billions before them have reached over the course of some 200,000 years, give or take a millennia or two. I hate these people and I hate their children. I suspect most people unable to have children of their own see posts of this nature in similar shades of black, covetous greed, not that there's anything wrong with *my* plumbing.

I scroll disinterestedly through my news feed, wondering why I subject myself to this. The tidy, drama-free lives of others are as artificial in social media as the over-the-counter dye Kelly's used to conceal the gray threading her hair since college. As I'm about to swipe the app closed, however, my eyes settle upon a link shared by an old acquaintance of mine from high school.

My chest tightens.

Additional Memorial Service for Nathan Kelson to be Held at Ogunquit Beach Accommodating Unexpected Overflow of Mourners

My finger moves toward the link, entirely self-guided. Facebook retreats to the side bar as my web browser opens to the write up, equal parts obituary and newsletter even though the accident is now well over a month behind me.

Nathan Kelson, 35 years-old, of Eliot, Maine died on May 4th, 2019 in Eliot as the result of injuries sustained when he was struck by an automobile while running.

Nathan was the loving husband of Mallory Kelson, 34, his high school sweetheart and wife of fourteen years. The two were married in York, Maine on May 3rd, 2005. Mallory was the center of his world, though she was not the only person touched by his love. Anyone fortunate enough to have known him, whether it be through various charity runs he participated in or within the local surfing community, was also touched by this wonderful man.

Nathan was born in York, Maine on January 9th, 1985 to his parents, Zachary and Melanie. He was a graduate of York High School and of the University of New Hampshire with a degree in Creative Writing. Over the course of his writing career he was published in Yankee Magazine and Downeast Magazine in addition to holding a staff position at the York Independent.

In addition to his wife, Nathan is survived by his younger siblings, Morgan and Sophie. He was very close with both of them and an amazing uncle to their children.

Nathan loved the outdoors and did whatever he could to spend time outside. His passion for surfing was rivaled only by his love for running and skiing.

A memorial service was held for Nathan on Sunday, May 29th at Potter Memorial Chapel in York, Maine. Due to the overwhelming turnout, another service has been planned for June 19th at Ogunquit Beach. All who knew and loved him are welcome to attend. The ceremony will start at 9:00 A.M. and carry on until it is finished. Everyone is encouraged to bring along a tale to tell of Nathan, in addition to their surfboards.

I lay the tablet on the couch beside me, my gaze drawn to Kelly as if by some unseen force. I wonder what she'd write about *my* untimely death, if anything.

I need another beer. Perhaps a shot of whiskey.

Definitely a shot of whiskey.

I rise from the couch, glancing once more at a softly snoring Kelly, undisturbed by the light jostling of what has, on many nights, been her bed. Heavy drinking opens most lounge spaces up as crash-spots. My current favorite of hers is the wedge of rug hugging the toilet, the same rug that catches my pee when my aim isn't quite true.

Turning away, I slip silently toward the stairs that wind up into the kitchen, which is a tribute to the '70s in a way that only the artsy and woefully nostalgic appreciate. The walls are an erratic pattern of tan, lime, and khaki tiles over an anachronous, speckled-stone countertop. At its center is a Stonehenge of wine bottles from days-past, winking in the failing light of a westering sun.

I open the fridge and go for the crisper where I stash the beers I don't want Kelly to pilfer in the seldomly occurring events when she runs out of wine. When my hand emerges with a bottle marked 4.9% A.B.V. I shake my head at it and go pawing around for something stronger. The next bottle is an IPA, 9.2% A.B.V. Sold.

Next, to the shot of whiskey I've failed to forget.

I'm already retching as I extract the bottle of Jameson Black Barrel from the liquor cabinet under the peninsula. The need to get drunk (*er*) is stronger than my body's preemptive rejection of the liquor, though, and I pull the cork with a *thunk* that leaves me wanting to congratulate myself on my conviction.

No sooner do I have the bottle tipped to my lips does the sound of Kelly's ire explode out of the living room.

"What the *hell*, Mark?!"

My first thought is that something particularly earth-shaking has hit in the world of TMZ, but the television is still off. I'd been in hopes we wouldn't fight this evening, but there's very little I can do to banish the feeling that one is imminent. I have developed over the years an immensely precise barometer for Kelly's emotional climate.

"Mark, where *hell* are you?!" she yells again, the heart-halting rage in her voice emerging in a way that feels like the only truth I've ever known.

I freeze and consider moving quietly up into the bedroom and feigning sleep, but she's pissed and won't hesitate to shake me awake. In the absence of other options, I draw a shallow breath and hoist the bottle to my lips. What would have been a single shot is a good four glugs which burn all the way down.

The sounds of the coffee table scraping the hardwood, followed in short order by a glass shattering, reaches me before I have time to set down the bottle. My cowardly instincts rarely push fight over flight, and as her heavy footsteps slam across the living room floor, growing louder with her approach, my first impulse is to dive behind the peninsula and hide.

But I freeze in terror, already aware of what she's found.

Kelly staggers up the stairs and into the kitchen doorway, white knuckles showing in the hand gripping my phone. Strings of blonde hair are a gossamer veil over eyes gleaming with antipathy.

"What... what is it, Kel—"

"You know *damn well* what it is!" she cries. She takes the final step into the kitchen and holds up the phone. For a moment I think she's going to throw it at me. Instead, she lifts the screen, holding it inches from her face as she recites my correspondence with Elora in a slurring drawl, breaking into moments of perfect clarity only as her rage flexes inside. "I haven' see-you inawhile. I'll be-staying... *overnight*. The hubby has-ta work so... *he'll be staying in Mass* – what the hell?! Are you seeing this woman again?!"

I have nothing to feel guilty about aside from hiding this from Kelly. I haven't cheated on her, though I'm not sure if I'd pass on the option if Elora made a move. That alone is enough to assemble an incriminating look on my face, and judging by the deepening redness of Kelly's face, it shows.

Kelly holds the phone obstructing her mouth as she continues reading through every part of the conversation, ending with my accepting Elora's invitation to meet in North Conway. Kelly has known about Elora since we first met in college. When she first came across me chatting innocently with her online in the early days of our cohabitation, I glimpsed her intense jealousy with the instant revelation that it was all-consuming when properly agitated.

Kelly finishes reading and pauses, that perma-scowl I've come to know quite well frozen upon her face. Her lips press together, bleeding out their color at the margins as her nostrils flare above. Without warning she hurls the phone at me, missing my head by a good foot. The handheld soars across the dining room to where it bounces off the wall and clatters to the floor.

I don't dare go after it. My gaze returning to Kelly, I take a deep breath as she unloads years of poorly suppressed jealousy and paranoia.

"You've been seeing her all this time behind my back, haven't you?!"

It doesn't matter how I respond. She's decided that I've been cheating, so I say nothing. I hunker down and weather the storm like a proper coward, impressed as always at how the slurring in Kelly's speech always tapers off when she's engaged in a proper screaming fit.

"We made *vows* to each other, Mark. We promised to love and stay faithful to each other, and here you are about to drive to the White Mountains to be with another woman!"

It's all I can do to keep from reflexively defending Elora.

Kelly continues for another few minutes. She slathers on the condescension and judgement, informing me that she would never break our marriage vows by sleeping with someone else. She even clues me in that there have been opportunities, and suddenly I'm left wondering if she isn't reacting this way because of some secret, buried guilt.

When she finally starts to run out of steam her lecture circles around to its beginning, revisiting our Greatest Hits. I'm not sure if she simply lacks the clarity of mind to remember which topics she's addressed or if she's really trying to beat the point into me. Most likely an even mix of both. My gaze drifts longingly to the bottle of Jameson. My hand begins to reach for it seeing as Kelly shows no signs of slowing.

I take a longer pull than the last time as Kelly's distant voice is lost in the fuzz. I drink until the bottle is swatted out of my hands and topples over on the counter, spilling across the unopened mail and food wrappers on the peninsula. The bottle rolls in slow motion to the lip of the counter then falls to the floor, shattering.

Silence.

My attention returns to Kelly, now leaning forward and gripping the peninsula, eyes boring into mine. Through clenched teeth she whispers, "Get out."

that
was
the
end
with
her

KELLY'S SOUL STILL loves you, Mark. What happened then means little.

That was the end of my life with her. I don't question this. I also have no idea why I said it.

All in adherence to the lessons you each went back to learn.

The weight of the simpering voice's truth is oppressive, yet a part of me can sense something wrong, something abnormal here in this empty, formless… whatever.

Your soul is beginning to open. Try doing the same with your eyes.

What lesson could we possibly have learned from five years of wasted marriage? A flickering image cycles through my mind's eye like a slide on a View-Master. I see Kelly slumped and broken over a steering wheel, snow pinging off the cold gelatin of her death-fogged eyes.

There is more you need to understand, says the voice.

I'm too drunk to drive, and considering how I'm leaning against Kelly's black Forrester, walking isn't really an option either.

My destination is of course my mother's house. I have nobody else in the world outside of her and my brother Walter, who happens to be my only real prospect for a ride.

I navigate into my contacts and thumb his name a little too hard, though fortunately not enough to shatter the touchscreen. It rings a few times before he picks up, addressing me as lovingly and eloquently as ever, "Whassup, loser?"

We usually exchange this flavor of brotherly banter for a good ten or twenty seconds before moving onto the meat of the call, but I'm in no mood for it. "I need a ride to Mom's, man. Are you good to drive?" Among my brother's many hobbies, alcohol, weed, and Adderall feature prominently. I hope he's sober enough to drive.

"Kell-Well finally kick you out?" he asks, using the pet name friends and family always use for Kelly. Kelly Wells, Kell-Well. It rhymes. Hilarious.

I nod slowly, head swimming. "Yes. Can you come get me?"

There's a lengthy pause on the other end. Then, with the exaggerated voice one might use in the middle of a stretch, he says, "Yeah, I think I can manage. Any chance you can hook a brother up with a little gas money?"

I try to keep the receiver from picking up the lengthy sigh that comes in this moment. The distance between my house and Mom's (incidentally also *Walt's*) is less than five miles. I could walk it if I weren't so apt to trip over my own feet into traffic.

I shiver against a vision of Nathan Kelson's face, wreathed in wet crimson.

Walt may be fishing for easy cash, but in this moment I decide it's fair, all things considered.

"Yeah, man, I'll give you some gas money. Just get here before I pass out in the frigging driveway."

"What'chu drinking? If you wanna bring it over we can hit it—"

"Just come get me, man... *please.*"

Another pause. Walt's childishly wounded voice returns, "...Okay. Fine. I'll see you in a few."

"Thanks, Walt."

There's a beeping in my ear as the call ends. The world spinning, I bury the phone in my pocket where it won't get me into additional trouble and lift my attention self-destructively to the kitchen window, where I know she's watching me. For a moment, dual swirling images of the same window orbit one another before clarifying around the gaunt silhouette of my college sweetheart, barren in every regard. Her hands grip her hips, rendering her the shadowed semblance of an all-seeing eye set ruefully upon me.

I swivel away, still gripping the car. The sun has already dipped beneath the horizon in the distance, its colors striking defiantly into the sky in hues that burn behind the arching trestle of the Piscataqua River Bridge. I remain like this, meditating on the sky's diminishing color until at last the stuttering drawl of Walt's busted muffler rises in the distance. It cuts through the quiet stillness of the cul-de-sac, growing louder until at last his black VW Golf rounds the street corner.

Walt pulls into the driveway. From what I can see through the windshield, he's in typical form: curls of pressed blond bedhead over a black form-fitting tank top. I assume he's wearing pajama pants.

Walt flips me the bird. I return the gesture and shuffle toward the car through a gathering cloud of black exhaust that speaks to its terminal nature. I don't dare glance back at the kitchen window even though a part of me wants to. Not that it matters, I can feel Kelly's contemptuous eyes slithering over me just the same.

Bracing against the trembling vehicle, I walk the remaining feet to the passenger door.

"You think she's kicking you out for good this time?" Walt's gaze moves past me to the window as I collapse into the passenger seat. His eyes narrow a moment before returning to me, waiting for my answer as I extract an empty bottle of Rolling Rock from under me. The car reeks of marijuana and cigarette smoke. It's a wonder he's never gotten an O.U.I.

"I don't know, man," I answer. "Can we just go?"

Walt is, indeed, wearing pajama pants. The design is an absurd arrangement of *barrel o' monkeys* daisy-chained in garish shades of red, blue, and green. They fit over his wiry legs like parachute pants.

"You, uh, got that gas money you said you'd give me?"

I fight back against the sigh that threatens to come as I fish out my wallet. I offer a ten-dollar bill, which he accepts with a look of resigned disenchantment before shoving it into his pocket and battling with the aged transmission to throw the car into reverse.

My younger (and only) brother has been losing weight steadily since high school. Now he's just skin drawn tightly over bone from all the Adderall he takes, something we were both prescribed as teens but only I outgrew. I can tell when he's on it, and I can tell when he's finished burning through his prescription, usually well before it's due for refill. The drug makes two people of him, one hyper-focused to the point of obsession for the two weeks he's on, the other lethargic and palpably *spent* the two he's off.

I understand the addiction better than most given my own limited history with the drug. I ended up getting off of it before college because I knew it was something I'd need the rest of my life and didn't want it to latch onto me. The stuff makes anything you do the best thing you've ever done. It shapes your interests compulsively around any task; even vacuuming is so invigorating on Adderall that you don't ever want it to end.

Right now, Walt does not have it. His eyelids sag in a telling way as he navigates the clogged lanes of US-1 reaching through the Kittery Outlets. The interconnected pods flanking the highway bustle with clueless tourists, hardly paying attention to themselves as they dart from outlet to outlet.

Kittery is the last town before the Maine/New Hampshire border. It's the first place most tourists stop on their way toward the ocean. Here, crosswalks and traffic lights are interpreted as mere suggestions by those vacationing and summering.

"You really okay to drive?" I'm watching both Walt and the road with equal trepidation. Walt's head lifts from its former decline toward his lap. As I ask the question, head still fogged with beer and whiskey, I wonder exactly what I'll do if he answers no.

"I'm good," he says, self-consciously correcting his posture. "I'm good, man."

Walt slows the car as it approaches a light transitioning yellow to red. He stops a good fifteen feet from the white line. I've lost count of how many times I've wanted to sigh or roll my eyes since entering his car. I turn my gaze to the crosswalk two car-lengths ahead as a red-faced father shunts his family across US-1. My head presses against the passenger window and I close my eyes.

"Yo, we should stop at the liquor store and pick up something," Walt says.

"Sure, man." I'll probably puke my guts up if I have much more, but I don't care. At least with Walt it might take my mind off of the dumpster fire my life has become.

"They've got Fireball up there now. You in?"

My eyes slowly lift open on the clustered neon of recognizable fast-food restaurants. Fireball whiskey is all the rage with the party crowd these days. Perfect for teens and college kids yet to warm to the burn of straight whiskey or scotch. Walt is 27, placing him right at the fringe of that demographic. Though he's tried to get me into Fireball, which is a cinnamon-infused whiskey schnapps, I've never taken to it. At this point I've given up reminding him.

"Whatever, bro," I say.

"You, uh, think you might spot me for it?" he asks, gaze trained upon the road so he doesn't have to look me in the eye.

Only a moment's hesitation before asking for more money, and that's just like my brother. It probably won't be the last time tonight, especially once we're at Mom's and he's had a chance to consider which of his long-term "goals" might become *our goals*.

"Sure," I answer, trying to conceal the irritation threading my voice. I turn to look at him as the car rolls onward with the changing light. Walt lifts a hand absent-mindedly to his scalp, itching through his blond curls with the erratic energy of a junkie about to fix. This is a decidedly *druggy* tic. He reminds me of a flea-bitten stray. It's one of many patterns of behavior our mother either overlooks entirely or fails to understand. If Dad were alive he'd have straightened Walter out in a heartbeat, or so I tell myself. Walt probably wouldn't have been permitted to spiral at all if Dad hadn't died in that fire when I was 16 and Walter 11, but fate is often cruel.

Thoughts of Dad remind me that the annual ceremonies for those who'd perished were due in the fall. Every year the same speech. Every year the same faces, some remembering things with a fondness that speaks to their owners' characters.

This year I'll have all kinds of police to rub elbows with. Suddenly I feel like throwing up, and it's just in time as Walt brings the car to a leisurely stop outside the Son of a Birch convenience store, tossing expectant looks my way long before fighting with the car to wrench it into Park.

Now I get to stumble drunk into a convenience store to buy booze for my brother.

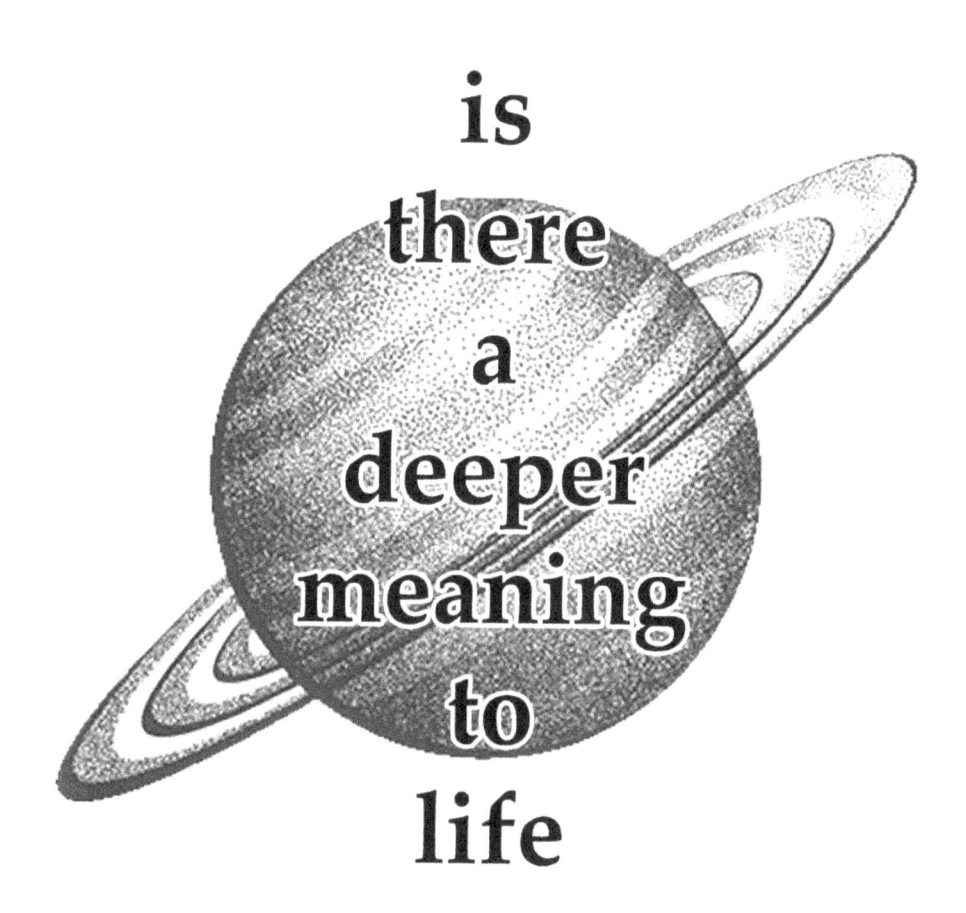

is
there
a
deeper
meaning
to
life

DAD? ARE YOU...

The sound of my voice alone is shocking despite its hollow, self-effacing cadence. I wait for the simpering voice to speak, but it remains silent, and I know it wants me to finish the question. It wants to hear me admit that I'm dead in asking if my father is present here.

You've no reason to be stubborn, the voice finally pokes through the ether. *Death is a celebration, like commencement. Mark, you've died and returned dozens of times since your soul was kindled, and each time it was when you'd finally understood the lesson of that life.*

Is there a deeper meaning to life? I ask, an image of Planet Saturn bubbling up through the clouds in my mind.

Transcendence is the only real meaning. The only true end-goal. When our lessons on Earth are finished, truly finished, and we go to God.

For some reason I think of Kelly, of the children we'd never have.

What about babies who die in the womb? What about children who die of cancer and leukemia?

The simpering character is back in the voice. *Some of us learn more quickly than others. Regardless of the contributing circumstances, each of our deaths comes when the soul recognizes its success in life.*

So I'm to accept that an infant who dies in the womb has somehow learned a lesson about life there?

Yes. You are to accept that, along with the real possibility that the loss is also part of the parents's lesson. The soul who grew in you for two months only to be lost could very well have been your mother or best friend, returned to Earth with *you to help with* your *lesson.*

A thought darker than anything I've ever known hits me, and I can't help withering beneath it. I open a mouth I know I don't have and ask the simpering voice: *What about people who commit suicide?*

A chill spreads through me, and suddenly I know I've been left alone for a bit.

Mom's cottage is nestled within a pocket of forest in Kittery, at the end of a well-driven, pot-holed dirt road in various states of neglect. The only light in this tree-shrouded corridor is that of a lone incandescent bulb, burning valiantly into the night through the whiffling foliage.

Walt is three deep into the Fireball nips I bought for him. As the car's suspension reckons with the potholes Walt has yet to fill, he seems to have forgotten his disappointment at my returning with nips instead of a handle.

I'm struck for a moment by Walt's coordination, steering with his knees leveraged against the bottom of the wheel and somehow able to drink without spilling a drop against the jostling car. I, meanwhile, place every effort I've got into keeping the contents of my stomach from joining the Rolling Rock bottle rattling around my feet.

Fortunately the ruts begin to smooth as the wilderness tapers, and the cottage comes into better view. The road curls into an oblong rotary, running up to the porch before doubling back. Sprawling in the center of the rotary is a white lilac bush, well cared-for in Dad's time though it's taken on a mangy character in its neglect. The lilacs have long flowered in that hurried, blink-of-an-eye space of time for which they're known. Withered bunches of flowers wash the car, shedding shriveled brown on the windshield as Walt coasts up to the cottage, already unscrewing another nip. The VW comes to a squealing stop behind Mom's parked minivan.

Eager to be out, I heave the door open and rise into the perfumed night. A breeze carrying the scents of flowers in bloom sweeps over me to play about in the foliage. Leaves flutter like summer's flirtatious whisper as branches rake the shingled roof of the cottage. The faraway baritone of car engines on I-95 is barely discernable to ears that haven't developed in this place.

Through the porch screen I catch the soft flicker of television light. Mom's probably asleep in her chair. It used to be you couldn't approach this place without her knowing about it. One of many behavioral oddities punctuating a resigned aging-out of her former roles as a mother and homemaker.

The car doesn't so much as sway as all 120 pounds of Walt steps out and starts toward the porch steps. As he ascends, emptying a fifth nip into his mouth, I follow, wanting to reach out in the most O.C.D. way and pluck the white paint chips flaking from the posts.

Walt walks to a purple Adirondack chair and plops down. Beside it is a small tempered glass table littered with empty bottles of Rolling Rock. They surround an ashtray overflowing with butts. From the pockets of his pajama pants he produces a pack of Marlboro Reds and a lighter. I pass by him as he lights up, feeling the rotting wood buckle under my feet. My gaze moves to the end of the porch where an outdoor dining table of matching tempered glass lists slightly toward the driveway, unable to find even footing on the bowing floorboards.

All that's changed since I was here for Easter are the cottage's advancing stages of disrepair. Walt is no traditional man of the house.

"Wanna butt?" Walt asks.

I halt, originally planning to bypass him entirely and go straight to Mom, but a cigarette sounds pretty good right now. Then I think of how it'll screw up my respiration during tomorrow's morning run. It's cute I still think that habit will endure when I haven't hit the pavement now for almost two months.

I decline politely. "Screw yourself." This is standard banter between us, especially when talk of cigarettes comes up. For a period of about four years I was a smoker – the Adderall days mostly. Walt likes to tempt me any chance he gets, knowing that a good chunk of the time I cave. If it weren't for my running, I'd have no power to resist at all.

My running. What was that anyway?

Walt chuckles as I continue past him toward the screen door, which is flimsy and duct-taped in places where its integrity is failing hardest. It swings back against my shoulder as I push my way inside, trying to keep as quiet as possible. This is dashed away by Mom's jingle bells hung from the inside knob; one of many familiar things I barely notice here.

More familiarities for my drunk eyes and nose arise as I step into the foyer. The mingling spices of leather and shoe polish are heavy enough to command their own presence. My right hand moves in the dark through garments swaying on an overburdened coat rack, searching for the always-concealed light switch. It conjures the sad ghost of a smile to my face as I think of my father, who'd decided to mount the hanger in such a terrible place. The odors of shoe polish are his, now gone sixteen years and still very much alive here.

I find the switch and throw it. A pair of incandescent lights flicker dimly to life, casting a gloss over the beige, 70's-era laminate reaching into the kitchen. I kick off my flip flops and step farther inside. The laminate gives beneath my bare feet in a way Dad always referred to as "broken-in."

I step into the kitchen, reaching unconsciously to my left for the light switch beside a humming, pea green refrigerator set in the wall. I pause, fingering the switch without throwing it. My gaze moves to the arched living room entryway. There I set eyes on Mom's thin form, draped in an afghan, reclined in her chair.

Curled in her lap is her black-and-white cat, Mouf, who regards me dismissively with the glare from the television catching in his eyes.

I step onto the brown, over-trodden fibers of the living room carpet. It feels greasy under my toes, probably hasn't been vacuumed since Easter. Were Mom capable, she would probably have tended it, but she hasn't been herself in years... at least not in ways that are... *helpful*. She's grown more and more reclusive for no apparent reason at all, and the idle life she's arbitrarily adopted has left her weaker, feebler by the day. When she needs groceries she sends Walter with money, and he returns with God-knows-what.

I step slowly toward her, chest tight. Here lay the woman who brought me into this world. Her face is the sun-bleached color of a tombstone, pale and sunken around pronounced cheekbones. Her snowy hair is frozen in an undulating drift over her shoulders and chest. From what I can see at the edges of the afghan, she's wearing one of the threadbare nighties she's had in rotation since my childhood.

I won't wake her, but I reach down and give Mouf a good stroke. He stretches and yawns lazily before rolling away.

A whispering breeze lazes in through an open window on the far wall, parallel to Mom's recliner. The floral scents of nature's renewal are imparted over the rattle of wind-driven leaves. It diminishes the stale, musty odor of dirt-pressed carpet and un-dusted surfaces.

Mom's television is an old Zenith tube from the '90s. I walk over and turn it off, for a moment carried back to my youth in its clicking and fuzzing to a black crackle of static. Turning, my gaze settles upon the couch on the far wall where I'll bed down tonight. It's a '70s relic like so many other things here. I can't remember if its brown, abrasive upholstery was ever particularly comfortable. As a kid I'd avoid sitting on it in shorts. Even its matching, flattened pillows conjure memories of sandpaper on my skin.

But it will have to do until I can find a more permanent spot.

As I start quietly toward the couch, still keeping quiet to avoid waking Mom, a heavy *thud* carries down the hallway from the foyer. Pictures rattle on the walls as Walter strolls into the kitchen, throwing on every light before hauling the refrigerator door open in a clatter of tightly-packed condiment bottles.

Swiveling back to Mom while I silently curse my brother's baffling lack of self-awareness, I watch with biting guilt as she's startled awake, eyes darting around the room before settling on Walt, presently extracting a casserole dish from the fridge.

Walt crosses the kitchen hugging the dish to his chest, oblivious. He sets the dish on Mom's lime green countertop, lid clattering, then goes about digging in the silverware drawer.

"Eric?" Mom's frail, whispering voice barely rises above the noise, calling me by my father's name.

I kneel beside her recliner. "No, Mom. It's Mark."

She blinks a few times in obvious confusion before nodding with sudden, cryptic emphasis. "Of course. I'm just a little dreamy."

"That's okay." I'm not sure what else to say. I can't just start with *Kelly kicked me out... roomie!*

Fortunately, she gets to it for me. "What are you doing here at a time like..." Her gaze lifts to the space between the windows on the far wall where a grandmother clock had hung throughout most of my childhood. There in its place for over a decade is a portrait of a bull fighter. For a minute she seems to strain at the wall, almost willing the clock to appear as she remembers it. When she fails to sort the situation out in her mind she turns to me with a defeated look she works quickly to banish. "What are you doing here so late?"

"I'm, um, going to stay here for a few days if that's okay." I shrug, studying her face for comprehension.

"Kell-Well kicked you out?"

Even Mom uses that stupid nickname.

The chirping of buttons on the microwave drifts out of the kitchen. I should be hungry, should maybe force myself to eat, but I'm reminded of the nausea in the car, and based on Walter's dubious inspection of the food on his spoon, Mom's cooking hasn't improved.

Our mutual attention comes away from the kitchen. Mom's face is the generic portrait of mother-in-law disgust seen since the inception of nuptuals. "*She's* the one should be kicked out. You work hard to pay for that house, she just sits and watches the internet all day." This is her decoding something she'd no doubt heard from Walt. The current of information running through a family as small as ours is like coffee hitting an empty stomach. Everything flows quickly. It's just the three of us after all. The only grandparent we'd ever known was Dad's mother, mostly due to Mom and Dad waiting until late in their lives to finally start a family. Mom is 68 with no siblings. Dad was also an only child, and dead at 49.

"I didn't feel like getting into it with her," I return. "Besides, it gives me an excuse to spend time with *you*."

I expect her to smile, but her face remains neutral. Either my charm is diluted by booze or Mom suspects I'm full of it. By the looks of her, she isn't going to address it anyway, which I support.

The microwave beeps in the kitchen and soon Walt is with us, stuffing his face with lasagna on the couch. He blows steam through puckered lips like a complete fool as he works over the too-hot food.

"Have you eaten anything?" Mom's attention gradually detaches from Walt. She begins to push herself up, drawing a reproving look from the cat.

"No." My hands go to her shoulders, gently gripping flesh-wrapped bone. "I'm fine."

She settles back in her chair, appraising me with a vacuous sheen on her eyes that makes my heart plummet. "Never known you to refuse food. Do you have any laundry from your dorm? I can put a load in before I go to bed."

My chest tightens. We just finished talking about Kelly kicking me out, but she's somehow pivoted to the days when I was a student at UNH, coming home for the weekend or a break. I look to see if Walter caught it, but he's oblivious, staring at the black television screen, forking food into his face. Cheese strings unmitigated onto his wife-beater.

"I haven't been at UNH in eight years, Mom." I realize how sad I sound the moment I speak, but something tells me she's not going to hang on it for long, assuming she notices it at all. Her gaze shifts to the cat, then to her folded hands as if searching for something tangible to ground her. Some mental compass perhaps. Eventually her gaze returns to mine.

"Of course you haven't," she insists, acting as though I'd misspoken. She supplements quickly, "It's been a long day... I'm *tired*."

"I can help you to bed." My hand perches on her bony knee. If I weren't certain of the flesh beneath her baby blue nighty I'd swear she was nothing but bone, a shrouded skeleton with a fleshed-out face.

"I can get myself to bed." She's already wiggling her legs, both to remove my hand and to inform the cat that his nap is over. Mouf's head rises idly from his front paws. Again he yawns, but remains in place until Mom heaves herself forward, dropping the leg rest on the recliner with an Amazonian grunt of effort. The cat lands on his feet, casting a contemptuous look about the room before sauntering into the kitchen.

I'm back on my feet and trying to avoid offering aid to my proud, independent mother, despite her obvious mobility issues. The television fuzzes back to life, and I rotate to see Walter lowering the remote. Nowhere has *he* offered to help. In fact, he's acting like our mother isn't even here at all, and the sharper side of me wonders if it has something to do with her obvious decline.

Mom's knees crack, her face scrunching up as she pushes herself to her feet. I say nothing, offer no help. I'm not about to challenge the ego of a widow who deserves every bit of dignity in the world, regardless of its base artificiality.

The voice of my grandmother, Nanny, enters one ear and flows out the other. She'd died when I was ten, avoiding outliving her son, my father, by six years.

Old age is hell, Marky. Hell.

I'm looking at my future in a woman struggling to navigate her own domain. I'm 32 years-old, in the prime of my life, the second stage on a three-leg journey to the grave, and here before me is the final leg, what waits at the end of my best years.

The nausea returns.

Mom wobbles but manages to keep her balance. Without a word she moves in safe, shuffling steps around me and into the kitchen, seeming to favor her left side in the way she distributes her weight. As she reaches the archway, hunched forward with her shoulders slouched, Walt calls after her from the couch.

"Ma' can I borrow some gas money for tomorrow?"

I've had enough drama for the night, and I successfully stifle the words that want to come. Our eyes meet, and I see before me the dumbest, most hammered face on the planet; a poster-child for substance abuse. His dull eyes tell me he doesn't remember already playing this trick on me. Gas money, my foot. He's putting together cash for a score. Cocaine, probably. My stomach turns over at the thought of Walt getting into heroin.

"In my purse, honey," Mom answers in that insufferably *silky* voice all youngest siblings know and enjoy. Her obliviousness is like a sledgehammer pounding my heart.

"I, uh, don't think you've got any cash," Walt says.

He's been through her purse. Again, I swallow back against the urge to rip into him.

Mom shuffles toward bed, down the darkened hallway where her and Walt's bedrooms face each other. Without looking back, she says, "I'll give you my debit card tomorrow. Goodnight, boys."

Mouf appears in the doorway and saunters lazily after her.

"'Night, Mom." The watery cadence of my voice makes me aware of the deeper emotions running beneath my anxiety; my budding existential crisis.

"What time tomorrow?" Walt asks.

He receives no answer.

"Mom! What *time*?!"

I lie awake, trying to trick myself into sleep. The odd, enveloping silence of voices that speak here at night is a familiar one; the low hum of the refrigerator motor, water dripping from the tap over the sink, the grating exhale of Walt's air conditioner (at one time *Mom's* air conditioner).

And with me in this world of nostalgic noise is the ghost of Nathan Kelson.

The itchy upholstery has me on my back with my knees bent, as little of me touching the couch as possible. My all-but-bald head is a landscape of agitated flesh, yet the discomfort isn't enough to distract from the man haunting my life.

Until today my thoughts had been unevenly divided between the fear of being imprisoned and the guilt of a murder – there's no other way to view it. I'd escaped everything unspoiled thanks to my arbitrary ties to Kittery, Maine's worst tragedy.

It was the memorial service announcement. I'd seen in the papers how three towns seemed to have come out for the funeral. Obviously not enough, they needed another ceremony on the beach where he apparently loved to surf because Nathan Kelson had been more than just a man, he'd been a humanist and philanthropist who'd touched countless lives.

And I'd taken him from all of them.

I'm a glutton for punishment, and I want this penance so much that I find my phone on the end table (toppling a couple Rolling Rock bottles) and open the browser app. Without a second thought to what I'm doing, I call up Nathan Kelson's pseudo-obit and read through it again twice. I pause on the same two sentences as images of Kelly pitching my phone across the kitchen cycle through my mind.

Nathan was the loving husband of Mallory Kelson, 34, his high school sweetheart and wife of fourteen years. The two were married in York, Maine on May 3rd, 2005. Mallory was the center of his world...

She must be so lost.

Fourteen years of marriage. High school sweethearts. When does real love *ever* take root in high school?

I think of Elora and my heart sinks for a moment before my attention shifts back to Mallory Kelson.

I've never met this woman, yet an odd part of me feels suddenly compelled – no, *obligated* – to reach out. To apologize. As if just showing up and saying, *I'm sorry and I'm probably broken forever* will be enough.

I hate myself. I should be in prison, but I'm a coward, come home to live with my mother at age thirty-two.

I thumb to the bottom of the press release.

A memorial service was held for Nathan on Sunday, May 29th at Potter Memorial Chapel in York, Maine. Due to the overwhelming turnout, another service has been planned for June 19th at Ogunquit Beach.

Do I have the nerve to attend the overflow funeral of the man I'd killed?

No. It would be disastrous if anyone found out who I was.

But nobody needed to know who I was, did they? My name had been mentioned in newspapers and on websites, but they'd focused more on my connection to the Shipyard fire than my personal history. And none of them had included pictures. I could attend the service anonymously, feel things out, see if peace might be found there.

I read Nathan Kelson's pseudo-obit again and again in my search for sleep, and with each pass I'm left more certain that attending his second service is a good idea.

I don't find sleep until much later as that up-all-night fugue builds fuzz around me. When I dream, it's in terse snatches. I see Mallory's face, and somehow it feels like I know her personally... even through the frozen, silent expression of loathing she casts my way in the dark.

Ogunquit Beach. I haven't been here since high school, and at that time I was parked with Elora, unconcerned with the Atlantic, my hand groping a girl's breast for the first time.

The place is, like so many others in Maine, an immensely successful tourist destination. When the season ramps up between Memorial Day and Labor Day, the beach is packed with bodies from the $20 pay-to-park lot to the fringe of the Atlantic Ocean. It's two hundred feet to the water at low tide, while the sand is erased entirely when the tide is high. A strip of adjoined buildings stand sentinel over the parking lot. Here tourists can pay $30 for a tube of sunscreen at the sundry shops or sit down to an excessively marked-up lobster dinner at one of the restaurants. There's also an oceanside hotel spanning the first quarter mile or so of sand, affordable only if $1000 a night for the crap rooms isn't a terrifying budgetary prospect. Those who vacation in that style are cut from a different cloth than I. Dress shirts tucked into khaki shorts? Sweaters synched at the sleeves over pastel-colored polos, collars popped?

No thanks.

I inhale sea mist and baked sand as I pause at the lip of the pavement where a concrete ramp declines lazily toward the beach. One look at the milling service-goers, most propping up cumbersome-looking surfboards, and I realize I'm overdressed in my jeans and black dress shirt. For a moment I consider fleeing to my car, but something keeps me here, the sun warming my face as I work through calming breaths to bring my emotions under control.

It works, by the grace of God or whatever. I bend over and unlace my shoes as people drift by, muttering in hushed solemnity. One at a time, I remove my socks and tuck them into the sneakers. Rolling up the cuffs of my jeans, I flag myself as the outsider I am and will myself forward until the sand fills the spaces between my toes.

I try to pick out Mallory as I walk toward the group. Most wear tight-fitting hoods and wetsuits, the majority trim and athletic, making it near impossible to determine their sex from behind. This isn't my first funeral, or whatever they're calling it, though I'll admit I haven't attended many. Still, I know what I'm looking for: a group clustered around a lone figure while others queue up behind to offer their condolences.

It doesn't take long to find her.

Mallory is not the rail-thin figure that her husband was. Her form-fitting wetsuit gives a good indication of how full-figured she is, though I wouldn't call her fat. *Thick* is what the kids say these days, or so I understand.

Mallory Kelson is a *good* thick.

She doesn't wear a hood like the others. Her chin-length chestnut hair is eerily unmoved by the wind. The foaming waters of the Atlantic advance up the sand, effervescing around her feet unnoticed, before retreating back. Before me is the peculiar form of a widow ankle deep in the ocean, attending her husband's *second* funeral.

I realize I'm walking toward her, coming so close I can see her swollen eyes and cheeks. As one-by-one mourners inch forward to take her hand or embrace her, Mallory's sobbing doesn't diminish, nor does it seem to worsen. This is simply her default state now and it's beyond palpable.

I halt in the waterlogged sand, feeling my feet sink into firm coldness. This is a stupid idea. I don't belong at this funeral. I belong behind bars. What was this anyway? Proof to myself that I'm not a coward? Did I really expect to find peace for *myself* here?

Every part of me tenses as my gaze meets Mallory's. At first I see recognition in those hopeless red eyes as the din of mingled conversation dulls out around me, leaving me cocooned in the silence of her sorrow. I'm paralyzed by her stare, every part of me rigid and conspicuous. For a moment it looks like she's going to leave the others and approach me, but I'm saved as she's drawn back to the steady influx of mourners, water sloshing around her ankles, face blending into neoprene until it's gone.

Time to book it.

Rotating away, I'm now blockaded by wetsuits as additional surfers queue up to see the widow I'd made. The noise of the world returns; crashing waves, blubbering voices, comingling misery.

"Excuse me." I realize the voice is mine, barely powerful enough to push through the din. I squeeze and wend my way through androgynous bodies shrink-wrapped and sheening, repeating myself with overflowing urgency. My gaze falls from the faces of those I'm passing to the sand, a landscape broken only by the curving tips of waxed surfboards and bare and booted feet.

My anxiety is a railroad spike to the heart. I feel it thumping so hard I know it will explode out of my chest in a minute, and I'm suddenly moving with greater urgency, now weaving through bodies spilling onto the beach. I can't breathe. Did I just knock down a kid?

My eyes to the ground, I press through like a surfacing diver holding my breath until breach. The legs and feet begin to thin out in the sunlit sand. The ramp appears.

"Excuse me!" A female voice snaps.

I'm aware of a pair of shadows parting in my path, but I don't stop until I reach the top of the sand-dusted incline. The feelings of claustrophobia diminish in a way that feels cooling. The pressure in my chest releases.

I turn and glance back down the beach. Mallory is no longer visible through the mourners massing around her, some of whom are now forming a single-file procession out to sea, bobbing with the waves as they paddle their boards toward the cloud-swollen horizon.

Swallowing hard, I backpedal without watching my footing, nearly colliding with a rotund tourist in swim trunks that fail to contain his bulk. He huffs and puffs, inspecting a paper tray of hot dogs before warning me to watch where I'm going in a heavy Massachusetts drawl. He waddles off licking mustard from his fingers.

My gaze moves past him to the seabound procession of surfers.

Just leave, I tell myself. I've already made the mistake of coming here, what else could I possibly take away, aside from more grief?

But something keeps me there watching from a distance. Without a thought I relocate to a wooden bench beneath a blue awning where trollies cycle through a small rotary, picking up Fat America and conducting them to the next lobster roll. Sitting there, breeze buffeting my face, I watch as every aquatically-minded attendee takes to the paltry waves of the Atlantic, paddling toward an ever-swelling circle of surfers rising and falling with the water.

The press release hadn't lied. Nathan Kelson was well-loved. As I watch those who cared about him tossing water in the air after each wildly gesticulated, inaudible eulogy, I can't help wondering if anyone will show up at my funeral when I die.

I should have left the moment I stepped off the beach.

is
nathan
here

IS NATHAN HERE? Even as I ask the question, I know its answer.

The simpering voice rises in the murk, *The living like to imagine the soul stays behind in the days following its liberation. Some do, but most of us lack the vanity to attend our own funerals.*

That doesn't answer my question.

Yes it does. You asked if Nathan is here. As I understand it, you still think you're on a beach back on Earth. Nathan Kelson is not there.

I want to press back against her, but to do so would validate her claims that I am, in fact, dead.

And I'm not.

For a time it's only the crushing silence of the void, then the simpering voice returns, *Many of us also steer clear of our funerals to avoid those we left behind, most specifically our soulmates. Sometimes they're bitter, angry over misperceptions that the person they loved was taken before their time.*

A shudder runs through me, rippling my very being.

Sometimes they're looking for someone to blame, I say, voice gobbled up in black. *Sometimes they don't have to look very hard.*

After about an hour the surfers paddle back to shore, some opting to catch one of the puny waves rolling in as curious tourists watch from the sand. Others crowd around Mallory before dispersing. Some return to the water, others stab their boards in the sand and walk off up the beach toward Moody. The majority, however, exit the beach en masse. I watch the burden evaporate from some the faces that pass… free now to move on.

I remain on my bench, flipping between Facebook and my Kirk Matthews novel. The majority of the time my eyes are on Mallory, watching as those still attending her thin out. After what feels like an hour she starts up the sand, escorted by a well-dressed elderly couple with silver hair (obviously not surfers) and a smattering of others who've just returned from the sea in glistening wetsuits.

This is another opportunity to introduce myself. It sits in my mind, running with the greasy drippings of an obviously bad idea. Yet I can't lift myself from this bench.

The other surfers leave her, dispersing and dragging their boards toward the mouth of the Ogunquit River. Beyond is a hillside sprouting hotels and extravagant seasonal homes.

Voices reach my ears as Mallory and the elderly couple summit the ramp. My heart slithers up into my throat, a fire burning beneath it. In a weepy voice, I hear her address one of the people as *Mom*, leaving no more mystery as to who, exactly, these people are. Just twenty feet away and closing, they walk behind their widowed daughter with expressionless faces, eyes trained on the ground.

Go. Move. Get out of here, Mark. This isn't a place for you, you murdered this man—

Mallory pauses at the top of the ramp, gazing upon me with recognition. Her parents come up and halt behind her. Sniveling, Mallory produces a white handkerchief, which she runs absently across her face, eyes still on me. She starts to walk my way.

I look away and try not to fidget nervously even though I'm absolutely fidgeting nervously. Perhaps she'll just pass by. Please, God.

"Do you mind if I sit?" a voice speaks above me, so devoid of hope it could be my own.

Horrified, I hear myself say, "Please."

I scoot to the far edge of the bench before reluctantly locking eyes with her. For some reason I expect a comforting smile on her face, something my waking dreams of her rarely showcased. I'm again reminded that I'm a selfish coward. She is, and rightfully should be, the sole recipient of today's comfort.

Mallory Kelson, up close and personal, is expectedly demoralized. She looks like a roadside pan-handler desperate for a handout, her bleary gaze holding me in its dark desperation as I'm sized-up.

The bench shifts slightly under her weight, though she seems oblivious. I glance at her parents, now waiting good-naturedly at the end of the lot, peering into the window of a sundry shop. A moment of uncomfortable silence stretches for what feels like minutes as waves break and gulls cry. For a moment I wonder if my lack of sleep is playing tricks on my mind, that I'm imagining the whole thing.

"I saw you down by the water. You looked like you wanted to talk to me," she speaks to the tumbling waves.

I'm unable to respond. I've never been so nervous and anxiety-riddled in my entire life. She seems to sense this and presses no further. Instead she asks a question I'd failed to anticipate despite the obsessive thought I'd already devoted to how this moment might play out.

"How did you know Nathan?" Her voice deepens as the name emerges. This time she waits silently for me to answer, studying the waves as if Nathan might somehow rise out of them.

What am I supposed to say? I want nothing more than to comfort this poor woman, yet I've done her the injustice of showing my face at her husband's overflow memorial. My selfish need for forgiveness can't compete with the guilt now driving me.

"I... I'm sorry..."

Our eyes meet, and I struggle to form words. My mind is scattered and disorganized. All I can think about is how much of a coward I am and how wrong it was to come here.

"It's hard, I know," she sobs. "He was so young. There was no way to prepare. One minute he was here, the next he was gone." Her voice cracks with the last word and her chin lowers to touch her chest. Though I would have thought Mallory had no tears left in her, fresh droplets patter the porous fabric of her wetsuit.

"I'm so sorry." This is apparently all I'm capable of saying. Then, the thought strikes that I'll never have another opportunity to tell her how truly sorry I am. And what if somewhere down the line she discovers who I was, that I'd sat silently beside her, sopping up her pity like... well, like a coward?

"Mrs. Kelson," I start, feeling like a love-addled kid trying to ask a girl out on the playground.

"*Mallory*, please," she says.

My eyes move submissively to the ground. I feel her gaze press upon me as she waits patiently, *compassionately* for me to continue. And somehow the words come on the wings of a confidence I'll never know again.

"I... I don't know how to tell you this. I'm hoping you'll see how terrible I feel... how much I wanted to *personally* offer my condolences here... now... not shy away from what I did like some..." I draw a long breath. "Like some coward." My jaw is trembling, my words emerging mostly in vowels. I swallow hard against the frog in my throat and tell her, "I'm Mark Wells. I'm the one who... who hit your husband."

It's in this moment that fate's cruel and precise will sees fit to join me with an image of my sentencing hearing last month. I realize with a sinking heart that Mallory hadn't been in attendance. She hadn't, in fact, attended any of the hearings, and I suddenly know why.

She didn't want to face me.

With the reluctance of a devout soul in the presence of God, my gaze moves back to her. A befuddled look crosses her face at first, every part of her seeming to slacken. Suddenly her eyes widen, glistening with renewed tears. All of the pity and sadness in those weary eyes dissolves, and my stomach turns at the rage building in their place.

"You..." she whispers, voice dripping with venom and nearly seized by the wind.

"It was an accident. I didn't want to do you the injustice of..." I struggle with my words, wanting to sound intelligent and well-meaning. I'm just as entitled to the world's empathy, right?

Naturally, I make it worse. "I wanted to give you the opportunity to say whatever you need to say to me... and I wanted to tell you I'm sorry." I could say more, but I leave it there for whatever reason.

"You took everything I had in the world," she growls. Her eyes, once so dull, are suddenly bugged with rage. "We were going to start trying for a *baby* this fall." The word *baby* emerges through suddenly-clenched teeth. I'm not certain what this woman is capable of, but as I watch her pot boil over, I begin to wonder if the fists she's formed will leave bruises on me.

"My wife and I can't have children," I find myself saying, immediately wondering why. I don't have time to chastise myself before a flash of movement leaves my right cheek stinging.

Mallory's open hand hangs in the space between us as she considers another slap. It slowly lowers to her lap, though her eyes continue to bore into mine.

"Were you *drunk*? *Texting*? How did you not *see* him?!" she cries, both hands suddenly flailing in frantic gesticulation.

I recoil, expecting another slap. My averted gaze finds her parents, now approaching with wild concern painting their faces. They move as quickly as their aged bodies will apparently permit, and in this moment

I'm struck with the odd observation that her parents also waited until later in life to start having children.

"The sun was shining in my eyes. He was coming around a dark corner. I didn't see him." I don't tell her that he was basically in my lane, nor do I tell her that I was, in fact, looking at my phone. Something tells me that it doesn't matter what I reveal, for better or for worse. It isn't going to change her opinion of me.

But part of me wants to fire back, *He wasn't paying attention. He didn't try to move out of the way. I hit him head-on at 38 miles-per-hour as I turned a corner!*

"How could you not *see* him? It's a law that you have to watch out for pedestrians—"

"Honey, what's wrong?" her father asks, shuffling up to the bench. His concerned gaze bounces nervously between me and his daughter.

Mallory ignores him, heaving herself up off the bench. Suddenly she's towering over me, fists white-knuckled and in striking position at her hips.

I wait for the punishment to resume and I watch her fists, telling myself I'll take all she's got for me. But all she does is glare, the silent wrath burning behind her pupils doing all the talking. The continued voices of her parents register like the distant cries of gulls, dulled out by the emotions ravaging me.

Never before have two strangers understood one another with so few words exchanged. She sees in me the guilty coward I am. I see in her the crushed widow from whom I've stolen absolutely everything.

"I wish you were dead," she says before storming off with her parents struggling to keep up.

I also wish I was dead.

i
just
want
to
go
back

YOU ARE DEAD, says the simpering voice, and for a moment I think it's Mallory's, that I'm still with her at Ogunquit Beach, waiting for her righteous retribution to redefine me.

Then a thought.

Hesitantly I ask, *Is Nathan Kelson my soulmate?*

He is not part of our chain, no.

Something is inexplicably intuited, its truth unimpeachable.

Mallory is though.

She is.

Then why was she with someone who isn't her – our – soulmate?

The answer lies in the mysteries you ventured to Earth to explore together. The voice darkens. Unseen connective tissue builds between us, and suddenly I'm cold. I feel through the contact an aching loss, and I wither, all of me withers against it.

Please, I just want to go back.

You shouldn't be this rooted in that world. What is it you're looking for, Mark?

I don't know. It's more like a feeling I'm chasing than anything tangible, but I know I must have it. Not simply for me, but for all of us.

Let me go back.

An ill-defined moment passes.

As you wish.

The next day I'm back at work again, on the road and feeling no different. My surreal encounter with Mallory Kelson continues to play back in my head like some demented movie. I can barely keep my attention on the road as it arches toward the green trestle of the Piscataqua River Bridge into New Hampshire.

I exit Interstate 95 at Woodbury Road and cruise into Portsmouth's retail sector of chain restaurants and unaffiliated strip malls. I nearly clip an oblivious pedestrian as I take inventory of my exhausted options for ridding myself of this guilt. My world is now a scratchy couch. What I'd had before, whatever it was, is gone.

I wish you were dead.

I've heard this in movies and song lyrics. Never have I heard it spoken in the real world with such unsettling earnestness. I can't banish the image of Mallory standing over me. It was with me when I started home from the beach, alone with my thoughts, and it was with me when I closed my eyes and tried for sleep that would not come.

It was with me when I sat up five minutes before my alarm this morning. It will probably remain the rest of my life.

I coast into the parking lot outside Izzy66, a retail store specializing in sports gear. It occupies the center unit of a strip mall, flanked by the likes of TJ Maxx, PetWorld, and Rent-A-Center. At 7:45 A.M., it's still early. None of these stores are open, though the majority are lit and staffed by workers preparing for the day.

It's a dark morning, a black storm head swelling above the smokestacks along the Piscataqua, mirroring my mood as I realize I've started my day outside my normal routine. Missing are my Monday Dunkin Donuts iced coffee and the antics of our local morning show. My radio is off. It was off when I drove absently past Dunkin Donuts in Kittery.

I roll down the driver- and passenger-side windows. A cooling breeze fills the car, the type that warns of an approaching storm with the tang of static electricity. I'm early for my 8:00 to evaluate a suddenly unresponsive mail server, so I take some time in my car, enjoying the pre-rain calm. Unclipping my phone from my belt, I thumb the Facebook app open. Beyond its blue splash screen I hope to see a red message notification from Elora.

But there is nothing. Not from her or anyone else. With a sigh, I begin to scroll through my newsfeed, rolling my eyes at how productive Walt seems to have been last night. Posted from his account are a number of right-wing infographics in bold, comic book typeface. The self-championed Defender of the Second Amendment, he's naturally posted a few pictures of handguns with a bunch of different threats amounting to "you can have my guns when you pry them from my cold, dead hands."

Walt doesn't even own a *cap gun*. If he actually found a way to get his hands on a real firearm, he'd end up shooting himself with it unintentionally.

It's a certainty.

I tap the search icon and blindly assemble Elora's name before stalking her profile a bit. Gone with haste are thoughts of Mallory Kelson, replaced with my obsessive love for a woman I'll never have. It's a nice break from the emotions that have haunted me, but with its finer points stripped away, it's just another flavor of pain.

A picture of Elora and her husband pops up as I scroll. I feel the frown forming as my lips tug downward and waste no time closing the app. As if on cue, the phone begins to ring. Flashing across its touchscreen is the name *Tim Massi*.

The clock says 7:51. He's a full minute late for his morning check-in.

Accepting the call, I press the phone to my ear. "Hi, Tim."

"Mornin', kid. How you feelin'?"

"Doing all right." I try to weave an artificial energy into my delivery but fail miserably.

"Eh, you still sound a bit dumpy."

Yep. Failed.

"I'm just tired," I assure him. While not the full explanation, this is partly the truth. I didn't sleep at all last night. Again.

"You're a bad liar. What's your first stop today?" He is chipper as usual. He's been pumping coffee into his body since 5:00 A.M. as he does every morning. I need to get some coffee.

"Sitting outside Izzy66. Got an alert from Exchanger Toolkit last night. Their site stopped answering S-M-T-P requests. Could be the I-S-P. I wasn't able to test remoting in because…" Crap. Now I have to tell him about Kelly. "'Cause my computer's down at home." Good cover. Let's see if he buys it.

"What's wrong with your computer?"

"Dead P-S-U."

"That sucks. Come by the office later, I'll hook you up with one of the 800 watt ones we've got kicking around."

"Thanks, Boss." I'm happy to have flown at least one thing under his radar.

"No prob. You need any help out there?"

"Should be good. I'll let you know."

A pause, then, "A little work is just what you need. Get your head off of things. No room to dwell on anything else when you've got fires to put out… or clients freaking out around you."

And we get a good mix of both.

"I sure hope so," I say through a sigh.

Another pause, as if he's trying to get a read on me through the phone. Before long he launches into our typical end-of-check-in exchange. "Okay, I'll be up in Concord all day. We saw a resurgence of Cryptolocker while you were out last week. It's like a plague. Grand Capitol was hit, and I'm on my way to restore their entire appdata volume from tape. If you need anything, *anything*, kid, you just let me know. Okay?"

"Will do, Boss. Thank you." I manage a genuine smile. Tim is a good man, and he's always looked out for me.

"All right, kid. Talk to you later."

I end the call. It's now 8:02. My gaze runs the glass façade of Izzy66, sharpening on the manager already standing in the doorway.

Time to go in and wave my magic computer wand. It's going to be a long day.

Two days pass, and like Tim assured me, work is like a glaring sun burning through the clouds over my mind. I'm still preoccupied with what happened between me and Mallory, but these thoughts are starting to come less frequently. My memories of her husband's final moments will never leave me, but a callous is forming now that the rest of the world has seemingly moved on.

But Mallory isn't the kind of wound that heals quickly. It's mostly at night when I rest my head on those abrasive couch pillows that I think of her and her parting words. I can almost still feel the bite of her open hand across my cheek.

Tomorrow I'm headed to North Conway, where Elora's band, *Staple You Shut*, is set to perform. In some ways this feels a lot like preparing to attend Nathan Kelson's overflow memorial.

As I lie on the couch, struggling to sleep even though I'm physically exhausted, I do my best to shift my thoughts from Mallory to Elora, to probe my empty feelings and attempt to understand them. I imagine Elora and me strolling along the sidewalks of North Conway, a bucolic village of mom-and-pop shops and restaurants nestled in the White Mountains of New Hampshire. We're holding hands, mutually enamored, walking as though we're the only ones on the sidewalk. Her hair, black as moonless midnight flutters over her shoulders, untamed. Her slim, gym-sculpted body rises and wobbles in all the right places, though I'm hardly interested in such things. It's her lips that I crave, pink and pure without a smudge of lipstick. I want them against mine, I want to breathe through her, I want to draw her close and absorb her entirely.

The fantasy is pleasant only so far as the reality of our situations will permit. I'll never have her this way. I'll never have *all* of her, and I know it.

A creak reaches my ears from the hallway. I crack my eyes enough to get a fuzzy look at the kitchen archway and Walter as he stalks slowly out of the shadows. He crosses the living room on his tip-toes, his embellished character rendering him the exaggerated villain of a silent film as he advances across the carpet. He's bare-chested with a pair of fraying boxer shorts clinging to his bony hips. He's coming right for me.

Walt pauses, every part of him seizing up as a creak beneath the carpet breaks the silence. For some time he doesn't move. Though it's too dark for me to see where his eyes are pointed, I'm certain they're on me, searching for movement.

What's he up to?

After a few seconds he resumes his halting trek across the living room, moving beyond the couch and crouching near me. I can smell his reek, a combination of skunky pot smoke and fruity body odor. I struggle to regulate my breathing, to feign sleep, as he begins sifting through my stuff on the end table. The sudden rustling of paper tells me he's going through my wallet.

I sit up. "What the *hell*, Walt?"

He recoils, scrambling back into the darkness, tumbling over his feet and crashing into Mom's recliner. My hand is already feeling out for the lamp, and when I finally locate and twist the switch, dousing the room in blinding light, I'm left considering the $300 in twenties I'd withdrawn for my trip, now scattered on the floor while Walter struggles to extract himself from the chair.

"Walter, you were going to *steal* from me?" I try to keep my voice down to avoid waking Mom. I fling the blankets off and launch to my feet, standing over him as every part of Walter seems to clench in the chair. His face is creased in an expression of oafish contemplation as he struggles with obvious difficulty to assemble a believable excuse. What he offers is beyond pathetic.

"I—I thought I left my wallet out here. I was coming to get it!" His spirited insistence works only to further illuminate the lie.

"That's a crock, Walter, and you know it." I step toward him, bending to retrieve my wallet and the bills strewn around the floor. When I finish counting, I'm left hunting for the $20 that will complete the $280 in my hand. Swiveling toward Walt, I set eyes on the missing note, resting incriminatingly on the bulge of his boxers. With a long, disappointed sigh, I step over to him and hold out my open hand.

Walt just sits there, looking at me with a combination of shame and fear that will ultimately do nothing to change his behavior. Taking a long sip of air, I speak though another, longer sigh. "You have a twenty on... on your junk."

His gaze falls to the bill. With a trembling hand he plucks it between his thumb and forefinger, seeming afraid now to touch it. His eyes lock once more with mine, still overcome with emotion. It's obvious that Mom doesn't often catch him raiding her purse, assuming she ever has.

Walt drops the note in my hand, averting his eyes and seeming now to make every effort to vanish into the recliner. To disappear entirely.

I stuff the bills back into my wallet and walk it back to the end table. Walt remains like a wild animal trapped in the headlights of an approaching vehicle as I fall back to the couch. He's too afraid to move, and despite his attempt to rob me, I can't help pitying him. He's high on a likely combination of Adderall, pot, and booze. Who knows what's going on in that drug-addled mind of his.

"Doesn't Mom give you enough?" I ask, endeavoring to keep my tone from offending him. For some reason the last thing I want is to further demean my brother. His helpless simpleton act (perhaps not so much an act) worked even when I knew he was using it. "What's so important that you need to rob me to pay for it, Walt? Please tell me you aren't in trouble with bookies or anything like that."

Walt's apparent unease melts away, along with most of the shame wrinkling his face. He slowly repositions himself in the chair, still facing me, now cross-legged. With a quick glance over his shoulder in the direction of the hallway, presumably to see if Mom is up and listening, he turns back to me and opens his mouth, his hesitation clear.

Then his lips press back together.

"If you want me to help you, you have to tell me what's going on," I urge.

Walt frowns. "I'm sorry, dude. I don't know what I was thinking."

"Are you in trouble?"

He shakes his head. "No, man."

"Then why were you trying to steal from me? And don't say you needed gas money. That excuse is so tired."

"I just needed money." Walt shrugs as if somehow, in some strange world, this is enough.

"For drugs? For booze? You don't *work*. You don't help with the bills here. Tell me what you need this for. Don't make me get Mom involved."

Once again he glances over his shoulder. When he turns back to me I see that my threat has stuck, though I hardly understand what he has to fear from a woman who will always see him as her *little baby*. A woman who would never dream of denying him a single thing his junkie heart desired.

"I want to buy a gun." His face is a sudden portrait of chilling earnestness.

An uneasiness ripples through me. It's as close to feeling raped as I've ever come. My brother's words, his desires, though not fully clarified, shake me to my soul. I open my mouth to say something, only to clam up and wait for him to continue. But he does not. He simply sits there, gazing pensively at folded hands like a guilty child unmoved to meet his parent's eye.

A voice in my head urges me to cancel my trip north tomorrow, to stay here and look after my brother and mother. But I remind myself that I *need* the trip. I have to get away from everything and into the company of a woman who unknowingly holds every key to my happiness. It's selfish, but I don't care. I've been made to suffer enough and I'm done with it until at least Monday.

"Walt, why do you need a gun?"

He shrugs, pupils flicking rapidly from corner to corner in their sockets. I can tell he's thinking hard, trying to blaze a pathway through the fog of inebriation. After a moment he turns to me, his face decked out in the most buffoonish, prideful look he seems capable of conjuring. "It's my First Amendment right."

I succeed in stifling my laughter, aided mostly by the gravity of this situation. With a sigh, I shake my head and correct him, "It's your *Second Amendment* right, Walt. And that doesn't tell me *why* you think you need a gun. Are you in trouble?" I hesitate, then whisper, "Are you thinking about hurting someone?"

He shakes his head with a vehemence I rarely see in him. "No, no." He stops and lowers his voice with another glance toward the kitchen. Looking back to me, face set with a sincerity I can actually read, he says again, "No. I would never – I *could* never hurt another person."

"Then what's up?"

"Forget about it—"

"Walt—"

"I said *forget about it, Mark!*" he cries, suddenly not caring about waking Mom. His back arches and he lurches forward a few times until he's able to free himself from the reclined chair. Once up, he teeters in place, seeming frozen mid-flight as I, too, launch to my feet. His gaze returns to me, a fire burning behind his eyes with an energy I cannot decrypt. "Just leave me alone, Mark. I'm sorry I tried to steal from you. It won't ever happen again. Just please leave me alone!"

His voice is so loud that I'm certain it's woken Mom, but he leaves it at that. Spinning with such haste he nearly loses his balance again, Walt steals off into the shadowed hallway, leaving me dumfounded. Moments later I hear the slam of his bedroom door, followed by the slow creak of another door opening. It isn't long before the hallway light comes on and Mom baby-steps into the archway, gazing sleepily at me.

"What the blazes is going on out here?" Her voice is hoarse and cracking with sleep. She chases an itch along her left hip, the frilled hem of her nightgown rising and falling at her feet.

I draw a long breath, stepping blindly backward until my calves touch the couch. I plop down, shaking my head. "Has Walt been acting strange lately?" I gaze up at her, hoping for something helpful, but she's already shaking her head with the same bullish insistence with which I'm accustomed. The one that silently, but *insistently*, maintains my brother's innocence in everything.

"Mom," I start, trying to overwrite the frustration in my voice with fatigue. "I just caught him stealing from my wallet. He was going to clean me out of $300."

She says nothing at first, pivoting toward the kitchen as if already planning her exit, then after a few moments she shrugs, "It must have been a misunderstanding."

"Mom, I caught him with the money in his hand."

She shakes her head again, lips pursed so tightly, so stubbornly that they're drained of all color. "You do better than him, Mark. He's not very bright. There's not much he can do for money."

"It doesn't take much of a brain to flip burgers down at Rich's Smokehouse." I'm readjusting my blankets, already resigned to going back to sleep without any resolution. She will defend him to the end. She always does. Walt could slaughter a family of kittens at the foot of a church altar and she'd insist he was just doing God's good work.

"He's different, Mark," she says, leaving it at that. I'm actually surprised she doesn't urge me to *give him* the money I'd recovered.

"Yeah," I agree, stretching across the prickly fabric and lowering my head to the pillow, still facing her. "He's different all right, Mom." I'm not going to tell her about the gun. What good would it do?

Closing my eyes, I attempt to find equilibrium as anger, frustration, and most importantly guilt and anxiety, flood my body. Yeah, I'm committed to seeing Elora tomorrow. I'm committed to slathering on the charm and wittiness that will almost *certainly* land her in my arms before the end of it.

Mom doesn't say another word, no doubt satisfied that she'd won the argument. Though I don't hear her tiny footsteps as she makes her way back to her bedroom, the creaking of the floor tells me she's off. Moments later, the pained creak of her door closing.

I retreat deeper into my imagination, back to strolling hand-in-hand with Elora. If my mind were a ship, my foolish hope would be the wind in its sails.

When I was a Sophomore and had just passed my driver's test, I was almost overcome by how much the world suddenly grew around me. Gone were the days when I had to wait for Mom to drive me into Portsmouth to buy a CD. Gone were the days of riding the bus to school. Most importantly, gone were my days of confinement at home.

Prior to this grand liberation, I was content to stay in my room all afternoon and into the evening after school. There I would finish my homework, listen to music, read, and write. While this existence lacked universal appeal, I was a happy introvert. But when that laminated card with my acne-pocked face entered my wallet, I suddenly felt the need to shake up the routine, to force my inevitable flight toward adulthood.

The local kids with wheels hung around outside a local gas station called "Mrs. Miles's" off of US-1 in York. When we'd occasionally pass by at night, usually on our way back from one of Mom's bridge games (back when she had friends), I'd ogle these kids leaning coolly against their beater cars, laughing and sipping Surge soda. I was jealous of their freedom, of their *confidence*. They smoked actual cigarettes without a care to passersby. What was it like taking smoke into your lungs? How did it feel to stay out past midnight or until the cops forced you to disperse?

What was it like to disappear with a girl into one of those parked cars?

My first car was a Ford Escort station wagon, one of the last in its line. As soon as I was legal to drive and took hold of that steering wheel, nothing was more important in my life than getting to Mrs. Miles's and seeing about a place for me in the hangout club.

I've never been particularly bold, even in my adult years. The closer and closer I came to Mrs. Miles's the more nervous I grew, my hands trembling at ten and two on the steering wheel. The auburns and violets of dusk had burned away, leaving an unobstructed starfield above. An orange moon bubbled up through the clouds scudding the treetops. Ahead, the glow of the Mrs. Miles's neon sign struck through the night, burning on a hilltop hugged by an estuary wending lazily inland.

As I cruised over the water and my destination loomed above me, I began to think about turning around, and probably would have if the gravel road shoulder offered more than enough space to change a tire. A quick check of my rearview mirror showed traffic stringing behind me toward Kittery in a serpentine line, no doubt having piled up as I subconsciously slowed my approach to Mrs. Miles's.

Don't be a coward, I remember telling myself. *For once in your life just be bold.*

Minutes later I pulled slowly into Mrs. Miles's as the traffic butting my bumper accordioned out over US-1 toward Ogunquit. The hangout kids were already gathered at the back of the lot beneath an awning of fluttering leaves. The nosier members of the group looked up, no doubt to see if my car was recognizable, before looking away almost as quickly.

I wanted to run away, but this was one of those rare moments where fate seemed to be urging me along. I had come this far, why not see it through?

I did it cautiously, cruising into a spot beneath the glowing store windows and walking inside for a Surge or Mountain Dew. I stole glances back at the hangout kids, one blowing jets of smoke impressively from his nose. I was so distracted that I was at the register with my purchases before I really knew it.

"That all?" a fortysomething woman asked behind the register. Her thin, graying hair drifted across her face like the unmoored fibers of a spider's web. On her cheek was a mole the size of Rhode Island, and as she smiled I noted she was missing a front tooth… because of course she was.

"That's it, thanks." My voice was shaky, but I wasn't left dwelling on it too long as the sigh of the front door opening drew my attention to the pixie stepping inside.

I'd seen Elora a few times in the hallways between periods and in our shared astronomy class, but at that point I wasn't even acquainted with her. Now here she was, unconcerned with me, her very presence coiling my stomach. She wore a black tank with those flair bellbottoms that had resurged briefly before dying forever as the natural world intended. Her black hair hung past her shoulders, down her chest and back. She looked me over briefly, offered a polite smile, then moved off toward the back of the store, disappearing behind the salty snacks.

The cashier cleared her throat with a wet rattle, recapturing my attention.

"Sorry," I said.

She smiled, revealing more missing gaps in the back of her mouth where teeth should rightfully have been. "That all?"

"Um, yes, please," I answered, fishing my wallet out of the brown corduroys I'd mistakenly thought were fashionable once upon a time.

"One oh-five."

I handed her two dollars and she made my change. I then took my soda and stepped back without looking, unexpectedly bumping an unseen person and sending a number of objects clattering to the floor.

"I'm so sorry," I said before I'd even seen who it was. As I swiveled around, I was horrified to find myself facing Elora once again, a half-dozen bottles of unnaturally green soda spinning at our feet. "I'm sorry," I repeated, "I didn't see you there."

She simply smiled and said, "No worries." It was genuine, but words rarely tamed this kind of embarrassment. My first instinct was to flee like a frightened animal, as always, but once more fate seemed to grip me in all the right places, and I crouched to help her collect everything. I tried my best to keep my gaze from moving down her shirt as she reached for a bottle that had rolled up beside my foot.

"You're Mark from Astronomy, right?" she asked as we stood, now clutching bottles to our chests. It took a few seconds of introverted silence to realize this girl knew my name. It was easy to overlook the nerdy kid in collared shirts and khakis, a kid who'd spent most of his life trying to stay off of everyone's radar, yet somehow I'd stood out to her.

I nodded with a forced smile. "And you're..." I trailed off intentionally, trying to play things cool. These moments were rare. I was grateful for each and every one that landed as intended.

"Elora," she said, smiling as she sidled past me and arranged her purchases on the counter. I followed, trying to keep from grinning as I placed the others beside them.

"Right." I backed away and allowed her to pay for her drinks. As the conversation ended, I began to move back toward the door, feeling like this meeting alone had been worth the trip. "Well," I said, smiling with surprising confidence that came as if distilled from the very air. "See you in class."

"Hold up," she said, lighting a bonfire of excitement in my chest.

I rotated back to see her coming up behind me, trying for a better grip on the paper bag in her hands. I stepped out into the spiced autumn air, holding the door for her. Once outside she paused, eying her friends occupying trunks and tailgates at the back of the lot.

"You wanna come hang out? That is, if you aren't doing anything else tonight." Her eyes moved down to my bottle of Surge soda, beverage of choice for the Mrs. Miles's Crew.

An eager excitement budded within me. It was like the anticipation of Christmas Morning though further refined and fueled by the always-reliable male libido.

I tried to keep my goofy smile from growing.

"Sure," I answered.

"Cool. C'mon, I'll introduce you to the crew," she said, already leading me toward the back of the lot.

One month later, Elora took my virginity in the back of my Escort wagon, parked beneath the moon at Ogunquit Beach.

The feeling is the same as it was on the ramp of Mrs. Miles's when Elora had asked me to follow her to the back of the lot. She will never truly be mine, and I understand this on every tragic level as she inhabits my mind, distracting from my northbound journey along US-16 in my newly-restored RAV. I'm still visited here and there by thoughts of Mallory and

Walt, but they don't last against the weekend I've built up in my mind with Elora Kennedy.

Early summer in the wilderness of Central New Hampshire is, in its own right, just as intoxicating as Elora. As my crossover bores through an endless tunnel of whiffling green foliage, shot in places with slivers of striking blue sky, the road rises and falls with the land, hugging its curvature.

A couple times the wilderness breaks, surrendering to the larger, settled areas. These are tourist hubs like Ogunquit Beach and the Kittery Outlets, though smaller in scale. Eclectic gift shops and fast-food joints mingle with mom-and-pop general stores, their Old American charm still largely preserved. There's one in each town I pass through, rocking chairs spaced beneath shadowed farmer's porches, anachronous pickle barrels set up as tables between them. I've been into one or two. They're a nice trip back in time, but don't offer much more than useless curios and novelties. Even their *homemade* items seem a little too similarly packaged not to have come from the same local bakery.

I cruise out of the last town I'll hit before North Conway, exiting its small strip of stores and restaurants flanking the crowded lanes of US-16 and entering another dark expanse of forest. An anticipation has been building in me for some time. Every mile I draw closer to North Conway seems to add to the constricting sensation that renders every breath shallow and unsatisfying.

A familiar song comes on the stereo, streaming from my phone. *Set the Ray to Jerry* by The Smashing Pumpkins. A raw, stripped down piece, it came as a b-side to one of the tracks they released from their most successful record of all time, Mellon Collie and the Infinite Sadness in 1995. I love this song, mostly because it reminds me of Elora. For a moment I entertain the idea that its playing is some sign that now, as I'm finally untethered from Kelly, Elora and I will rekindle our love.

I crank the volume, singing poorly but passionately along. My and Billy Corgan's voices crack together, so simultaneously poetic and pathetic.

My mood is set.

you
were
listening
to
that
song
when
you
died

YOU WERE LISTENING to that song when you died.

I want to argue with the voice, but I can't. I'm joined with the images of sheeting snow and ice pinging off a castle made of glass. I hear the song in the hollowness of this void, and for a moment I start to drift toward my final moments in that life.

But something stops me, the impulse feeling somehow... *planted* in me.

You're trying to steer me away from this. You don't want me to see what happened in North Conway, I say, aware of the resentment in my voice.

The simpering voice is unfazed by my tone, saying, *I actually fail to see the point in most of this, but I'm going along with it because you've never acted this way after transitioning.*

A dark thought. *Is something... wrong with me?*

No, the voice answers in a tone that suggests my question was anticipated. There's an undercurrent of loss eroding its simpering character, the depths of which I'm presently being spared. And for the first time I entertain the idea that I might actually be dead.

But there is... something wrong.

Nothing that concerns the soul of a man still tethered to his former existence.

Fine. Be that way. I have plans with the love of my life anyway.

I arrive in North Conway just after 1:00 P.M. Traffic is tight along the main strip of US-16 striking through the center of the village. The sidewalks barely contain the disorganized bustle of tourists pointing at shops and gripping small children by the wrist as they're shunted through gridlocked traffic.

North Conway is an idyllic mountain village surrounded by bald, pointed peaks, many still capped with snow. Farther down US-16 the quaintness dissolves around a sprawling outlet mall. Here the highway shifts into two lanes with crosswalks and traffic lights every block. Chain restaurants abound. It's exactly like Kittery, only tax free.

I had first thought to book a hotel at one of the more rustic bed and breakfasts in the village, but the chain hotel rates were lower. The idea that I might be paying alimony in the near future helped seal the deal.

My hotel is a Motel 8, a brick box lacking any semblance of character or charm. The mountains rising behind it leave me considering just how out-of-place it looks, as if Motel 8 is a species indigenous only to highway offramps and low-income urban areas.

Considering how out-of-place I've felt in my own world lately, this hotel will suit me just fine.

I pull slowly into the parking lot, allowing an Indian family to scurry across the street toward a McDonald's where drive-thru traffic is presently backed into the far-right lane of US-16. I coast up to the motel, passing beneath a brick overhang situated before a pair of glass entry doors. I park the RAV and emerge into a hotter environment than the one I'd departed hours earlier. It seems as though the summer has actually come to the White Mountains of New Hampshire. I haul my backpack out from where it's fallen behind the driver's seat and head inside.

To the left as I walk in is a utilitarian breakfast nook devoid of charm. Plastic dispensers hold cold cereal above a basket brimming with untouched fruit, and dual banks of toasters stand ready to burn bread. To my right is a small gathering area with pleather couches and chairs arrayed around a tempered glass table piled with magazines.

The lobby smells of fresh flowers with a nibbling edge of dollar store cleaning products.

"Afternoon, sir," an Asian twentysomething says cheerily, face barely rising over the lip of her recessed check-in desk. Smiling, she says, "Checking in?"

I step up to the desk, extracting my wallet. "Yes," I say, sliding out my driver's license and a credit card that's about 80% maxed out. I push them across the reflective onyx countertop, but she isn't ready for them yet and doesn't bother to look down.

"Name?"

"Wells."

Her tiny, manicured fingers become a pastel blur over a wireless keyboard. Her eyes sweep a monitor built into the desk. "Mark?"

"Yes."

"Okay, I have you for two nights in a standard non-smoking room with a king-sized bed. Is that correct?"

"Yeah," I answer, decoding my own behavior and realizing I'd booked a room with only one bed in hope that it would be shared with someone. Should Elora need to stay with me, there would be no other option but to sleep with me. The extra night was simply wishful thinking.

I live in a dream world.

"Great," the girl says, now reaching across the counter and picking up the cards. "Is this the same card you used to book the room?"

"Yes."

"Awesome." She slides my driver's license back without even looking at it. I guess identification isn't necessary anymore.

I pivot back toward the entry doors, watching as an Escalade piloted by a slim woman of the anorexic-chic variety stops millimeters from kissing my bumper. She's mid-fifties with the kind of blonde hairdo that comes with hours of meticulous sculpting. She's yapping on her phone, barely paying attention. Judging by the car, she's one of those entitled types. Affluent as an artform.

"Okay, you'll be in room 619, very top floor." The receptionist slides a pair of card keys my way along with my credit card. "Take the elevator to the right of this desk and go right as you exit. Is there anything else I can do for you today, Mr. Wells?"

"Is there a liquor store anywhere nearby?" I ask, suddenly feeling exposed. It's as if admitting I'll be drinking alone somehow violates a long-established Acceptable Use Policy. These are the frankly *stupid* thoughts that I endure.

"Yeah, just head back out to Route 16 and take a right. It's down the road in a little mini-mall, right between the new Big Daddy's Ice Cream and Dunks."

"Thanks," I say, feeling the corners of my lips tug upward for once.

"You're welcome." Her eyes move to the Escalade woman, now strolling with an intolerable air of privilege, of *ownership*, through the entryway.

I toss an up-and-down look at Miss Privilege on the way to my car, unsurprised and oddly unaffected by the derisive look she returns. I can't help feeling embarrassed for her, but these types are so lost in themselves that they're completely oblivious to the little people cycling through their world.

"This is the last time I'm going to tell you – I made these reservations *weeks* ago. If you can't honor them I can't promise that I won't report you to the Better Business Bureau and the Chamber of Commerce, and tear you down all over the *internet!*" She brushes past me as if I'm not there at all. The displaced wind as she hurries along, suitcase in-tow, washes over me. Left in her wake is the scent of luxury perfume. I turn to watch her, aware I'm not the only one as others in the lobby pause as well. The woman's flat ass rises and falls in form-fitting white pants, a bronzed sliver of skin showing beneath a matching white blouse. She angles her body to keep the phone pressed to her ear as her rolling suitcase catches on the lip of a rug.

I may be a murderer, but at least I don't go around like this woman, unconcerned with the misery I sling.

I have a couple hours before the concert so I pass the time watching television in my room. For some reason TV is always better in a hotel. I find myself watching things I'd never consider at home, not that I currently have a real home.

My texts to Elora informing her of my arrival go unanswered. Big surprise. I'm here, there isn't any posturing or luring left to do. The gig is at a bar called The Dirty Moose. I've already checked it out. It's small, built out of an old log cabin back in the village. From the looks of it, it's a dive, but I haven't seen inside yet. Perhaps it's another wilderness-themed *adventure* bar. I have my doubts.

Staring at me, unopened, beside the television are the bottles of Grey Goose and cranberry juice I'd picked up at the liquor store. A couple of times I'm inclined to make a drink, but I back myself off, fearful I'll be completely smashed by the time I actually get to speak with Elora. I've got to stay coherent in order to apply the proper charm, otherwise I'll end up running my mouth about nothing, or worse...

I think of Kelly, probably dead to the world back home, the couch slowly eating her.

My show ends, another cookie-cutter reality program, this one about bad tattoos and ways artists fix them. Rolling over in bed, I'm held in place watching the sun sink outside my window. The clouds are ablaze in fiery colors that bleed through the gossamer curtains. I feel a million miles away from my life back in Maine, and I'm grateful for it. If I take away nothing else from this trip, it's the brief reprieve from my ongoing dumpster fire of a life.

Commotion in the hallway draws me away from the stunning picture nature is painting outside. The sound of a million tiny feet thunders past my door, small voices shrieking in the aftermath and trailed by the weary, flavorless voice of a mother issuing empty threats.

I guess in some ways it's good Kelly and I couldn't conceive. Little reminders like the scene outside my door help thicken my veil of self-delusion. Suddenly I'm depressed again.

I turn off the television and sit up. Sliding my feet into my flip-flops, I grab my keys and wallet off the nightstand and walk toward the door, intent for some reason on getting out of the room. As the sounds of free-range children begin to fade down the hall, I step out and set off to God-knows-where. I need to get out and into the world, force that feeling of *vacation* upon me or face the consequences of hitting the bottle early.

I end up cruising the outlets on foot, stopping to buy a few work polos and treating myself to a Big Daddy's ice cream as the street lights sputter to life and strings of Christmas lights along the eaves of the outlets offer a festive twinkle. The heat of the day lingers a bit, edged out only by a light breeze that carries down from the mountains. It imparts the earthy scents of maple and pine, which mingle nicely with the aromas of fried dough and roasted Bavarian nuts from vendor carts.

As I sit alone on a bench outside Victoria's Secret, I can't help feeling enchanted by the place. The ambiance kindles feelings that I haven't known since the Florida vacation we once took with Mom and Dad – really the *only* vacation we ever took as a family. As I shovel chunks of smashed blueberry pie in vanilla ice cream into my mouth, all is right with the world, and I am at peace again.

It's a pity I'm not more disciplined. It would be nice to hold onto this feeling. As I start to entertain the idea that it will inevitably slip away, I find myself missing it before it's even gone.

Has there ever really been a point in my life when I wasn't completely out of control?

After a long sigh I spoon the last bite of ice cream into my mouth and set the cup down on the bench beside me. I fish out my phone and check for messages from Elora with the excitement of a high school kid waiting in the bushes outside his girlfriend's house for her parents to retire to bed.

But there isn't a single notification on my home screen. And why should there be?

I try to keep from becoming annoyed, from going back to the dark places I've been. This will inevitably lead to resentment, and I don't want to be all hot-headed when I start drinking. Elora has always been a bit detached from the world. In fact, she lives in a different world entirely. She's oblivious to *most things* in a way so innocent and innocuous it leaves me wondering if that's why I love her so much. In any event, it's one of many qualities that escaped me in the waning days of our final high school summer. The summer when I broke things off in order to *properly enjoy* the university experience.

I'm a proper *idiot*.

A notification pops up on my phone, accompanied by a little jingle. *Concert at Dirty Moose*. The reminder is set to go off one hour before I need to be there. Elora goes on at 9:00, it's 8:00 now. I suppose it's okay for me to head over and put my claim on a seat at the bar. Who knows, I might even be able to chat with Elora before their first set.

The Dirty Moose is a dive as expected. I knew it the moment I made my drive-by, but it isn't confirmed until I step onto the sagging planks of the front porch and make my way uneasily inside, shaking my head at the deer antlers used in place of door handles. I'm so tired of overused backwoods motifs in New England.

The bar room is open-concept with the sharp presence of comingled sweat, skunked beer, and urine. There are no walls separating the billiards and darts on the right from the tables, dance floor, and platform stage on the left. Neon signs advertising every mass-produced pilsner on the planet hang arbitrarily from the walls. The floor is dirty and strewn with peanut shells. In the center of the room is a square bar with a conical arrangement of liquors in the middle. It's lit from beneath because that's what all the bars do now. The light catches in cold shades of glass.

Two men tend bar, each dressed in what I imagine to be management-mandated flannel and blue jeans. Both are overweight as an apparent lifestyle choice, wearing yellow trucker hats with the bar's name emblazoned on them. Both remind me of Kelly's backwoods cousin Larry from Sanford, Maine, a man who has somehow managed to exemplify every redneck and white trash stereotype ever gifted to the world. His usual pairing of sleeveless flannel over honest-to-god jean cutoffs represents his commitment to a lifestyle I'll never understand and baselessly condemn.

I'm appraised upon entering by locals and tourists alike. Even the townies wrapping up their game of Eight-Ball pause over the felt to have a look at the tourist who's clearly lost his way. Surely a man on vacation who shows up at this kind of place has done so in error, though that fails to explain the parents in the corner trying to force pub food on unyielding children.

The bartenders look as though they're sizing me up differently. Perhaps as the type from whom they'll farm some solid tip money. Who knows? Like most things, it's probably all in my head.

It doesn't take long for the men and women at the bar to return to their drinks and conversation. The sound of a man's voice calling his shot from the billiards area informs me that the game has resumed. The experience feels like something out of a movie, and I need a damn drink.

I walk to the bar and sit opposite the locals on the other side. The bar itself is surprisingly clean, despite the odors testifying otherwise. I'd expected tacky patches of dried grenadine and untended puddles building beneath perspiring glasses, but the polished wood is pristine despite the general character of the place.

Larry #1 approaches. I differentiate him from Larry #2 by the blond curls poking out from under his cap. The stubble on his face and neck is so fine it's barely noticeable without the light.

"First time at the Dirty Moose?" he asks, lacking the southern twang I'd expected.

"Yes it is," I answer, folding my arms on the bar.

"Well, welcome. We've got six beers on tap, can mix anything you can think up, and we've got live music at nine."

"What's on draft?"

"Miller, Bud, Coors, and Allukalana IPA."

"What's Allukalana IPA?"

Larry #1 smiles. "Microbrew out of Rangeley, Maine – 9.6% A-B-V."

"That's for me then," I say, smiling in anticipation of the buzz I'll soon enjoy. Hopefully it'll take the edge off.

"Right on, right on. Sixteen or twenty ounce?"

I raise my eyebrows and give him my best *what do you think?* look.

"Twenty it is, brother."

He throws back a cooler lid beneath the bar and extracts a frosty glass, not stopping on his way to the taps at the other end. As he pours my drink, I swivel toward the stage, where Elora's band has already set up their equipment. My gaze falls upon her green, glittery guitar. It looks lonely just sitting there on its stand, waiting for her to strum life into it.

The guitar and I have a lot in common.

Behind the microphones and guitars is a drum kit with the band name "Staple You Shut" hand-painted on the bass drum.

"One Allukalana IPA," Larry #1 says from behind the bar. I spin around in time to watch him lower a colossal beer onto a napkin printed with a cartoon moose struggling out of a mud puddle of all stupid things. "You want to start a tab?"

"Yes, please." Something tells me I'll be buying a lot of drinks for my high school girlfriend. I pull my wallet from my back pocket and extract my credit card.

"Right on, man." Larry #1 nods and tugs down on the frayed brim of his cap before snatching up my card and shuffling to a cash register at the base of Liquor Pyramid. He drops it in a pile, scrawls something down on a notepad, and raises his voice over the crowd. "You're number seven!"

Lucky seven, I think. I give him a confirming nod and lift the beer greedily toward my lips. It's bitter with a fruity, citrus finish. I try my best to savor it, but I've wanted to have a drink for hours at this point. The first sip spirals hastily into three enormous gulps that leave the glass half empty when I set it down.

I draw out my phone. Moving past the lock screen, I see that I'm still absent notifications of any kind from Elora. Thumbing my way through my messaging app, I count the number of texts I've sent her, all unanswered these last twenty-four hours. The total is five. She probably thinks I'm pathetic. There's really no hiding my feelings for her. They may be shadowed in the subtext of our correspondence, but I don't trouble myself to hide them all that well.

As the warmth of an imminent beer buzz kindles in my belly, I set the phone on the bar and refuse myself another outgoing text. This doesn't however mean that as I grow more inebriated I won't change my mind. For a moment I entertain the idea of leaving, of allowing Elora to play for the townies without a familiar smiling face to greet her. But I don't, because I love her despite it all.

The next hour is a series of phone checks, tentative conversations with Larry #1 while ordering additional rounds, and more self-destructive introspection. As the time for live music draws closer, more locals trickle in alongside occasional tourists, unsure about the looks tossed their way as they cross the threshold. By the time the small stage door opens and Elora emerges ahead of her bandmates, the bar stools around me have filled with bodies.

I try not to stare too intently at Elora. She's clad in black boots bolted up to her knees. Red fishnet stockings cling to toned, athletic legs beneath a black dress that swishes at her thighs in a way that drives me crazy. On full display is her diverse collection of tattoos: a red, white, and black snake curling down her right arm with its head ending just shy of the first knuckle on her index finger; a blue bird with red eyes perched above her left breast; a human skeleton seductively straddling her left wrist with its head thrown back in demonic elation.

This is my perfect woman.

She doesn't seem to look for me as she takes the stage and lifts her guitar. Her fingers curling around the neck of the instrument, she slings the strap over her shoulders and turns to the microphone, speaking in a deep, sultry voice that could tell me to do anything and I'd comply. "How we doing tonight?"

Flavorless whoops and whistles are offered up by the townies. The tourists clap politely, unsure of what might be coming. My gaze remains held by Elora, who seems unfazed by the lack of enthusiasm.

Oblivious is another word for it.

"We're Staple You Shut." She strums her guitar a few times, giving us a taste of the heavy, electric distortion to come. She stops, cymbals whispering behind her over a few pumps on the bass drum. "We're here to rock you *stupid.*"

Our eyes meet, she gives me a friendly half-smile and a wink before glancing behind her to make sure her bandmates are ready. She's the only woman in the group. The drummer is slightly overweight with long black hair that falls over his shoulders. He's wearing a t-shirt riddled with ovular holes. The bass guitarist easily stands at over six feet tall, dressed in ripped blue jeans and a plaid flannel. He watches Elora through gold-rimmed, circular eye glasses. Short-cropped blond hair is parted down the left side of his head.

Elora looks to the rhythm guitarist last, nodding her head as she counts quickly upward. He nods his head along with her, locks of black hair obscuring his eyes. They seem more in tune with one another than the other band members. He's sleek and athletic just like her, sharply dressed in skinny jeans and an untucked crimson dress shirt which hugs his torso in a way that dispels any thoughts trending toward *dad bod.* In any other situation I'd swear he was her brother, but given my ability to conjure up negatives for any situation, I jump to the absurd conclusion that they're lovers. Probably.

I upend my beer and order another.

Fast-paced rock music fills the bar, catching me off guard. I almost drop my empty glass, but manage to set it gently back in its sweat puddle. Pivoting back to the stage, my gaze is hauled by the harshest of mental gravity back toward Elora as she plays, legs splayed, eyes on her fretboard. Her lips part, teeth nibbling at the tip of her tongue a moment before she leans into the microphone, singing softly in contrast with the grating instrumentals. It's different, and it works for Staple You Shut in all the best ways. Or perhaps I'm biased because the front-woman is my own personal rock goddess, or so I fervently wished.

They play a couple original songs before Larry #2 moseys up to the stage for an inaudible chat. After a brief gap the band resumes their set, now switching over to cover songs. Both the locals and the tourists are fairly liquored up at this point. From the bar comes a slow trickle of people who pool around the stage, dancing. We get some AC/DC, Rolling Stones, Beatles – the usual fare. It seems live bar music has never found its way out of the '70s. Though every member of Staple You Shut missed that glorious decade (as did I), they still seem to understand this, and for a band that clearly keeps to the Metal side of things, they do pretty well.

More bodies fill the bar as the hours turn, much to my genuine surprise. I can only assume that the place is a local haunt – perhaps even the only place catering to locals in a town almost exclusively structured around tourism, but the locals don't seem to mind the likes of me and the scattering of other obvious out-of-staters.

The clock on my phone marches steadily toward midnight, and I lose count of the beers I've put away. As the band launches into their final set, they brazenly perform a half dozen original songs that succeed only in clearing the dance floor. A part of me expects Elora to end with something she can use to properly flex her passions and abilities in ways the Greatest Hits parade stifles. I'm struck by a spark of hope as she pauses before the mike and meets my gaze, the room now shifting around her thanks to the beers I've consumed.

Elora says, "This last one is for a special friend of mine who came all the way up here from Maine just to see us." She winks my way, sweat glistening on her brow in the warm, incandescent glow of the bar. "Still like Smashing Pumpkins, Mark?"

For a moment I think she's going to play *Set the Ray to Jerry*, but there's no way she knows that song. Still, I can't help appreciating the odd coincidence that I'd just been listening to them on the ride up. I return her smile, unable to smother out the enamored looks I'm projecting her way. I'm sure she sees it, but she continues to look at me like some… relative.

"This is *Stand Inside Your Love*," she says, her booted foot tapping a pedal before the amplifiers bleed with heavily distorted, static-laden guitar. I recognize the song immediately from the last album the band released with their original lineup. It wasn't the most amazing record, but it holds a special place in my history and inspires its own memories, provokes its own emotions and feelings.

This particular song though. Why did she choose it? It certainly isn't their most popular. Nobody outside of the fan base would even know it. Was she trying to say something to me? Its lyrics are an obvious declaration of affection, of rebuilding oneself around the person they love.

Our eyes are locked as she sings. She's singing to me, I'm certain of it, her message a clear profession of love.

Elora's voice is lost in the instrumental fuzz, but I know every word to this song and don't need to listen closely to follow along. I can't help the mixture of rapture and anxiety that coalesce within me. My fingers and feet cease tapping as all but the woman I crave, the woman I *covet*, dissolves away. Her intentions, her body language, her expressions, all suddenly shift from friend to lover. It's all there in her eyes, in her *voice*, in the way her hips swivel and her fingers pick at the strings of her guitar. It's a spark that sets a short fuse burning from my head to my heart, leaving me with moments before I explode.

But when the song ends and the din of conversing voices rises in place of the music, that fire in her eyes seems no longer fanned. It diminishes to a spark, a flicker, and once again she tosses me a half-smile and a wink before setting her guitar down and speaking into the mike, "Thanks, Dirty Moose, you got us off hardcore."

She goes to work helping her bandmates break down the stage.

What the hell was that?

She joins me at the bar half an hour later, after the stage is emptied of their equipment. Since their set wrapped, I've found it difficult to keep from tracking her down and following her like a dog from stage to van and back again. I'm still with it enough to see how pathetic that would look, so I wait, enjoying my eighth or ninth beer and wondering what kind of tab I've accumulated.

Then all at once she plops down on the stool beside me.

"How we doing, Mark?" she asks, arms opening immediately. I'm drawn into them under the same gravity as a black hole sipping light off a neighboring star. I'm awkward, rigid. I can feel it in the way I hug her back. The contact is euphoric though. I remain there, my body pressed to hers as long as she'll allow, breathing lilac and scotch on her.

"How've you been?" I ask as we separate. She pulls an elastic from her wrist and draws her hair into a tight ponytail. She's traded her stage outfit for a red tank and form-fitting jeans.

"You know," she smiles, glancing to Larry #1 as he approaches. "Busy, busy, busy. I can't stand still for a second." Her gaze shifts to Larry #1 as he places his hands on the bar and leans inward.

"Couple good sets there." He makes a decent, albeit obvious effort to keep his eyes from falling to her chest. Based on the glowing smile she forces his way, it's obvious she's noticed. Now my opportunistic love will work him over with the patient prowess of an expert con artist.

"Thanks," she returns, her voice high and flirty, eyelashes batting just enough to avoid overselling it. "You guys have a nice spot here."

"Been a work in progress for a few years now, but it's coming along," Larry #1 says. He adjusts his trucker hat, pinching it by the bill and lifting it up and down a few times. "So, what's your poison?"

Seriously? What is this, 1987?

Elora assesses me and my half-drained beer. She oscillates toward the bartender. "I'll have whatever he's having."

"You got it," Larry #1 says, turning reluctantly away from her with a goofy smile still plastered on his fat face. He's clueless to what she's doing here, my enchantress working her social magic on this credulous rube. He'll pour her free drinks until cutoff time.

I wonder, only briefly, if this is what she does to me.

"So," she says, rotating on her stool and facing me head on. She leans on the bar, clearly intent on listening and absorbing, as usual. "How's life?"

Have I really not told her about Nathan Kelson or Mallory or Kelly? My lips crack open as I prepare to fill her in on everything, then I quickly seal them shut again. If I went into details about the last few weeks, we'd be talking about it all night, and that is not what I want. There is, however, one item I lack issue sharing.

"Kelly and I split up. For good this time, I think." I do my best to exude equal parts grief and relief. My intentions, I hope, are only obvious to me: I want her to realize I'm available.

She frowns and says, "That sucks," in a lachrymose voice. Her treatment of this news as an apparent formality leaves me losing hope for the first time that night. But I soldier on. I am, after all, happy just be in her company.

"How are you and... um—"

"Gary," she says.

"Right – Gary. How are you two doing?" I realize as I ask the question that she probably assumes I'm hoping for the same flavor of answer. Not that it matters, I'm convinced she's known of my feelings for years.

"We're great. *Never better.*" Heavy emphasis on the last part. "I guess it helps when you don't have to see each other every day. He's always off traveling for NeoGris and I'm always on the road." Larry #1 sets her beer down, receiving a roguish smile and wink for his troubles. He grins back and turns to another drinker, not once asking for payment.

Elora rotates back to me, beer in hand, and gives a shrug before lifting it to her lips.

Peering into my own beer, I suddenly wish it was a shot of whiskey. But it's my turn to stoke the conversation, so I try not to picture Gary's coffin sinking into the ground as I continue with my feeble propositioning. "That still must be tough though. Not having your partner around all the time leaves a hole, I'd think."

She cocks her head in a knowing way, and I realize I've overplayed my hand. "You know me – I've always been pretty independent," she returns, brushing cruelly past the meat of my statement.

And now we dance the periphery of the *Friend Zone*. "Makes me wonder why you got married in the first place." I know the moment I speak that I've had too much to drink. I understand this in the same way that I understand I'm powerless to stop.

Taking a long sip of her beer, Elora begins to nod, staring pensively *through* Larry #2 at the far end of the bar. "Nobody wants to be alone *all the time.*"

"I know all about that." I hoist my empty glass until it catches the attention of Larry #1. He nods, eyes sliming over Elora before producing a fresh glass and pouring. I'm already plodding up-current in unsafe waters, but at least I have the self-control to keep from moving onto the hard stuff.

"What d'you mean?" she asks, a current of reluctance flowing beneath her words.

"Nobody wants to be alone. Even when I was with Kelly, we just, you know... *existed* together. There hasn't been any kind of spark in years, no attachment. We've just been roommates." A darkness I don't understand flexes in me. "I know all about being alone."

"I'm sorry, Mark." She turns away, taking a lengthy sip of her beer, eyes averted in a way that tells me my words are far from well-received. Larry #1 approaches with my beer, lowering it and carrying my used glass away.

I take a hard pull, drinking out the uncomfortable silence. When I set the glass down it nearly topples, but I catch and steady it in time.

Both Elora and Larry #1 cast uneasy eyes on me now. I don't let it stop me. "Yeah, it sucks. Hey, why'd you pick that song at the end there?"

She smiles uneasily. "Smashing Pumpkins was always your favorite band. I thought you'd like it."

"I did," I return, though my dismal tone does little to sell it. "I'm just curious why you picked that *particular* song."

She rotates her glass thoughtfully before lifting it, no doubt revisiting the lyrics of clearly professed love with a sharper mind. "I just always liked that song, I suppose. I was never crazy about the band, but that song wasn't so bad."

"They aren't for most people," I agree, reaching for my beer and drinking it half-empty. For the moment I have nothing more to say, my mind a blank slate waiting to be chalked up with the best foot-in-mouth material my imagination can summon.

A minute or so passes before she takes it upon herself to jump-start the conversation. These long gaps aren't like us, and we're both painfully aware of it. "So I was in Eliot last month. You'll never guess who I had lunch with – Andersen Sullivan. You remember him? He literally just popped up on Facebook. Nobody's heard from him since graduation."

Jealousy blazes in me. "You were in Eliot? Why didn't you tell me? We could have had lunch or something." I'm acting possessive. I'm out of line. I realize both these things, yet I'm powerless stop. It's been building too long.

The color drains from her face. She begins uncharacteristically tripping over her words. "I was just passing through really. I'm sorry. I thought of you, that's why I sent you that text about the concert. I felt bad that I missed you and really wanted to see you."

This isn't the first time she's bragged to me about reconnecting with old friends and acquaintances. She's always been a social butterfly – I met her at the biggest party spot in town for Christ's sake. Still, I'm pressed upon by the heaviest of existential revelations that the object of my undying affections doesn't so much *make friends* as she *collects people*. It makes me wonder if I'm just another of her possessions, a stuffed animal relegated to the closet, played with out of guilt-driven obligation and only long enough to satisfy her before I'm returned to my dark solitude.

"Why?" I want to pick up my beer and toss it back, but I want this more. I want a straight answer from her. I *deserve* a straight answer.

"Why what?" She's growing nervous again.

"Why did you want to see me? Why here? Why not while you were in Eliot?"

"I told you, I was just passing through. If I had time I would have... I'm sorry." Again with the forced frown. Then the inevitable, "Are you okay?"

"No," I growl. I feel my emotions spiraling as the firewall between my brain and mouth crumbles. "No, I'm not okay. I'm far from okay. My life has turned upside down – I killed a man with my car, was told by his wife that she wishes I were dead, then my wife kicked me out for good measure. For the first time since all of that stuff happened I've been excited, happy to come up here and see you, only to find out I'm just another keeper in your card collection."

Those in our immediate proximity go quiet. Or perhaps they've been quiet since the beginning of my tirade. I don't know. What I do know is that both Larry #1 and Larry #2 are looking me over in a way that says I'm not getting more drinks tonight.

As my gaze drifts back to Elora, I'm overcome with guilt. She looks like someone just punched her in the gut. Her bottom lip trembles in the early makings of a tear storm. A voice, distant and muffled as if sifted through a dream, asks her if she's okay. Her eyes remain on me.

"What—what is that supposed to mean?" She's struggling to keep herself together, eyes glistening in the soft light. I've only seen this woman cry once... the day I broke up with her.

I let out a long sigh. "You're a collector of people. You cultivate friendships like a hobby. I'm sorry, but I can't take this. I feel like you've been leading me on for years. Elora, you know that I still love you, right? You must. You coax me up here, making sure to point out that your husband won't be around, then you play a song that's an obvious profession of love. What, exactly, are you *getting* out of this?"

Her pupils dart to the corners of her eyes as she breaks contact and stares off toward the stage. She says nothing, tears brimming and threatening to spill over.

Larry #1 is suddenly in front of us, gut puddling on the bar. His attention rests exclusively on Elora. "You okay?" he asks, only then shooting a look my way. It's a look that says, *I may tend bar but I do side work in attitude adjustments.*

"I'm fine," Elora answers blandly, staring off.

"You sure?"

"She said she's fine," I answer for her, not sure why I've opted to push back against a man with the unambiguous desire to put me in the hospital.

He glares at me. I glare back. I've just destroyed the last good thing in my life. I don't care.

Larry #1 backs reluctantly away and joins his partner at the far end of the bar. There they seem to discuss the situation with a pair of townies who've obviously been following our soap opera.

I have little time before I'm kicked out. Whatever I want to say, however I intend to wrap this up, I have to do it now.

And so it comes.

"Breaking up with you before I went to college – *losing you*. It's the greatest regret of my life. I love you. I'll *always* love you. I'm sorry."

With that I'm up and striding toward the door. She doesn't call after me. She doesn't pursue me despite the revelations I've laid at her feet.

Elora Kennedy lets me go.

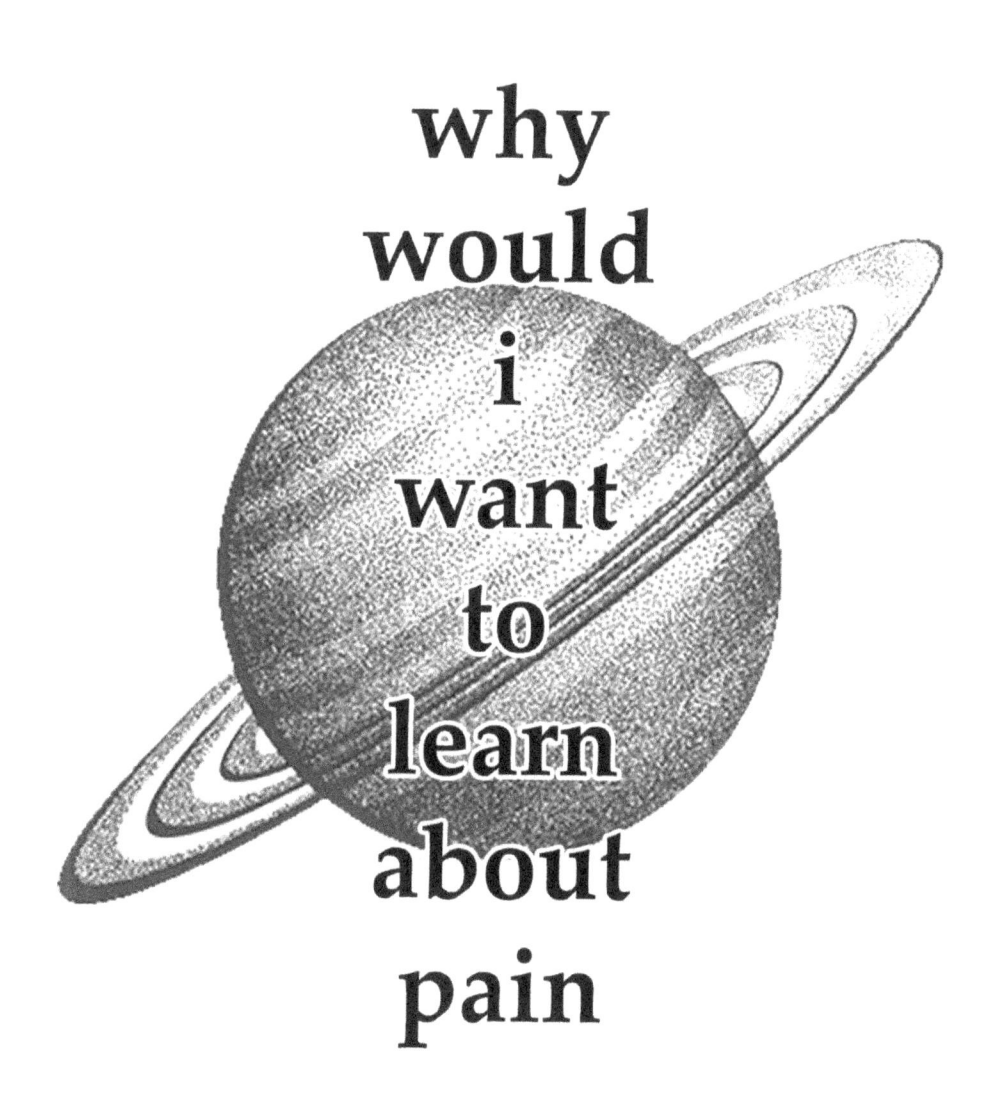

why
would
i
want
to
learn
about
pain

THE PAIN OF taking a life is nothing compared with that of a broken heart.

I thought those kinds of things were trivial on this side, I return, still full of emotion from the bar.

You obviously returned this time to probe the depths of pain, to make its understanding your lesson in life.

Why would I want to learn about pain?

Transcendence is about knowing all things, about going to God with a pure and enlightened soul.

The word *Transcendence* alone is enough to ground me here in this nothingness, to bring a semblance of form to the murk. For a moment I see pitted stones and boulders rotating and undulating against a striking field of star-shot black, and then it's gone. The crushing weight of oblivion presses back upon me.

If I wanted to learn about pain… if I wanted to suffer… a life without Elora would certainly do it.

And she'd never refuse you anything. If you asked her to return with you to walk the periphery of your life, never to be possessed, she would do it without hesitation.

Because she loves me.

Because she loves you.

I end up at the first gas station I encounter on my way back to the hotel. I've never driven so drunk in my life, and I don't care. I park diagonally across two spaces and step out with the engine still idling. The vehicle rolls forward, I panic and fall back into the driver's seat, this time throwing it into Park before venturing into the convenience store.

I'm in search of the thing I need most now that I'm thoroughly liquored-up: cigarettes.

So I'll have respiration problems when I run over the next few days. For the first time in weeks I acknowledge that I haven't gone out for a single run. What purpose does it serve anyway? Maybe I should adapt Walt's approach to life and just do what feels good. Screw responsibility, just drink and do drugs and tool around on the internet all day.

"Marb Reds," I say before I've even reached the counter. The old woman manning the store in these early morning hours assesses me with healthy suspicion. She squints through thick bifocals, sucking her dentures as she decides whether or not to card me.

I fish my wallet from my pocket and realize with a sinking stomach that my credit card is gone, left behind at the bar. Like so many other things tonight, I don't care. I pull my debit card from its slot and hand it over. "Make it two packs." I select a lighter at random off of one of the impulse racks. It's one of those stupid zodiac ones – Elora's sign, Sagittarius.

I'm out the door, butts in-hand, and strolling back toward my car before I know it. The world I pass through feels frail and artificial, and it moves of its own volition as I struggle to tear open my cigarettes and extract one from the pack. I light up as I fall into the driver's seat, reclining beneath a night sky hindered by gas-pump fluorescents.

I draw deeply, lungs swelling with smoke. I'll be chain-smoking for the rest of the night. A gentle breeze laps at my face and disperses my clouded exhale. The euphoric effect of nicotine coursing through my blood is almost instant. I close my eyes and begin to play back *Stand Inside Your Love* in my head as I take the cigarette all the way to the filter and light up another.

The rumble of a car passing on the silent, early morning lanes of US-16 draws me out of my little coma. I glance to my left at the street meandering down through the village, past the shadow-delineated geometry of local gift shops and restaurants. A white van cruises slowly along. I can't see inside. I wonder if it's Elora and her bandmates off to whatever hotel they'd booked for the night. Perhaps they're headed home.

As the humming of the van's engine dwindles in the distance, its red taillights are swallowed up in trees. Replacing the sounds are the voices of kids out somewhere in the night, laughing and fooling around, no doubt up to no good. It immediately sets memories of my time with Elora at Mrs. Miles's playing across my mind's eye. The best days of my life, never to return.

"Well," I say aloud. "At least I don't have to worry about being friend-zoned anymore."

There's no way Elora's ever going to speak to me again, and in a way that's comforting. At least now I can try to move on, or at the very least devote more serious time to contemplating suicide.

The acrid, chemical taste of burning foam fills my mouth as my latest draw burns through the filter. I toss the cigarette to the ground and spit until I've fooled myself into believing the taste is gone.

I consider another, then decide to get back to the hotel instead. There I can move on to hard stuff, get drunker, and rip on all the butts I want without worrying about a DUI.

It feels like twenty minutes before the silhouettes of the outlet malls sprout like gravestones on the horizon. Soon comes my hotel, a true sight for sore eyes, and despite this being the worst night of my life, I'm relieved to have gotten back without spotting or being *spotted by* a single cop.

It's straight vodka now, no mixers. This isn't a vacation anymore. I'm not here to lounge and enjoy my drink – I'm here to get plastered and forget about my life, and after three back-to-back-to-back shots, I pour myself a fourth and move over to the bed, lifting the remote control to the television. I settle on an infomercial for some male enhancement pill called Maxomizer, clinically proven to enhance the male libido and all that garbage.

Double-blind test studies.

I leave the TV on as I forget the shot in my hand. At least I'm not pathetic enough to need penis pills.

The only thing you're screwing is yourself, Kelly's voice drips over me with tar-thick contempt.

It's not long before my body begs for another cigarette, and suddenly I'm aware of the weight of the shot glass in my hand. I toss it back, leaving the TV on as I set the glass absently on the nightstand, throat burning.

I find the presence of mind to pat myself down before venturing out, making sure my wallet with the key card is on me, but more importantly making sure the pack of cigarettes is still in my pocket. The presence of each verified, I draw open the door and pass into a silent corridor.

Something in my drunken mind leads me to believe I'd be best to take the stairs, so I hang a left outside of my room and descend to the ground floor slowly and carefully, hands white-knuckling on the bannister. It's a wonder I don't fall and hurt myself. When I take the final step I'm clued suddenly into the subliminal train of thought that had me picking the stairs over the elevator: there is a side door. Beside it is a small block of wood no larger than my hand, no doubt used previously by other smokers to keep the door from locking behind them. I'm unsure if I'd noticed this previously or just assumed it would be there based instead on past experience, but I spend little time ruminating, instead snatching up the block of wood and letting myself out into the night.

In the powdered light from the half-moon, along with that cast by the stars and parking lot LEDs, I'm able to make out one of those potted ashtrays with the long, narrow stems. Wasting no time lighting up, I draw greedily and billow cloud in the dark, knowing I'll be back multiple times tonight.

I enjoy the quiet around me, finding it another world against the sounds of fervent shoppers descending upon daylit outlet stores. My only company is the wind whispering through the trees, tossing leaves and pine bristles.

Then the door is thrown open, startling me. I stumble backward, groping out for something to steady me and miraculously finding balance before kissing the pavement.

The reedy silhouette of a woman steps through the door, a 100's style cigarette drooping from her lips. As she bends over to replace the block of wood, slowly guiding the door closed, the metallic click of a Zippo lighter stabs the silence, and a massive flame reflects off the brick siding.

She's all legs, and petite to the point where she isn't simply flat-chested, she's *no-chested*. Shadows sharpen along the arches of her heels. As her Zippo winks out, she turns finally toward me, gasping and recoiling from my silent shadow in a fit of coughs.

Apparently the presence of a block of wood already propping the door open hadn't entirely resonated with her.

"Sorry," I say, the word emerging as *sowwy* in my drunken state. "I didn't mean to scare you."

She plucks the cigarette from her mouth, pressing her free hand bracingly to her chest. As my eyes readjust to the low light, I notice her low-cut skirt, and heat swells between my legs.

"They—" she coughs, the fit starting to calm, "they should have *lights* out here." Her voice is familiar, but I can't quite place it.

"No respect for smokers anymore," I lament, feeling like a relapsing heroin addict. I know I'll regret everything in the morning, but that holds zero consequence *in the now*.

"Don't get me started. This country is beyond hope," she says with a final hack before returning the cartoonishly long cigarette to her lips and drawing expressionlessly. Silence settles between us until she exhales a jet of smoke broken by each syllable as she continues. "So you on vacation or do you work for the hotel?"

"Neither," I answer blandly. "Came up to see an old friend. Turns out that was a big mistake."

"Bad night, huh?"

"The classic mixture of heavy emotions and too much to drink." I pull another cigarette from the pack and pinch it between my lips. Using the cherry from my first one, I light it, take a pull, and toss the butt to the ground without a thought to the stemmed pot beside me.

"Been there."

"So what brings you up here?"

She doesn't answer at first, obviously hesitant. After another drag she shrugs and says vaguely, "I was lured up here by a pack of lies on a dating website by some lowlife *cat-fisher* or whatever they're called."

"Enough said." Social Engineering in the cyber realm is one of my specialty areas. "This your first time up here?"

"Yes. Long drive from Boston."

It isn't, but whatever.

"I take it you aren't the outdoorsy type."

"What makes you say that?" There's a playfulness in her voice now that I don't expect.

Chuckling, I return, "Can't say I've met many mountain-faring granola types that dress like that." I wonder for a moment if I've overstepped by commenting on her clothing (or lack thereof). Guys with confidence can say these things and get away with them, but not me. In a panic, I rack my brain for a quick way to clarify what I'd meant, but she saves me the trouble.

"What? You don't think this is good for a hike?" She laughs, twirling a heeled foot for emphasis. I laugh along with her. It is genuine, not my usual social fakery. It's not often I feel so immediately comfortable with a person I've just met, but I don't question it. I don't even consider that it might be the mixture of booze and nicotine dripping poison on my mind.

"Definitely good for a night clubbing, but I don't think there are any places like that around here."

"There's one, but they book up months in advance, and seem to have a problem with their records. Pisses me off just thinking about it."

I'm missing background here, but I don't care enough to press her. "Sounds like we're on the same kind of trip. I was going to stay another night, but I'm thinking I'll just head home tomorrow. No point staying in a place that makes me miserable."

"You've got the idea." She clips her cigarette between her fingers again and measures the dwindling distance between the cherry and filter with one eye. The shadow she once was is taking further form, features refine here and there as my eyes adjust. Her face is roundish, pronounced cheekbones over recessed hollows that speak to an unhealthy relationship with her weight.

She turns with a final drag and deposits her cigarette in the receptacle pot. Reaching for the door, she pauses before turning back to me. Now, I've never been hit on so unambiguously in my life, so when she propositions me I'm first inclined to believe I've misheard her.

"I have some wine in my room if you'd care to join me for a drink," she says, her voice soft and inviting. It's the underlying implications, undeniable in her body language, that force me into a double-take.

"Excuse me?" I ask like a dopey teenager hoping to decode *sex* in a girlfriend's innocuous invitation to study at her house.

"Would you like to have a drink in my room?" she repeats, eyes suddenly devouring me.

Anticipation spreads through me like fire. "I'd love to," I answer, starting toward the door.

I get my first good look at her in the stairwell. I recognize her immediately as the woman from earlier, the one complaining into her phone about reservations while I was checking in. Everything she's said suddenly makes more sense.

She leads me to the elevator, my mind running with thoughts of every flavor. I'm going to have sex with this woman, a stranger. I'm struck by the odd memory of the restaurant I'd worked in during my summers in

Ogunquit. There the kitchen boss Steve maintained that *every* young man need find himself a *cougar* to fool around with, that she'd *teach you more and do crazier stuff than any girl your age.*

Beside me in this elevator, teetering out-of-sync with my tottering, is a woman decades my senior. A full-bred cougar, every qualification satisfied.

I feel myself harden as my gaze sweeps ravenously over a body that would tonight be mine. A second later, the doors slide open again, and it's only a few steps to her room.

"So what do you do in Boston?" I ask as she extracts a key card from her bra. She fumbles it into the reader and the door unlocks with an electronic *click.*

"Unhappy Homemaker," she answers in a monotone, elaborating no further. She steps into the room without glancing back.

I wait in the threshold a moment, allowing myself a final opportunity to reconsider things before following her toward certain sex.

Kelly has kicked me out.

Elora has been stringing me along for years and made no attempt to stop me leaving.

The last woman I spoke with before Elora told me she wished I was dead.

I wish I was dead.

With a conscience scrubbed preemptively clean, I step into my cougar's room, slapping Do Not Disturb on the door handle and closing the door behind me.

I wake to the sun warming my face. The light bites at my eyes, trickling over the bald peak outside my window.

Feeling through the knotted blankets, I roll over and away from the light, taking what I can with me. I return effortlessly to sleep, only to be woken after what feels like minutes but turns out to be hours by knuckles rapping gently on the door.

"Housekeeping," an accented voice pokes through the door.

Panic constricts my chest. My eyes snap open and I'm sitting up cross-legged on the bed, trying to bring order to the memories suddenly blitzing me, each hazier than the last, all punctuated by booze and cigarettes. My mouth tastes like I licked an ashtray clean.

Suddenly the memories clarify, pummeling me like a rogue wave. Hazy images of rough, unprotected sex flash through my mind, each more disturbing and decidedly *not me* than the last.

This isn't my room. It's *hers*.

Another, louder knock on the door. "Ma'am?"

"Just a minute!" I bellow at the door, startled by the volume of my own voice. No answer comes from the other side, leaving me to assume that the housekeeper moved on to the next room.

I rub sleep sand from the corners of my eyes before really inspecting the bed and realizing that my *cougar*, as it were, is no longer here. Glancing toward the open bathroom door, I find she's not there either.

She'd already left. Her suitcases are gone, the bottles of wine we'd killed are arranged neatly before the trashcan.

I throw the blankets off and swing my feet over the side of the bed. I'm completely naked. A quick survey of the floor finds my hastily shed clothes scattered everywhere. I gather them with equal haste, dressing as if suddenly exposed in this empty room.

I need to get back to my room, pack up, and get the hell out of North Conway.

The corridor outside the room is empty, save for a housekeeper's cart a few doors down. I have no idea why I'm so timid, I've done nothing illegal. My brain is simply incapable of letting me do things like this without the guilt that marries itself to every aspect of my life.

A wave of kids go running past out of nowhere. I wonder, strangely, if they're the same free-rangers from last night. I stand watching them charge down the corridor, bouncing off one another and nearly taking out a housekeeper emerging farther along.

It's a short walk to the elevator, one of many things I recall from last night with unfathomable clarity. I select my floor and ride to the top, anxious to brush my teeth and have the taste of my mistakes flushed from my mouth. When the elevator doors open, the same horde of kids goes rushing past. The last and smallest of them halts, looking me over with crossed eyes through thick-lensed cat-eye glasses. Even in this *child* I feel judgement falling upon me.

Turning back to the group, now farther down the hallway and not looking back, she hollers irritably after them, "Cece, Evy, wait for *me*!" and sets off again.

I step out of the elevator shaking my head, again trying to tell myself that it's a good thing Kelly and I couldn't have children. This leads naturally to guilt over the unprotected sex I'd had last night.

I'll make an appointment with my doctor for an S.T.D. screening first thing Monday. That's enough to quiet the bully in my mind as I walk the remainder of the corridor with snatches of bare flesh from my one-night-stand playing like a beaten-up VHS in my head. As I reach my room I enter another phase of panic, struggling suddenly to remember where I'd left my keycard. Fortunately the fog burns away over my mind, and I'm reminded that I left it in my wallet. Pulling it from my pocket, I'm relieved to see that Unhappy Homemaker didn't clean me out of cash for the hell of it.

Something tells me she wouldn't have been interested anyway, that hers is a life of wealth that fails to satisfy any of her needs.

I let myself into my room, striding immediately toward the trash can where I toss my cigarettes along with the Sagittarius lighter. The unopened pack from the nightstand joins its depleted brother, and I resolve never to light up again. The resolution hits like a bad joke more than anything else, further darkening my spirits.

I spend about five minutes brushing my teeth and rinsing with mouthwash which I'm tempted to swallow afterward. When I'm done I do it all again, the taste of cigarettes still lingering afterward. Perhaps an enormous, greasy breakfast will eradicate it completely. Baked beans and corned beef hash feel right. Throw in some sunny side up eggs and we're in business.

Breakfast is the exact lure I need to carry me forward and out of here. For a moment I consider a shower, but the messages coming suddenly from my stomach do so with escalating urgency that I'm disinclined to ignore.

I perform a onceover of the room, making sure I haven't forgotten anything, then move out of the bathroom, collecting items from the floor and reviewing a shoddy mental inventory of all I'd brought. Everything is crammed hastily into my backpack.

The last item I lift is my phone, still on the nightstand where I'd left it charging last night. I approach it guardedly, afraid it might bite me, and in many ways it can. After my meltdown at the bar, this was where the reprimands would arrive in neat, 160 character SMS format.

I power up the handheld and wait for it to boot while sweeping the room for any missed items. The phone vibrates, rattling audibly across the table minutes later. The lock screen shows three text notifications.

I draw a long, shallow breath, my stomach already folding over on itself.

All three texts are from Elora. I read through the entire string twice, my heart sinking further with each pass.

1:14 A.M.: *I can tell you have a lot going on, but what you said at the bar was really hurtful. I'd never do anything to upset you, Mark. Please tell me we can patch this up.*

2:32 A.M.: *Can't sleep. You still up? I've been thinking a lot about us. I'll always have deep feelings for you too. I may regret this, but screw it. I'm at the Red Leaf Inn, room 207. Come over if you want.*

7:41 A.M.: *You know, it's all for the best that you didn't come last night. I was drinking and wasn't thinking clearly. I'm sorry. Give me a call today. Please. I want to talk this out, and I need to know that we'll always be friends.*

The phone falls to the carpet, landing face up with the message feed open. My body lurches forward in that universal, arched posture of impending purge. I swallow back in a futile, last attempt to keep it in, the world doubling, but it's of no use.

Moments later I'm retching over the sink as I wash my sick off the face of my phone.

she
was
there
to
cheat
on
her
husband

YOUR UNHAPPY HOMEMAKER died in a car crash on her way back to Boston. Do you feel the mark you left on her?

Somewhere in the enveloping gloom I feel something reaching to me. Or am I reaching toward it? Here I intuit something that surprises the simpering voice.

She wasn't part of our chain of souls.

A stunned moment. *No, she wasn't.*

But I helped her with the final part of her lesson.

You did. The simpering character returns to the voice, *Do you know what that lesson was?*

Yes. Same as mine. A life learning the depths of pain and despair. She was there to cheat on her husband. Another detail drips into my consciousness, seemingly out of the ether. *Her* rich *husband.*

Like actors in a play, we all exit when our performance has ended. Her death was a joyous event for her and those awaiting her return.

Death is the reward at the end of our individual journeys. I try to wrap this around the tragedy of a woman I'd met once and with whom I'd been intimate, dying hours later in a car wreck.

She thought she was coming to North Conway to meet some guy from a dating site, but she was really coming up there to be with me, and I her. North Conway was never about Elora...

Was...?

I'm not dead.

T he more I think about North Conway the more I'm certain this is some rock bottom for me. This helps me turn an odd corner where I freely acknowledge that drinking no longer helps with anything.

Back at work Monday, I force myself through the grind, embracing the idea of simply riding out my lingering feelings. But fresh thoughts of Elora renew themselves in my mind with cruel abandon, drawing me back to the opportunity I'd missed with her.

I haven't answered any of her texts, and she hasn't followed up. Maybe she's ashamed of inviting me to her hotel room, of showing vulnerability with me.

It all feels like a drunken hallucination. But it was not, and I still sadly have the texts to prove it.

I pull into my office parking lot, a narrow, evergreen-shrouded business park in the woodlands of Berwick. The company I work for, *ReqTek,* occupies the last two units in the otherwise empty park.

The day is over, but I lack the mental fortitude to return home to Mom's odd behavior and Walt's idiosyncratic world views. If I could get away with sleeping here I would.

An unmanned reception desk sits in the entryway even though we've never had need for a secretary. Beyond is a cluster of gray cubicles and an open diagnostic area where a half-dozen workbenches lay strewn with modular components, keyboards, mice, and other digital detritus. With so much of our work performed in the field, time at the office is typically solitary, alone but for the collective exhale of server fans expelling hot air.

I enjoy the silence as I check email in my cube and update billing notes. When this fails to occupy me for long, I pivot to my diagnostic bench and go to work socketing processors, reseating RAM, and changing out PSUs for no reason other than to keep myself busy. I do this in a fugue, not stopping until the sound of the door swishing open announces the arrival of my manager, Tim.

"How we doing, kid?" Tim's voice startles me out of my shallow trance, sending the RAM stick I was mindlessly thumbing to the ground.

As I swivel a little too forcefully, my elbow knocks a red plastic cup to the floor, scattering peanut butter pretzel nuggets everywhere. Tim shakes his head comically and lets loose a long sigh as a couple roll around his foot. He sets down his messenger bag and grips his narrow hips, khakis barely holding on for dear life. Assessing eyes gloss over me under an elevated brow.

"Hit it a little too hard this weekend?" he asks.

I shake my head. "Just tired. I'm still having trouble sleeping."

"None of that business was your fault. It'll pass in time."

His words would carry more weight if, A) it truly wasn't my fault Nathan Kelson was dead and buried, and B) Kelson was the source of my current woes. Still, I nod, again to the floor, and thank Tim for his assurances. When I finish cleaning up and find him still standing silently over me, I ask him point blank if he needs anything. I'm slightly ashamed of the tone that emerges, but he doesn't seem to catch it.

"Yeah," he sighs, somehow knowing where this is going. "Kevin's been flaking out while you've been in-and-out the last couple months. For all we know he's always been flaking out and we just haven't noticed because you've been around to pick up the slack."

This is exactly the case. Kevin is a co-worker of mine, the only other field tech in the company. He's also a complete screwup, never shows up on time for work (especially early shifts and weekend work), and he doesn't know a Class A IP Scheme from a Class A cigarette. The company's been carrying his dead weight for almost a year while I've made both subtle and unabashedly direct attempts to get him fired.

"No problem," I say. "Where's he dropped the ball?"

"Cliffside Resort in Bartlett. Seems there was a virus on one of their front desk systems. From what I can tell, Kevin tried some registry cleaner software – messed the whole thing up. Gonna have to wipe it."

"I'm sure there's a good reason he couldn't stay up there and wipe it himself," I say, slathering on the sarcasm.

"You bet – it was a Friday night and he was already there past five. Add to that a two hour drive back, and, well, you can put the rest together yourself. He didn't want to be late hitting the bar."

"You'd think the overtime would make him want to stick around."

"He said his wife was sick and he needed to get home to take care of her. Again, I'm pretty sure he just went somewhere and hit the bottle."

I've suspected Kevin to be an alcoholic almost since the moment I'd met him. There have been a few occasions where I was certain he was even drinking at work, but I could never prove it. I wouldn't put it past him to carry a flask around, absconding to the bathroom every now and then for a nip.

"You want me to head up tonight?" I hope he says yes, even though Bartlett is a town over from North Conway. The last thing I need after a long day is to be tossed back into the epicenter of my emotional issues, ground zero of my slow mental implosion, but the idea of going home also sucks.

"Naw," he says, gesticulating like he's trying to wave me down. "Go in the morning." He checks his watch. 5:24 P.M. "By the time you get there it'll be 7:30. With two hours to format the system, load the OS, and reinstall drivers – not to mention loading and configuring software – you'll be there way too late."

"You're the boss."

"Damn right I am," he says, voice deepening. He steps up to me and delivers a couple playful punches to my shoulder. I hold my hands up in exaggerated defense. Such is our father and son dynamic. "You hangin' around much longer? Wanna grab a beer?"

"Wish I could, but I have to get my notes updated and remote into Strout Holdings to watch their backup. Been failing after the initial buffer since last Thursday apparently."

"You take care of it?"

"I think I have. Won't know until I watch the backup run."

"Your devotion is inspiring, young man," he says, chasing an itch over the glossed dome of his head. He claps me on the shoulder as he lowers it. "Don't stay here too late. The wife'll think you're up to something." He chuckles and walks away.

The wife. Right. I'm sure she's worried sick.

The next day is a literal guilt trip.

My sudden return to the White Mountains invites back that familiar darkness, and I wonder if I'll ever feel any differently about this place or Elora again. It seems certain now that I'll never speak to her again.

My route to Cliffside Resort – the only route – takes me past The Dirty Moose, past the hotel where I trysted with Unhappy Homemaker, and inevitably past the Red Leaf Inn where I could have spent the night with the lost love of my life. I picture each of these places engulfed in flames as I speed past, unconcerned with the posted limit of 35MPH.

Work at the Cliffside is quick. The staff is relieved it's me and not Kevin. All it seems to take is one visit for him to completely turn clients off on his "abilities." First impressions are most definitely everything, and when you're all bluster and no muster, people pick it up. Sometimes quickly, sometimes gradually, but they always find you out eventually.

I wrap the system wipe in a tidy ninety minutes and treat myself to lunch on the way home. Mexican food at a local café hits the spot nicely, and the hour or so I spend there is a renewing reprieve.

Days pass and my emotions temper. By Friday I'm back on something of an even keel, leaving me nervous that something horrible will soon go down. But it doesn't, and I enjoy a weekend with my e-reader on the scratchy couch, polishing off my Kirk Matthews novel and about three pots of coffee. I steer clear of booze with encouraging ease.

The next week is business as usual at work. Monday flies by in a storm of Cryptolocker infections. This sucker is mean, and comes as a welcome challenge as Tim, Kevin, and I tag-team impacted clients. That night the three of us go out for beers. It's the first time I've had a drink in almost two weeks, and the difference in company is enough to overwrite most of the lingering feelings from North Conway.

Walt's car is gone when I arrive back at the cottage. He and I haven't spoken much since I'd caught him trying to rob me. His reduced attention span limits his occasional periods of shame to a just few days. After that he's forgotten and moved on.

But I know he's avoiding me, just as I know I'm avoiding the gun topic with him.

I let myself into the mudroom, wondering if Walter has forgotten any beers in the fridge, when I halt at the sound of Mom's urgent, exhausted voice.

"Eric? Eric, help me."

The messenger bag slips down my arm and I'm almost in a sprint into the kitchen. Mom is sprawled on the floor, seeming pinned. It's obvious she's been here for hours, unable to get up. As I go to her, she starts trying to drag herself across the tiling, pawing and sloshing around in what I first mistake for water. It's not until I crouch that I'm struck by the smell of urine puddled around her, soaking into her white capris shorts and t-shirt. Beside her is one of the kitchen chairs, overturned ominously. Her hair is a snarled mess.

"Mom. What happened?" As I lean in, the smell of feces clarifies over the urine. Her face is wild, eyes gaping. She's only partly lucid.

"Eric?"

"It's Mark, Mom," I scuttle around her, trying to avoid the puddle. As familiar emotions build, I try not to focus on her confusion over my identity. "Let's get you up and—"

"Where's your *father*?" She's suddenly irate. All at once she stops fumbling on the floor and goes still, head lolling up and down, now staring off into nothing.

"Mom, Dad's been dead for almost seventeen years. We need to get you to the bathroom."

Her eyes spin wildly before locking with mine. Her confusion melts gradually and there's a shift in her body language. Her jaw trembles, signaling that she's returned to me. "I tripped over the cat."

"That's okay, Mom." I gather her in an awkward hug, willing the persistent odors away. She groans but doesn't resist. "Let's get you to the bathroom, clean you up."

It feels like an anvil is perched on my chest. Every breath is shallow and unsatisfying and seems only to grant greater presence to the odors wafting off her.

"Okay," she answers in a mousy mumble. She sounds like a child.

"On the count of three. One, two, *three*." I hoist her carefully, nearly losing my balance before finding equilibrium with Mom mostly limp in my arms. She wriggles briefly, reminding me of a fish drowning in oxygen, offering its final, lethargic flop. Though her feet touch the floor, she's not standing on her own.

"Can you stand?" Grunts punctuate my speech as I struggle to gain a better hold on her.

For a moment she puts in the effort, and I support her as she teeters, knees knocking and threatening to buckle. Moving around to her side, I keep my arms looped around her as I sling her arm over my shoulders and steady her. After this, it's a careful trip down the hall to the bathroom, feeling like I'm conducting a bag of dry bones.

"Do you have to use the toilet?" I ask of empty eyes.

She shakes her head, silver hair brushing my cheek.

"Okay. I'm going to sit you down and get a bath going. That sound okay?"

"Where's Walter?" she asks. She's not angry even though I, for one, have no doubt he's out smoking pot or snorting blow. No, she speaks of Walter as though he's some lifeline even though she'd still be on the floor if I hadn't come to live here.

"I don't know, Mom." It's obvious he's been gone most of the day. He's lucky *I* don't have a gun.

I steady Mom on the toilet, watching to ensure she stays upright, before turning to the bath and starting it filling. Another symptom of Dad's absence is the black mold growing in the grout between the blue tile. Mom's not with it enough to keep up the house anymore and Walt is useless in nearly every regard. The smell of mildew is strong enough to slice through the odors coming off Mom.

I rotate back in time to catch Mom listing to the right. I steady her as she watches the rushing tap water filling her bath. She's staring at it in a way that tells me she's humiliated and terrified somewhere in there. And why shouldn't she be? What mother wants to have her filth scrubbed from her naked body by her son?

Mom has been ravaged by the world and she deserves none of it.

I crouch into her field of vision. "Mom, I'm going to go and get your nightgown. Are you okay here by yourself?"

She nods, though her eyes are glazed in a way that leaves me doubtful. As I stand there, grappling with the idea of leaving her alone, she lifts a surprising hand to my shoulder.

Our gazes meet. She's drifting in and out.

"Mark." Her eyes are watery now, voice desperate. "I'm thirsty."

My hand grips hers. "I'll go get you some water," I hear myself croak as I guide her hand to an area not smudged with Walt's toothpaste spit at the lip of the sink. "You just hold on here, okay?"

"Okay."

Standing slowly, I attempt a final read on her before dashing into the kitchen. The sink is piled with Walt's unwashed bowls and plates, which I have to unload in order to fill a glass for Mom. From the depths of it comes the rich funk of unchecked decay. I've never seen Walter wash a single dish.

With the extra time it takes to fill the glass, I'm relieved to find Mom still upright on the toilet when I return.

"Here," I say, offering the glass to her. She reaches for it with her left hand, which she'd been using to steady herself.

"No, Mom, you keep holding on with that one. Take it with your right hand."

She lifts the hand with halting difficulty, as though she's clutching a dumbbell. An uneasy look dawns across her face, every feature seeming to droop in defeat.

"Are you okay?" I ask, voice timid as I try to make myself small for her.

"I..." she works quickly to banish her emotions and lifts her hand toward me, face scrunched against palpable, heartbreaking effort. "I'm fine. Can I have the water, please?"

Hesitantly, I deliver the glass into her twitching fingers. Her arm sags toward the floor as I release its weight to her, but she steadies it, and for a time sits there staring at the glass in a way that tells me she's terrified and lacks the strength to lift it all the way.

Fresh anxiety blooms as I'm struck with the sudden idea that she's suffered a stroke. This means she'll have to see a doctor, and... well, Mom's had an unflinching, baseless distrust of doctors for as long as I've known her.

There will be time to worry about that later. Though my mind wants to dwell, as it's given to doing lately (to no end), I have a job to do in getting her cleaned up.

Mom's gaze is fastened to the glass of water. Her arm begins to tremble. If I don't help her she will absolutely drop the glass, but again I'm conflicted – wanting to avoid further damage to her pride at all costs.

"Let me help," I say softly, doing my best not to sound like a parent addressing his child. I'm relieved as Mom surrenders the glass without argument, and I lift it with deliberation to her lips, regulating the flow so she doesn't drink too quickly. The smell of her is all-assuming.

She finishes and withdraws, leaving a mere sip in the glass.

"Good?" I ask.

She nods, drawing a long breath that smacks of deep frustration. She's back to leaning against the sink. I set the glass down before a trash bin brimming with toilet paper and used strands of floss. The tub is a quarter full now. Scooting to the edge of the basin, I dip a hand in the water and swirl it around, making sure that the temperature is consistent and mild enough for her.

I angle my head to peer back over my shoulder. "Do you want anything else before I help you into the bath?"

"I can get *myself* in the bath," she insists, suddenly sounding like herself. As much as I want to grant her the license to take care of herself alone, my thoughts are dominated by the frailty I'm seeing in the right side of her body.

Frowning, "I don't want you to fall again."

I expect her to fire back, and for a moment her lips pooch in an obstinate expression I've known since I was small, but she seems to reject the impulse, gaze falling wearily to the floor.

"I'll get you some fresh clothes. Just stay put, okay?"

She peers up at me again, misted eyes like dull portals to a world of eroding control. This woman never relinquished command. She'd raised two boys alone, never dating or remarrying. She'd sacrificed everything and this was her reward. In the blink of an eye she's become an elderly woman, helpless in ways the child in me cannot endure.

"Are you going to be okay?"

"Go, Mark," she says in clear defeat, head sinking toward the hand gripping the sink.

I want to tell her I love her and that everything will be okay, then I consider my position in line behind her. Forty years from now I'll be exactly where she is. I have no one to care for me, no children, no wife.

I'm out of the bathroom and in Mom's room before I realize it. The bed is shabbily made, though clearly to the best of her abilities, with her fraying quilt draped unevenly atop the mattress. Mouf stretches his front paws and releases a long, lazy yawn before rolling over on his wadded-up afghan at the foot of the bed.

"Nice to see you, too," I say to his back.

I go right for the mirrored sliding door of Mom's closet. Throwing it open, rattling on its aging track, I strip one of her nightgowns indiscriminately from a hanger.

With fresh clothes, I round the bed on my way back to the bathroom where, to my relief, Mom is still upright on the toilet. Next comes the most difficult task of my adult life.

I wash the woman who'd once washed me.

***

It's 1 A.M. and I'm still waiting for Walt. Perched at the edge of my couch, I'm awake as the milky face of the moon traversing a cloud-choked dark. I'm unable to banish images from my mind of Mom collapsed and enfeebled on the floor.

She'd said nothing, seeming to escape somewhere inside her head, as I dressed and assisted her to bed.

Now I lurk in the veiling darkness like a parent keeping his teenager honest with curfew. To say I'm irritated with Walter doesn't cut the mustard. I've been left to stew on this for hours, my anger swelling with each passing minute.

I've made an inventory of all he takes from our mother, living rent free, devoid of motivation, pathetically averse to working for a living. It wouldn't take much to do the dishes from time to time or maybe fold his own damn laundry, but these things require effort and independent thought, things Walter regrettably cannot smoke, snort, or drink.

I'm going to throttle him.

Another hour sees my temper cooling, and I begin to worry that something might have happened to Walter. I pluck my phone from its charger.

No missed calls or texts.

Habit has me on Facebook in no time, blinking lethargically at a picture of Elora's husband, every part of his fat, cheese-wheel face engaged in a smile so genuine I find it offensive. He's got an arm draped over Elora's shoulders, gripping her with an air of possession as Boston skyscrapers nibble at a cloudless blue sky behind them.

Elora's obviously happy to have avoided cheating on him in North Conway. The days since the trip have left me feeling that it's better to live without her than suffer beside her.

In the bowels of my newsfeed I unearth a series of insufferably grinning faces. It's not until I feel my fingers tingling that I realize I'm actively trying to crush my phone. Like a shooting star slicing through the heavens, so does my rage suddenly return, but not for Walt. No, I mash the status update button hard enough to crack the glass and bang out my message to the Happily Ever After world.

Screw you all. Screw your wives. Screw your husbands. Screw your kids. Screw your happiness. Screw EVERYTHING!

My thumb hovers millimeters above the *post* button. It's like a belt is cinched tightly across my chest, my breathing shallow and rapid. This is what mania looks like.

Closing my eyes, I work to force calm on myself. I'm a mess. I was stupid to believe these last weeks that things would improve in any lasting way. How could they? I destroy everything I love, ruin everything I touch. My life is nothing but pain and suffering.

I clear the field and lock the phone, cradled once more in the unassuming comfort of darkness. I need to get away from everything, *everyone*. It's the only way I'll find peace, by running like a coward.

Light suddenly slices across the ceiling. The undulating sputter of Walt's rust-eaten muffler bleeds through the walls until his car pulls into the circle outside and the lights and engine cut.

Silence returns until the sounds of footsteps crossing the porch and the aged protest of a front door tactlessly flung open fill the cottage. Then comes a moving shadow stealing across the cold light cast by the incandescent over the sink.

"Walt." My voice cracks, startling the sneaking shadow, which jumps a half foot off the floor.

Walt spins toward me wildly, steadying himself against the kitchen table before searching the darkness as though oblivious to who'd spoken. He's lucky he didn't roll in an hour earlier, then he'd have been greeted by the thundering voice of his elder brother, not the cracking chirp of a wholly broken man.

"Mark," he sighs, "dude, don't *scare* me like that." He steps away from the table, right into the spot where I'd found our mother and later cleaned up after her.

"Where've you been?" I ask.

"Out with friends," he answers, his pinched voice giving him away. Walt's never been a particularly good liar, but I can't blame him for not sharpening the saw over the years when Mom literally takes everything he says at face value.

"At 2—" I check my phone, "2:17 in the morning?"

"Yeah, man. We got a thirty-rack and snuck into Fort Foster – you know, the old park down by the river—"

"I know it, Walt. I'm still calling shenanigans."

He manages a pair of rigid steps toward me. "You know what? Screw you, man. You aren't my father."

Suddenly my rage rebuilds itself, and I feel like I could kill him. He should know better than to say something like that. "Why do you live here if you can't be bothered to help Mom? Are you really so selfish you don't care about the woman who changed your diapers and made your dinner and, and *washed your clothes* all these years?!"

"Dude, of *course* I do!" he insists, gesticulating wildly, tone darkening with deep resentment.

"I found her on the floor today. She'd been there all afternoon, unable to get up. What would she have done if I wasn't staying here, Walt? She would probably still be there now, at two in the damned morning!" I'm on my feet now. It's only when the ache of my fingernails biting into my palms registers that I realize how close I am to losing it.

Walt says nothing, seeming instead to process things quietly in the dark. I can't see his face, can't determine if he's silent with concern or appraising his new future with her like the opportunist he is.

For a time there's only the humming of the refrigerator motor, then he says, "A couple weeks ago the cops brought her home. She'd gone to Portsmouth and… and she forgot how to get home."

I'm advancing on him before I know what's happening, ready to seize any convenient part of him and shake until his brain starts working properly. "This happened and you didn't say anything?!"

"You're never here," he gasps, cowering suddenly behind shielding arms. I stop short of seizing him by the shirt collar, then with a sigh, I close my eyes and wait for him to realize he isn't going to get the beatdown he so rightfully deserves.

Naturally, he doesn't come around without prompting.

"Walt," I say. "We need to get her to a doctor. She's been saying weird things, and today she couldn't get herself up from the floor. Poor Mom..." my voice deepens, suddenly watery, "...she *peed herself*, man. When I got her to the bathroom to clean up, she could barely move one side of her body. I'm no doctor, but that's a stroke or something."

"She won't go to a doctor," Walt says, speaking stubbornly *for her*. "I've tried for other things—"

"*Minor* things," I interrupt. "This is serious. I don't care if we have to call an ambulance and have her *dragged out* by paramedics, she needs to be seen."

More of Walt's contemplative silence. After a few seconds he wobbles as if moved by the weight of these revelations. He steadies himself, gripping the chair Mom had overturned in her struggle to get up.

"You're high aren't you," I say, no effort to hide the contempt seeping out in my voice. "I don't smell weed on you. Please tell me you haven't gotten into hard stuff."

He comes back at me a little too insistently, further incriminating himself. "No, man. No way. I'd never do that. We were smoking outside."

"At Fort Foster."

He nods persistently. I still don't believe him, but as is common these days, I have issues beyond the antics of my brother. Still, I file this away with the gun talk in my mind and resolve to get to it after we sort Mom out.

I draw a long breath, speaking as I exhale, "Get to sleep. We'll talk about this in the morning."

Walt hesitates, then comes in with open arms for a hug. At first I don't know what to do with him – our family has never been big on physical affection. When he fails to intuit my discomfort, I step reluctantly into his arms, feeling more or less obligated. On him is an amalgam of smells, some I fail to recognize.

Again, I wonder what he's been up to.

When after a few seconds we part, I'm left struggling to determine what I'd expected to accomplish in waiting up for him, by cornering him like this. Whatever it is, it isn't coming tonight. I need to catch him when he's sober.

"G'night, brotha," Walt says, clapping me on the shoulder and backing into the kitchen.

"Goodnight," I return, watching as his silhouette joins the darker hallway shadows.

"Walt," I whisper after him. "From now on one of us needs to be home at all times. No excuses. No more late nights. No more flaking out. Understood?"

"She's dying, isn't she..." Walt's voice pokes through the dark, running with a current of defeat.

I have no answer. At the bottom of me I sense dark times ahead, but I'm incapable suddenly of conjuring my own voice. A moment later I hear the click of Walt's door closing.

Three hours later I'm up for the day, zombie-shuffling across the living room, into the kitchen, and down the hallway to Walter's bedroom. My morning routine can wait. I'm still struggling with whether or not to call in sick anyway in light of Mom's accident.

I stop beside Mom's door and grasp the handle. I give it a nervous turn and peek in at her thin figure, draped in a single sheet with the comforter she'd kicked off in the night pooled at her feet. Sunlight slants through the windows, delineating her receded features. I wait for her chest to swell with breath, and when it doesn't I'm left with the stabbing revelation that she's died in her sleep. Then the feelings evaporate as the barely perceptible rise and fall of the blankets grants me license to move onto my next charge.

Closing the door in the rehearsed, gentle manner I'd perfected as a teen, I turn to Walt's door and let myself in without so much as knocking. My brother's laziness is showcased in the character of his room. The floor is hidden beneath clothes and other debris. Band posters from the nineties cling, most askew, to baby blue walls.

The residual skunky smell of pot smoke seems to rise from the carpet and the untidy knot of blankets on his bed. He's overwritten it to the best of his ability with incense and air spray, which mingle *alongside* the odor in a way that calls up memories of a friend's basement in high school, one I'd visited often with Elora.

Walt's bed is situated at the far-left corner of the rectangular room. Beside it, a varnished white pine nightstand with an out-of-place stained-glass lamp. It's a knockoff – one of Mom's from back in the day. Beneath it is his pay-as-you-go flip phone, a prescription drug bottle, and a crushed pack of cigarettes... necessities. Situated between windows hung with repurposed towels and bedsheets to block the sun's glare (for better daytime sleep), is a dresser piled with relics from our childhood; Power Ranger figurines; a plastic case of stacked comic book cards; and an old military ammo box no taller than my knee and padlocked to protect who-knows-what. Beside it sits an old desk bedecked with eclectic stickers.

Walt is on his back sawing wood, leg jutting out from beneath his comforter. I'm visited briefly by a childish impulse to stick something in his gaping mouth.

I walk to the bed, gliding soundlessly through the debris. Stopping shy of his protruding leg, I reach for his shoulder, smelling the smokey stink of him as I shake him gently awake. He grumbles a moment, mouth opening and closing a couple times, then rolls over and away, tugging his tangled blankets with him.

The fart his body offers up feels like some Darwinian defense mechanism. His are always the foulest.

Backpedaling through the trash, I pull my shirt up over my face. "Walt," my voice is muffled, but my growing exasperation is edging out my directive to avoid harsh tones with him. I stare, hoping it's enough to wrest him momentarily from his dreams. He stirs, then immediately stills again.

"Walt! Wake up!" I'm shaking him now.

"Erm. Go away," he groans, voice groggy and marinaded in confusion.

"I don't have time for this." Drawing a long breath, I gather up fistfuls of blankets before hauling them off him. What I'm left with as the blankets fall absently from my hands is the slender, nude form of my addict brother, painted in the building daylight. Beside him in the bed are a number of crumpled tissues at which I can't help shaking my head. My attention doesn't linger on them, instead drifting along in appraisal of Walt's willowy features. The shadows cling more firmly to parts of him suddenly recessed and concave in adulthood. He's dangerously underweight.

Walt cringes blindly away after a few seconds exposed. Slotted eyes doused in immediate, belligerent confusion bore into mine. "What the *hell*, dude?" He gropes out frantically, realizing that he's naked. "Dude, gimme my blanket."

"C'mon, Walt. We need to talk about Mom. If you aren't in the kitchen in five minutes I'm coming back." I rotate and exit the room, tailed by questions like *what time is it?* and *why do you have to be such a jerk?*

I leave them unanswered as I shuffle into the kitchen to make coffee, still shaking off my own fatigue.

Again the thought to call in sick flashes through my mind. It's trumped by the heavy weight of duty and responsibility, things as alien to Walter as sober daylight hours. I've only got a few appointments this morning, then I can cut out. I can do this.

Walt slinks into the kitchen after a few minutes, seeming guided by the smell of coffee. I'm at the table now, watching him over a steaming mug as he enters. He's pulled on black gym shorts and a t-shirt. Our eyes meet for a moment before he continues along, beyond the refrigerator to the cupboard, where he extracts a mug and pours a sloppy cup, leaving spilled coffee cooling on the counter.

"Okay," he says, back to me as he shovels an ungodly amount of sugar into his mug. He takes a measured sip. "What's your plan, Mark?" He swivels toward me, lazing against the countertop.

I sigh, gazing into the cooling black of my cup. The truth is I was thinking about it long after Walt went to bed.

"There are two options," I say, casting a sideways glance down the hall. "We either bring her into the hospital ourselves and force her into the emergency room, or we wait until this happens again and call an ambulance." There's no denying that neither idea sits particularly well. Both are a betrayal, the former characterized by its naked deception, the latter by its negligence in allowing Mom to suffer another accident. I'd already made up my mind before trying for sleep, reasoning that if Walt reached the same conclusion he'd see himself as the driving force and arbitrarily take on more responsibility. Perhaps put in more effort than the bare minimum of *none*.

"We can't let her fall again," Walt says, shaking his head. This restores some of my faith in him even though he seems to lack more to say. He sips pensively beneath eyes lit with uncharacteristic resolve. Despite this, he simply nods and says *okay*, seeming to agree with himself more than anything before tossing back the rest of his cream-cooled coffee and going back to the pot for more.

"Okay then, we're in agreement. It needs to be done as soon as possible. I'll cut out of work after I get my morning appointments out of the way and we can bring her. Make it seem like we're going out to a late lunch in York. I need you to stay here and keep an eye on her until I get back. I want you to see how she's walking and if she's still weak on one side." Walt nods with a slow rhythm that leaves me instantly vexed and wondering if he's really listening at all. His vacant gaze as he approaches and sits, staring *through* the kitchen table, is not encouraging. "Walt?" I ask. "You got that?"

He snaps out of it, gaze sharpening on his coffee as a finger runs absently through forested blond curls. "Yeah, yeah, dude. I got it."

"What did I say?"

"Stay here until you get back. Watch Mom. Watch how she walks." His eyebrows lift, creasing his forehead in a way that makes him look older and reminds me of Dad.

"Watch to see if she's weak on one side," I repeat.

"Yeah, yeah, of course."

I'm about to repeat it with him when a xylophonic series of notifications arise suddenly from my phone. I'd forgotten I had morning server maintenance. Now I'm running late.

Normally when I'm running on less than four hours sleep I'm able to push through the morning on caffeine and willpower. The fading doesn't start until the afternoon, when suddenly an impossible monolith falls along my day's trajectory. Today, however, I'm dead on my feet from the get-go, and no matter how many cups of coffee I drink, I'm never quite able to get an edge on the woken world. It's like slogging through quicksand in a dream, illusory and impossible.

I'm the only tangible part of a world rendered artificial.

Server work is a typically solitary job, testing the limits of my eardrums with grating music while downloading and installing patches, checking system logs, and testing backups. This is actually my favorite part of the job, blissfully alone with my music and a machine that – typically – does what I tell it to do. Most of the time this work is performed at a client's office before staff arrives, but this server is a special case, dropped off while its parent company shuts down for a scheduled staff vacation.

Must be nice. Good timing though.

The office is dark by design today, lit only by the rising sun. It's 7:30 A.M., so others will start trickling in shortly, but for now I've got the place to myself.

My legs are rubber as I totter before my workbench, a six-foot deskspace littered with RAM, CPUs yet to be socketed, and eclectic tech detritus from gutted ATX cases and server chassis. Humming away in the center of the particleboard desktop is the blade server I'm tasked with configuring, its front LEDs winking chaotically despite the system never breaking a sweat. I realize as the lime and amber lights begin to leave shimmering chromium imprints behind my closed eyes that I've been zoning out for an indeterminable amount of time.

My gaze shifting back to the monitor and the notifications, warnings, and errors generated by the system these last four months, I will my arid gaze along the white and yellow log entries in search of red warnings. These bad boys are really all I'm concerned with. Most are fortunately benign and safely ignored as I probe deeper. To my relief there are no others, just stubborn DCOM errors generated by a server looking for laptops that rarely see the inside of the client's office.

Clearing the log, I step away from the workbench and check the time on my phone. 7:45 A.M. Tim is due in five minutes, reliably early by at least ten minutes since I've known him. Part of me wants to finish work and hurry out before I have to face anyone in my current fugue. I'm reminded of the days abusing Adderall with Walter, when I'd go all night, rolling on amphetamines with vampiric dismay toward the rising sun. But another pill was often ready to carry me through the day.

I can't help wishing I'd asked Walt for a tab, not that he'd offer up anything for free. Without it, I'm a zombified mess that would do best to bug out before anyone else arrives.

I try not to rush through the remainder of my work, and I finish with a few notes scrawled on a legal pad. Glancing at my computer as I rush past my cube, man-purse swaying, I try to convince myself I'll be in early tomorrow to get my billables done.

In a flash I'm out the door, stopping half way across the parking lot, realizing I'd neglected to lock up.

"Damn it all," I say, loud enough for my voice to carry across the empty lot. Backtracking to the door and locking it, I'm once again set on fleeing the scene.

My worries at being caught by an incoming co-worker aside, I'm able to escape without incident and point my car toward my first appointment. I'm happy to have caught a break, but as my car begins to drift between the double-yellow and the road shoulder I realize I'm in worse shape than I'd thought. Making matters worse, I can't bring myself to believe Walt hasn't dozed off on the couch or gone back to bed at home, leaving Mom to care for herself.

Heavy eyelids seduce me toward sleep despite my building anxiety, now an apparent constant in my life. When I can take it no longer, I dig my phone out of the trash in the center console and dial my office. I pray it'll run through to voicemail as the outgoing call begins to ring. I can't help thanking good luck as the line clicks over to the company mailbox. I'm then greeted by the owner's forced, overly cheery voice, inviting me to leave a detailed message with my time of call and preferred callback number. I'm then encouraged to have a *splendid* day.

"Tim, it's Mark. I'm having a problem at home – gonna have to cut out early this morning. The server work for CortoWorks is all set. I'll pick it up and deliver it tomorrow. I need you to call Green Clean and let them know I'm going to push them to tomorrow. I might be able to do it this afternoon—" not a chance in hell "—but I need to get home right now." The phone falls out of my grip as I react late to a car stopped at a red light and hammer on the brakes. It's not so close that it's noticeable – at least I don't *think* it is – but it's enough to know I have no business operating on such little sleep. Not, apparently, at my age.

Straining to keep an eye on the light, I hunt through the gravel peppering my floormat, eventually settling on the phone and hauling it back up to my ear as traffic starts to accordion out beneath a green light.

"Call me back if you need to." I toss the phone into the passenger seat and scold myself for nearly getting into another distracted driving accident. Lifting my travel mug to give up its final drops, I upend it, shaking what's left onto my eager tongue, already driving distracted again.

A gas station takes form down the road, one of the newer convenience stores springing up in the Berwicks over the last couple years. Late-stage capitalism at work, they'd driven out the last of the mom-and-pop places.

I need caffeine.

I coast into the gas station and park outside the door. The street-facing façade is all glass and glare from the rising sun. A bustle of morose-looking construction types in tan Carhart coveralls, carrying impossibly *extra-large* cups, edge wordlessly past their white-collar counterparts. It's probably just my frustration with Walter and worry for Mom, but I wouldn't mind stepping into this crowd with fists flying indiscriminately.

As if navigating a dream, I step out into the sleep-deprived surrealness of the world. It's only as I reach the entrance door and push inside that a familiar voice re-grounds me.

"Mark, brother! How we doing?" Stepping away from the register and advancing on me is my manager, Tim. The pneumatic whoosh of the door opening prompts me deeper inside, closer to him. "Already done with CortoWorks?"

"Got an early start," I answer shakily, hoping I don't appear outwardly guilty of anything.

He eyes me up and down appraisingly. "Must have. You look like garbage." He lifts his coffee and draws emotionlessly for a moment, waiting for me to come out with everything.

"Didn't get much sleep last night. My mother's been having issues and…" the wind leaves my voice as I realize just how little I've told him of Kelly… of Mom and Walter. I take a moment watching the blue-collar crowd doctor their coffees, not so much deciding *whether* to tell him as struggling with *where to begin*. "It's a long story. When's your first appointment?"

"I'll be at the office until eleven or so. You all right, kid?"

"Let's step outside," I return. And so we do, settling on either side of a circular umbrella-shaded picnic table that seems not to have been cleaned in any serious way in years. Embossed driblets of dried ice cream and sickly-colored condiment puddles smatter the surface. Cigarette butts garnish the crushed gravel at our feet.

Here I spill my guts about everything, with the exception of Elora and the trip to North Conway. I don't hesitate, dumping everything on him and actually finding it therapeutic when I'm done. Like shedding diseased skin. Kelly, Mom, Walt… even Mallory Kelson, I tell him everything as if purging myself through some unseen release valve.

When I'm done we're left with a silence between us that feels almost physical. Then, all at once, Tim locks gazes with me and nods. Tipping the rest of his coffee up, he places the cup on the table and says, serious as a heart attack, "We need to get drunk tonight."

I choke back the laughter that wants to come as his eyebrows lift and a sly smile builds itself on his face.

"I'm serious, kid. You need a night off with someone who isn't trying to fit you for a straightjacket."

"I've gotta get my mother taken care of—"

"Of course!" He's gesticulating now, always making with the bigger parts of his personality when topics like respecting one's elders arise. He glances around us in a rare showing of self-awareness before shaking his head and turning back to me. "You take care of your Mom. Go home, get to it. Then tonight, old Massi's gonna take care of *you*. Got it?"

"I don't—"

"Enough of that. Chop chop – go take care of Mom. Meet me at Rough Ruby's tonight around eight. If you can't make it—" he wags his finger at me, "—legit excuses only, just let me know and we'll go *tomorrow* night instead."

I lean forward to speak, but he cuts me off with a sweeping hand. The smile teasing behind it all reminds me of my father. It's impossible not to completely adore this man. He's the best boss I'll ever have.

"No, no. Nope. You'll do as the boss says. Now go. Off to Mommy," Tim says, waving me away.

And so I go, *off to Mommy*.

Walt is still awake and on the job when I skid into the driveway and dash on borrowed energy for the door, kicking up gravel and other loose debris behind me. I find him sprawled on the living room couch watching television with Mom, who is reclined almost horizontally, legs up, Mouf warming her shins. She's still wearing the nightgown I'd dressed her in, which tells me she hasn't had any more accidents.

At least none I can see or smell.

Two sets of eyes lift to me as I slip into the living room, passing through a shaft of sunlight in the otherwise stifling drear.

"Mark? What are *you* doing here?" Mom asks, confused. Lifting the remote, she balances it on her upturned palm as all members of the TVgeneration seemed to do and depresses the volume-down button with an index finger until she's stolen the voice from the television.

"I came back to see if you and Walt wanted to go out for breakfast with me." I smile down at her, feeling like the world's most inept conman. I'm with it enough to realize we're earlier than expected, with lunch hours away. But breakfast might work better given Mom's lifelong belief that eating out for lunch is an unforgivable waste of money.

Mom's feeling characteristically obdurate just the same. This is evident as she scowls at the clock on the wall, or at least the spot where a clock had hung once upon a time. "But you should be in *school*," she grumbles, seeming to gloss over the confusion at the absent clock. "I'm not paying tuition for you to come up in the middle of the week for *breakfast*."

My eyes find Walt's. He shrugs, silently informing me that she's been like this all morning. I nod toward the hallway, urging him to go and dress. He glances down at his gym shorts and tee, seeming prepared to make the case for venturing out *as is*, but even *Walt* understands that loungewear isn't hospital attire. Not unless you're the one being admitted.

He sidles wordlessly past me and vanishes down the hallway. As his door clicks, I step closer to Mom, whose attention has drifted back to her *stories*. "Mom," I say, kneeling at her chair and placing my hand on hers. "I've been out of college for almost ten years."

Suddenly she's peering back at me dubiously, eyes flitting this way and that before hardening and locking with mine. "Well of *course* you have," she barks with a confidence that makes me feel idiotic for even clarifying.

"Let's get you dressed and we'll go out, Mom." I expect resistance, just as it's come with everything else the last couple of weeks, but surprisingly she backs off and wriggles her legs until the cat abandons his bed. Mouf touches down and stretches his paws before going to work digging at the carpet. Mom's immediate, bellowed reprimand sends him skittering in panic out of the room.

I offer Mom a hand, which she eyes with a look of unconcealed insult before heaving herself up. She walks slowly, almost arduously out of the living room, limping now and shifting her weight noticeably to the left. Though not as weak as last night, she's still struggling with one side of her body. Her right hand sways almost lifelessly at her side, fingers twitching as she goes.

I want nothing more than to follow and aid her into her room, but I know she won't accept my help. Better to keep her in something of a good mood if I want to get her out of here. This day is going to be hard enough without inviting the inevitable anger born of frustration.

My gaze moves to the coffee pot in the kitchen. As I walk over I assure myself a cup of hours-old coffee will do in keeping me sharp until we get to the restaurant.

"Where we going to eat?" Walt asks, drifting into the kitchen. I pivot toward him, drinking in the outfit of blue jeans and a wrinkled white dress shirt he's assembled, no doubt plundered from the bottom of the dirty laundry pile. He's opted for church attire for a hospital visit, and I'm left wondering what, exactly, had last compelled him to unearth that shirt.

Walking to the kitchen table, I lower my mug and plop into a chair. "I'm thinking Rich's Smokehouse," I answer.

"Don't you think we should pick something closer to the hospital? She's gonna get suspicious if we don't go right home after we eat."

I'm vaguely aware of my mouth falling open. I really must be tired if Walt has considered something I haven't.

"Good idea," I say, giving him his due. I take a moment to think, sipping coffee with that burnt, hours-old taste. "How about that place next to the gas station by the rotary? The hospital is right down the street."

Walt sits across from me, nodding. His face darkens a moment, features scrunched in a look of sudden panic. "We splitting checks? I'm a little short on cash."

"I got it, Walt," I say, too tired to be annoyed.

Moments later Mom shuffles into the kitchen having decided to pair white capris and a blue blouse with the ever-fashionable resting scowl on her face. Her hair is still pressed from sleep in the back where she can't see herself in the mirror.

"Ready to go?" I ask, glancing into the shallow mire of my mug. Tipping it up to my lips, I take the rest in one shot. My gaze returns to Mom.

"We going to Rich's?" she asks, more rhetorically than anything. She starts assumptively toward the foyer, still favoring her left side.

"We were thinking about trying someplace new," I answer reluctantly. I walk my mug to the sink and turn back to find a bemused look taking up all of her face. Textbook oppositional defiance, just like a small child.

"Why not Rich's?" Mom's a true Baby-Boom Mainer – once you've discovered something good, there's no need to try the rest.

"We've been going to Rich's *forever*, Mom." I try to laugh, to play it off as minor, but it emerges so forced that even Mom seems instantly wise. Finding some semblance of *center*, I advance, guiding her into the foyer. "Let's give something else a try. If you don't like it you can tell me you told me so. I'm treating anyway."

For a moment she's rooted to the floor, unbudging, the dim energy in her eyes informing me of the struggle taking place within. She doesn't trust me. Even when she isn't completely with it, Mom is still reasonably sharp. She knows something is up.

My stomach coils as I reconsider the ambulance option.

"Where were you thinking?" she asks, very much to my surprise. Glancing at Walt, I see he's just as floored. Of all the days I've needed her somewhat malleable, today it's like hitting the Megabucks.

"That place by the rotary in York," I answer, still trying to pluck the name from memory.

"The Egg Basket?" she asks, brow lifting in an expression I struggle to decrypt. I can't tell if she's consenting.

"Yeah, that's the place."

She starts down the hallway toward the foyer. "Your father always went there with his Shipyard friends. I never understood why they'd drive so far out of the way for it, and he sure never took me there to find out." This is all she says on the matter as she exits the kitchen.

I look to Walt.

He shrugs.

Michael Wilford

Onward to breakfast.

i've
never
lived
past
50
have
i

I'VE NEVER LIVED past 50, have I?

The simpering voice assembles itself with an undercurrent of impish prodding. *Have you finally accepted that you're dead?*

Truth told, I don't know that my question was born of any conscious thought. More instinct, something intuited in those final moments at the cottage before we shuffled Mom off to lunch.

Why 50? I ask, skirting the question in a way that reminds me of Walt and reinforces my cowardice.

Who wants to see old age? the voice asks, assuming a darker character that feels deeply personal. *Who wants to suffer the indignity of no longer being able to care for yourself, of having your license revoked, your freedom rescinded?*

I thought you said physical existence is trivial. What purpose does it serve to... well, to check out *while still on top? Fifty isn't old.*

Only you know the answer to that question, Mark. Maybe Elora.

The name explodes in the formless nothing, warming me as though I'm suddenly tending a blazing bonfire. Suddenly the question I'd asked doesn't matter, and for a time, minutes, hours, years, I stay cradled in the void, waiting for my thoughts to find order.

The simpering voice stays silent.

Soon, the aroma of pancakes and eggs cooking on a grill...

Mom either isn't hungry or simply doesn't like her food. After a few bites of her blueberry pancakes she folds her napkin neatly and sets it on the table. A liver-spotted hand, corded with violet veins eases a hardly-touched plate toward the ketchup Walt spilled earlier at the center of the table.

Walt and I take our time eating, both preoccupied with the next step – the real reason for dragging Mom out. On a certain level I think we're avoiding the inevitable, justifying in our own minds our unspoken decision to idle the time away.

We know it's going to be bad.

But eventually Walt and I gaze upon clean plates, with nothing more to justify our delay. My belly is full of eggs and corned beef hash, his stuffed with one of the thickest Belgian waffles I've ever seen, mounded with whipped cream and drizzled with chocolate syrup. The restaurant itself is nothing special, another breakfast joint sparsely decorated with framed prints of country landscapes and a pair of bulletin boards flanking the entry door, each filled to capacity with business cards and flyers. Exposed wooden beams run overhead, varnished to the point of *glowing*. They're topped with plants and the ever-reliable rustic décor which could easily have been lifted from an abandoned barn: milk cans, butter churns, and antiquated tools gathering all manner of rust and dust.

The majority of the tables are set into the wall, booths with varying views of Colonial York, Maine. Ours overlooks one of the last gas stations still lawfully grandfathered into York Village's tourist-focused businesses. To my knowledge it's the last of its kind in a town desperate to preserve its old village charm against an American economy of convenience and innovation.

Walt swallows his last bite and chases syrup around his lips with a napkin. Our gazes meet then pivot simultaneously to Mom, staring out the window at the pumps next door.

"You not hungry, Mom?" I ask, certain I'd already done so but unable to touch the memory.

She either ignores or doesn't hear me.

"Mom?" I ask, louder.

Her gaze detaches from a minivan at the pumps, currently spilling a litter of children out toward the gas station doors. "What?"

"Not hungry?"

She answers with a slow, stubborn shake of her head, then returns to the window. My gaze follows, settling on a squat woman as she falls out of the van's passenger seat and sets off after her children, hollering unintelligibly as her oafish-looking husband pumps gas and yanks on a pair of overburdened chinos.

I'm left puzzling over Mom's interest in the family. Her elbow is now planted on her napkin, hand supporting her chin as she studies them.

"What is it, Mom?" I look to Walt, currently angled away, fiddling with a prescription drug bottle. If he has a fresh Adderall prescription it explains a lot about this morning. I'm surprised he's taking inventory here. An addict never draws attention to his stash.

I wait for him to pop one, but he seems to decide against it. It's probably because he feels me watching him. The bottle soon disappears back into his pocket, and I reach for Mom's arm, trying not to startle her. Her body trembles briefly at the touch. She turns back to me only after stealing another look out the window.

"Old age is *hell*, Mark," she sighs, sounding just like her mother-in-law once upon a time. Her eyes stay with me as I read their despondence. In these eyes is a longing so palpable that my eyes mist over as I watch her turn back to the family. "I never appreciated my youth. Just drifted through it, taking everything for granted. Now it feels as false and hollow as a dream to me."

"I think that's the way it is for all of us," I return.

"No," she says, swiveling back, eyes hardening on mine. "Every day is a gift, baby. Live each one like it's your last or you'll discover they're numbered and… and…"

"What?" Walt asks, answering to *baby*. A part of me miles away wants to laugh, but I don't because it's obvious she knows something is up. Was it the accident yesterday? Had it left her pondering her own existence? Her own mortality?

"We should go," I say, suddenly on my feet. It's time to get this over with and move forward. Good or bad.

Fishing out my wallet, I drop a pair of twenties on a $28 check and look to Walt, now engaged in some game on his phone, lips puckered in concentration.

"Walt," I say, snapping him out of Snake or whatever he's playing. Out gazes meet, and in his I see preemptive reluctance. "Make sure she gets out okay. I'm going to go get the car started and get the air conditioner going."

I step out onto the sunbaked pavement, my caffeine buzz waning immediately, not that it was much to write home about to begin with. I wish I'd changed out of my work clothes and into a pair of shorts as an unseasonably oppressive sun does its best to broil the world.

My RAV unlocks as I touch the fob-sensitive handle, and I open the door with a difficulty that speaks further to my lack of sleep. Falling into the driver's seat, I press the ignition and crank the A/C, and closing my eyes, I take a moment to bolster myself against what awaits.

I'm not given longer than a couple minutes before the restaurant door opens and Walt steps out, squinting against the sunlight. As he holds the door open for Mom I'm already coasting toward them, hands shaking on the wheel. Drifting to a slow stop, I nod to Walt, observing his Adderall tics, out today in full force. He's cracking his knuckles one-handed, working his thumb across every finger of his free hand. A serpentine tongue laps at his lips.

Mom's gaze lifts from the pavement, coming to rest in confusion on my car, then me in the driver's seat. She doesn't recognize the RAV, and my presence behind its wheel isn't helping. In her usual way, however, Mom is able to dismiss everything she fails to grasp before Walt can even open the door for her.

She doesn't so much plop into the passenger seat as she *collapses* into it. For a moment she simply gazes about the interior, thinking I'd bought a new car but not trusting herself enough to fully commit.

"Why do they have to make these things so *high* now?" she wheezes as I reach out and draw the seatbelt across her narrow chest.

"I dunno, Mom," I say, clipping the belt and noting how suddenly small she looks in the seat. "That too tight?"

"I'd prefer not to have it at all," she says, her left hand (her *good* hand) tugging at the strap.

"Well, you have to wear it," I return with an authority that feels perverted.

She doesn't fight me. Within a few seconds Walt climbs into the back seat and settles quietly. Our eyes meet once more in a weightless exchange of solidarity in the rear-view before I throw the car into Drive, bound for the hospital before I lose my nerve. After a quarter mile I ease the RAV off the main road, coasting down a tree-shrouded street flanked by the canting, pitted gravestones of a colonial cemetery on one side and the Colonial York Visitors Center attached to a burgundy-colored tavern house on the other.

"Why are we going this way?" Mom asks, an ominous thread of irritation in her voice. "This isn't the way home."

"We have another stop to make, Mom." I swallow hard. A sign reading *York Hospital* rises suddenly in the roadside lilacs.

"Where are we going?"

I take a moment to consider how I might guide the conversation toward a more seamless reveal. Sucking absently at the air, chest feeling as though a belt has been drawn tightly across it, I'm pressed to find a new avenue of deception. "Mom, your accident yesterday. Do you remember it?"

Silence. I can feel her eyes crawling over me.

"You need to be checked out. You need to see a doctor."

Suddenly Mom is fully animated, no longer content to let her silent contempt do the speaking for her. "I most certainly *do not*!" she yells, gesticulating wildly, voice so condemning that I nearly swerve off the road. Righting the car, I gaze back at Walt, now biting his lower lip and peering out the window in that absent way I hate, endeavoring to minimize himself to the point where he's overlooked entirely.

"Mom, you were on the floor all afternoon. You… you *soiled* yourself. You couldn't get back up on your own. You have to at least get checked out."

"No! No doctors!" She's shrieking now, each syllable lacerating my ears.

I turn into the hospital, saying nothing. Rising ahead is the brick ER building hugging the edge of a hill as if recently sprouted there.

"No!" she wails, now fumbling desperately at the doorhandle. As the car meanders up the winding driveway, Mom's gaze fixes itself on the awning shrouding the ER entrance and its serif *Welcome* sign. She begins to paw at the windows in a manic frenzy, eyes darting and settling on nothing for longer than the space of a microsecond. She reminds me of a dog trying to escape confinements beyond its understanding, and my heart divides at the sight of it.

"They're not going to hurt you—"

"No doctors!"

I pull up in front of the ER. My gaze falls upon one of the wheelchairs folded up in the foyer beyond a wide automatic door. I feel like punching myself as images of me and Walt tying Mom to one of them seeps into my mind like poison. Throwing the car into Park, I rotate toward Walt, who continues to gaze out the window, withdrawn. "Walt!" I hear myself yelling, anger spilling out freely. It rocks him in a very satisfying way, and he pries his gaze from the periphery of the parking lot. "Go get help, please."

It feels like we're having her committed.

Walt struggles with the door before disengaging the lock and stepping out. The door slams, then Walt's speeding around the car and inside the ER as Mom continues to unravel.

"They'll put me in a *home*. They'll take my house away!" she cries, her erratic, jerking struggle suddenly calming. She tosses a look my way, narrowed eyes burning with incensed betrayal.

"They're just gonna check you out."

"That's how it *starts*!" she shrieks. "Then some *stranger* in a white coat is making my decisions for me!"

"I won't let that happen!" I struggle to lower my voice and keep my frustration with her, Walt, and the rest of the world from spilling out.

She returns to fumbling at the door. With a sigh, I turn back to the hospital entrance and try to will myself elsewhere in my head. It isn't long before the automatic doors slide open and Walt emerges, headed back to us down a red brick pathway, tailed by a pair of nurses, one male, one female. They're dressed in navy blue scrubs with black Crocks. Their faces are, at best, uncertain.

I exit the car as they reach us, ready to spirit my frantic mother into her own Hell. The nurses size me up in a way that suggests Walt told them all he could but evidently floundered with the details.

The *biggest* detail, as I quickly discover.

"Do you have Power of Attorney over this woman?" the male nurse asks. He's slender with auburn hair curling over his ears. His face is a constellation of freckles, densest beneath his eyes.

The female nurse is a matronly block of solid woman, looking arbitrarily hostile. She stops beside her male counterpart with her arms crossed like a bouncer, hair drawn back in a fraying plait. "Your brother here wasn't sure."

More like he has no idea what it even is. Unfortunately I do, and my hopes for getting help for Mom are dashed away in an instant.

"She needs help," I answer, skirting the question and working urgency into my voice. "Please help me get her inside."

"We can't take a patient who refuses treatment," the male nurse says with bland ambivalence. His gaze drifts to the car, eyes narrowing as he searches the moisture-fogged windows for signs of the woman bludgeoning the silence between us with her muffled ire.

"She doesn't know what's best for her. Please, she needs help."

Walt stands idle, voiceless, useless. A part of me wonders why he isn't picking his nose or off chasing butterflies. You know, doing things suited to his mental aptitudes, lacking as they clearly are.

"I'm sorry, sir, but without Power of Attorney you can't force her to be seen."

He starts to turn with his bouncer tailing. I should have known from the beginning there was nothing I could do, but I call after them just the same, desperate and alone against the entire world.

"Please! She's had a *stroke*!"

The man stops, and I feel a slow trickle of hope wet my emotions. But as he turns around, I see only cold indifference on his ginger face, the kind you'd expect from a store refusing to accept a one-dollar coupon, not a hospital.

I hate this man.

"If it's an actual life or death emergency we can take her, otherwise we can't force her to do anything." He starts back again.

"How can you know without *looking* at her? How can you know this isn't life or death?!"

"Your brother already told us that she had an accident last night but has been fine all morning." He starts toward me, but my gaze has already narrowed at Walter.

The male nurse grows in my peripherals as he steps up to me, continuing, "If she comes in an ambulance, we're legally obligated to check her out. But we can't take her like this."

"I can't just wait for her to have another accident!" My hands are now fists. The nurse takes note without reacting, remaining cold and statuesque, insinuated between my mother and the help she needs. This is just a job for him, nothing more.

Already feeling defeated, the fight flees me and my chin is drawn with sullen gravity toward my chest. "I think she's had a minor stroke. She's having trouble with one side of her body," I whisper, watching as this horror of a human being shakes his head at me.

"I'm sorry," the man says, placing a hand on my shoulder in an empty gesture of naked pacification. Though he speaks sympathy, his expressions say *I don't give a damn*. "I truly am, but we're legally bound to these rules. If she falls again, call an ambulance. They'll bring her here and we'll have a look at her."

He rotates back toward the building and walks off with his *muscle*. Suddenly I'm aware of how silent Mom is in the car. I step back toward the driver's side door, cupping my hands to the windows for a look inside.

Mom's hunched over with her chin on the dashboard, head canted back unnaturally. Her body writhes and convulses as if suddenly running with an electric current.

"Oh, my God, Walt! Help!" I'm already sprinting around the car. Gripping the handle, I haul the door open with enough force to tear it from its hinges.

"What's going on with—"

"Just go get that nurse back here!" I cry, easing Mom upright and holding her there. Blood pounds in my ears as she starts to shake, at first with a weak tremble, then so violently I'm left in terrified awe of her sudden, inexplicable power.

"Mom," my voice is a whisper, contrasting with the maelstrom churning in my belly. That artificial tint returns to marinade the world in dreamlike hues. Yet somehow I remain grounded with Mom, pulling her as close to me as I can, wanting to weather the storm with her.

"Mom, it's going to be okay. We're gonna take care of you… get you through this. It's gonna be okay."

Contact registers at my shoulders, though I don't look to see who it is. I'm eased up and out of the car. Bodies in scrubs fill the void closing around me, voices spiking with urgency, hands in motion. It's all I can do to keep from collapsing on the pavement.

For three hours I wait, unable to lift myself from the chair as if pinned by the weight of existence. Even Walt looks crushed, face pressed to his palms across the room, hands parting occasionally like shutters on a window to draw breath. He gazes now through splayed fingers at the floor, eyes dull, like an old man in the twilight of his life returning to the same haunting memory, the defining regret of his life.

Suddenly I wonder how I look. If someone as selfish as Walt could be so impacted by Mom's condition, what will I see when I eventually give in to my screaming bladder and consider my reflection in the restroom mirror?

The waiting room is upscale by hospital standards, not that I'm particularly interested in much outside the occasional body stepping out of the exam corridor, a place into which we've yet to be invited. The room is vase-shaped, Its padded chairs are divided by end-tables toppling with picked-over and abused magazines. Somewhere is the aroma of burnt coffee and the excited voices of children circling a twelve-foot tank teeming with reef-dwelling fish.

Walt and I sit separated by a sea of ashen carpet. Every time the frosted glass doors open on the unseen inner nervous system of the ER, I glance up for the doctor who will inevitably inform us that Mom is going to be okay. When each time a nurse or ER tech walks casually through without stopping, my eyes find their despondence mirrored in Walter's before we return to our self-guided meditations.

At least with Dad there had been no waiting, just a visit from a cop and the news, "Mrs. Wells, we regret that your husband died heroically in a shop fire this evening." It had been quick and clean, not like this, where we've been forced to wait hours without word if our mother is even still alive.

My gaze falls to the hours-old cup of coffee beside me, and for the briefest of moments I want to laugh at how little good it's done me. My gaze seeking out Walter, I consider asking him for a pill, and not for the first time today. The cylindrical bulge of the prescription bottle in his jeans pocket is like a siren call.

No. It had been hard enough to kick that stuff before college. One pill would lead back to a world of addiction I'd be struggling to wrench myself from for years. Gazing back to the coffee and trying to stimulate some interest, I lift the cup for a cold sip before replacing it and standing, no longer able to ignore nature's call.

Walt removes his face from his hands to watch me go. Suddenly I'm sprinting against an overburdened bladder, wincing with each footfall.

"Just running to the bathroom," I inform him, speeding out into a busy corridor.

I'm passed by knots of people on my way to the restroom, some cradling flowers from the apothecary and gift shop, others paused in conversation beneath a gilded plaque reading "In Memory of David Wilford, Our Halls are Darker Without Your Light."

A cluster of scrub-clad nurses pass, prattling away. I reach the bathroom and step inside as that sheen of artificiality suddenly coats the world once more.

An automatic light stutters to life overhead, casting the single occupant restroom in cold fluorescence. Locking the door, I turn reluctantly to the mirror and take myself in.

My eyes are bloodshot, and my entire body seems to sag with the weight of the world.

I turn away after a moment and go about my business, finding that remaining bipedal requires more discipline than usual the further the clock ticked. I teeter for a moment and lift a bracing hand to the wall, closing my eyes as I purge.

When I finish, my feet carry me dreamily back. I'm not quite on autopilot just yet, but I'm getting there. As I reach the waiting room doorway, however, my mind is suddenly firing on all cylinders.

Walt is gone.

Had he been called into the exam corridor? Were the doctors and nurses now discussing my mother's condition with the absolute worst-qualified person?

Anxiety ripples through my body. I rush toward the doors where I'd observed countless doctors and nurses exiting, my heart beating so fast that a voice in my head starts to whisper, *heart attack*. I take comfort in the knowledge that I couldn't be in a better place for it.

"Sir?" a voice asks from my left. I turn, my frantic gaze falling on a receptionist I'd apparently missed on our way in. She stands gripping a podium with one hand, a pair of clipboards angled before her. She's thin and petite. Her shoulder-length almond hair pokes out of a headband that has long failed in taming the bunches of fuzz and wiry outliers sticking out. "Can I help you?" she asks, following my gaze toward the exam corridor with diluted concern.

I take a long breath and nod to her. "My brother – was he called in to see our mother? Is there any news on her condition?"

"The man with the curly blond hair?"

"Yes." Another long, shallow breath. I tell myself it's calming, but the truth is I'm teetering at the edge of control.

She nods toward the exit doors, her gaze returning to mine as she reveals with poorly-repressed denunciation, "He's out smoking a cigarette."

My shoulders slump and a cooling relief loosens the knots in my chest. Walt is indeed standing just outside the entry doors ripping on a butt with zero regard for people entering and exiting – one, an elderly man wheeling an oxygen tank. That's my brother, Captain Inconsiderate.

I hate him.

An hour later a doctor so young he seems fresh out of pre-school enters the waiting room carrying a tablet computer. I'm afforded a quick look into the exam corridor. There, a cluster of nurses huddle around the lip of a nurses station, calmly discussing… whatever. I suppose I'd rather see this than some frantic rush.

"Mr. Wells?" the doctor asks, glancing up from his tablet at the mostly vacant room. He eases a pair of thin, square-rimmed glasses up the bridge of his nose with theatrical flair. I can't help my gaze seizing upon his prematurely bald head, shadowed with dark stubble around a glistening pate.

I suppose my own baldness could be worse.

Walt and I stand to receive the twentysomething doctor, who makes an alternating assessment of us before correctly determining that I'm the one in charge. His face is expressionless, not a single muscle engaged.

"You're her sons?" he asks.

"Yes," I answer.

He nods, eyes glossing over the tablet with a stagy exaggeration in his every action. His gaze returns to me. "I'm Dr. McWilliams." We shake hands. His grip is of the cold fish variety, which always leaves me thinking *your father didn't teach you the importance of a firm shake*. I'd known my father for only sixteen years before he was taken. Somewhere along the line he'd imparted this wisdom, and it stuck.

"Your mother is stable," says McWilliams, "but we have her heavily sedated. A C-T scan was necessary after our initial tests came back inconclusive." He seems to darken a moment, his practiced *doctor* act faltering slightly as he adds, "She woke part way through and was... uncooperative."

She must have been terrified. My heart sinks.

"What happened to her?" I ask. "Was it a stroke?"

His lips purse then pucker to one side. His gaze flows up and down the glowing tablet screen, and suddenly I'm sidling up to him for a look of my own.

"It wasn't a stroke," the doctor answers. He withdraws the tablet with an aggravating appearance of possession, hugging it to his chest like a child unwilling to share a toy. "I think it would be best if you came with me."

Walt and I search each other for reassurance neither can offer. Without a word we follow McWilliams into the exam corridor beyond the now empty nurses station. Sunlight trickles in through skylights above. The nibbling odor of sterilizing agents is pervasive, filling every part of me as numbered exam doors pass every twelve feet.

Mom's room is the fifth on the left. The doors are closed, blinds lowered. Dr. McWilliams reaches gingerly for the doorhandle, glancing back to ensure we're still with him, then carefully eases the door open. Sunlight chases shadows along an unremarkable white tiled floor. Centered against the far wall is a hospital bed, and in it is our sleeping mother. Monitors on either side of the bed tick away, collecting biometric information.

I step inside, silently tailing the doctor.

Walt hangs back in the doorway.

"How long has your mother had mobility issues?" Dr. McWilliams asks, voice hushed as his gaze settles apprehensively on Mom. He approaches a narrow metal cabinet on the wall, opening it to reveal a thin-client computer that is little more than the standard mouse, keyboard, and monitor trio. He beings to click away, his progress through the browser-based software application punctuated by complaints muttered so softly I only catch snatches of phrases. These include *the old system was better* and *it used to be there* and the bane of IT workers worldwide: *this is so slow.*

It isn't, you're just impatient and don't understand the limits of what you're asking the machine to do. This moron made it through medical school.

"It's been getting worse over the last few months," Walt answers, still occupying the doorway, reluctant to step inside.

I shuffle toward the doctor, studying Mom's motionless form before looking back at Walt and gesturing him in. He comes reluctantly.

"Why didn't you bring her in sooner?" Dr. McWilliams calls up an electronic file in the program with which he's waged battle the last couple of minutes. There isn't much in there aside from the personal information Walt and I provided during the first hour of our wait. Beyond that I understand little of what I'm seeing, short of how the information is stored, gathered, and presented.

"I've no doubt you saw how much she hates doctors," I answer. "No offense. It's this irrational fear she's always had. I don't think she's been in a hospital since my brother was born." I gesture to Walt, but McWilliams doesn't see, nor does he respond as he navigates the clustered windows on the monitor with his clear absence of prowess. Eventually, he's able to call up the image file he seems to have been hunting for.

"What's wrong with her?" I'm not sure if I want to hear his answer.

The screen fills with a top-down view of what I imagine to be the interior of Mom's skull. It looks like an Xray – all black and white and fuzzy in places. Dr. McWilliams plucks a gilded pen from the breast pocket of his lab coat and lifts it to the monitor, circling a swollen white spot over the left hemisphere of Mom's brain.

"This is the cause of her issues," he says in a flavorless voice. I wonder angrily if bedside manner is still a thing. The tip of the pen orbits the white spot for another second before McWilliams tucks it back into its pocket. "We've sent this image and others to our staff neurologist for clarification, but it's important you know that this growth is massive—" He pauses in a way that feels done for effect. "It's," he starts, frowning and drawing a long breath, "most likely final stage."

I feel my thighs touch the bed behind me, halting an unconscious retreat that illuminates my operating cowardice. The room assumes a shifting character; the world moves while I stand tottering on the verge of collapse.

"I don't know how to say this," he says, his face creased in a forced look of compassion. I feel like I'm in some kind of television drama. Even his words seem scripted and generic. "So, I'm just going to come right out with it. Based partly on your descriptions of how she's been at home – the mood swings, the confusion, the difficulty moving around and getting up, the lack of control over her bowels – and given the *size* of this growth, your mother seems to be in the final stages of brain cancer."

My mouth opens, but I have no words. A question hangs unasked in the silence between us.

"It's not likely she has more than a couple months," he says, his face a slab of stone-chiseled impartiality.

"Are—are you certain of this?" I suddenly find my voice.

"We'll be getting the final prognosis from the neurologist, Dr. Bishop… but the signs and evidence stack up pretty clearly."

"I want to hear this from the neurologist," I say, suddenly defiant. All at once this balding child before me is an incompetent *quack,* as the old folks used to say. Even med students have a bottom of the class. There's no doubt in my mind this man was cut from the soiled end of the cloth and has no idea what he's talking about.

As if sensing my baseless appraisal, Dr. McWilliams levels his gaze with mine. I'm left glaring at a man in clear denial of his ego, waiting for him to add more toneless commentary to an already crushing situation.

My eyes flit away, first to the floor, then to Mom, then back to the doctor as he responds.

"I'm very sorry to have to deliver this news to you. It's never easy. I hope to God that Dr. Bishop finds some way around this, I really do, but I pride myself on telling my patients *how it is* and not sugarcoating or giving false hope." He pauses for a moment, enamored of himself, then steps closer, laying a gentle hand on my forearm.

"Do you have any questions for me? Anything at all." His gaze lifts over my shoulder, making me aware once more of my silent brother. I feel a tear trundle down my cheek and I turn away, peering through running water at Walt, now crouched beside our mother's bed.

Dr. McWilliams leaves it at that. His job, after all, is done here. He's delivered the bad news like a champ and now it was time to brag about it at the country club. I'm barely aware of him as he slinks quietly out of the room, drawing the door closed and snuffing out the sunlight.

A couple months to live.

I'm startled awake by the vibration of my phone, still clipped to my belt. I shake my head, eyes darting around the foreign space for something to ground me.

Ah yes, the emergency room. Mom.

The natural light from the corridor outside has diminished with the onset of night, replaced with cold fluorescence. It makes the hospital feel even more like... well, a hospital... a place of death.

A way station to God.

I shuck my phone from its holster, squinting in the darkness against its soft glow. We've spent the entire day wilting in this room, unwilling to turn on the overhead lights for fear of waking Mom. Something building in me like the precursor to a total mental breakdown wishes we could keep her asleep for the remainder of her time on this planet.

I shift off this train of thought and parse through my missed messages and emails. It's 8:32 already. I've slept most of the afternoon, finally succumbing to my body's needs after all hope for Mom's recovery was sapped out by Dr. Bishop, a bearded man, mid-fifties, who reiterated Dr.

McWilliams's prognosis word-for-word. The news held more gravity coming from this man – a doctor clearly long-separated from his first foray in the proving grounds of medicine. This man was a veteran, and clearly distinguished from McWilliams in the way he presented the news, acting as though he'd legit return home this evening and cry himself to sleep over it. Though I wanted to argue, to push him to try *something*, he disarmed me with a prowess I couldn't help but envy. We could attempt to operate, maybe grant Mom another few weeks or months if lucky, or we could make her as comfortable as possible and be with her until it was over.

Given Mom's hatred of doctors and hospitals, there was really only one option.

Dr. Bishop then gave the names of a couple non-profit in-house hospice providers. He informed us that Mom would stay at the hospital for another day or so, then be discharged, and he gave me his cell phone number, telling me to call him if I needed anything.

Anything, he emphasized in a way that eased the building emotional friction in me.

Shortly after, at some point around 4:00 P.M., I submitted to sleep. It was nice to have escaped this horror show of a world for a few hours, but now, regrettably, I'm back. And glancing over my phone, it seems that several parties have missed me, most notably Tim, who has texted me asking where I am, and Kelly, wondering why I haven't responded to the email from her—

Lawyer?

I navigate to my home screen and launch the email app. There, mingling with the junk messages and client correspondence, is an email from a law firm in Dover. It seems Kelly isn't interested in a trial separation, not that this surprises me. Her lawyers, whom I've never heard of in my life, want to expedite divorce proceedings. Their email is vague and contains no official summons or petition.

I delete it immediately.

Thumbing back to my text app, I delete Kelly's message and enter into my chat string with Tim. *Sorry, man,* I type, letting autocorrect compensate for my imprecise fingers, *things are worse here than we originally thought. My mother is terminal.*

I stop and delete the last part. I know Tim will understand and sympathize – his own mother died from stomach cancer – but it all still feels like a part of some terrible nightmare. That to acknowledge it will somehow draw it out of the despairing depths of my mind and make it real.

I apologize to Tim and tell him to have one for me. Then the string of texts begins.

Tim: *Everything okay?*

Me: *We're waiting to find out.*

Tim: *What are they saying? They can't keep you waiting that long without at least an update. You need anything?*

Me: *They're still running tests. I'm all set, thank you.*

Tim: *Well, you let me know. I'll be here for a little longer.*

I lock the phone and go to clip it back to my belt. With a sigh I remove the holster and drop it and the phone on a nearby table, feeling odd about lying to Tim but not necessarily remorseful. There are parts of me that simply can't accept reality right now. My gaze settles upon Walt across the room, leaning into the low light, quietly scrawling away in a notepad.

I have no idea where he got it.

"Has she been awake at all?" I whisper.

Walt shakes his head, not looking up. His pen moves in a frenzy across the college-ruled paper. He doesn't pause for a moment to consider the words he's putting to page, he just continues scrawling hastily. Is he keeping a journal? Perhaps writing the Great American Novel? I have no idea, and I don't really care. The little punk's rolling hard on Adderall. He could be writing *I love pills* over and over again and be no less fixated.

I lean back in my chair with a sigh, feeling my back pop in ways it never did in my twenties. A groan from my stomach reminds me that I haven't eaten since breakfast. The thought to venture out to the cafeteria and grab food slides in and out of my mind, accompanied by the familiar baseline guilt. I can't leave Mom. Not for a moment. And I certainly can't leave her alone with Walt. He's so high and thoroughly out-of-it he'd probably launch into the prevailing prognosis, tactlessly and senselessly informing her that her days are numbered.

No, this needs to be handled delicately. By me.

"Walt," I whisper, eliciting an acknowledging grunt. He leans into the pad, pen hurrying. "Why don't you go get us some food in the cafeteria? I'll give you cash."

"Not hungry," he says, itching at his scalp through blond snarls before returning to work.

Typical. Adderall suppresses the appetite better than any drug I've known. I knew girls in college who took it for just this reason. My heart sinks as the combined thoughts of girls and college deliver my mind invariably to Elora and my decision to break things off before heading to UNH. I do my best to shrug it off before my brain feels the need to revisit North Conway.

"C'mon, man. We need to eat. I'm starving." My voice falls upon deaf ears. He's engrossed in his writing.

Anger, long overdue, twists my insides as I consider the addict seated at the feet of my dying mother. Not once today has he contributed in any useful way. Sure he went in after the nurses, but that had nearly ended with *Your brother already told us that she had an accident last night but has been fine all morning.*

I'm only vaguely aware of the fists I've formed. My eyes narrow, the room darkening around my brother. Never have I been closer to striking him. I'm literally perched on the edge of my seat, grasping for reasons *not* to launch across the room and give him the beat-down he so deserves. Fortunately, the universe is looking out for Walter Wells tonight.

A gentle rapping on the door draws me, startled, out of myself. It cracks open, a strip of fluorescent light slicing through the shadows as I settle back in my chair. Peering upward, I take in the dark silhouette of a woman, face doused in shadow as she hesitates in the doorway. She says nothing. She does not enter.

"Can I help you?" I ask, gaze falling to my half-tucked shirt. Rising to my feet, I straighten and rub the sleep from my eyes, wondering if I look as horrid as I feel.

In the Arms of Saturn

The woman slowly steps in, easing the door open. Her unease is palpable, communicable. It makes me feel as though I've somehow repulsed her.

My eyes slowly adjust to the light. Bits and pieces of the woman gain clarity. She's short with chin-length hair, medium build. Not skinny but not overweight. She walks first over to Mom, her face still consumed by shadow. Leaning in, she lifts one of the biometric feeds ticking out of equipment at the back, studying it pensively.

"Is this just a checkup?" I ask, suddenly submissive. The silent power of this nurse is strange. She's put me in my place without a word. I look to Walt. It's possible he might have glanced up briefly as she entered, but he's already back in his notebook, putting to page social and philosophical commentary that would rival Socrates (or so it would seem given his abject lack of awareness).

The nurse turns slowly, the light from the doorway spilling over her chest. She steps further into the light. First an ear, then a cheek. Before I know it I'm gazing into the glistening eyes of Mallory Kelson. Mallory Kelson, RN, it would seem.

My mind is rendered a pile of clay. Not a single spark or synapse fires. My mouth cracks open like I have something to say, and for a moment she seems to wait on it, then after a few seconds she seizes control of the situation.

"We're moving your mother out of the E-R and up to the I-C-U for the night. I'll need you to sign some paperwork." Her words are a rushed, syllabic drawl. She's having trouble keeping it together, but she's forcing herself along just the same.

"Whatever you need to do," I find myself saying. My voice cracks. I fidget like a child before her.

"We'll be back to move her shortly." Mallory brushes past me, so close the fabric of our clothing swishes. Flowery perfume wafts into the air, applied conservatively, detectable only in close quarters.

I watch her leave, stepping out through the doorway and into the light. She turns, gripping the doorhandle, and for a moment I think our eyes meet again, though I can't be certain as her face suddenly gathers shadow.

Every part of me wants to scream *I'm sorry* as once again the emotional storm from the beach makes landfall in me. But something in me is able to break through the cowardice and the guilt. The time for seeking Mallory Kelson's forgiveness is over. I'd said my piece and she hers. We might as well be living in a different world now.

Without a word she closes the door.

I trail the rolling bed, gaze returning with unflinching gravity to Mallory, who is hunched over Mom's feet, steering. This poor woman. I've now intruded on both halves of her life.

My gaze shifts to Walt as he walks alongside the bed, still writing furiously with no attention spared to his footing. I'm amazed he hasn't tripped or crashed into anything or anyone. At this point I'm so disgusted with him that I don't want to speak with him at all. A part of me wonders if I'll ever cool enough to look at him differently.

Ahead, a bank of elevators seems to be our first stop. When the silver doors retract, we step into an almost awkwardly long car, and my gaze strays toward Mallory as she swivels and mashes the second-floor button.

The questions begin to spring up in my mind.

How often will she be lucid over the next few weeks?

Will she even know she's dying?

How quickly will she decline?

The elevator dings and I press myself to the edge of the car, making room for the nurses to wheel the bed into the hallway. I follow. Here the smells from downstairs seem to surrender – though not entirely – to intermingling flavors of *sanitary sick*; Iodine, Neosporin, that deep, stinging aroma of disinfectant. We pass rooms exhaling the odors of urine and feces. One of them is spiced with the pungent onion reek of an unwashed body.

Ahead the hallway seems to taper toward infinity, lit with garish fluorescents. We move with deliberation, pausing only now and then for the odd doctor or ER tech to edge past. When we finally arrive at Mom's room I'm relieved to find that it's not a shared space. That she'll be waking up in a foreign place – and a *hospital* at that – is bad enough. To have a stranger parked beside her would push her into an immediate fit.

The nurses maneuver the bed into the dark room using the light from the hallway and park it beneath a row of monitors and other electronic devices. Wires connected to my sleeping mother are patched to the new equipment as one of the nurses flips switches in a series of bleeps and chirps. The other nurses are dismissed by Mallory, leaving me understanding that she's a supervisor of some kind. She then goes to work checking Mom over, drifting through each task as if second nature, gentle hands repositioning their sleeping patient. I'm left not simply impressed, but *grateful*.

After a moment she turns to me, slinging her stethoscope over her shoulders and rounding the bed. Walt has already parked himself in the corner beneath a standing lamp.

"She's stable and should sleep through the rest of the night," Mallory informs me, stopping at arm's length between me and the edge of the bed. She's more composed than she'd been in the ER. She speaks with equal parts authority and compassion, seeming to have found what she needed to temporarily divorce herself from her feelings toward me... or she's at least set them aside for the time being.

"Thank you," I say in a whisper, no less intimidated.

For a moment there is only silence. We're held together in the strip of light cutting in from the hallway. I would give anything to know what she's thinking.

Whatever the flavor of her thoughts, none of the voices in me suggest they're anything I want to know. With this I'm once again able to win the battle with myself and avoid placing our unresolved issues on the table.

She seems to decide the same.

"We'll be in every few hours to check on her. Doctor Bishop wants us to cut off the medicine sedating her around 4 A-M. He'll be in tomorrow morning to speak with her... and you." Mallory speaks mostly to the floor. Her eyes only lift at the end.

"I appreciate everything you've done for my mother," I say, offering another *thank you* that goes largely unanswered.

Mallory draws a long breath and nods. "Hang in there," she says, edging past me and out of the room.

I watch her go.

I snap awake to a frail moaning, cracked every so often with a high, piercing note. This is the second time I've been startled awake in the last twenty-four hours. Such is my life of late.

My eyes roll dryly in their sockets as I soldier through the disorientation, eventually gaining a better grip on my surroundings. Blinding light filters in through a window at my right, the sun burning up the clouds over the eastern fringe of Old York. The silhouette of a man, Walt, rises from the chair across from me, momentarily blotting out the sun as he steps over to Mom.

I stand as well, underused muscles voicing pained protest. Mom is pawing at the blankets, favoring her left hand. Her back is arched, face twisted and angled toward the ceiling. Strings of unintelligible words thread into her moans.

"Mom," I whisper, nearly tripping over my feet as I hurry to her. Reaching the edge of the bed, I try to insert myself into her field of vision, currently fixed on the drop-ceiling above. Not once do her eyes meet mine.

"Momma," Walt whimpers with the helpless cadence of a toddler.

"It's okay, shhhhh," I continue. I place a gentle hand on her cheek and try to guide her toward me. She resists, and though I could easily overpower her, I relent.

"Walt." Our eyes meet. "Go find a nurse, please." For a moment he looks like he's going to argue, his gaze falling helplessly to Mom before nodding apprehensively and shuffling out into the hallway.

With him he takes his precious notebook.

Walt soon bursts back into the room, speaking excitedly, even optimistically in a way that only illuminates his disconnected grip on the situation. I pivot toward the door as he enters, expecting to see Mallory again, but the nurse accompanying my brother is instead the red-headed jerk from yesterday.

"Is she really *awake*?" Walt asks, his voice wavering. He tails the nurse to the side of the bed opposite me and hovers around the man as he goes to work.

"She's in shock," the nurse says, voice steady enough to suggest competence, even concern, where yesterday he'd made himself an obstacle and nothing more. He evaluates the equipment above her bed before switching back and heading toward the door where he pauses, face blank. "I'm going to go get a doctor." And with that he's off.

A minute later Walt is in the doorway peering expectantly down the corridor. In no time at all he's shifting aside as the nurse rushes back into the room with the last person I want to see. Every part of me clenches as I take in the fluorescent light sheening off Dr. McWilliams's bald head.

McWilliams rounds the bed at a leisurely pace, his tv doctor persona flexing in a way that has my fingers digging into the flesh of my palms. He leans over Mom, first checking her IV and the pouches of fluids strung above her before lifting a pair of receipt-style printouts one at a time for pensive study. I can tell he enjoys posing like this for the little people, basking in silent, if misperceived adulation.

"One and a half milligrams of Ativan," he says, cocking his head to the nurse without eye contact. The nurse beats feet out of the room, returning minutes later with a small syringe, which McWilliams plunges into a tube in Mom's saline drip, depressing the plunger. Mom seems to find the most horrible presence of mind in this moment, eyes snapping over to the doctor as he feeds the medicine into her. She begins to thrash, terrified, though fortunately the drugs take quick effect.

Mom's eyelids rise and fall languidly, her body stilling. Moments later her open eyes roll toward the window, where they remain as she drifts back off.

"Where is Dr. Bishop?" I ask, glancing at my watch. It's 7:23 A.M.

"He'll be in shortly," the nurse answers as McWilliams edges past us toward a yellow wall-mounted container marked *Biohazard*. It looks like one of those mailboxes mounted outside someone's door. He dumps the syringe and swivels around, our eyes locking over the shoulders of Walt and the nurse.

"I feel it's best to keep her sedated until she's discharged," McWilliams says. I think back to what Mallory said earlier that morning about Dr. Bishop wanting her off drugs when he visited. I can't pretend to understand the situations that supersede such calls, but my distrust of this man leaves me aggravated at best. "She's obviously unsettled. It would be best to get her home, explain the situation – I'm sure Doctor Bishop would come to you – and make arrangements for hospice care."

He's so *matter-of-fact* that I want to wring his little neck. *Sure, Doc, that's easy enough, let's just cart my dying mother home, explain the situation and bring a couple strangers into the house to change out her soiled linens for the next few weeks. Easy-peasy.*

Still, I remain where I am, silently loathing this man.

"How soon can we get her out of here?" Walt asks, peering up at the doctor like a leper in the presence of Christ.

"That'll be up to Doctor Bishop," McWilliams answers, extracting a tablet from its sconce at the foot of Mom's bed and glossing over it. He mutters something I can't make out before lowering it back and turning to Walt, identifying him correctly as the more agreeable brother. "I think he plans on seeing her out of here today, provided she doesn't suffer any more seizures like the one yesterday." He thrusts his hands into the pockets of his scrubs and tilts back on his heels as if we're just shooting the breeze now. "Do you have any other questions for me?"

Yeah, I think. Would you mind tossing yourself out the window, please?

After a moment McWilliams takes a deep breath and backsteps toward the door. "I'll inform Dr. Bishop of the situation when he arrives. I'm sure he'll be in to see you as soon as he's settled."

Die, worm.

With that the doctor and nurse leave together. Walt remains over Mom for a moment, angling himself in an effort to force a meeting of their eyes. His face sags in disappointment as he fails to draw recognition from her, and I pity him. Walt may be a substance-dependent simpleton, and he may be very easily and obsessively distracted, but moments of genuine, crushing emotion like this help remind me that he cares for our mother in his own odd way.

For a moment I feel bad for my shortness with him.

Of course the moment doesn't last long. Wearing a despondent frown Walt straightens and our eyes meet over our dying mother. His mouth slips open like he has something to say. He seems to grapple internally with the words before allowing the dull look of lost hope spreading over him to do the speaking instead.

And speak it does.

I almost start around the bed toward him, but he rotates away, returning to his chair and the work in his notebook. I study him for some time. He seems completely unaware of everything but the words he's scrawling in that book. He's obsessed, and I know that the cylindrical bulge of the prescription drug bottle in his pocket is mostly to blame.

He's been up for twenty-four hours straight, most of it apparently spent on whatever he's poring into that notebook. It's half full already. I wonder how much further he has to go.

I'm drawn away from my thoughts by a groaning stomach. All I've eaten in the last twenty-four hours is a late breakfast yesterday, a few cookies, and a handful of mini-muffins scrounged from waiting areas. Walt has eaten even less, propped up by the Adderall.

It will catch up with him, and I hope to God I don't need him when it does.

Turning to Mom, I reason that now's as good a time as any to find the cafeteria. She's not going to wake up. Not, apparently, until she's back home in her own bed. I suppose a part of me is resigned to the idea even though Dr. McWilliams was its champion. It's best we break the news to her in a familiar environment.

"I'm going to go get some breakfast." I speak in Walt's general direction, but he's too absorbed to latch onto my voice. "You want anything?"

He continues scribbling in his notebook.

"Walt."

His head lifts, eye-contact is established, then he refocuses on his work. "What?" he asks, seeming miles away.

"Do you want anything to eat?"

"I'm good."

"You *have* to eat."

"Just an orange juice or something. And water."

With a deep, aggravated breath, I spin and exit the room. As I walk toward the cafeteria, making my way by memory even though I can't remember why or when I was last here, I offer a silent plea to the universe that my brother burn through his Adderall before Mom dies. If not, I fear he'll miss his only opportunity for a sober goodbye.

who
is
carter

WHAT'S THE DEAL with Walter? What lesson was he struggling to learn in life? Better Living Through Drug Use?

I expect the simpering voice to slather its often condescending commentary all over these questions, but the voice doesn't answer. In its place is a darkness that seems to spread out from the core of me, darkening the formless void in a way that makes me feel... broken...

I'm alone here, and in this moment I intuit from the ether something that leaves me reaching toward my childhood, toward events that failed to resonate with clear meaning at the time, but now hold weight I'm powerless to understand... or avoid.

Who is Carter? What has he done?

The margins of my reality fray enough to inform me that the simpering voice is listening.

But it will not answer my questions.

It doesn't want to answer my questions.

Perhaps it *cannot* answer my questions.

I'm not certain. Soon I'm back with Walter in another *where* and *when*, long before our concerted effort to force medicine on our mother.

It's the second snow day we've had in as many days, and while Mom isn't a fan of Kittery's decision to scrub lessons in the interest of safety, Walter and I have been over the moon at the four-day weekend the Nor'easter's afforded us. Though our interests have diverged with age (at eight-years-old Walt can only pretend to understand the majority of my 13-year-old interests), it's on days like this, when we're anchored to home and isolated from our social groups, that we still come together.

And the last couple days we've come together on a major project out in the snowdrifts and mounded piles left by the plow guy – a friend of Dad's from the Shipyard who Dad maintains *won't screw us*. Yesterday had been productive enough, boring into the snow far enough to carve three sizable rooms. It's easily our most ambitious snow fort ever. Today we've been gifted additional daylit hours to expand our warrens in the snow.

"Hey, wait for *me*, Mark!" Walt calls from the covered porch as I'm already vaulting over the railing into the snow. As I make for the closest snow pile I can't help grinning at the sounds of Mom fussing over him in the doorway, making sure poor baby Walter doesn't go out with any patches of skin exposed.

I can't remember the last time she fussed over me like that, not that I'm about to complain as I fall onto all fours and crawl into the dark tunnel we'd dug in the embankment. Walter's urgency to unstick himself from our mother continues in his whining and her attending retorts, each beginning with words like "you need to be careful..." and "I wish you'd listen to me when..."

Being more free-range myself, I can't say I'm subjected to Mom's insecurities in *half* the ways Walter is. A part of me, old enough now to understand the finer points of their relationship, wonders if she'll ever let Walt leave the house. The thoughts don't remain in my teenage mind for long before I'm crawling through the snow-slopped dark into the farthest of the rooms we'd dug. It's not long before Walter's trifling, whining voice begins to originate from the anterior rooms of the fort, and when he comes scuttling into my room he's already wearing an expression of pained betrayal.

"I said to *wait*, Mark," Walter grumbles, his wooly cap already falling down over his eyebrows, rendering him sightless as he closes the remainder of the gap between us.

"What I gotta wait for *you* for?" I return, purely for the sake of riling him up.

But Walter only frowns at me as he fixes his hat and tugs down on his white and purple nylon jacket, one I'd worn until it no longer fit. "It's our fort," he says, seeming to fix himself both inside and out. "Not yours, *ours*."

I've already started on a new space in the wall where I'm hollowing out another tunnel. Mom's gardening spade works best for this, while we use the larger snow-shovel to clear out the excavated snow. Walter had spent most of the day yesterday on snow removal duty, and I'm more than aware today of his desire for a more constructive role. I hear him lift the snow-shovel, scraping it through the snow a few times before his tiny voice makes with its inevitable discontentment.

"I thought I was going to make the tunnels and you shovel the snow out today," Walt says, sounding already defeated as he no doubt studies me shaping the threshold of our latest warren.

"I've changed plans. If you're allowed to do it you'll cave the whole thing in because you're a *retard*," I fire back, smiling into the hole slowly taking shape before me. A part of me wants to glance back and drink in the look of betrayal on his face, but I know I'll be able to milk it longer if I continue prodding carefully, not engaging directly.

To the elder sibling, such was life's greatest boon, needling at the younger for as long as possible before the inevitable meltdown. Walt's wiser these days though. Pokes and prods that had previously pushed him over the edge no longer worked, rendering my tactics more and more cruel with each year I've been forced to adapt.

"I won't cave it in," Walt snivels, already most of the way toward the mental cliff where I'm driving him. "I'm eight-and-three-quarters, Mark. I'm not a kid anymore."

It's with the utterance of this absurdity that I cannot help myself swiveling to face him. I can't say why I'm so intent on destroying him in this moment, on seeing my brother scramble out of our fort in tears so that his mother – *his* more than *mine* – spends the rest of the day mopping his tears inside.

But I will do it. I'll destroy everything about him purely for the sake of doing it.

"You'll *always* be a kid – all coddled by Mom, under a microscope, helplessly controlled by her."

His tiny, cherubic face scrunches in the makings of an inevitable fit. Tiny eyes try their darndest to go hard against mine, but they're already glistening with tears set soon to spill down his flushed cheeks. His stubby chin trembles a moment before he fires back with the only remaining argument he has. But it's a good one. The one I always fail to see coming.

The one I'm powerless to stop myself reacting to.

"You're just jealous."

I feel my gloved fingers tighten around the handle of the spade. I unconsciously angle its pointed tip toward Walter. Through gnashed teeth, I whisper, "I'm not jealous."

"Yeah you are," Walt returns, suddenly finding a confidence that fills him. I can't help withering in his presence as he's suddenly channeling the presence of a man, something I struggle to place in any one quality of his behavior.

It's something in him. Something inside that I don't like or understand.

"I'm not jealous, Walt." But I am. It's clear in the way I'm growling-out my words.

And then he does the thing he knows will push *me* over the edge. He simply grins back at me, that tiny face doing all the talking. My mouth falls open, and for a moment I know exactly what I want to say in shutting him down, then I lose it. With nothing in the way of a snappy retort, I default to the behavior I've yet to grow out of at age 13 and hurl the spade at him blindly. It soars over his shoulder like a javelin, narrowly missing his face.

Walt whips around, surprised. In the microseconds it takes him to glance backward I see on his face the terrified expression of a little brother aware suddenly of the monster he's been looking up to his whole life. The spade embeds itself in the wall, its handle caught in the slanted daylight from the entrance two rooms back.

I know I've screwed up. In my head I watch the spade soaring inches from Walter's face again and again before sticking into the wall and going still.

Slowly Walter turns back to me, tears renewed. In this moment I know we're both thinking the same thing, that I'd almost killed him. Nowhere in my brother's tear-choked eyes do I see the impulse I'd expect, to flee into the house and the safety of our mother. Walter shows no signs of flight, only deep, existential hurt.

"Mark..." Walt blinks a pair of tears down his wind-kissed cheeks.

"Walt, I..."

There is only silence between us. Silence and a sour flavor of betrayal that seems to reach beyond our brotherly bonds. Though his face shows the blackest disillusionment toward the sudden change in our dynamic, he says nothing. Like me, I feel like a part of him struggles to understand exactly what's just fallen off between us, but the emotions it leaves hold nothing to decode.

Slamming my fists in the snow, I scramble past him though the slush and out of the fort, leaving him there. I'm in the house before I know what's happened, kicking off my boots and shucking my snow gear as Mom steps out of the living room with an expression of crazed concern on her face.

"Where's your *brother*?" She asks, already annoyed with me.

"Outside," I answer as I continue to fumble with my gear.

"You can't leave him out there *alone*, Marky!" She's already rushing toward me, and before I know it she's forcing me back into my gear.

"Mom – *ow*! C'mon I don't want to play outside!"

She's already so worked up she's out of breath. "Walter can't... be... out there... alone."

"He's eight-and-three-quarters," I fire back sardonically, resisting the hands drawing the jacket back onto my body. "He can do things *alone*!"

"Your... brother... is *special*, Mark." She fumbles a moment with the zipper on my jacket before hauling it up with enough force to pinch my chin as it reaches its apex. Gripping the doorhandle, she hauls the cottage door open once more on the blinding sheen of winter coating the land. I'm being ushered out the door to her still prattling voice when suddenly she goes silent.

"Oh my *god*," Mom gasps, shoving me to the ground as she launches herself out the door and into the cold in a house dress and stocking feet.

I'm left struggling to understand her outlandish behavior until my gaze settles upon the hillocks of snow beneath which we'd carved out our fort. While five of the six peaks retained their drifting form, the third one in – the one under which I'd recently argued with my brother – was flat to the point where it was concave.

The fort had collapsed while I was inside.

A fire in me unlike any I've ever felt has me launching out the door to join Mom, already slogging through the drifts on her way to the site of the collapse. Before I know it I'm ahead of her. Scanning in a panic for any snow displaced by Walter's small body, I rack my brain to recreate the interior of the fort from this outside perspective. I need to determine where I'd left him.

When nothing outwardly apparent presents itself, I trudge to the spot where I'd been excavating our latest tunnel. Without thinking, my now bare hands are digging in the snow, heaving chunks of dislodged ice over my shoulder as Mom comes up beside me, collapsing to her knees and tossing up manic fistfuls of her own.

She's panting like a wild animal in a frenzy.

Over the sounds of the wind whistling through the trees and the sounds of our exertions, I swear I hear her mutter a few times, *Damn you, Mark, damn you.*

This makes me dig more feverishly. I shudder, even at age 13, to imagine what Mom would be like without Walter. I can no longer feel my fingers. I'm unaware of how much time has passed, but as I suddenly grip something firm, something not of ice or snow, I'm certain we've lost him. For a few seconds I try to extract him from the ice before collapsing and digging around him, eventually unearthing his tiny face in time for Mom to notice and shove me off of him.

From where I roll in the snow, I watch her press her lips to his, I watch her breathe into him, and as his coughing fit announces that he'll be okay, I watch every part of her not already devoted to Walter commit itself to him, to her life's charge.

"Mom, I—"

"Shut up, Mark!" she yells, sobbing as she clutches her baby to her, blue housedress jostling in the icy wind. Now fussing over Walter, she's whispering all kinds of things I cannot hear, holding him out from her every now and then and looking him over as though she'd missed something. Several times I catch her apologizing to him, most likely for me, before he's whisked into the house, muttering odd things which Mom would later dismiss as the incoherent ramblings of a child in shock.

But I hear him repeat the same part several times as he's spirited inside, and he utters it again to himself later as he's sipping cocoa at the kitchen table and shooting the occasional silent, reproving glance my way.

"Carter saved me," he says. "Carter saved me."

your mother loved you

WHAT WAS THAT? I inquire of the void, aware on a deeper level that I'm still alone here, that the simpering voice doesn't approve of the sudden change in trajectory regarding my wanderings.

It isn't until all of me seems to darken at the memory of my mother treating me so cruelly that the voice rises in the formless nothing. Its simpering character seems shed in place of an odd, feverish insistence now threading her voice.

Your mother loved you, the voice says defensively.

Oh, I know she did, I answer, able to intuit the unspoken connection she and I had shared. But with it comes so much more, not the least of which is the understanding that our lives hadn't gone untouched by those here on this side.

Something had drilled into Mom the feverish impulse to get me back out that door. Something... perhaps *someone* had interfered in our lives that day.

There are things you're touching here, Mark... and your interest in them confounds me. There's nothing in the past that will benefit you here. Not now.

A shiver runs through me.

'Not now' she'd clearly said. This means there's something missing here, something that's broken us on this side. I'm certain of it.

Who is Carter? I ask, receiving no answer.

We leave the hospital after another day of Mom under meticulous sedation. Dr. Bishop agrees, though I sense reluctance, that it's best we break the news to her at home. He reminds us – more me – that this isn't the usual way he does this type of thing, but he can see no other way given Mom's irrational fear of all things *healthcare*.

I'm bold enough to ask that he come to our house in street clothes when it's time. He agrees in an instant.

Chalk off another day of missed work for me, plus the day I'm taking today. I'm rapidly burning through my PTO options. At one point in my life – really just a couple of months ago – this would have riddled me with anxiety and plagued my thoughts. Now that I've been plowed over by the world, I can't help viewing my professional life in shades of irrelevance. I have far more important things to worry about. Like making hospice arrangements for Mom... and getting started with funeral arrangements.

We don't see Mallory beyond that first night in the hospital. Odd feelings join me at the thought of her, none entirely pleasant, though thankfully they aren't born of guilt. As Walt and I wheel our sleeping mother out of the hospital and to the RAV, I can't help glancing back a few times, searching the sun-gilded windows for signs of Mallory. It's strange, not being able to read oneself. I'm certain that forgiveness is no longer my endgame, its space now filled by something else entirely. I'm at a loss to what, exactly, I want from this poor woman.

We get Mom home and into her bedroom. Her eyes flutter as we ease her into bed, but she doesn't wake. The drugs are still wearing off. Walt holds the doors open for me. His interest in composition has tapered only marginally after filling his entire notebook and moving onto another. I've no idea where he's getting them, though I suspect it's the hospital gift shop. A part of me wonders if he'd stolen them.

I join my brother in the living room. Settling on the couch, I consider changing out of the clothes I've worn the last three days and freshening up ahead of Dr. Bishop's arrival. Just sitting down in a familiar place after days away is in itself immensely restorative, and for a while I flirt around a nap. I don't know how long I'm sitting there, cocooned in silence broken only by the hum of the fridge and the soft scraping of Walt's pen. It's not until he grunts loudly in Mom's recliner and submits to a long stretch that my eyes open on him and I'm finally moved to ask.

"What are you writing?"

"It isn't finished yet."

"Is it a journal? A story?" I think back to my Adderall days, up for 24 and 48 hour stretches writing just like Walter is now. Guilt moves in and pricks at my heart as I lament my lost art. I haven't written anything since Elora and I parted ways before college.

"It's personal," Walt says, clutching the notebook melodramatically. His mind is fried. He needs rest.

But I don't linger on these things for long, worried instead about Walt's suddenly evasive behavior. It's not like my brother to be secretive about these kinds of things. When it comes to his drugs, he's closed up tighter than a dolphin's blowhole, but he's never shied away from celebrating accomplishments, regardless of their frequent "Participant Award" nature.

What's so important about this thing he's writing?

If I wasn't so exhausted I'd push him further, but I have more important things to do. I have yet to meet the person or persons who will be attending Mom over the coming weeks, the last of her life, and I already pity them. Mom isn't likely to make things easy, especially for strangers in her home. She's always been so distrustful of anyone outside her circle. It's clear why the house was always so empty and quiet when I was a child.

Mom pushed people away.

My thoughts pivot to the inevitable funeral. Will Walt and I be the only ones in attendance? I honestly can't think of anyone else to invite besides Kelly, then I consider the spectacle of burying the wife of Eric Wells and force myself to abandon my train of thought.

Digging around in my pocket, I extract a folded leaf of paper Dr. Bishop had given me. It's a printout of two in-home hospice providers. I'll end up paying double or triple the cost of a bed in an established facility, but it's the only option for Mom. One of them is right off US-1 here in Kittery, and that's as good a sign as any to pull the trigger on their services. Unsnapping my phone from its holster, I lift it to observe a depleted battery notification.

I'm floored the handheld lasted even *this* long.

Scooting across the abrasive couch, I fish the charger cable out of the cushions and plug in my phone. My eyes close, and I wake moments later – or perhaps it's been hours – to a timid knocking on the front door. I find Walt through the fog of sleep, he's looking me over expectantly, obviously not about to answer the door himself.

I heave myself to my feet, wincing at a spike of pain shooting down my back. Too many nights spent sleeping in a chair. Staggering at first, I exit the living room and make my way down the hallway toward the mud room. When I open the door, I find Dr. Bishop standing there in blue jeans and a tangerine t-shirt reading *Saunders at Rye Harbor 10K*. I recognize the race, having run it myself many times.

"You got a shirt," I say, nodding toward the logo on his left breast.

For a moment he's confused. His entire beard seems to droop in the makings of a frown.

"Saunders at Rye Harbor," I clarify. "Only the top finishers get a shirt."

"Oh." A relieved smile. "Yeah, ran it for the first time last year. You?"

"Ten years in a row – got a shirt every time." I feel like I'm coming across smug and dial it down. Runners are such elitists. "Can't say I was at the top of the qualifiers, but I suppose some people are just built for running and the rest of us have to be happy competing with ourselves."

"You got that right," Bishop says, peering past me into the shadowed interior of the cottage. It seems the time for small talk has come and gone. "How is your mother?"

"Asleep as far as I know," I answer, waving him in. As he steps into the house I curse myself for not tidying up. The kitchen in particular is a mess, sink overflowing with dishes and teeming with fruit flies stirred aloft by each passing body. What a picture this must paint of our little family – two men living at home with their mother in a filthy, crumbling house.

I lead him into the kitchen, glancing briefly into the living room to see if Walt is going to join us. His face lifts for a moment before returning to his writing. He finishes what I imagine to be a final thought before lurching upward and jamming the recliner's footrest home. Teetering a moment, he collects himself and shuffles over to us.

"Walt," Dr. Bishop says.

Walt gives him a nod. It's best he not say anything anyway; when he's been awake this long he tends to say some really random stuff.

Turning to Dr. Bishop, I ask, "Should we wake her?"

"She's been in something of a medically-induced coma for two days," Bishop says, his tone carrying restrained disapproval. He turns with a face so strikingly grave that I backtrack a few paces. "It's best you wake her. I'll wait outside until you feel it appropriate to bring me in."

"Okay." I nod several times before turning and walking down the hallway to Mom's bedroom. The footsteps of the men tailing me are so soft that I have to glance back to make sure they're following. The darkness of the hallway is all encompassing, mirroring the despair gripping my heart. I've never had to tell someone they're dying, let alone my own mother.

I stop before Mom's door. My hand lifts of its own slow, astonishing will and eases the door open just enough for me to get a look at her. She's still sleeping with Mouf curled up beside her.

Vaguely aware of what I'm doing, I see the door open, and I'm walking to the edge of the bed. Walt appears on the other side and descends to his knees, folding his hands atop the mattress like a child offering evening prayer. I lean over our mother, gaze running despondently over the creases on her face. Her silver hair drifts like windswept sawgrass over her pillow and chest. She breathes softly, the swelling intake barely perceptible under the blanket draping her.

My hand finds its way to hers. I caress the bandage left from her IV. "Mom," I whisper, a part of me actively trying *not* to wake her. She doesn't so much as stir. "Mom," I repeat, louder.

Her eyelids flutter before slowly rising. She blinks a few times before assessing the room, her attention eventually returning to me before shifting to Walt. "What's this?" Her voice is crackly with sleep. Her gaze returns to me. "Mark... is it Saturday? Why are you home?"

She's back to thinking I'm still in college. What is it about that period that resonates with her? Is that when the cancer first started assembling itself in her? I try to pluck moments of odd conduct in her from memory. The truth is Mom's always been more than *off*, her behavior at the hospital a glaring testament to this.

"Mom, I graduated ten years ago." I caress her hand and force the biggest, fakest smile to my face, hoping to exude enough love to burn through the confusion fogging her mind.

She looks to Walt for corroboration, then back to me. "'*Course* you did." She clears her throat with a wet rattle and scoots up in bed. Her right hand barely moves beneath mine. Most of her strength seems sapped toward the left side of her body, and after a moment struggling to move upright, I gently take her by the shoulders and ease her back against the headboard.

"Do you remember much from the last two days, Mom?" I look to Walt. In his eyes is the same dread I feel, flickering dimly.

"Well, I..." She speaks at first with confidence, but it's chased away in short order by a heavy, settling confusion. Her mouth slowly closes. She looks between me and Walt, waiting for us to clarify things.

"You've been in the..." I pause. "You've been in the hospital."

Her eyes widen. Suddenly a fire roars to life in her, fueled by a seething mixture of panic, incredulity, and rage. "You took me after breakfast! Tried to *force me in!*"

"Calm down, Mom. Please. We had to do it for your own good."

"You'd turn on your own mother! After everything I've done for you — everything I've *sacrificed!*"

"It's not like that," I argue, trying to keep my voice from elevating. She's quickly working herself up, and the last thing I want is for her to fall into the grip of another seizure. "Please calm down, Mom. You're not there anymore."

Her eyes bore into mine. Her voice is heavy and sullen. "What did they do to me? What did they *put* in me?"

"They just ran a few tests—"

"Tests? What tests?"

There's no way I can answer this question without further agitating her. I never should have used the word *test*. But it's too late to backtrack now.

"It—it doesn't matter," I say through a long sigh, hoping she'll accept it. Naturally she doesn't.

"Mark *Cedric* Wells, you tell me what they *did* to me right now!"

I've never seen someone transition so rapidly from sedated to fully awake in my life. She struggles to wrench her hand out from under mine, but I can tell it's giving her trouble. I lean in closer, staring deeply into her eyes with as commanding a look as I can maintain. "Mom, this is very serious. You aren't well. Please, calm down so we can talk about it."

Her lips crack open, and for a moment I think she's going to fire back. Then her brow furrows over a look of tight unease that rises quickly to dominate her face. The anger and resentment still flare behind her eyes, but she's disarmed now to a degree. Her lips pucker, then, "Wha—what's wrong with me?" Her voice quivers like that of a frightened child trying to cope with a sudden, unexpected reprimand.

I swallow hard, unsure how to do this. "You remember the other day when you fell and couldn't get back up?"

Her eyes narrow. Slowly, she nods.

"You couldn't get back up because your right side is weak." I watch her gaze fall to her right hand and I tighten my grip. "The doc— the *people* at the hospital found a growth on the left side of your brain. It – I'm sorry... I..."

The look on her face will haunt me for the rest of my life, all color drained, every muscle slackened. Her mouth is slotted, and though she's gazing at me, it feels like she's peering *through* me.

And suddenly I know I can't do this.

"There's someone here from the hospital," I say, already blinking against the world of water building itself in my vision. I turn to Dr. Bishop, standing in the bedroom doorway, waiting for his cue.

Mom's gaze finds him. Within the anxiety assembled on her face is a wholly debilitating terror, and I wonder if she's going to just lose it completely.

"Mrs. Wells, I'm Harold Bishop, a neurologist with York Hospital." He walks haltingly into the room, seeming poised to snap backward at the first sign of hostility. Mom's reputation, garnered through moments of fleeting lucidity with Dr. McWilliams, seems to have preceded her.

Bishop stops and stands abreast with me at the edge of the bed. Our eyes meet for a moment before he pivots toward Mom. She gazes up at him like a primitive in the shadow of a furious deity. I've never seen her so yielding in the presence of a doctor. Her hand trembles weakly in mine.

"What your son says is true. We've isolated a growth in your brain, stretching across most of your frontal and parietal lobes. The growth looks to have been spreading across the dorsal areas of the left hemisphere for some time now. That's why you're so weak on your right." He swallows hard, showing vulnerability where McWilliams would have flexed his ego and delivered the news with the presence of a man concerned exclusively with his own status. Dr. Bishop, a veteran in his field as far as I can tell, has no soul-sheathing callous between him and my mother. He lets her existential woe flood over him, taking it freely. "Had we caught this sooner there may have been a few treatment routes for us to explore... but this is very late stage."

I grow aware of Walt's heavy breathing across the bed, and my gaze goes to him. His skin is porcelain. In fact, every part of him looks suddenly *drained*. His vapid eyes cling to the man in the Saunders t-shirt.

"How—how much time do I have?" Mom speaks in a ghostly whisper, asking the question countless other unfortunate souls have asked before her. She looks to her right hand, still resting in mine. Her fingers twitch slightly as she tests the hand. Here she finds hard evidence of a situation from which she cannot escape. This isn't the same as feigning a momentary lapse in memory when she thinks I'm visiting from college, her stubbornness will not be enough to brute-force her way out of this.

"It's difficult to know for certain," Dr. Bishop says, boldly taking a seat at the edge of the bed. "I estimate maybe a month."

She doesn't react. Not even a twitch. I'm left wondering after a few seconds if she'd even heard him. Then pointed questions that are so tragically *Mom* emerge.

"Will there be any pain?"

I look to Dr. Bishop, equal parts interested and uneasy, anticipating his coming answer. I breathe a sigh of relief as he shakes his head. "It's different for each patient, but typically there isn't much pain."

"What can I expect? What will happen to me?"

Now Dr. Bishop looks to *me*, silently probing the virtues of providing additional detail. I nod, already aware of what he's going to say.

"Your mental faculties will start to degrade. You're likely to become annoyed with certain noises. There will be moments of disorientation..." he trails off, glancing up at me again, and again I grant him license to continue with a wordless nod. "You'll lose control of your bowels. You'll spend the majority of your time sleeping. Visual acuity is likely to diminish."

My vision doubles. I try to keep from blinking, knowing the tears will come in earnest once I do. But I can't control myself, and soon water is spilling down my cheeks. Through the blur my gaze finds Mom studying her right hand as though she expects it to detach and crawl away.

Across the bed Walter is also weeping, head sagged.

"We'll make you as comfortable as possible right up through the very end," Dr. Bishop says after a deep breath. His face is genuine.

Mom says nothing. A part of me wonders if she'll recall any of this in the coming days. I try not to consider how unbearable it would be to break this news to her daily.

"Do you have any other questions for me, Mrs. Wells?" Dr. Bishop shifts in the early makings of his escape. I don't fault him for the discomfort Mom inspires. She makes grown men tremble as an artform. The doctor has been so gracious, coming here when nothing obligated him to do so.

Mom's chest rises and falls slowly. She eventually shakes her head, gaze settling on Walt as she extracts her good hand from the covers and reaches for him. Walt runs the sleeve of the dress shirt he's failed to change out of the last few days across his face before inching closer and taking her hand.

"I think I'd just like to be alone with my boys," she answers. Her voice is laced with submission and it's beyond crushing. My stomach folds over on itself as I consider all I've done to protect her dignity only for her to spend her final weeks defeated.

"Of course," Dr. Bishop says, now moving to his feet. He sidles behind me, and I feel his hand grip my shoulder. "I'm very sorry. Is there anything else I can do for you?" He gives me a look that says he'll truly do *anything*.

This man has restored much of my faith in humanity.

I shake my head. "Thank you, doctor."

He pauses, face set as though he has more to say, but he seems to swallow his words before rotating and walking out. I wait for the sound of the front door opening and closing. A million miles away, Bishop's car roars to life before diminishing, edged out by the pressing silence between us three.

Walt and I wait, our gazes alternating between Mom and each other. Before long we're drawn in closer. My fingers lace with Mom's. Walt clutches her other hand in both of his in a gesture of unconscious protection. My head finds its home on her shoulder, and within seconds

I feel her shift gently as Walt follows suit. We stay like this for some time, emotions piled, before she finally speaks again.

Mom's voice lacks power, seeming muffled like neighbors conversing on the other side of a shared wall. "Have I been behaving oddly? Have I done anything embarrassing?"

Daggers pierce my drumming heart. No person should have to suffer such humiliation.

"No, Momma," Walt and I say in one voice. I haven't called her *Momma* in more than twenty years. Not since Walter nearly died in the last snow fort we'd been allowed to build.

Not since childhood's end.

She snivels, chest expanding and contracting with each sharp breath, tears running through the time-sculpted valleys in her flesh. "Please don't think poorly of me when I start to lose it," she weeps. I keep tight hold of her hand and feel around with the other until it finds Walt's.

"Never," I say. I breathe deeply the lingering scents of perfume still present beneath the sterile-smelling traces of *hospital*.

"You'll take c—care of each oth—other," she stutters, chest heaving in the early throes of an existential breakdown. "And *Mouf*."

"We will, Mom," Walt sobs.

She grows silent once more, and for a time we remain there connected, weeping freely. We don't get up to eat. We don't get up to use the bathroom.

We talk of days passed and of things to come.

We rise and fall together on the waves of our pooled emotions.

does
the
forest
show
your
way
home

AS A CHILD I had this recurring dream, I whisper.

You suddenly have a lot of interest in your childhood. Tell me about the dream, Mark.

I'm in a forest at night. The sky is an onyx slab, bruised over by clouds. Starless.

Describe the forest.

It has a voice. It speaks, but its words are formless... like this place.

Stay with the dream, Mark. Tell me more about the forest.

There's a breeze always playing in the trees. It has a mischievous character, a sentience I don't so much know as I feel. *The chittering music of nocturnal insects is a boisterous symphony of sexual proposition.*

Are you lost in this forest?

No. I mean, yes, but... I know where I'm going even though I don't know where I am. Does that make sense?

Probably more to me than you. So you're in this forest, which has a **presence** *of intelligence beyond your understanding...*

Yes.

What happens there?

At first nothing. I just sit there, listening to it speak until the words begin to hold meaning.

What does the forest say?

It asks me if I'm lost, if I belong in this place, if I want to... have it light my way home.

Try to visualize home *right now. What comes to you?*

This feels like another task designed to convince me I'm dead, but I go along with it in a way that feels wholly natural and instinctual, like a bird's impulse always to point its beak into the wind. I try to visualize *home*, but all I can conjure is an image of the planet Saturn. In my mind's eye I see myself as a grain of sand floating over iconic rings that have belted the gilded titan since time was young.

Mark?

The planet vanishes, and I'm left gripped in the silence of the void.

It was the planet Saturn.

The simpering voice says nothing at first, then, *You're drawing closer to us. Whatever has you so firmly tied to your old life is going to reveal itself soon. What made you think of the dream?*

The first word that comes to mind is *escape*, but it quickly distills into purer form: *early release*.

Though I possess the answer, I fail to understand it. I don't answer the question.

Does the forest show your way home?

I hear the forest's voice rising up from the bottom of me: "Come home. It's not too late. You still have time."

I start into the forest, suddenly aware of a monster at my heels, I say. *Its footfalls are the pounding of thunder along the leaf-dusted ground, its hulking body crashes with raucous abandon through the trees. It wants me out of its domain.*

What happens?

I run, feeling like the beast is gaining two steps for every one I put forward, but there's a light ahead in the trees. I force myself into a sprint toward it, the entire world seeming all at once to bite and scratch as I fight through the last of the foliage. I ignore it, my thoughts divided between the advancing monster and the gilded light building in the trees. I stumble, plowing through a wall of branches before bursting out and falling to the ground.

I pause, wondering if the simpering voice *feels* this memory as I do. I have only a second to acknowledge that I'm out of the forest and standing in a clearing. Windswept sawgrass is frozen in static waves. I'm up quickly and dashing through it, blades lacerating my bare legs as I consolidate my willpower and sprint through the pain, away from the forest. When I see it, the oddly misplaced orb hovering in the center of the field thousands of feet in the distance and pulsing with ethereal, lemon-tinted light, I understand that the voice I'm hearing is not the forest but in fact that of this inexplicably earthbound... planet.

I point myself toward it, knowing nothing else and nearly screaming as the monster behind me breaks through the trees with a ravenous ROAR that shakes the earth and sets new patterns streaking through the tallgrass.

But all I see is Saturn, trimmed in a way suiting its earthly visit, suspended twenty feet above the ground. And I'm drawn to its siren call, running now through the tall grass with unnatural speed. A car doing 70 wouldn't catch me, yet the monster is gaining.

I'm nearly there, just another fifty feet, but this is where the monster catches me.

Paws like the hammers of God shove me from behind, and I'm soaring suddenly over the grass. When I land it's without pain, sliding through the grass as the world is reduced to the pounding footfalls of my monster. But its eagerness has only betrayed it as I rocket to a skidding stop beneath the glowing face of Saturn.

Then the beast steps over me, obscuring the earthbound planet and renewing my panic. The ground shakes as it straddles me, panting in steamy gusts that speak to the dead things it's recently eaten. I feel saturated in it and scramble to free myself only to be met with more pounding.

It's only when I give up struggling that I see the monster for what it is, a black bear, its mangy coat broken by festering wounds that sit like islands in swatches of bald flesh, each running with blood and puss and reeking of death.

The bear levels its foam-fringed muzzle with my face and washes me in the stink of its bellow. Gobs of syrupy mucus spatter my skin.

I pause, seeing the dream as though it were playing out in this formless place. I remember how much the bear frightened me as a child, how bears would end up an irrational fear I'd carry until the day I die...

A part of me insists I should flee...

The simpering voice doesn't wait for me to finish. She finishes for me.

But you don't, she says. *Instead you begin to pummel it anywhere your fists will land. In the nose and muzzle and ear and shoulder, blow after blow lands upon ropes of engaged muscle under loose fur. Four-year-old hands beat back against a creature built of impulse, indifferent to the artificial concepts of right and wrong. Yet somehow it's enough, and the bear recoils as if suddenly challenged by a superior predator. It exits the light cast by Saturn, and in its frustration the bear halts at the edge of the planet's influence, tossing up clods of dirt and grass in its ire.*

Suddenly the space I share with the simpering voice, formless as it is, feels smaller. I don't have to tell her she's right. She already knows it. Just like I know on a deeper level that I am dead.

I pick up where the voice leaves off. *Before I know it I'm on my feet wiping strings of mucus from my face. My eyes meet with the bear's beneath the roiling churn of Saturn. The bear's lips furl, brandishing rows of jagged teeth, but I don't recoil or even flinch. Instead I plant myself beneath my mother planet and stand defiantly against my enemy. My tiny hands are fists, my body dips into the preparatory crouch of a predator soon to pounce. My back arches and my mouth falls open, roaring back at the bear with the ripping voice of God Himself.*

The simpering voice picks up again, *The bear cringes against your power. Such palpable terror in the eyes of a creature never meant to understand fear is staggering, almost unnatural. All at once it whirls around, kicking up dirt and grass in its sudden haste toward the forest… and just as quickly as it had come, it is gone.*

She's either dreamt the same dream, or she's drawing the memory from me. Somehow, I know it's both.

You're left doused in the bolstering glow of our celestial mother. And out of the settling silence, broken only by the swishing of grass and whiffling of wind in the trees, the voice of Saturn speaks, 'It's not too late. Should you change your mind, you will have another chance.'

Crushing silence. Vast nothingness.

The dreams were an out provided by my subconscious. A way of fleeing life and abandoning its lesson, I say, feeling the margins of the stifling void fray in the presence of such bare truth. *I'd simply have died in my sleep.*

A way of returning safely to the ether, regrouping with your soulmates, and trying again, the simpering voice clarifies.

Wouldn't suicide accomplish the same thing? I ask, gripping myself as a sudden rush of black despair floods my soul.

For a time I think the voice has left me, then, grudgingly, it speaks, barely loud enough to hear.

No. Suicide does not *accomplish the same thing. Suicide is the greatest possible failure a soul can endure. It traps the soul in a state of never-ending confusion...* violent *confusion, from which it can never emerge. Not ever,* the no-longer-simpering voice states, sounding as though it is painful, *physically* painful, to speak of such things.

Why is it so devastating? So... final?

Again I think the voice is gone. Then, *Suicide is the result of a soul confounded by the lesson it returned to learn. It's one of two final destinations for us. We either finish our lessons and Transcend, returning to God, or we suffer in the madness of our failure.*

The blackness draws me tighter into its embrace, darkening along with my thoughts. *Lots of people commit suicide.* I'm not sure why I say it.

Yes, the voice says, now sullen, seeming weighted down by the darkest of existential truths – truths I can *feel. Lots of people commit suicide, and left behind in the ether, unable to ever return to physical existence, are its chain of souls.*

I don't understand.

Each of us is bound to at least eight others. After every life we reunite for a time before returning, usually together, to life on Earth and another lesson learned. When one of us kills themself, it anchors the rest of us here in the ether. We are simply... stuck, never again to return to an earthly life, unable to pursue Transcendence, unable to join with God. We're left aimless... forever.

Forever, I repeat, tasting the word. It holds different meaning to me from its eternal inferences. I feel like I've tied this word to a feeling of love, and as I submit to the feeling I'm warmed to the point where talk of suicide slips the borders of my consciousness.

I'm left with a mind intent to wander as the margins of my reality grow suddenly porous and shot with winking stars and gaseous nebulae.

Behind it I see the face of my mother slowly building itself in the murk.

"Help! Somebody help!" Mom's wraithlike voice pierces the nighttime stillness. I snap awake, shooting up off the floor outside her door just as Walt's door thuds against the wall across the carpet. I've been sleeping in this spot every night for the past two weeks, yet Walter can't commit it to memory. His frantic rush to Mom's rescue sees his foot catching on my sleeping bag, and he topples into Mom's bedroom, landing with a weak *whump!* that barely registers beneath the screaming.

"Help! Help me!" Mom continues with ear-splitting urgency as Walt and I scramble to our feet. He's consistently more worked up than I, almost always dialed up to eleven these days. I get it, neither of us wants to see Mom like this, but with Walter it's almost like he sees an extension of himself in her. This isn't the first time she's woken up in a frenzy, though her outbursts typically occur during the day when she wakes to one of her hospice nurses reading in the recliner beside her bed.

Every day she meets the same pair of strangers, while every day I feel more and more like I'm in this alone. Walt is seldom helpful, only seeming to work on his writings now. He doesn't even go out with his loser friends anymore, though I suspect it's guilt keeping him moored to the cottage rather than any dimly-firing thoughts of shame.

"Mom," I say, trying to reduce my voice to a soft mewling. A part of me, naïve and irresponsibly optimistic, hopes that it will inspire calm in her. "Mom, it's okay." I move to my feet, feeling up the wall until I find the light switch. I flick it on, flooding the room with light.

The blankets are kicked off the bed toward the left. Her bare legs piston weakly, catheter tube slapping back and forth between. Her right hand rests limply on the bed while her left thrashes at the tubes and pouches strung over her, feeding into her body.

The room reeks of body odor and urine. Fortunately she hasn't soiled herself tonight.

Walt is already at the bed. He draws the covers back over our mother and grips her gently by the shoulders, easing her back to her pillows. "Momma," he whispers, arms trembling against her. "Momma, it's okay. It's me, Walt. Look," he gestures toward me with a flick of his head, "there's Mark."

Her eyes flit from his to mine, and for a moment a spark of understanding flares there. Her panicked breathing declines to a light pant. She gazes about the room as if visiting the site of a dim memory.

Then a spark of awareness lights behind her eyes.

Things are suddenly familiar. She knows this place, but it will take a few minutes for her to *trust* it as her own.

"Oh, a-no, a-no, a-no, a-no," she stammers. She's been doing this a lot over the last week, usually in moments where she's *with it* enough to acknowledge she's done something embarrassing. I've decoded the *a-no*'s as *oh no*'s. "Di-I wake y'up?"

Did I wake you up?

"It's okay, Mom," I whisper, walking toward her and feeling the mattress sag as I sit beside Walter. Here the smell of her is strongest. Her swift decline saw an end to baths six days ago. Her caregivers have been sponge-bathing her since. Though the odor is borderline unbearable, I'll endure it with gratitude. The last thing I want is to tip her off that something *else* is wrong with her.

"Mark ah hope ye' on't hava test 'morrow."

Mark I hope you don't have a test tomorrow. She's regressed so far that she can no longer rid herself of the misperception that I'm a college student visiting from UNH. I've chosen to go along with it to spare her the grief of being corrected.

"Not tomorrow," I whisper. "It's Sunday." Only a half lie.

In the Arms of Saturn

"Mmmm," she mumbles, her eyelids falling heavily. Her mouth cracks open like she's got something else to say, but sleep claims her before she can spit it out. I watch, relieved, as her breathing slows and she goes under.

Walt and I tip-toe cautiously across the room. Mouf is waiting at the door, tail raised self-importantly as he rubs his whiskered maw against the molding. His back arches as we approach, and he presents himself for affection.

I can't help obliging him, reaching down and scratching behind his ears. He runs his mouth and whiskers over my hand, licking my fingers a few times before plopping down for a few good strokes. I feel bad for the little dork. Half the time Mom doesn't even realize he's there.

Walt sidles past me into the hallway. He pauses and glances back as if silently asking if I intend to play with the cat all night. With a sigh I collect Mouf, gathering him to my chest and carrying him, purring, out of the room as Walt kills the lights.

"Wanna smoke up?" Walt asks without hesitation or preamble.

"Yep," I answer, and we step together into his bedroom.

Among the many things to change around this house since Mom's decline, I've given up thinking of myself as a runner and committed to solving my problems through drugs and alcohol. More of the former since I still have a slight aversion to booze since North Conway. A part of me insists that things will change once Mom passes and my world shrinks, and that's enough to allow my conscience a pass on a little weed. With each fleeting day I'm growing more adept at submitting to my vices. Of course, I'm under the oblivious tutelage of my younger brother, who may as well be a Shaolin monk for the wisdom he commands in this area.

I pause a few steps into Walt's room and turn back. Stepping into the hallway, I find my phone in the polyester and nylon folds of my sleeping bag and go to set the cat down.

"No, bring him in," Walt whispers behind me. "Let's get him high."

I turn to him, eyebrows raised, Mouf's feet dangling over my sleeping bag. "What are we, fifteen?"

He turns away without arguing and goes to work extracting his *stash box* from under the bed. I stroke Mouf a few more times before urging him with one of my bare feet down the hallway and toward the kitchen. He stops and circles back, purring loudly. "That's all I got for you, man. Catch you in the morning." With that I side-step quickly into the room and shut the door before he can pursue.

I navigate loose articles of clothing and empty food containers as I pick my way toward Walt's bed. There, he's already breaking apart a nug and cramming the pieces into his massive calabash-style glass pipe. The weed is mine, or at least was purchased with my money. Once Walt figured me for a born-again smoker he made sure to send the party supply invoices my way. Of course, this didn't grant me the right to keep hold of the stash. I'm surprised I didn't see it coming, but after everything we've endured with Mom, it's not like I've been firing on all cylinders. I haven't even been going to work, and though the time off is scheduled, paid, and part of my contract, I can't help feeling I might not have a job anymore once I bury Mom. Tim's been cool, still trying to coax me out for beers a couple times a week, but the higher-ups, the ones I don't deal with regularly... they're the ones I'm worried about.

Walt finishes packing the bowl and lifts the stem to his lips. He always takes first hit. That skunky smell of burning flower fills the air, dulling out the earthy reek of mold spores growing beneath the carpet's top-layer of detritus. My gaze is held for a moment by the pile of socks on the floor near the headboard and I frown at their probable use behind closed doors.

"Your hit man," Walt chokes out, holding the smoke in his lungs as the pipe bobs in his hand, offered my way. I take the pipe, drawing at length until I'm suddenly hacking up my lungs.

Walter mutters *amateur* just loud enough for me to hear.

I give him the finger and return the pipe, already starting to feel slightly euphoric. I thumb past the lock screen on my phone, noting the time (1:37 A.M.), and launch the messaging app. Waiting for me are several notifications, some from Holly, Mom's more tech-savvy caregiver, some from Tim, and a ton from Kelly. She's been riding me hard this last week to get with her lawyer. The soulless wretch doesn't seem to care even slightly about Mom, she just wants to claim her half of my life so she can "move on" with hers.

I scroll further, pausing as Elora's name drifts past my thumb. I hover over it for a moment, tempted to open the string and send a message, but my better judgement prevails. I hit the lock button and drop the phone on the bed. My timing is perfect – Walt passes the pipe and goes to work muscling open the window beside the bed.

I take another extensive pull, challenging my lungs in ways that illuminate the ten odd years since I'd last smoked weed. Despite my best efforts these last two weeks, I'm still a total lightweight, and I'm stoned before my second coughing exhale.

Walt senses this as I pass the pipe back. "You good, bro?"

I nod breathlessly and scoot backward as the world fuzzes. I lean against the wall, legs splayed and feet dangling over the opposite edge of the bed. I note the receding tone in my legs and try to bite back against the guilt of abandoning my ten-year running routine. Fortunately I'm in the perfect state to forget *most things.*

It's not long before Walt sets the pipe down and scuttles back until we're sitting shoulder-to-shoulder. I cant my head toward him, studying his emaciated features as though miles away. My gaze pivots to the nightstand where a half-dozen notebooks rest in meticulous vertical alignment.

"What are you writing about, Walt?"

His gaze detaches from the wall and drifts toward me. He swallows hard, studying me wordlessly as if offended I'd asked. It's unlike Walter to shy away from forcing even the most miniscule of his achievements upon anyone who'd praise him.

Everything about this whole writing project is decidedly *un*-Walt.

He lets out a long sigh, his attention moving with palpable reluctance toward the notebooks. "I'm writing about death."

"Death?"

"Yeah, death. What it all means, how it affects us, what exists after all of this."

"Is it fiction?"

The muscles in his face tense up. He doesn't understand.

"Is it a story? One you're making up?"

He considers this a moment, hand rising toward his pillow-pressed curls. Scratching absent-mindedly at his scalp, he shakes his head. "It's what I believe. It's my religion."

I think back to when I was a kid going through my religious doubts. During this period I'd picked up and read the Satanic Bible, a playbook on unchecked carnal indulgence written by a circus carny. I'd read pieces of the bible, too, but it didn't hold my interest enough to carry me through all the way.

"So you're writing, like, the Bible of Walt?"

He doesn't answer. He thinks I'm making fun of him.

I wait a moment before reaching toward the stacked notebooks, asking, "Can I read it?" But before I know it his hands are on me, pawing in their odd, manic directive to keep me from touching his niche-faith manifesto.

"It's *personal!*" Walt grunts, finding little resistance from me as I retreat to the wall.

"Okay," I sigh. "Sorry, Walt."

He scoots off of the bed and gathers up the notebooks, clutching them like baby to his narrow chest and delivering them to the top shelf of his closet. There he deposits them gingerly beside a tottering stack of porno tapes – yes, actual *tapes*, the ones with the comically oversized sleeves.

Walt swivels back to face me. "Promise me you won't go digging around my personal stuff, Mark. Please."

I raise a hand as if taking some oath. "Dude, I promise. What's wrong with you?"

"It's personal," he repeats, eyes boring into mine. I've never seen him as intense as he's been with this project. It's a coping mechanism, of that I'm certain. He's having intense trouble dealing with Mom's impending death. I suppose we all weather these things differently. I've been sleepwalking through it one day at a time, figuring that life will sweep me along its natural course once Mom goes.

"You won't understand." He remains there, standing sentinel over his treasures, partially-eclipsed by the slanted shadow of the door. His eyes find mine, seeking additional assurance as his fingers dig thoughtlessly at his scalp.

"Walter, I swear I won't touch your notebooks." I do my best to convey the most categorical sincerity. I watch him as he watches me, searching for signs of treachery. It's probably just that he's high – this over-the-top inquisition – but you never know with him. You could live with Walter for years and think you've got him figured out as a dim-witted druggie with no real ambition, and then he throws something like this into the gears of life's shared machine.

Slowly he begins to nod. "Cool." He slinks back to the bed where he joins me. "You wanna watch TV or something?"

I shake my head. Things have gone too weird too fast. "I think I'm gonna just go back out in the hall and listen to music. That cool?"

His lips pucker to the side. He nods wordlessly.

I lurch up and off the bed, teetering in a brief search for balance. Walt chuckles and calls me a lightweight again. I give him the finger. Again.

I find my stability and start toward the door, avoiding the laundry and trash hazards on the floor. Without turning back to my brother, I bid him good night and slip back out into the darkness.

I'm writing about death, he'd said.

As I settle in the folds of my sleeping bag and fumble with my earbuds, I can't help my mind clinging to the subject of death while in the room next to me my mother lay dying. I've never given much thought to what might await after death. I'm not a firm believer in God, I mostly don't believe in Him at all, but that doesn't mean I haven't always assumed there are mysteries to be probed in the next life. This system of belief implies the existence of an afterlife.

What if there isn't anything at all after this? What if our consciousness simply slips away and we never perceive again?

* * *

A couple days later I'm off to Rough Ruby's to meet Tim. I can't blow him off any longer, and I need a read on my continued employment prospects now that I've missed so much time.

I don't feel terribly comfortable leaving Mom with Walt, but if I time things right he'll only have been alone with her for an hour or two after Holly leaves.

Good old Holly. She's been great these last couple weeks. A part of me thinks she'd work the same job even without pay. When she found out I was considering going out for a beer, she was all but *shoving* me out the door, insisting I needed the escape.

She'd even offered to stay later with Mom.

It's refreshing to stumble across people like Holly in the world, though I'll admit that when I first met her I was a bit turned off. I've never been particularly comfortable around people who speak their minds as bluntly as she. Full-figured and sassy, her mouth started flapping the moment she first entered the house, speaking to Mom as though she were a lifelong friend, temporarily misplaced.

Rough Ruby's isn't my kind of place. I don't think I really *have* a kind of place. It sits off US-1 in York in what had long ago been a working lobster barn. The rustic charm of the place is only superficial. Once you get inside and work your way through the sea of obnoxious townies crowding the bar, your failure in choosing the place is made obvious. At least for me anyway. I can't fault the boisterous patrons for their *in-my-face* good time – the bar lifestyle simply isn't mine.

I push through the front door and into a vacant breezeway. Cheering voices waft down from the bar upstairs along with the oft-trysting odors of sweat and beer. To my left is a coat rack where a number of people have brazenly hung jackets ranging in value from worksite Carhart to soon-to-be-unseasonable styles of leather. Directly ahead, two steps up to the bar, is a host station where a slender middle-aged hostess places me as the outsider I am and favors me with a smile that fails to touch her eyes.

"Headed to the bar or can I get you a table?" she asks, tone doing little to mask her contempt for the job. Her hand settles atop a stack of laminated menus as she anticipates my answer. Something about a man in khaki shorts and a polo in a place like this just screams *table*.

"I'm actually meeting a buddy." I glance up the steps into the dining room. The bar is off to the right, isolated from the restaurant proper save for the persistent, unintelligible chorus of drunken voices. I look back to her, "Mind if I look around?"

"Be my guest," she says, that fake smile making its half-hearted encore. I return it with rivaling sincerity before slipping past the host station and ascending toward the bar.

As if on cue a voice stabs through the din.

"Mark, brotha'!" Tim's bellow silences the other patrons for the space of a couple seconds.

My gaze finds him waving to me from a corner where he sits beneath a barrier of varnished wooden lattice. Beyond, an empty function room largely comprised of arching windows that sit like black mirrors in the unoccupied space. It reminds me of a solarium. He's alone at a small table, and judging by the three empty pint glasses before him, he's already loaded.

I feel the corners of my lips droop, and I quickly work to straighten out. With a deep breath, I push into the crowd, wending through bodies casting off heavy cologne and rich, fruity perspiration. I gather a few dirty looks, most from good-ole-boy townies looking to throw around what little weight they retained from their high school days when they'd peaked.

"Sit down, kid," Tim commands, slamming down his fourth empty glass and gesturing at the empty seat across from him. I do as I'm told, and he says, "What are you drinking?"

"I dunno." My first thought is water, but I know he isn't going to let me hang without drinking. My thoughts stray naturally to North Conway and the woman who'd used me for sex; to the booze and cigarettes; to Elora.

"I'll have a P-B-R," I say, feeling as though I've conceded something.

"You got it, brotha'." He considers the glasses he'd emptied while waiting for me, hesitates, then leaves them to continue gathering condensation as he's swallowed up in the crowd.

I wish I were at home reading. Or toking up. Then I think about how quickly Mom's condition has worsened, and I'm suddenly neutralized, left impartial to both the bar and my home life. With a sigh, I'm surprised to find myself relaxing. The collective drawl of voices is no longer a threat to my introverted self for reasons I don't care enough to evaluate.

Perhaps I'm back on autopilot.

"Here we *go!*" Tim's voice suddenly tears me from my trance. I wonder how long I've been zoning out as my eyes leave the latticed wall and lift to a grinning face. In each hand he holds a massive, frothing beer stein, easily 25 ounces. If I didn't know the guy so well I'd swear he was trying to get me liquored up, though he'd certainly have his work cut out for him with PBR.

He lowers the glasses to the table, dewy beads of moisture tumbling through frost. Taking his beer in hand, he holds it up and pauses, looking me over with eyebrows lifted. "Well?"

I slowly reach out and lift my beer. My gaze locks with Tim's, and his mischievous smile morphs into one of benign friendliness that disarms me of any lingering irritation at having been dragged out. "To your mom," Tim says, "God love her."

He's never met my mother, but the sentiment is appreciated. I return his smile, surprised to find it unforced. "Thanks, Boss." Our steins come together, beer spills over the sides, and we each take a good, long pull in the name of my poor mother, stuck at home in bed and probably unsure where she is, assuming she's even conscious.

"Sixty-eight," he sighs. "Still a young lady. God's cruel sometimes."

I can't help the guilt washing over me as I realize how much Tim knows about me and how little I know about him. He must have listened to and locked away everything I've said since I started with the company.

Men like Tim are the true salt of the earth. I don't remember *anything* about *anyone*.

He takes a swig of his already half-empty beer and sets down the stein. His gaze lifts and all semblance of his smile fades. My chest tightens as I absorb his suddenly hardening features.

Tim asks, "How much time are the doctors giving her?"

I sigh, "Bishop says if she keeps up like this..."

"You don't have to—I didn't mean to—"

"No," I say, reading the guilt now stealing across his face. "It's okay. Doctor Bishop estimates she's got a week and a half. Ten days probably." I lift my beer and finish the rest.

Silence settles between us for a moment as we each seem to struggle with what to say next. It's not typical for us to encounter gaps in conversation. Then Tim shrugs, his voice slicing through the background chatter, "Anything you need. *Anything*. You let me know. And don't you worry about the time off. You do right by Mom. You'll always have a place at ReqTek."

"Thanks, Boss." The alcohol I'd hastily put down kindles a tiny fire in my stomach, and my body is warmed.

"How's your brother doing with all of this?" He asks, giving me a look that suggests he's gleaned the proper subtext in stories I've told about Walter, none of which spring presently to mind.

I shake my head and lift my glass, getting all of my words out just as it reaches my lips. "Lost in himself. Odder than usual."

"How so?"

"He's writing some kind of book."

Tim shrugs as if to emphasize how minor this revelation is. "We all deal with things in our own way."

I just nod, unsure what to say to a man who knows Walt through stories I can't remember telling. I decide to conduct the conversation elsewhere. "How are things at work? How's Kevin doing?"

The stein lowers gradually from Tim's face, barely a swig sloshing around at the bottom. His face drops, and for a moment I think he's going to unload on me for some reason. "That little *loser*." His eyebrows lift and his face blows up in mock disbelief. "Trashed a RAID array at Red Door by initiating a rebuild from a blank replacement disk."

"What?" My stein slams down. "How stupid do you—"

"I know—I *know*! The whole server's pooched. We'll be going bare-metal tomorrow. Lucky they had a good backup." He tips his glass toward me before putting the rest of his beer away. I look down at my empty stein, then to Tim, already rising from his seat. "Another?"

I nod. "See if they've got a good I-P-A."

Welcome back, alcohol.

Tim nods, smiling. "Attaboy."

I settle back in my chair and watch Tim as he once again braves the crowd. He walks in a way that reminds me of an orangutan, holding the steins up over his head instead of pulled to his chest. I start to chuckle at it, but quickly freeze, every part of me seizing up.

Mallory Kelson is sitting at an adjacent table. She's dressed in loose jeans and a pink blouse. One of a dozen anachronistic lanterns flickers above her, painting odd shadows on her face.

For a moment I do a double-take, convinced it can't be her. But as our eyes lock and all color and expression drain from her, the panicked impulse to flee already has me inching up out of my chair.

The conversation she'd been having with the woman across from her abruptly ceases. Her friend swivels toward me to see what has captivated Mallory in such a way, her black shoulder-length hair swishing. Her face twists in confusion, and she rotates animatedly back to Mallory, no doubt asking *what's wrong*.

I avert my gaze, settling submissively back in my seat. I'm obviously not going to run, but I'm unsure if I'll have another beer now. Drinking to excess didn't work out so well at the *last* bar.

My gaze is drawn back to Mallory at odd intervals when I hope she isn't looking my way. Sometimes our eyes meet, while other times she's looking at her friend, no doubt recounting the details of our odd meetings. This would be our third, seemingly via cosmic coincidence.

"Here we go," Tim says, nearly startling me out of my chair. He places another frosty mug before me, this one a deeper amber than the PBR. I note as he sits that he's gone back to drinking from a pint glass, slowing himself down. "What's the matter?" he asks, looking me over like a father evaluating his bullied son. "You look like you've seen a ghost."

I debate whether to tell him, then after a few seconds I divulge it all in a rare moment of *I don't give a damn*. "There's a woman sitting over there – don't look. Her name is Mallory Kelson. She's the wife of the man I…" the guilt-spiked pain of revisiting Nathan Kelson dead in the street, blood pooling around his head, stabs at my heart for the first time in weeks. "She's the wife of the man I struck with my car."

His eyebrows lift, "Brotha' you've got the worst luck of any man I know." He shakes his head, and for a moment I think he's going to turn and glance over at Mallory. Fortunately he does not. "You wanna go?"

I look over his shoulder, my gaze finding Mallory's. She draws a deep breath, showing similar incredulity at this latest chance meeting. Has she perhaps drawn the conclusion I'm arriving at lately? That we're consistently drawn together by otherworldly designs?

"I'm good," I answer, seizing my beer and gulping it down despite my better judgement. It's bitter and delicious. I smack my lips as I set it down. Glancing back to Mallory, I'm happy to see her engaged in conversation once more with the woman across from her.

Over the next couple of hours, Tim and I shoot the breeze across a wide range of topics. We hit books, television, and the inevitable subject of computers. Tim starts to slow his drinking right around the time I begin to notice his speech slurring. He switches over to water, and I marvel at his discipline. I continue to let him buy me drinks, mostly because he's watching my progress like a hawk ruminating over a rodent in the bush. Every time I finish that last swig he jumps up and sets off once more for the bar. It's going on 11:00 by the time he plops down across from me for the last time, a beer in one hand (which he promptly slides my way) and a water in the other.

"Well, brotha', I'm thinking about calling it and heading home. One of us has to get into work tomorrow and keep Kevin from running the company into the ground." He stretches his arms and considers the glass of water without taking it up. "You gonna be good to drive?"

I'm hammered. "I'll probably just hang around a bit longer. Grab a burger before I head home."

Tim fiddles around in his back pocket and produces a wallet so overstuffed it's a wonder he doesn't have back problems. He plucks out a twenty and slaps it on the table. "Dinner's on me."

"It's all right, man, I—"

"Naw, enough of that. I dragged you out here. I'm buying." His face takes on the character of a mobster sizing up an underling, searching for signs of cognition, ever-primed for a fight.

With a smile that I'm sure is as goofy as they come, I nod to him. "You got it, Boss." I want to say more, to tell him how much tonight has helped, but I don't. Feelings don't weave well into man-banter, and I'm a minority in that I'm as sensitive as men come.

"Good," he says, picking up his water and taking the tiniest of sips. He sets it down and grunts to his feet, peering out over the thinning crowd, now diminished to a shadow of its former glory. He steps over to me and lays a hand on my shoulder. I lift my gaze as he says, "You take care of yourself. Anything you need, you just let me know. Understood? Anything."

"Thanks, Boss."

He claps me on the shoulder. "Make sure you're sober when you drive out of here. Last thing you need right now is to be popped for D-U-I, what with what happened…" he trails off, nibling at his lower lip. "You know."

"I know. Thanks again… for everything."

"You take care of yourself, kid."

With that I watch him slip into the hallway and around the corner, and then he's gone.

I can't help my gaze straying back to Mallory. She's already looking at me over an arrangement of thinly-stemmed martini glasses. Her friend is nowhere to be seen. Alone, Mallory seems stripped of burden, not drunk, but operating with the ease of a woman unmoored from her life's problems, albeit temporarily.

Alone, she seems to take on a different character entirely.

Are trips to the bar a nightly coping routine? That guilt I'd felt in her at the beach floods over me in a dark reunion that erases much of my buzz. My mind is suddenly coursing with all I've stolen from her.

Which parts of her have I unintentionally claimed since that day on the beach, all for the sin of repeatedly and innocently intruding on her life?

I nearly fall out of my chair as she moves to her feet, our eyes still locked. Lifting her half-drained martini glass, cherry liquid sloshing, she teeters a moment before starting toward my table.

I swallow hard.

As she draws close, Mallory's eyes lower to Tim's empty seat before finding mine again. "Mind if I sit down?"

I feel my face slacken in almost horrified confusion. I'm left gaping up at her, struggling for a read. Am I about to be worked-over a second time? Is this chemically altered widow looking for a fight?

She starts to turn away in my hesitation, and I react by fumbling out the first words that touch my tongue. "You – you can sit. Yes. Please, sit." I gesture toward the chair for good measure, nearly toppling my beer. Mallory studies me a moment before nodding, seemingly to herself, and settling tentatively.

"I've never seen you here before." She breathes deeply, peering into her drink. Had she approached me on a whim and now regretted its lack of a payoff?

"I'm not usually one for these kinds of places," I return.

"Not much of a drinker?"

I think of North Conway, stifling the grimace that wants to build itself on my face. Suddenly my mouth is festering with the taste of cigarettes. "No, I drink. I'm just not a bar guy."

"An introvert."

I nod. "I suppose so." Reaching for my glass, I lift it to my lips and take a measured sip, intent to make it last or risk growing sloppy. The awkwardness of our exchange is like a fog hanging over the table. We both feel it, yet here we remain, each intent on seeing where it goes.

"I'm an introvert, too," she sighs. "I used to come here all the time with Nathan, but I didn't really care for it. Now I just come out of habit, most nights alone."

"Mallory, I—"

"You've already apologized. The whole *world* has apologized. There's nothing anyone can do to change the fact that my husband is dead. Let's just... move forward."

Silence settles again, thick and pensive. From it I'm surprised to mine a strange comfort. *Let's just... move forward.* Is this her way of saying she's forgiven me on some level? I can't help speculating, and it's all I can do to keep from asking for clarification.

"How's your mother?" she asks, fingers lacing around the stem of her glass, swirling her drink. She's tired. Not simply exhausted from work though. Her eyes show the weariness of a woman who's walked the periphery of a storm rather than boring through and having it over with.

I swallow against a new lump in my throat. "Doctor Bishop gives her a week and a half."

"I'm sorry to hear that."

I toss back the rest of my beer. "Thank you. It's a lot to take in all at once." I stop short of drawing a comparison between our lives. I can tell by her loosening body language that she's already thinking it. Her hand shows a slight tremble as she directs a strand of chestnut hair over her left ear. She reaches for her drink and puts the rest of it away. As she returns the glass delicately to the table, I find myself asking if she'd like another.

She nods, and I ask her what she's drinking. A pomegranate martini. I repeat this in my mind, fearful I'll forget it as I meander through the ever-thinning bar crowd. The bartender is already cleaning up for the night even though they'll be open for another hour. I place my order and offer her my I.D.

The bartender recognizes my name with flaring eyes and wastes no time asking about my relation to Kittery, Maine's most celebrated martyr. She launches into questions about what Dad had been like and how my family coped in the aftermath.

For my troubles I'm spared having to pay for the drinks.

Mallory regards me with a soothing neutrality as I return. Handing her drink over, I'm tossed a half smile that seems to startle her, tailed by an awkward *thank you.*

"What happened to your friend?" I ask, sitting.

Mallory shakes her head dismissively. "She's been gone for an hour or so. She says she has to work early, but I wonder if she was just looking for an excuse to get away. It's no fun drinking with a downer like me."

"I don't mind drinking with you." The statement makes me feel like a high-schooler hopelessly trying to impress the object of his affections.

We sip in silence for a time.

"It's funny how the death of your husband shows you which friends were yours and which were his." She stares into her drink as if divining the future from it. In a way it seems more an acknowledgement of what, exactly, has loosened her lips with such abandon. "Everyone is supportive – some are *overly* supportive, but that's about as far as it goes with them. They hang out with me like it's their duty. They grieve with me... observe silence with me. They treat me like Nathan's widow, not the friend I always thought I was to them. It's been almost three months, now only my girlfriends from high school bother to ask me out. The rest... all the folks Nathan brought into our lives... they email or text me, checking in to see *how I'm doing*. They don't come to see me. It's like I'm some morose reminder that the man they all loved and looked up to is gone."

"I'm sure they still care about you."

"Just you wait," she says, gaze hardening in a way that leaves me wanting to recoil slightly. She seems to realize this and dials it down. Drawing a long breath, she shakes her head and goggles absently at the table. "Just you wait, Mark. You'll see how differently people treat you once... well, you know."

I shrug, "I don't have many friends. I don't have any family outside of Mom and Walt. My ex-wife hates my guts. The only person I'll have to test your theory on is my mother's cat."

She shakes her head and sips her drink. Her lips are inked red until she licks them in a way that makes me pause a moment as a full-blooded man. She looks back to me, suddenly guilty. "I'm sorry. Here I go again, Mallory the Miserable."

"You're fine. Please, vent all you want with me. I don't think there's anyone else in this bar who could understand you better. Maybe not even in the entire town."

There's silence again, then all at once her face blooms in a massive smile. "This is so messed up," she laughs, shaking her head and lifting her drink.

I can't help returning the smile, though I fail to understand it entirely. "Yeah," I agree. "Yeah, this is truly messed up."

We laugh a moment then drink some more. It's not long before the laughter feels forced and is permitted to fizzle and die.

"I'd never have thought after that day on the beach I'd be sharing a drink with you."

"I'm still not really sure why you are," I admit. "Not that I'm complaining."

"I've learned a lot about people over the last month, but you already know." She stops swirling the drink, her gaze lifting over a settling whirlpool of pomegranate red. "You didn't have to come to the funeral. You didn't have to seek me out and try to make amends. I know I said some hurtful things then," her eyes soften. "I thought a lot about it over the following days. It's not like I had much else to do. And the more I revisited it the less I was able to keep hating you. I made my peace with it, ready to return to work weeks later… and then there you were."

"I couldn't believe it either."

"I almost apologized to you that night, but somehow I convinced myself that I shouldn't, that it was just sympathy for the situation with your mother. So I forced my emotions back and pressed on."

I'm silent, waiting for her to reach the end of a story with which I'm already quite familiar. Or, at least, I *think* I am.

"So here you pop up tonight." She shakes her head, a half smile cropping up on her face. "I'm half – no *three quarters* convinced that the alcohol brought me over here, but it's just too coincidental that we keep running into each other."

There it is. She feels it too then. I'm able only to nod along, no doubt looking like some spectacular buffoon.

"Do you believe in soulmates?"

I swallow hard, anxious and nervous to determine where she's going with this. "I'm not sure." Only I am. Elora's face falls like a curtain over my mind, and for a moment nothing else exists.

"Why do you ask?" I'm no more aware of asking the question than I am of the dark tone with which I'd voiced it.

She shakes her head and frowns into her drink. "I've been thinking about it a lot these last few weeks. That and the whole nature of life."

This steers my thoughts toward Walt, Elora's face blinked suddenly out of my mind's eye.

"It's a curious word," she continues. "*Soulmate*. As in, the mate to your soul, the other entity that completes you. If we're so cosmically bound, why don't we exit this world together? Think of it as symbiosis – are you familiar with the term?"

"Yes," I answer, though my knowledge of a shared existence doesn't translate into any tangible, scientific experience. Mostly just Star Trek.

"You remove one of the organisms bound together in symbiosis, and what happens?" She leaves me no time to answer. "They both die."

I nod, suddenly very much in awe of her mind's depth. All the surfer stereotypes offered in books and film have failed me.

"So if we truly have a soulmate, and that person dies, how is it that we manage to remain alive?"

"Lose an arm and you might find it difficult to ride a bike, but you're still alive." I take another swig, suddenly wanting a shot of whiskey as well.

"An arm is a physical extension of the body. I'm talking about something—*someone* external."

I'm confused. "So what you're saying is you don't believe in the existence of soulmates?"

She tosses back the rest of her martini, sets the glass delicately back down. "I don't believe in anything anymore."

"Can't say I've *ever* believed in anything. Maybe when I was a kid, but it feels like I've always strayed from the spiritual side of things." I consider taking hold of her glass and getting her a refill, but that nagging, irrational voice in my head insists she might think I'm trying to get her liquored up. Always so paranoid.

Plus I don't need another *Eric Wells The Hero* conversation tonight.

"I was raised Catholic," she says. "Had a Catholic wedding – Communion and all. Went to church every Sunday. Now the idea that there's some ghost up there in the clouds watching us and snatching up those we love because He has *some plan* seems as ridiculous as Ancient Egypt worshipping *cats*."

"Like we're insects in some experiment or something. What purpose could we possibly serve to some enlightened higher power?" For a moment I'm impressed with my analogy, then I understand we've both simply had too much to drink.

I cock my head, glancing about the still-quieting room before looking back to Mallory. She's lost in her head, gaze penetrating the varnished tabletop once more. The electric flame from the faux oil lamp above reflects in the curvature of the glass, assuming the wraithlike appearance of dancing fire elementals. Mallory remains lost, oblivious, for a minute or so before letting out a long sigh and pushing the glass away as if she's now just decided she's done with it. "Have you ever had dark thoughts... like a voice in your head that isn't yours, trying to convince you that suicide is an acceptable way out?"

"Yes," I answer without hesitation.

Her eyes meet with mine once again, flashing respite and release. "I'd never be able to do it. Never. I'd never even *thought* about it until Nathan's passing. It's like the part of me that was stripped away with his death was perverted and replaced by some shadow of itself."

"It's normal to go to dark places when faced with death. Be it your own or someone else's." I speak with confidence, though I'm mostly drawing from unsubstantiated philosophies I'd collected over the years. "I've been going through the same thing since the accident."

I'm relieved to see her relax further, shoulders falling in a way that speaks to the cryptic bond we suddenly share. We're inmates in the same prison. "I guess that event left us both broken then, huh? I can see it in you. Even that day on the beach, I could see how troubled you were. I'm glad we spoke tonight." She glances at her watch, "I wish we could talk a little more, but I'm on the clock in seven hours."

I stand with her. "If you ever need anyone to vent to – just a listening ear – please don't hesitate to..." For a moment I wonder how, exactly, she might take me up on this offer. The idea to give her my number seems perverted. Perhaps I'll friend her on Facebook. I'm relieved as she fishes a smart phone out of her back pocket.

"What's your number?" she asks.

I give it to her. Pulling out my own phone in the process and asking for her number, which she offers freely. I'm not sure if it's because we're drunk or if we've hit the same bottom of despair, but whatever the reason, our coming together feels right.

I see her to the door, thinking I should ask her if she's good to drive, but nervously deciding against it. I don't know her well enough to tell, and she's a grown woman with what seems to be a good head on her shoulders. I'm encouraged by her perfect speech and unwavering posture as she walks ahead of me, taking the stairs with apparent ease as I grip the banister for dear life.

The hostess bids us good night as we pass, coming to a stop at the exit door. There Mallory turns and extends her hand. A smile lights her eyes.

"'Til next time, Mark."

I gently shake her hand. "I look forward to it."

"I hope your Mom's passing isn't too hard. If you need anything or have any questions, just call or text me."

"Thank you."

For a moment we remain there, searching each other for answers to a question neither of us knows.

She turns and disappears into the night.

* * *

Walt sits across from me at the kitchen table, hunched over the latest volume in his masterwork – another tiny 5-Star notebook, pages away from capacity like the others in a now towering pile. I count ten of them, eleven including the one he's currently wrapping up.

Mom's voice echoes down the hallway, a phlegmy drawl devoid of discernable words. She's conveying her grievous urgencies as an infant would, having lost her ability to speak coherently over the last six days. What exactly she wants is anyone's guess. Holly and Dr. Bishop have both carefully explained to us that she's more out than in at this point, meaning that the cancer growing on the soft tissue of her brain is crushing away what little cognitive ability she has left. She doesn't seem to know where she is, and when she's up sitting in the recliner (now moved into her bedroom), she often stares at her feet for hours. Mouf has ceased trying to jump into her lap as she's often surprised by the sudden movement and recoils in a way that sends him shooting vertically into the air before touching down and skittering out of the room.

I stir my bowl of Spaghetti-O's and spoon a sizable clot of rings and mystery-meatballs into my mouth. I hated the stuff as a kid. Odd that it's a taste I've acquired in adulthood. As I chew I focus on the mid-afternoon sunlight sifting through the open window over the sink. The drifting dust catches the light like a million tiny insects soaring over Walt's blonde curls. Yet another reminder that the house is a mess.

Digging back into my lunch, I shovel another bite into my mouth just as Holly speaks up from the end of the shadowed hallway. "Having a bad day today, boys," she says, pausing outside Mom's door and toeing the latch on a biohazard disposal bin. She drops a cinched bag inside and turns toward us with a reluctance we rarely see in her. "I'm thinking it might be time to call Doctor Bishop."

"She's dying," I say, pushing my lunch away. I speak in a sigh, "Every day is a bad day…"

Holly rounds the table, floorboards bowing under her. It's not that she's fat – chubby more than anything – she just walks in exaggerated lopes. There have been a couple times when I've passed her in the hallway and had to press against the wall to avoid being checked.

"It's not just that," Holly says, settling in a chair to my left. She considers my lunch before looking back up. Her usual spunk and sass seem edged out by grave solemnity. I can't help my heart sinking. I've anticipated this moment for weeks, and I'm used to the saccharine feelings it inspires. I feel guilty because in a way, after all we've been through, I kind of want it now. "She's stopped eating. Her urination has lessened in frequency and she hasn't had a bowel movement in two days. When I change her she can't move to help me reposition her body." Holly hesitates, and in this moment I glance across the table at Walt. Though reliably oblivious, his eyes are set on Holly.

"Is she going to pass soon?" I wonder if I sound eager and spend a few moments hating myself.

Holly chews at her lower lip, glancing momentarily to Walt for God knows what. "We should call Doctor Bishop. I can't say for sure."

I grab my phone up off the table and unlock it, finding the still-active text string I've maintained with Mallory since the night at the bar. Every time I receive a message from her I can't help wondering if some cruel psychic force is playing tricks on me. That night seems so surreal I just can't get past it. But I've enjoyed our correspondence thoroughly. Each deep reflection on life and the mysteries of existence we share is like an odd sedative, numbing me while filing down the world's fangs. I imagine it's doing something similar for her. Why else would she keep talking to me?

I thumb to the home screen and my address book. Dr. Bishop's number is pinned at the top. For a moment I hesitate, my thumb hovering above the illuminated glass. I look to Walt, watching me, nearly bursting with fear and anxiety that set his jaw trembling. His face is paler than usual.

I tap Dr. Bishop's name and lift the receiver to my ear. My gaze shifts between Holly and Walt as the phone rings. After the third ring I know that I'm going to be re-routed to his answering service since this has happened before, and sure enough I'm able to make out the slight click of the call passing over to a different network. A female voice speaks up.

"Doctor Bishop's answering service, is this an emergency?" the woman's accent smacks of New York City. Her question catches me surprisingly off guard.

"No," I answer, though a part of me – a very insistent part – wants to say yes.

"Doctor Bishop is with a patient at the moment. Can I take a message, sir?"

"Um, yeah," I answer as eyes silently and urgently implore me for unspoken details. "This is Mark Wells, my mother Shannon Wells is a patient of his. Her condition is growing worse, and we were hoping he could come out to see her."

"Okay, Mr. Wells. It looks like Doctor Bishop is in and out of appointments for the rest of the day, but I'll make sure he gets your message." Her ambivalence makes me wonder how she reacts in an actual emergency.

"Thank you," I return, feeling powerless.

"You're welcome, Mr. Wells. Is there anything else we can do for you today?"

Yeah, get Dr. Bishop over here now so that we can get a proper read on Mom.

"No," I answer. "Thank you."

"Have a nice day. Goodbye."

"You do the same." I end the call, ruminating a bit over her parting words. Have a nice day? This seems wholly inappropriate, but I suppose it's imperative for all people working in medical to keep things positive wherever possible.

There's no positivity here though. As I set the phone down my eyes meet once more with the morose faces of my brother and Mom's caregiver. "I left a message for him." Gazing down at my half-eaten bowl of Spaghetti-Os, I sigh and push it farther away. Down the hall, Mom's voice has gone silent. Holly is already in action, leveraging her hand against a shifting table as she heaves herself to her feet.

I watch her go, then turn to Walt.

"You okay?" I ask. He stares down at the tabletop, a hand laid protectively over his notebook, the other clutching a pen. He doesn't seem to notice that I'm speaking to him, and I wonder how many days he's been awake. "Walt?" His attention snaps over to me, eyes wild in a way that leaves me thinking about the night he tried to rob me. "You okay?"

"There is no *okay* anymore," he sighs, seeming offended I'd ask. A part of me acknowledges that I want him to ask the same question of me, if only to mine comfort from similar feelings, but Walt simply waves a dismissive hand and returns to scribbling in his notebook.

Resting my elbows on the table, I bury my face in my hands, drawing air through the slits of my fingers, feeling poised to break down entirely. I'm yanked out of it by the chime of a text notification from my phone, and I emerge from the darkness to reach for it, finding a message from Mallory.

How's your mother today?

My fingers go immediately to work, my anxiety dissipating like thunderclouds over the ocean.

Mom sleeps the rest of the afternoon. She barely moves, save for the silent words mouthed in her dreams. She's no longer observably distressed or confused, but there's no real way for us to know what's going on in her mind. Though she wears a cap fitted with electrodes to measure her brain activity, it fails to paint pictures of her thoughts.

I sit in the corner watching her between texts with Mallory. Though Mallory's prognosis is as dismal as Holly's, I still find comfort in her assurances that Mom will likely sleep her way toward death and exit the world peacefully.

The blips and chirps of the monitoring equipment are the only noise in an otherwise soundless room. I know the names of some of these machines. I'm also now savvy to some of the finer points of

Electrocardiography and Electroencephalography, not that I ever hope to put this experience to use again.

The sun is a glimmering dollop of butter melting over the eastern woodland as Dr. Bishop arrives. Fiery evening light shines in through the gossamer curtains at Mom's window, painting her wizened face in hues of surreal exuberance. I hear Dr. Bishop's car rumble up the driveway, followed by the cutting of the engine and the slamming *thock* of his car door. I remain with Mom even as the doctor lets himself in. I hear him greet Walt as he passes, unanswered, through the kitchen.

"Mark," Dr. Bishop acknowledges me as he steps into the twilit room. He moves over to the EEG biofeedback machine on the other side of the bed and studies a small monitor mounted above the headboard. His stethoscope dangles from his neck above an open lab coat, surprisingly-paired with slim-fitting blue jeans. He strokes his beard thoughtfully as years of hard-honed experience and training make sense of the data lolling out of the machines above my dying mother.

I push myself out of the chair, limbs stiff from hours of sitting, and slowly make my way toward him. I sense Walt stepping into the doorway as I approach. "How long?" I ask, suddenly aware of the sweat beading my forehead and dampness wetting my shirt at the small of my back.

"She hasn't been eating much these last few days, I take it?" Bishop asks, addressing the monitor.

"Hardly anything."

With a sigh he straightens out and rotates toward me. In the ever-encroaching darkness I can see how chiseled his expressions have become. His unblinking eyes flash hopeless empathy, and it's genuine.

"Mark, Walter... I'm sorry boys. She's got twenty-four, maybe forty-eight hours tops." He steps toward me with the presence of a mourning relative and places a hand on my shoulder. I feel Walt step closer. It isn't until my vision blurs that I realize I'm crying. All at once a rush of self-discovery settles as I acknowledge the quivering jaw, trembling knees, terse breathing. My phone, still displaying a string of texts with Mallory, falls soundlessly to the carpet.

"She won't feel any pain," Bishop continues, "She's likely to sleep right up until the end. I'm going to contact your hospice provider and request that someone be here full time until... until she passes."

All I hear is *she's likely to sleep right up until the end*. Finding Mom in my water-colored double-vision, I struggle to recall our last substantive conversation. What had my last words to her been? I can't remember. I didn't realize she would decline so rapidly, so all-at-once.

Had I told her I loved her? Had I thanked her for her life of sacrifice in raising us?

What were the last words she'd heard from me?

My head sags and my chin touches my breast bone. I brush past Dr. Bishop and collapse at the edge of the bed. A trembling of the mattress brings my attention to Walt as he settles in similar defeat on the other side.

"I'll leave you alone for a bit," Bishop whispers, a million miles away. "If you need me I'll be outside making some calls. I won't leave without checking with you."

I'm not aware of his having left until I hear the front door open and close moments later. I pad about the covers, searching for Mom's hand. It takes me a few seconds, but I'm able to isolate its bony bulge beneath her comforters. I close my hand over it, squeezing a few times to see if I can draw a response, but she doesn't stir. She remains with her head canted toward Walt, electrode cap making her look strangely suited for synchronized swimming.

"Do you think we'll be able to say goodbye?" Walt asks, his cracking voice startling me out of my head. As I think over what he's asked, I find comfort in our parallel trains of thought, even if the answer is one neither of us want to hear.

"I don't know," I return, my voice watery. "You heard Doctor Bishop – she's likely to sleep right until the end."

"Do you think there's anything we... could have done to save her?" His chest shudders against the bed. He's fighting hard against his emotions, still afraid after all these years to wittingly show vulnerability.

The saddest part is he's too oblivious to understand how the world truly sees him.

"Nothing *we* could do, no," I answer, my gaze falling once more upon Mom's silver-shocked head. It's the hardest thing I've ever endured – even harder than standing over the twitching body of a man I'd run down in the street – sitting here over my dying mother, seeing what she's been reduced to. A catheter tube snakes out of the shadows beneath the bed. All manner of tubes and wires curl their way to various points on her body, measuring, collecting, documenting. She smells of sanitizing agents and her own filth.

"What do you mean, *we*?"

For a moment I'm impressed that Walt picked up on my singling us out. Perhaps he hasn't burned through this month's Adderall supply just yet. "I mean, the guilt and blame for her condition is hers and hers alone." Anxiety rips across my chest. I hold my breath as long as I can to keep it muted, knowing full well that it will be back once I exhale. It's difficult not to feel in the wrong for acknowledging the truth about someone as you prepare to attend their death, but it is the truth. "Mom never went in for checkups or physicals. She outright refused to see doctors. They might have caught this sooner – I doubt it, but they might have – if only she'd been rational."

My gaze locks with Walt's long enough to catch the grudging understanding there. He turns back to Mom, "It's not fair. It's just not fair."

His face vanishes into the blankets delineating our whisp of a mother.

No, it's not fair. Not for any of us.

Hours later I'm sitting on the couch in blue lounge pants and a white undershirt, staring expectantly at my phone. With Mom in her bedroom is Cynthia, a hospice nurse we haven't met before this evening. She'll be with Mom for the overnight until Holly arrives tomorrow morning. Cynthia is so thin I'd reference cancer in describing her if it wasn't so distasteful. She's mid-fifties with thinning gray hair in a tight, tapering plait to the small of her back. She's in surprisingly high spirits for a woman called-in to attend a dying woman on what I presume to be her night off. I suppose you have to be ready for anything in her line of work. Considering all she needs to do is sit bedside with her face in a romance novel, I reason it's not all that bad.

My phone vibrates just as the screen begins to dim from lack of activity. I look down to a text from Mallory asking if I minded her coming over tomorrow night with a couple beers. We've been passively circling the idea of getting together again. Her initial suggestion was that we go back to Rough Ruby's, but she immediately backtracked with a follow up text, apologizing for suggesting I leave the house now. I responded that it was okay, though I could use a drink. And, here we've arrived.

I begin to type a response. My fingers are able to assemble *yeah, I could certainly use it* before I'm distracted by the lights of a car washing the living room in electric blue.

I move to my feet and approach the window, squinting against the glare. Whoever this is, they have their high-beams on. It's almost what you'd expect a vision of God to manifest as, stifling and suppressive in its power. As I lift my hand to block the glare, I murmur out loud, "Cut the lights. Jeez."

My first thought is that the hospice provider has sent someone to relieve Cynthia. Following this, I entertain the idea that Dr. Bishop might be returning to check in. Neither scenario holds much weight, but who else would be coming by at – I glance at my watch – 9:30 at night?

The car pulls around the oblong rotary, headlights illuminating the rear bumper of Cynthia's tan sedan, license plate, *CARES4U*. I squint out into the darkness as the cabin lights wink on in an SUV which I suddenly recognize with paralyzing dread.

A woman stumbles out the door. I recognize her, too.

"Kelly," I whisper, backing away from the window and shuffling toward the arched kitchen entryway. Curling my fingers around the molding, I peer down the shadow-strewn hallway and into the foyer like a child waiting for his abusive father to stumble in, fresh from the bar.

What is she doing here?

Fists pound against the front door. I turn and peer down the bedroom hallway, searching for signs of movement. After a few seconds of constant pounding, a strip of light divides the hallway shadows, and Cynthia's confused face pokes out of Mom's bedroom. I hold a finger to my lips, make a shushing noise, and silently urge her back inside. She hesitates.

"It's..." I struggle to draw breath against a belted chest. Shaking my head, I come right out with it. "It's my ex-wife."

Cynthia's lips pucker queerly. She nods without a word. Shadows mass in the hollows of her face as she leans out for a prolonged look at the ongoing pounding. It's now joined by Kelly's shrill voice, informing me and all of Kittery that she knows I'm inside, that she saw me in the window.

Again, I urge Cynthia back into the room. This time she complies, pushing a pair of reading glasses up her nose before disappearing with obvious reluctance.

There is no sign of Walt. He's either passed out or too engrossed in his writings.

My gaze moves back to the door as the pounding intensifies and Kelly's voice grows louder. Somehow I avoid putting my fist through the wall as I step all the way into the kitchen and make my way reluctantly toward the door. Never in my life have I so wished we had a chain lock. There's no doubt in my mind that she'll force her way in as soon as I crack the door.

I stop and grip the tarnished door handle. With a sigh I decide to jump right into things, reasoning that the sooner we start, the sooner it'll be over. As the click of the deadbolt disengaging makes itself known between thudding fist-falls, the pounding and yelling suddenly cease, and I crack the door for a look at the wraith darkening my doorstep.

She's a disheveled mess, hair sleep-pressed to her head on one side and curled and snarly on the other. I'm left to wonder if she's recently woken from some alcohol-induced coma. Matched with a pair of short-shorts that I've never particularly cared for (the bottoms of her cheeks stick out of it) is a red tank top with a lollipop-shaped stain at the cleft of her breasts.

It doesn't take long for me to catch wind of vodka, spiked with rotten onion body odor. She's been drinking so much she's *sweating* booze.

"What do you want, Kelly?" I ask, shocked that she hasn't already launched into some verbal attack. Her texts of late have been particularly colorful.

"Why haven't you responded to my lawyers?" she hisses. The reek of cigarettes rises into the mix.

Kelly steps forward, advancing on me like a predator as I backtrack, mostly in disgust. There's this enveloping darkness to her, as if while left alone she's finished transitioning into the wretched crone she's always been inside. I only halt and find the initiative to hold my ground when I realize we're in the kitchen and I'm still backing toward Mom's room.

"You do know about my mother, right?" I ask, halting and tossing what I hope to be a piercing look her way. I won't let this go any further.

"You've told me." She teeters slightly before catching herself on the molding at the kitchen entryway. By the look of things, it's a wonder she's made it over here. This goes beyond sloppy. It's clear in the languid way her eyelids rise and fall.

It's also clear in her struggle to remain bipedal.

"Every penny I'm not already giving you is going to hospice. You know Mom. She doesn't have insurance, she hates doctors, and —"

"I want out of this marriage!" she snaps.

I toss a glance down the hallway in time to see a sliver of light quickly snuff itself out. This new nurse is definitely a busybody.

"I know what you want." I swivel back to her, this woman I'd convinced myself I loved for so many years, now a creature who stirs the most exotic dread in me. I seek out her eyes in the darkness, hoping that she senses my resolve. "I have no money to pay for a lawyer. It'll be a while before I can. You're already getting half of my paycheck, you've got the house – you have my blessing to move on with your life, do whatever you want."

"That's not *good enough*," she bellows into a quiet that's remained undisturbed these last weeks, gesticulating so fiercely she nearly topples forward. "I want my life back. I want my last name back. I want this to be *over with* so I can move on."

I clench my eyes shut as spittle peppers my face. Drawing a deep breath, I hold it a moment, enjoying the fleeting reprieve it grants from the anxiety swelling beneath my ribs. I try to tell myself that she's drunk and not thinking clearly. A part of me suspects that she hasn't been sober since our split. Is she coming after me out of spite? Is it really this important to her that our marriage be legally voided? Now?

I seriously doubt it.

"Look, Kelly," I sigh, acknowledging inevitably that this is going to get nasty. "My mother is on her death bed. Her doctor and care people are giving her another day at the most. Your timing couldn't *possibly* be worse. I'm begging you, *please*, just leave me alone until I can bury my mother. She always loved you."

This seems to resonate with her a bit. I mean, why wouldn't it? I've found a way to make this about Kelly. She sips at the stale air, and for a moment I think she's going to force her way in. To what end, I have no way of knowing. Relief washes over me as she suddenly lets go and steps backward.

"For Mom," she says, the rancor in her voice all but melting away. What's left is compassion and a saccharine sweetness that feels ancient. I'm struck by déjà vu. It's like I'm just recognizing this woman as someone who'd once been my wife, not a lifelong enemy. Then she dashes it all away, her tone assuming its black character from before. "But you promise me we'll get this finalized once all of this is over."

Does she ask to come in and see the woman who was her mother inlaw for almost six years? Does she care that this woman is dying? No, she doesn't. All Kell-Well cares about is scraping us off of her boot and "moving on with her life." I'm unsure if I've ever truly hated her before this moment. I want to hurt her, not physically, but mentally, *emotionally*. I want all of this revisited upon her in the most soul-crushing way.

"I promise." I step closer to the door, silently repulsing her. "Are we done?"

She's silent for a few seconds, then, "For now." With that she staggers off of the porch and back to her car. She seems to overestimate the distance between the gravel and the front stoop, losing her balance and crashing against Cynthia's car. Recovering, she glances up at me to see if I'd noticed.

With a shake of my head, I close the door and walk back into the living room. Once more I stand in the window, watching as her headlamps wash CARES4U. She backs onto the lawn, jostling over a pair of neglected rose bushes planted by the community in the aftermath of the Shipyard fire, then hauls off down the driveway, narrowly missing a gnarled oak at the edge of the rotary.

Cell phone in-hand, I dial Kittery Police Department. Seconds later I'm speaking with a hard voice, reporting a black Forrester swerving along US-1 near the outlets.

I feel petty.

I also feel better.

but
there
is
a
god
right

DOES KARMA TRULY *exist?* I ask of the formless void, now suddenly shot through with pinpricks of light and swollen clouds of bright, nebulous vapor. My reality here, the reality my soul has made for itself is deteriorating. I must be close to what I need to move on.

I am dead. I know it, but I will not admit it aloud. Not yet.

In order for Karma to exist, the concepts of good and evil must also exist, says the simpering voice, thought its impish current of mischief is gone.

I barely notice, already forgetting what has drawn me back here, knowing full well that an end of some kind is coming. The part of me still mostly grounded in the past-life of Mark Wells instead grasps the underlying truth here and responds with a very human air of *aha!*

So organized religion is all based on a lie...?

You may feel inclined to look down on the devout as ignorant children lacking the most basic understanding of God, but I'll have you know that the religious among us have a history of early Transcendence.

I search my limited understanding of things on this side, finding myself still anchored mostly to the doctrine, or lack thereof, that had driven me in my former life. *So people who sexually abuse small children, people who take entire countries to war on the basis of some religious ideology... they've got things figured out better than you or me?*

A current of what I decode as pity weaves its way into the voice, now sounding less playful with every word spoken. *For every atrocity committed, there are countless acts of altruism and benevolence carried out in the name of that religion.*

But there is a God, right? I ask.

You can hear God's voice now, can't you? As the walls of your self-imposed prison crumble, do you not hear it speaking to you across the living universe?

I close my eyes, even though I'm aware on a deeper level that I have none. I open the ears I also lack in this place, straining to hear something, *anything*, in the vacuum I've existed within for the last day, week, month, year, century... whatever. It isn't until I'm about to give up and ask the simpering voice to guide me that I detect it.

Like a note in a song held indefinitely, an unintelligible drawl suddenly gains presence, not simply all around me, but sifting through my very soul. I realize in this moment that I've been hearing it this whole time, that what I'd naively dismissed as a vacuum, as an absence of sound, was actually the voice of God calling ceaselessly across its infinite domain.

Suddenly I think of Walter and curl defensively against what I can only describe as a stress fissure opening down my being, dividing my soul.

You'll pay no penance for getting Kelly in trouble with the cops, Mark. For that was your original question, right? Will there be some kind of karmic retribution against you?

I can't answer. The pain is all-encompassing. It tears at me with cruel, natural indifference, as if to say, 'I'm just doing my job, this is the nature of things.'

What's happening to me? I ask, gasping and clutching at my chest in a way I know is pitiably *mortal* given my lack of physical form.

We're nearing the end. Whatever this is, it will leave you shortly to cope with things on this side.

It feels like someone is... tearing me apart.

I know it does, says the voice, now entirely devoid of its former character.

Kelly is caught and arrested. I'm clued into this the next morning through the Kittery Police Department's Facebook page, updated diligently with the previous day's traffic reports. There was Kelly's name, right beside a D.U.I. writeup that made me feel surprisingly terrible.

I'd gone to bed thinking perhaps she'd made it home without getting caught since I wasn't called to bail her out of jail. She must have called her parents or one of her remaining friends. Probably left with a court date already set – one I hope will tie her lawyer down with something *other* than the divorce.

I lock my phone and set it on the table. I toe an emotional line dividing remorse and relief. This woman has been coming after me for weeks with hardly a scrap of proof I'd been cheating on her. And I hadn't. Still, something feels so inexplicably wrong here, as though I'd betrayed a lifelong friend and not a woman actively trying to destroy my life.

The sky outside is leaden. It isn't hot enough for lightning, though the threat of rain is not an ambiguous one. The patter of thick drops on the roof comes eventually like the sigh of a god.

Drawing a deep breath, I gaze into a half-eaten bowl of Cheerios, now soggy with my disinterest. I spoon a few bites into my mouth, forcing myself to eat even though I'm not hungry, then shove the bowl away. As if on cue, Mouf leaps onto the table out of nowhere. He saunters toward the bowl with an air of possession. He's a sausage propped up on toothpicks. His whiskers bristle as he sniffs at the bowl then begins to drink, unchallenged, face dominated by that cat-grimace they all seem to wear when lapping something up.

I leave him to it, suddenly up and walking toward Mom's room. I pause in the living room, finding Walt sitting on the floor in the corner, hair pressed to his head from sleep. The fire in his eyes that kept him obsessed these last few weeks has inexplicably snuffed itself out, now just a lone pilot light. He's definitely run through his Adderall, confirming my suspicions that his sudden creative drive was born of the drug.

Now he'd have to wait until the pharmacy refilled it under rigid Controlled Substance Laws that counted the days since his last refill. He stares vacuously at the floor, notebooks absent.

For a moment I consider what will become of him after Mom goes. With no one left to support him, the responsibility will be mine. Suddenly I'm thinking of the inevitable drug intervention, and a stabbing hopelessness forms in me. I'll have to find a way to dry him out and keep him clean. I can't expect any kind of life working 50 hours a week to support an ex-wife *and* my little brother.

I push the thoughts away and walk into Mom's room. One thing at a time.

Glancing to Holly, whose spirited arrival had woken me at 7 A.M., I ask how Mom is doing. Holly pivots away from the equipment she's monitoring, which seem less and less important to the people tending Mom each day, and attaches a stylus to the side of her tablet computer. The corners of her lips drag downward. "Most of her vitals are slowly declining, with the exception of her heart rate." She points to the EKG, sharply spiking in narrow waves. "This is the kind of thing we see in the last eight to twenty-four hours. She could go at any time."

I swallow hard, suddenly aware of Walter in the doorway. Mom's completely still now, not a single observable movement all morning. The muscles in her face have disengaged, her lips are cracked and parched with a flaking membrane of snake's skin. Were it not for the white comforter slowly rising and falling, her heartbeat a metronomic ripple, I'd swear she was already dead.

"You don't think there's any chance she'll wake up again?" I ask, thinking of Walter and *feeling* his hopelessness.

Holly's lips droop further. She gazes at Mom with nothing short of love. "I don't want to give you false hope, Mark. Even if she wakes up, she's not going to be lucid. She won't have any idea what's going on or have the ability to communicate verbally." She steps over to me, smelling of flowery perfume and alcohol-based hand sanitizer. Resting her hand on my shoulder, she says, "If you've any last words for her, you should give them to God."

I consider this a moment, contemplating how a sentient and compassionate god could allow things like this to occur.

"I'm sorry if I've overstepped," Holly says, reading something in my face.

"No, no. You're fine," I assure her, the hand still resting on my shoulder. "I'm sorry, I've just got a lot to sort out, and I've never been a particularly... *spiritual* man."

"I'll say no more on the subject." She returns to her machinery, and I notice for the first time that several of the machines are no longer powered. This observation, combined with the sudden departure of Holly's optimism, is unsettling to say the very least. For a moment I consider reengaging her, but instead I turn away. There is nothing pleasant, no hope to be mined from those attending a death bed.

Turning to Walt, our eyes meet for a moment before his submissively find the floor. My fingers loosening, I close the gap between us and consider taking him into my arms as I ask if he's okay.

Walt shakes his head. No, of course not. None of us are okay.

"Do you want anything to eat? Some breakfast?" I ask.

Walt shakes his head, informing me in a distant, dreamy voice that he can't eat.

Not that he isn't hungry. He can't eat.

I consider asking him if he wants to smoke up, but quickly discard the idea. I don't want to be under the influence of pot when the end comes.

I grasp at straws, searching for ways I might draw Walt out of himself. Feeling somewhat defeated, and for multiple reasons, I return to Mom, patting the blankets until I find a hand.

"Mom." I can feel my emotions swirling into some storm. Above, the patter of rain pelting the roof intensifies. "I'm sorry for every time I've ever wronged you. I'm sorry for stealing from your purse in high school. I'm sorry for missing curfew and making you worry." I choke on spit as I recall her panicked breakdown at being forced by her sons into the emergency room. "And I'm... sorry I tried to make you go to the ER. I—I just didn't want something like *this* to happen to you." I study her unmoving face. Suddenly I'm alone with her and the rain.

I'm vaguely aware of my jaw trembling, and I'm unable to stop an adjoining frown from assembling on my face. "I wish you would wake up. Just one last time so I can say goodbye." My hand tightens over hers. "I don't want you to leave like this."

"Stop." Walt's voice is startling, snapping me out of the mental seclusion into which I'd withdrawn. I turn to him, now settled in Mom's recliner, scowling at me. In all my life I don't think I've ever felt my brother's judgement.

"What's—"

"Just leave her alone." His voice is low and almost... otherworldly. His fingers curl into the armrest fabric, digging in as he stares *into* me, daring me to argue. I don't know if it's because he's overtired and grumpy or if it's the aftereffects of the drugs he's coming down from, but this is not like my brother.

"Walt," I say, assessing him carefully, shocked to find myself intimidated. "I just want to say goodbye to her."

"Then say goodbye. Don't make her feel guilty because she can't wake up for you. Don't leave her all alone in there, feeling that way." He leans forward commandingly, voice and body suddenly imbued with passion I'll never know.

I want to push back, argue that she's vegetative, but I'm able to do nothing but wither in his gaze.

"I'm sorry, Walt."

He reclines without a word, gazing at the ceiling, offering nothing more. I look back to Mom, blinking tears. Is this how I'm going to spend her final hours? At odds with everyone around me? Made small by the last person in the world who's never come down on me?

Is this the culmination of everything I've endured these months?

A part of me hopes so.

"Mark," a frail voice pokes through the darkness of the cottage. I hear my name several more times, uttered with the same strange absence of urgency despite the condition of its owner.

I'm long past the confusion that gripped my mind every morning and night I'd wake in this house in the aftermath of Kelly kicking me out. When my eyes open, it is to a familiar black void, the same corridor I'd walked every night and morning in my youth. On one side, a closed door and a man forcibly unanchored from his stimulants, impossibly dead to the world. On the other, the open bedroom where my mother lay dying.

Where my mother lay *awake* and *asking for me*.

I'm not certain what keeps me from springing to my feet, anxious to say what needs to be said with no grasp of how long this moment will last, but I don't. Instead, I rise slowly, noting that's she's stopped uttering my name now, seeming aware that I'm up.

Uncertain where her head is, I hope I at least *resemble* the child she'd raised into adulthood.

"I'm here, Momma," I whisper into the black, shuffling carefully into her room as my eyes adjust. Asleep in the recliner is another night nurse we've only ever seen recently, and only after sunset. Her name is Lindsay and she's given Mom a run for her money in the sleep department.

"Come here," Mom whispers, her voice carving through the darkness beneath the blinking amber and lime LEDs above her. I make out the movement of her stronger hand beneath the white comforter, held in a rectangle of powdered moonlight.

I obey, shuffling the rest of the way toward the bed and kneeling beside her. From under the blankets comes a frail hand which struggles to free itself until I lift the blankets and guide it into my own. She pumps it a few times, seeming to test her strength while confirming I'm real.

"I'm here, Momma," I repeat, suddenly a child.

"Water," she returns in a rasping rattle. I reach for the pitcher beside the bed and pour her a glass. Lifting it carefully to her lips, I'm transported back to the moment it all started in the kitchen. It's with great difficulty that I keep the cup steady as she drinks, cooing and grunting with each swallow until she's drained it all.

"More?" I ask, noting the wet character of my voice and wondering how I'd been blindsided by tears. Tears are par for the course these days.

"No," she answers, licking at her parched lips and drawing a long breath. "Thank you."

"You're welcome," I return. I wait for her to speak again. I haven't been beckoned here for water. This feels like divine providence, a true miracle, for I shouldn't be *speaking with her* at all.

My eyes adjust enough to see the whites of hers. She's gazing right at me, chest rising and falling slowly as we're serenaded by the equipment above and the soft snores of Lindsay the Nurse. After a minute or so, just as I'm considering the idea that it had all been a fluke, Mom speaks again.

"I need you to promise me something, Marky," she whispers. All of her seems engaged in this. She doesn't so much as stutter or pause to rethink her words. It's as though this has been practiced and stored away in her for decades, and for this exact moment.

"Anything," I return without hesitation.

She swallows, eyes never leaving me. "I need you to promise me you'll take care of Walter when I go. I need you to keep him out of trouble. Keep him from hurting himself."

For a few seconds I can only gape at her. Of course I intended to take care of Walter, whatever *that* looked like. Was this all she could think about as her mind spat its final sparks? Was she truly this concerned about Walter lasting on his own?

I open my mouth to answer and am silenced by my mother.

"He has it harder than most," she says with a confidence and understanding I cannot impeach. "He's been alone all this time, *struggling by himself*."

"Mom, he's hardly *alone*—"

"Mark, promise me, please."

Without hesitation: "I promise, Momma."

She stays looking at me for a few seconds in the darkness. Though I can only see the whites of her eyes, I can feel her pupils probing me for commitment, searching the lines of my face for disingenuity. Her hand tightens around mine, flexing a few times against her fleeing energy. I want to ask what she means by Walter being alone and *struggling by himself*, but I don't. Part of me writes it off as the confusion of a soul about to flee its mortal prison, while another part of me intuits something cosmic in her words, something far above my powers of perception.

"I want to tell you something, Marky. I want it out before I go so I don't take it across with me." Somehow her voice finds a current of power, banishing the wet rattle of an unexercised throat. She hesitates a moment in a way that strikes me as rehearsed for flair, then, "I never forgave your father for running back inside that fabrication shop. I never forgave him for trading his life for the ones he'd saved, dashing back through those flames over and over. He was *safe*, Marky, *safe*. His decision to spend his life on those... *other people* came at the expense of our family... and I've *hated* him for it."

I'm wordless. Suddenly everything I've known about my mother's life, post-Dad, is a lie. Everything I'd gone through these last months in trying to spare her dignity, in trying to *keep her proud*... I'd done all that for a woman who resented the most celebrated man in Southern Maine, my father, Eric Wells.

"But you—"

"Yes, Marky, I went to all those ceremonies, I let them parade me and you boys around like the only remaining artifacts of a man who suddenly *defined* us. Oh, how I hated your father for that, for making me a celebrity widow. Do you know how many businesses I had to stop going to because they wouldn't take my money anymore? Because they suddenly saw me as a *charity case*?"

I'd seen none of this, but then again, Walter and I had still been too young and naïve at that time to appreciate the nuances of adult bitterness. We'd simply grown up seeing our father as the hero who'd saved three lives in a shop fire that had claimed nineteen, not as a man who'd gambled and lost with his life in a moment of misplaced, maybe even overdone heroics.

My proud mother had her dignity stolen from her when I was sixteen. As with her rigid impulse to brush off misunderstandings during my visits, she'd spent more than two decades doing the same in the community.

I consider her friends who'd drifted off the radar over the years. I'd always known Mom was to blame, but now there was a clear reason: she'd weeded charity out of her life.

"I'm sorry, Momma. I never knew you felt this way."

Her hand tightens, "'*Course* you didn't." Her face lifts slightly in the moonlight with a smile that fails to completely lift the corners of her lips.

It's a playful smile, a *simpering* smile.

Her amusement not diminishing, she lays it all out for me. "Nobody's ever known more than I'd let them, and those who pressed too much or said the wrong thing went quickly. No need for 'em. I've carried this with me to my death bed, Marky, and it's here I confess." A tremble shakes through her body. Her hand tightens. "Somehow I always knew it would be to you."

"But Walter—"

"I love your brother – I suspect you've believed all this time that I love him more, but it's not true. I love your brother for his innocence, for his old soul, but he's not here to leave a mark on the world like you are. You've always been my determined deep-thinker, Marky, out to conquer one thing or another, and I love you for it. Always have. The day you graduated UNH was one of my proudest as a mother. My secrets are for you, not Walter, because you will take them and make something with them. I've always known yours is a soul made to travel, one that collects and makes use of life's lessons in ways Walter…"

She trails off, finally and abruptly losing her train of thought. It doesn't matter. Her words fall upon my weary mind, melting over my fears and anxieties as if dripping from the lips of God Himself.

The LEDs above streak suddenly in the dark as my tears renew. "I'm sorry for everything I've ever done, every time I stole from your pur—"

"It's okay, Marky. Don't force yourself down this road. There isn't a single slight against me for which you haven't been long-forgiven. You were my first baby. You got all the best parts of me and your dad."

In their own way, these words are all the forgiveness I need to cool the long-burning guilt fire in me.

"I love you, Mom."

"I love you, too, Marky."

We stay like this until she's sleeping once more, never to wake in this way again. Her lips have spoken their final words. Her secrets are my secrets now.

I'm almost certain I hear a door clicking shut across the hall.

Mallory arrives in the early evening with one of those odd *eight*-packs of Guinness under her arm. I meet her at the door, immediately realizing I'd neglected to tidy up the house. I apologize to no end for the state of things as I lead her into the kitchen. Each time she assures me with escalating insistence that things are much worse at her house and that her *clean-freak* proclivities went with Nathan.

After a day wallowing alongside Mom's unchanging condition (not to mention the conversation from the night before and the ever-devolving moods of both Holly and Walt), it's nice to have someone to talk to who isn't embedded in our situation.

"How is your mother?" Mallory asks, setting the beer on the kitchen table and smoothing down a form-fitting red thermal. Along with the jeans she wears, the outfit molds itself to her in all the right places, delineating curves that I'd see so much differently were this any another time.

My cereal bowl from this morning is still on the table. The Cheerios are bloated mush. I quickly snatch up the bowl and deliver it to the kitchen sink, speaking as I walk. "Nothing's really changed since this morning. Holly says that's normal at this point." I deposit the bowl in the sink and wipe my hands on my khaki cargo shorts. The window over the sink is a dark mirror in which I check my appearance, running a hand over the stubble on my head and tugging down on a Dandy Warhols concert tee.

I turn to find her watching me, lips compressed. She asks, "Are you okay?"

It's difficult not to marvel at how our relationship has progressed in spite of literally *everything*. Before me stands a woman showing palpable concern for me, the man who'd made a widow of her.

I nod and work to stifle the discomfort that runs through me at this revelation. "I'm... a... hanging in there, I suppose." Swallowing against a lump in my throat, I step around the table and peek down the empty hallway before sitting across from Mallory. Her gaze goes to the beer before lifting back to me.

"It'll be tough for a while, but it will start to get easier," she assures me. The hollowness of her voice makes me wonder if her words are arbitrary, the same bland, tired proclamations she and others made to suffer have heard and dismissed for centuries.

I nod toward the beers, "Should I get some glasses?"

"Sure, though I can't drink too much. Got work in the morning."

It seems that, for both of us, the beers were just an excuse to get together and talk. To further probe the weird depths of our bond.

"I'm probably only good for one myself. Just enough to take the edge off. I don't want to be out of it..." our eyes meet. I feel the corners of my lips drag downward. "...If Mom passes tonight."

"That's a good idea."

I don't get up at first, held in place while chasing a thought. Eventually it flutters out of reach and is lost, and with a soft grunt I rise, walk beyond the dishes heaped in the sink, and open the cupboards. A cooling relief gusts through my body as my gaze settles upon a pair of clean glasses, the last in the house for all I know.

Small as it is, I'm grateful to have caught a break. Reaching into the dusty darkness, I grasp the glasses, one in each hand, and turn around, examining them in the light for soap marks or dust.

"So how have you been?" I ask, now back at the table and extracting a can.

"'Bout as good as I can be. Work helps take my mind off everything. I'm not sure if I'll ever get used to living in an empty house."

"I've never felt comfortable alone myself." I tip one of the glasses and pour.

"It's not being alone that's the problem, really. It's seeing his stuff there in the same spots. His surfboards in the garage, his running gear in the bedroom closet… his keys still hanging on the key rack." She stares down at the table, nibbling at her lower lip. "Cliché as it may sound, I feel like I'm living with a ghost."

I finish pouring and push the first glass to her before going to work on mine. I bite back against the urge to advise her to pack Nathan's things away. Mallory's grieving process is her own. Oddly enough, she seems to pluck the thought right out of my mind anyway.

"I know I should probably pack everything up and give it to charity or something." Her fingers tap out a harried rhythm on the glass. "It's just hard because I know it will signify that I've chosen to move on, and I don't know if I'm ready yet. I mean, what's the standard for mourning? Do I have a minimum amount of time?" She chuckles. It sounds hollow and forced. "There should be a rule book for this, if just to save us from the guilt."

Mallory's eyes lift back up to mine. I shrug, "Maybe the two of us should write it." An image of Walt pouring his soul into all those notebooks enters and exits my head with View-Master speed and clarity. I gaze into my beer, suddenly unsure if I even want it. One look at Mallory, her fingers still drumming on the glass, and I understand the feeling is mutual.

She chuckles, "Yeah, I can see the tagline now: 'most depressing book ever written.'"

"I guess you're right." And I'm surprised to hear myself add, "My brother's writing a book."

Mallory's eyes shoot to the corners of their sockets as though she's working suddenly to extract a memory. "That what he was doing in the hospital that night? With the notebook?"

"It's like *twelve* notebooks now. Maybe fifteen. I dunno."

"Have you read it? What's it about?"

"He hasn't let me read it – he gets really defensive when I bring it up. Apparently it's some spiritual… *something*. He says it's about death and the meaning of life."

"Perhaps he's starting his own religion." She lifts her beer and takes a measured sip, licking away the foam beneath her nose in a way that's unbearably cute.

"Who knows what he's doing." I take her lead and have a sip of my beer. I run my bare arm across my lips as I return the glass to the table. "I'll tell you this much – he hasn't been himself these last few weeks."

"That's not difficult to believe. I'm sure you're different, too, you just don't realize it. Having to sit, powerless, through a family member's slow decline… I almost think I had it better with the way Nathan went."

This stings me a bit, but as our eyes meet and I see her absence of resentment, my anxiety effervesces like the diminishing head on my beer. "My dad died in a fire at the Shipyard when I was sixteen. I got up in the morning, hugged him goodbye, and when I went to bed that night he was dead. At the time I was beside myself, couldn't cope. Still, it was preferable to… to *this*."

The conversation ebbs. We go to work more aggressively on our drinks, the silence a clear indicator of our mutual desire to move on to other topics. I set my beer down after a couple long gulps, ready to move onto the always reliable topic of *the weather*, when the sudden sounding of alarms explodes down the hallway.

I start, staggering eventually to my feet and knocking the chair out from behind me. It clatters to the floor, its sound barely registering over the sudden shriek of frantic voices and the thudding of footfalls.

"Holly!" I yell, nearly tripping over the chair as I'm suddenly sprinting toward Mom's room. "Walter!"

Walt comes barreling out of his room, door thwacking against the wall. He charges across the hallway into Mom's room. I'm right after him with Mallory behind me. As I enter, my gaze falls upon Holly, hands engaged in a cartoonish blur, silencing the shrieking equipment.

"What is it?" I ask. "Christ it sounds like a damned *heart attack*."

"Her heart-rate is dropping. Her breathing, slowing," Holly answers, suddenly all business as her years tasting every flavor of trauma take over. This is the final encore to her every gig.

Walt is already on the opposite side of the bed, eyes brimming with tears that glisten in the lamplight as he gazes helplessly down at our mother. Alarms find their voices stolen one-by-one by the practiced hand of Nurse Holly.

"Walt," I sob, unsure what else I intend to say to him. I rush around the bed only to be shoved aside as Walt launches to his feet and dashes out of the room. His shoulder smacks mine with the force of a charging bull. "Walt? Walt!" I call after him in a watery voice. My vision doubles, and I watch two identical versions of my brother disappear from the room. "Walt!"

His answer is the bathroom door slamming.

"Mark." Mallory's voice blazes through the confusion, drawing my attention to where she stands behind Holly, placing obvious effort into staying out of the way as she watches. I gaze at her through a world of flowing water, my cheeks wet and swollen. "She's going quick."

I collapse beside the bed and shove my hand beneath the blankets. It's as if I'm drawn right to her hand because I don't have to feel or fumble around for a second. Her flesh is cold and damp, as though the warmth has already fled. Though I pump the hand a few times, it remains limp. My attention lands on the sleeping face of the woman who'd brought me into this world, the woman who'd sacrificed her entire life and suffered a secret pain in the aftermath of Dad's death.

"Mom," I whisper. "Mom, I love you so much." I bury my face in her, feeling the labored inflation of her lungs, the stuttering patter of her heartbeat. She draws breath only every few seconds, throat rattling with mucus.

I channel every bit of spiritual energy in me and offer it up to God. *Take her. Just take her quickly, please. Don't let her suffer. Just end it.*

I start as her chest heaves, driving me off of her. My retreat takes me as far as the edge of the bed, my hand still clutching hers. Mom's eyes flutter a bit. She lets out a long, drawn out sigh, and then she's still.

Suddenly and definitely still.

"Is that it?" My gaze shifts maniacally between Holly and Mallory. Above my mother the biometric devices that had prolonged her life and cataloged her decline continue to tick away, flatlined. The crushing analog drawl lets me know, from every hospital movie I've ever seen, that she is gone.

My chin trembles, shaking tears onto the bedspread. I study the form of my departed mother for a few seconds in deep, oppressive disbelief before I'm startled backward, nearly off my feet, as her chest rises.

"What's going *on*?" I all but yell.

"Reflex breathing," Holly answers. "All involuntary. She's just winding down, Mark." She doesn't look at me as she speaks, still working over Mom. Suddenly I'm aware of a hand on my shoulder. I follow it up to a sodden face gushing with empathy.

Mallory's face.

I can't help my gaze being torn back to Mom as she shakes out a pair of final breaths, then is still. Her eyes crack open, lifeless and glazed, yet there's a certain euphoria in them that brings a moment of pause before the emotions overtake me.

My mouth drops open, jaw still trembling. Holly checks her watch and fishes the tablet computer out of its sconce at the foot of the bed. She unsnaps the stylus and scrawls something down, the time of death perhaps, then turns to me, seeming to shed the chaos of the past few minutes like a snake slipping its skin. What remains is naked empathy in the place of solemn duty.

"I'm so sorry, Mark." There are tears in her eyes. Real tears. For a moment she's silent, standing there as if leafing through mental notes on death etiquette. After what seems like an eternity, the three of us pressed beneath the silence of this room, Holly asks me if I want to be alone.

I shake my head. I do *not* want to be alone.

Where the hell is—

you've finally woken

WALT?

I open my eyes, though I have no eyes. I draw breath, though I have no lungs. All around me is the drawling voice of God. Gone is the formless void, the reflective vacuum in which I'd cocooned myself.

Enough dreaming, enough looking back. It's time to be in the now.

Where am I exactly? Where is the simpering voice?

Before me is a field of floating debris, rocks ranging from grains of sand to house-sized boulders. They float in a state of constant, languid motion, against a sea of star-shot black. I set my sites farther out to where these millions of rocks blend in striking lemon-colored bands, and at the center of the formation, half-eclipsed, is the planet to which they are bound.

To which I am bound.

I feel my body rising, the debris seeming to fall around me. I gaze at my hands and feet, my nude form. All of it is something of a contrivance, for even in this moment of slowly inking enlightenment I understand that my soul is finally untethered.

I'm awestruck as I'm lifted more swiftly, the debris fusing into additional bands until I'm flying over the rings of Saturn.

My gaze sharpens on the colossal planet, wreathed in teeming segments of lemon cloud – turbulent storms fuming, undisturbed in the black vastness of space since time immemorial.

And all around me is God's voice, that pressing silence of something simultaneously everywhere and nowhere. This must be what it feels like to be deaf – the sheer absence of sound taking on a character of its own, like a million voices singing in chorus, unintelligible, muted against a distant, obstructing monolith. Its power penetrates the bottommost depths of my soul.

Tightly packed, luminous stars are like crushed diamonds against far off galaxies and stormy nebulae. A part of me is aware that I've visited most of them in the spaces between past lives. Beetlejuice, Coma Berenices, Andromeda – names given by living men. I can't conjure up their true names just yet, but I know they'll come in time.

Solar wind passes through me with an odd tickle as I'm drawn forward toward the planet. I plummet toward the yellow rings banding it before streaking across them like an unmoored star flung into the cosmos.

I'm skating across the rings of Saturn, held in a peace that feels like homecoming. This is where I belong, where I'm meant to experience true consciousness.

I'm startled for a moment as I'm spun and swept farther inward toward the planet. It grows in an instant as I traverse the gaps in its bands. The shadows draping the planet's surface recede until I'm facing away from the sun, gaping at the titanic face of Saturn, my guiding celestial.

My true home.

I pass beyond the rings, arcing now toward the northern pole where streaks of green, fibrous light shift erratically. I feel content to remain here forever. Larger and larger the planet grows until I'm saturated in gold.

The crushing whisper of God informs me that the planet intends to consume me. Nothing has ever felt so right.

Then, all at once, I stop. I'm still thousands of miles from the membranous margins of the planet's atmosphere, its rings curving into and lost in its own shadow. Even in this state of building insight, I am powerless to escape the awe that crashes over me. I'm growing less and less aware of a *need* to breathe with every second, yet I begin to pant, sucking fake air as I'm held in the presence of undistilled nature.

Of God.

Hello, Mark, the simpering voice pierces the din, and I rotate toward my mother, now floating beside me. She is trim and healthy, the sprig of a girl in her mid-twenties. Her hair is blonde again, not the white that tinted silver in certain light as her days wound down. Like me she is nude, though the *physiological* is hastily growing irrelevant now.

Mom, I say, feeling my soul smile at her. I correct myself, *Shannon*.

You're still adjusting. It's fine. I'm glad you've finished glancing back. She swivels, cradled in the same nothingness as I, gaze sweeping with palpable reverence over the planet dwarfing us. *I've always loved that we return here. To this place. God's love is big.*

God. The great ghost in the sky, right? That is what Mallory and I always called Him, sarcasm dripping ignorance from our lips. How blind we'd been.

I understand everything Shannon is saying on a level that feels *low*, existing at the very bottom of me. It speaks with the voice of a small child, difficult to understand, relentless in its nagging. I gaze into the planet's atmosphere, watching as clouds swollen in shades of darkening amber flare with strikes of blue lightning.

Where are the others? I ask, glancing behind and around me as if there should be more here. I don't know how I know it, it's simply intuited.

Your father will be here shortly. Kelly – Kell-Well, we called her – will be with him.

I nod, suddenly aware of the years that have passed since I was at my mother's deathbed. I'm aware of those of us who've passed, but this again is like a feeling more than anything of substance in this place. I know it will gain clarity in time.

What about Walt?

Shannon's soul darkens, a sullen look sweeps across her face, and I feel my soul wither as if in the grip of madness. I feel a fissure dividing me, and I lurch forward, knees to my chest, the voice of God now crushing down harder upon me. My soul feels like it's fraying at the edges.

You remember? Shannon asks. In her I feel the same disturbance. She's been coping with it longer on this side. There's a callous she's built in her that I can identify but fail to understand.

I –

Imagine my horror when I materialized here, as you have, to find him already waiting for me…

I'm already reaching back to those final moments. The moments right after Shannon – Mom – offered her final exhale to the corporeal world.

Mallory's grip tightens on my shoulder. "You don't have to stay in here. It's okay if you need to get away."

My hands gather up snatches of comforter. My knuckles are white. Any remaining vitality has fled my mother's face. What's left is a body lacking even a whisper of life. She smacks of emptiness. All that's left is this husk.

How long has it been? How long have I been kneeling here?

I turn away, rising through a dreamlike fugue to my feet. Mallory's face enters my field of vision. The oddest compulsion to collapse in her arms washes over me before receding against sudden, maddening anger. "I'm sorry," I whisper to her, trying my best to keep it together. I edge between her and the bed, already searching the hallway for my brother, for the vermin who'd abandoned our mother in her final moments.

"Walter!" I call, recoiling against my own voice reverberating back. I'm vaguely aware of Holly covering Mom's face and Mallory tailing me out. I nearly trip over my feet as I traverse the grimy carpet and stumble into the hallway. "Walt!"

Movement in the kitchen catches my gaze. There is Mouf, seated unfazed in a patch of moonlight on the linoleum. He sniffs in my general direction before arching his back, hissing, and scrambling off into the living room, claws skittering across the reflective tile.

I have no time to sort out the cat's odd behavior. I'm fueled by a gnashing sense of loss and sudden exasperation with Walt. Without thinking, I shift my weight with the prowess of a blackbelt and deliver a kick that thunders Walter's door open in a chaos of swirling dust, splinters sifting through the cloud.

"Walter," I sob, eyes sweeping his vacant, moonlit room, my emotions like the wavering lines on Mom's EKG. I feel around the wall until I find the switch and throw it.

The room is in its usual disarray. No sign of Walt.

There's only one other place he can be. Rotating to the bathroom door, I note immediately the band of light creeping out and sluicing across the carpet. I remember seeing him go in there. I'm so frazzled it's escaped me. I step up to the door and shock myself with the restraint I channel, lifting a hand and knocking gently.

"Walter?" I wait a few moments without an answer, then knock again, harder. "Walt?"

I grip the knob, unsurprised that it won't turn. Now I'm pounding on the door. "Walter! Open now or I'm gonna kick the door in!"

No response.

"What's *wrong* with you? Are you *that* detached, you can't face your mother's *death*!" My weight shifts once more to my left leg. "Son of a –"

I kick as hard as I can. The door flies open, thudding immediately against an obstructing object, only about a quarter open. It's enough to see a bare leg, stretched out across the floor. The rest of him is blocked.

"Walt...?" At first I'm dumbfounded. It takes time for me to decode what I'm seeing.

My anger evaporates in an instant, and suddenly I'm no longer thinking of Mom.

"*Walt!*" I cry, angling myself sideways and forcing my way in. Everything is blood, and I think immediately of Nathan Kelson.

Walt is turned on his side, looking as though he'd been sitting just long enough to do what he needed, then lie down on the floor to wait it out. One leg is bent awkwardly against the bathtub, blood inking into the grout between tiles, rendering the tub an island floating in a lake of crimson. The opposite shore: Walt's nude body, siphoned of all color.

"*Help!*" I cry, the reality of the situation collapsing upon me. "Oh, God, *help, please!*" My knees mash into the floor and I snatch up one of Walt's wrists. I immediately avert my eyes at the sight of the ragged lacerations he'd made there, streaking all the way up to his elbow. Dry-heaving and blinking fresh tears, I'm suddenly lost here.

I'm not sure how much time passes, but Mallory and Holly push their way in at some point.

"Get out of the way!" Mallory cries, stepping over Walt and shoving me back with a force that knocks something off the toilet. I peer down at my feet where it's landed, finding Walt's clothes crumpled but still holding the folded form in which he'd left them.

I fall against the wall, my attention whiplashing toward Holly, currently dialing 9-1-1 on her phone. She vanishes into the hall, her diminishing voice a slew of medical jargon too serious in tone for me to endure.

Mallory muscles Walt onto his back and begins administering CPR. As his arm flops lifelessly on the dry portion of the floor, I realize with a back-flipping stomach that he is no longer bleeding. I push my back against the wall as if trying to retreat into it, and I slide away until my shoulder finds the groove of a corner. My gaze finds Mallory, now inadvertently gathering Walt's blood in her jeans as she struggles over him, his body shuddering lifelessly beneath her.

I can't watch this. But as I slap my hands over my eyes, I continue peering through the crack between my palms. It's in this moment that my gaze locks on the straightedge razor occupying an unblemished tile beside the toilet. It's one of those slotted ones with a disposable blade. My vision blurs, tears now spilling out in a torrent as I acknowledge how characteristically *cheap* this is for Walt.

Even the instrument of his destruction is a dollar store special.

My knees knock. I feel my shirt lift behind me as I slide down the wall. There's nothing left to do but cry.

"Ambulance will be here in less than five," Holly's voice reaches my ears. My heart sinks further as I pick up on the hopelessness garnishing her words. She already knows that Walt is gone and not coming back.

Mallory says nothing, though her grunting and the thudding of her body inform me that she's not ready to give up. Not like Holly.

I press my face deeper in my hands. It's over. I know it's over. Everything.

Here I am, crumpled into the corner like dirty clothing as the woman whose husband I murdered works desperately to save the life of my last living relative. Even now, as waves of emotion break mercilessly upon me, my heart thuds with clear designs of escape. I can't help appreciating the irony. After everything, could it really end any other way?

I can feel myself letting go now, inviting death to come claim me as well, until all at once I'm startled out of myself by the slamming of doors and the thudding of footfalls in the hall.

"In there," Holly's voice urges, hopeless.

"Watch the door!" Mallory cries. My hands fall away and I watch as she lurches forward and shields Walt's head with her hands. The door thuds hard against her knuckles. I wince for her, but she doesn't so much as pause to consider the broken flesh of her fingers.

A pair of EMTs edge their way into the bathroom, lugging suitcases and duffel bags with caduceus symbols emblazoned upon them. I don't see their faces until one of them commands us out of the room, and even then I find myself gazing only at Walter as I'm spirited through a dreamworld into the hallway.

Away in the darkness, I'm able to get a look at the blood-smeared hands that ushered me out. My gaze lifts to the disarming face of its owner.

"I'm s—sorry," Mallory stutters, working against a trembling jaw, eyes glistening in the bathroom light. "I t—tried to…"

I know it isn't her fault, that he was too far gone by the time we found him. Images of the crude lacerations he'd made continue to drill into my mind.

For a moment we just stand there, reading the guilt and dismay in each other. Nothing seems real. I feel as though I'm in the throes of some terrible nightmare. I might awaken at any moment.

Please, God, let me wake from this dream.

The voices of the EMTs grow more urgent behind me. Then suddenly the voices seem distant, filtered through the same artificial lens as those who'd attempted to revive Nathan Kelson. For all I know they're the same EMTs.

"Mark." Mallory's hands travel down my arms, trembling, until she's holding my wrists. Our eyes meet. "You should... *we*... should get away from here."

"I—I can't j-just la-*leave*!" I manage to choke out, suddenly snatching at each breath, barely able to find the wind to push out my words. Mallory's face is an ill-defined silhouette behind a wall of flowing water.

"Just outside the house," she urges. As I blink and my vision clears I see that she's crying harder now, though clearly keeping it together as much as she can for me. Staying strong for me... the man who'd taken her husband away months earlier.

I don't realize we're on the porch until the smells of wet leaves and years-old mulch reach my nose, raising sudden and striking awareness of my former world of urine and sanitizing agents. Scents I'll forever associate with death. Mallory leads me beyond the frantic strobe of the parked ambulance, to the right side of the porch. The chirping symphony of nocturnal insects plays for us alone. Through interlaced branches above comes word that the clouds have broken. Winking stars garnish the edges of a waxing moon, framed in the fluttering leaves.

"It's better out here, right?" Mallory says, face upturned to the moon.

I move up beside her, gripping the rotting, splintered railing. Breathing deeply, I hold in the nighttime coolness before releasing my breath in a stuttering exhale. It does feel better to be out of the house, but my nerves are far from calmed. Even with their lessening I'm left aware of a fissure in my soul that will stay with me the rest of my days.

Mallory seems to sense the minor shift in me. She considers her bloody hands a moment before wiping them with odd nonchalance on her jeans and lifting her shirt to sponge at the tears. Sipping pensively at the air, her hands find the railing and her gaze lifts again to the moon.

"There's... nothing that I can say to make you feel better." Her voice darkens only momentarily before shifting back to sympathy. "I hope it's of some comfort, though, knowing that you're with someone who understands where you are. How you feel."

"Thank you," I say, tears stringing down my cheeks and neck. I do feel comforted by her. It's the strangest feeling given our history, but it is real. I've come to know myself and the vast spectrum of misery over the last couple months. I know when something is real. It's the only truth I know in the world. "I should have seen this coming, I—"

"No. Don't." She says, swiveling toward me. Her hand finds and settles on mine, and for a moment a spark lights in parts of me that have been dark since I broke up with Elora. Her eyes are washed diamonds winking in the moonlight. "There's nothing good, nothing helpful that can come from that kind of thinking." Her voice deepens. "We're drawn to thoughts of how we could have changed things in moments like this. Don't do it to yourself."

The eye contact doesn't break, now we're probing each other for hints about what might come next. My thoughts whip me this way and that, circling reliably back to the images of my brother's lacerated arms.

The groan of the front door has me swiveling to see who'd stepped out. Mallory turns with me, contact is broken. Holly walks slowly across the bowing floorboards, every part of her seeming to sag. Though I can't see her well as she advances through the shadows, I can feel her eyes on me.

"Mark," she says. And it's all she has to say, really. Her tone tells me everything.

"Don't," I snap. I'm immediately ashamed of myself. Somehow my breathing grows even more shallow. "I already know. Ju—just *don't*. Please."

Holly halts at armlength in the darkness. I make out a slow shaking of her head. "I'm so sorry."

My attention is seized suddenly by the chaotic blue strobe of an approaching police cruiser, its lights cutting luridly through the whiffling foliage. More cops. More questions. Will they recognize who I am when I give them my name? I'm the only remaining member of a family forever carrying the mantle of my father's heroism. A mantle Mom didn't want, and I'm no more interested in adopting.

Then another thought. What if the police start to notice patterns in my life? What if they become curious about all the people dying around me. Suddenly the nightmare of prison returns, something I haven't considered since before the beach funeral. Is this what my life has become? Am I merely probing the depths of pain, ignorant to my actions?

Mallory's hand falls on my shoulder. "Don't worry," she coos as our mutual gaze holds the flashing, bobbing vehicle.

The lights of the cruiser shift to illuminate the neglected shrubbery beside the porch. My vision is a blur until I blink the latest tears free.

Mallory's hand slips into mine. Our fingers knit together unconsciously. "We'll get through this," she assures me. "Together."

i
was
born
to
die
in
that
fire

HE WAS HERE, convulsing before me, hanging in the face of Saturn as I came to, Shannon reveals. She turns her gaze to the churning chaos of our mother planet. She speaks as if separated from those moments by a length of measurable time, and somehow I know she's doing this for me. So far on this side, more is felt and intuited than *known*, and a part of me understands that time is formless to us.

I went to him, Shannon says, *somehow I was able to will myself toward him, still thinking of him as my baby. When I pried his head from his hands, he recoiled in horror, insisting that I was dead and that I shouldn't be there. He had no grasp of where he was, only that I was his mother, and his mother had just died.*

Where is he now? I ask, stretching my limited conscious, feeling across the cosmos for Walter.

On Earth. In the house we shared. He suffers in what was once his bedroom, trying to touch the souls of the living. The years have passed, faces have changed with age, and his confusion has worsened.

Please take me to him.

Not yet. You're still acclimating. She sounds broken, defeated, and a part of me wonders if I, too, will be the same in time. *First you'll meet the rest.*

The rest.

What feels like a solar wind blustering through the deepest fibers of my soul rapidly and without warning assembles itself into the form of a person. Like a shot of adrenaline to the heart, my soul flares with warm, inviting energy.

Mark, a voice speaks where the wind anthropomorphizes itself into the stout body of a young man in the prime of his life, pink flesh drawn over mountainous landscapes of muscle. The rings of Saturn arc behind him, swallowed in black where the planet eclipses the sunlight.

This man was my father.

Eric, I say. My soul is a furnace burning with the heat of this reunion. I feel my soul smile upon him. It's difficult after decades of separation to push beyond the overriding feelings from my mortal life; the long and supposedly lost pain of a child in the aftermath of his father's untimely death. It's all I can do to keep from throwing myself into his arms.

You look... learned, he says, soul smiling affectionately back.

I don't feel—

It'll all come in time, he assures me, speaking of the lesson I'd brought back with me from my prior life. I have yet to consider decompiling, not that I'd know where to begin. The fissure in my soul aches in a way that leaves this revelation feeling minor. There's a fracture in our link. Our very existence has been upended in the most catastrophic way. Even on Earth I'd felt it. So had Mallory and Kelly and Elora and Tim. We didn't realize what was happening, what had come over us, but it placed us inextricably on the same altered trajectory. One I'm certain we never intended to follow.

Is that why Mallory and I—

Come out of it, Eric urges softly. I can feel him in my thoughts, peeking into my soul in a way that is strangely sightless. It feels natural, though a part of me still clinging to my former existence feels violated. He senses this and stops. *There will be plenty of time to revisit the past. For now, enjoy this reunion. It is the only comfort that remains for us.*

That warming, they feel it too, and they're exposing me to it one at a time instead of overwhelming me as a group. I'd felt it strongly with Shannon, stronger still with Eric. The feelings will no doubt carry more weight when Kelly arrives.

What sensation awaits upon my reunion with Walt?

Eric, I say, searching a youthful face I've never known for that of my father. The guilt I've carried with me, both passed on by Mom and cultivated in the moments I'd taken advantage with the police in life, is no less potent here. *The fire at the Shipyard. There's so much I've wanted to—*

It's okay, Mark. There's no deeper meaning to be found there. It's meaningless to all but those of us who perished in that fire.

But, you... you left us behind. A twinge of resentment builds in me, something I recognize easily for its absence of consequence here, yet I'm unable to stifle it.

Eric can see it all, can apparently *feel* it all, and he moves immediately to disarm me. He's already drifting closer as I finish speaking. Lifting a hand to my chest, he presses it to my heart, and the fires in me cool as his meaning comes through.

You returned to learn about sacrifice, to build courage... I'm unable to translate the rest into words, but I understand him through the transference of emotion. Then something else. *The souls you saved are part of the same chain. Doctor Bishop and Holly the Nurse's chain.*

All as was intended. I touched their soulmates same as they touched you and Walter and Shannon, Eric says. *I was born to die in that fire, Mark. Your soul returned to Earth knowing that I would be leaving, and that was part of your lesson in pain.* Eric, too, struggles at points to translate the language of the soul, but I give him a nod. From my limited understanding, he's got my side of it just fine.

Eventually Eric drifts off, and for some time, *centuries* for all I know, I simply lie there, cradled in the ether, enjoying the warmth of the others before the watchful face of Saturn. 746 million miles away, past Jupiter and Mars and the Amor Asteroids, life on Planet Earth continues as it has for thousands of millennia. I know this because I feel it, even from here. Though the barriers of our separate dimensions stand between us, we are still able to peer into the world of the living like a one-way mirror. A part of me still latched onto that life wants to go there, to see life from this side again, but my soul urges otherwise. Now is the time to be with my soulmates, to bask in our lingering grace and harden ourselves against what we've lost.

And so we do, energy and essence flowing in open exchange as the Voice of God prattles busily along the margins of existence. For a time I try to process the unintelligible drawl, probing it for meaning, listening for anything familiar. Then, sensing we aren't meant to comprehend His words, only to know that God is there, I spare myself the trouble. We exist *within* Him, as does all life across the vast reaches of corporeal existence.

It's good to have you back with us, Mark, Shannon says at last. *The more of us on this side, the less broken we feel.*

We're going to leave you for now, Eric says. *Kelly is anxious to reunite with you.*

You can't stay? The very *idea* of their withdrawing leaves my soul feeling empty. Without their warmth I suspect the fissure will spread, dividing me in two.

Given the way the two of you parted in the last life and your current diminishing bindings to it, it's best we leave you alone. Shannon's hand falls on my shoulder. The warmth of the contact is like a current of shared euphoria. She remains the simpering voice that had guided me here. *We will be together again soon.*

Eric's hand falls on my other shoulder, kindling another fire. *Very soon.*

I turn to look at him, but he's gone. Turning back to Shannon, she is gone as well. I'm left alone, suspended in a sea of black pierced by stars that wink as if in defiance of the oblivion in which they're strung. For a moment I swear I can feel Walt. My gaze lifts over the hazy bands of gold and black circling the planet, settling upon a bright dot in the murk of space.

Earth.

Yes, I can feel Walt.

I lurch forward, eyes clenching against the sudden renewal of soul-shaking agony. I cry out, spinning forward in the empty vacuum of space only to be caught and righted by hands suddenly gripping my shoulders. Gasping, my eyes shoot open to find a familiar face. Like cracks in a window retreating back to the ding they were born of, my soul is warmed and bolstered by the most unlikely of entities given our former relationship.

You must try not to seek him out. You're not ready yet, Kelly whispers. Her face is the one I remember from college. I can't remember the name of the fraternity, though I remember the reek of pot smoke and skunked beer. I remember sighting her across the room and falling instantly in love. Or at least what I *thought* was love.

Blonde hair touches her shoulders, parted in the middle, framing her face. That athletic body she'd garbed so appropriately in form-fitting active-wear is now nude, her more *human* features dulled to the point where they barely require a look. She seems healthy, glowing in a way she never had in life. Gone is the bitter, emaciated alcoholic she was the night I watched her die.

She is strikingly beautiful.

Are you okay now? Kelly asks.

I swallow hard, a curious sensation given I have no throat. My gaze still locked with Kelly's, I nod slowly. As with the others, now that she knows I'm okay, her soul brightens with a smile, and warmth settles between us.

Your soul will try to drift toward him for some time. It's best you try to ignore the impulse. There is only pain for us on Earth. We seldom venture there. I can see in her face a crushing despair. It's as if they've abandoned Walter entirely, something with which Kelly in particular seems unable to cope. I can't help judging her, judging all of them, though a voice at the bottom of me insists I'm being naïve.

I look away, debating whether or not I should push the topic. Shannon and Eric had avoided it, but Kelly feels more open, less sculpted in her shorter time on this side. Turning back to her loving face, I feel her peer into me, sensing my observations.

He's the oldest of us, you know. He's been there and back again more than... well, most *of us.*

Walt? I ask, flabbergasted.

She nods solemnly, eyes like building storm heads.

This was to be his last life. His final lesson before Transcending... before returning to God and allowing a new soul to be born. Every part of her dims, and the darkness inks into me like black dye. Even the universe cradling us seems suddenly tarnished. *The final lesson, Transcension, is always the hardest. There's no way for us to know what drove him off track, but whatever it was, he couldn't handle it. He took his own life, now his soul is lost.*

Lost. Never before has a word hit me with such cruel gravity.

There must be a way for us to straighten him out. Get him back on track. I must sound like a babbling infant to her.

His soul is divided between two planes of existence. It would take the strongest of emotional resonance to make him whole again.

So you've given up on him?

Given up, no. We visit him, though we must do it together. With you here, the pain should be lessened.

But you've given up on him.

You don't understand, she says. There is no judgment in her, nothing that leaves me feeling dismissed for my ignorance. Perhaps it's because she's been here the shortest amount of time aside from me. I've no concept of how long it will take for me to leave my former life behind, but I'm comforted that Kelly clings to bits of hers.

Is that why she wanted to meet alone?

I want to see him. I want to see my... I stop myself before calling him my brother. He's so much more than that. I'm thinking too small. All at once my mind is driven back across the eons of my soul's existence. I've called Walter by names like Kurt, Billy, and Kilgore. And then my names return. Abby, Erin, Raney, Melanie, Ryan, Josephine, Sheila... too many to find all at once. With each of these lives I'd honed a deeper understanding of the living universe.

A deeper understanding of God.

Your soul is expanding, Kelly's voice is the softened mew of a kitten. Her grip tightens on my shoulders before falling away. My gaze locks with hers and my soul begins to weep. She floats softly alongside me and drapes an arm across my shoulders, drawing me into her depths and warming me again.

It's a lot to absorb even without a break in our chain. I remember being where you are now, after my life had reached its end. The knowledge of what we are, of where we are, comes in spurts. Some big, some small. I am here to help you through them.

Did you try to help Walter?

She hesitates, and I know why. I can feel it in her soul. She wants to spare me the hindrances she'd experienced after crossing over. The emotional transference smacks like a punch to the gut.

I did. I sat with him in what was his room, trying to draw him from the confusion with the others. We must always be together when visiting him. By the time I'd arrived, you and Mallory had already turned his bedroom into a den. I'm told that when you boxed up his things and moved them out he was particularly disturbed.

A spike of guilt stabs at a heart I must remind myself I don't truly have in this place. I remember that day. We'd left his room alone for almost five years before repurposing it. Previously, I'd spent numerous nights alone there, lying in Walter's bed and staring at the ceiling, waiting for some part of him to present itself.

There's no way you could have known, she assures me, feeling what I feel. She's silent a moment as we read each other, then continues. *I kept trying to explain to him that he was caught between worlds and that he needed to let go. He'd answer by insisting I'm not part of the family anymore and that I should get out before 'Mark gets home.' He called me – he* still *calls me Kell-Well when he's composed enough to resist… violence.*

Violence. I swallow hard, thinking about the night he'd tried to rob me. Thinking about the gun he'd wanted in life.

He was always stubborn. Somehow I'm certain he was equally stubborn in each life, I say.

Kelly's soul grins. *He was absolutely just as stubborn in each life.*

The conversation ebbs. I want to push harder, to *force* them to take me to Walt, but I know it will benefit me little. Not now anyway. The last thing my soulmates need is my fledgling grip on existence further burdening them. I'm still seeing him as my brother, still besieged by a pain first ignited the night he killed himself, threatening over the decades to extinguish the light in my soul.

I never got over Walt's death. None with us in the aftermath of his suicide recovered in any substantive way. We dug in and fortified ourselves within the confines of our mortal existence, oblivious. Mallory and I came together in a way we were never destined to in that life. We dated, then moved in together, then were married. Tim and I broke off from ReqTek and started our own tech support business, just the two of us. Kelly spiraled further into alcoholism and alone, became a recluse. Elora and I...

It was all the result of Walt's death, the break in our chain. Whatever purpose we'd had in our lives, whatever reasons we'd had to be there, had been irrevocably altered.

I had originally gone back to learn of pain and suffering. To brighten my soul through it and understand its nature.

This seems to catch Kelly off guard. She swivels away from her thoughtful study of our mother planet, its clouds lit from the interior by flashes of electric blue. She says, *It's interesting that you're already aware of this. You and I returned together for the same lesson.*

And it was ruined. I think to clarify this, to inform her that it wasn't ruined by Walt, but ruined by the situation, but she knows.

Everything was ruined.

There haven't been others? Others brought back from suicide by their soulmates?

At the mentioning of suicide that fissure in me cracks again, only to heal once more under Kelly's soft touch. Within her warmth comes a frustration she makes no effort to conceal as she answers, *We would need to convince him that he's dead, and we'd have to pinpoint exactly what drove him off the rails.*

My heart sinks. What drove him off the rails? That could be anything. Walt made nothing of himself in life. He coasted along, depending on Shannon for everything. He was a druggie and a schemer, and I struggle to see him as anything more despite his soul's obvious depth.

Shannon and I worked on him until we nearly lost ourselves.

I draw a deep, anachronous breath. *I know him better than anyone else. I'll find what we need to bring him back. Please, Kelly, take me to him.*

She pivots slowly away, gazing out at the fluidic maelstrom of agitated cloud with deep, palpable longing in her emerald eyes. Her soul drifts over to me, and she draws me into her.

I hear it when she speaks, but I'm already drifting into another *where* and *when*.

Kelly says, *We'll need the others.*

It feels wrong, clearing out his stuff. For the last five years we've done little more than bring order to the chaos and venture in for bi-yearly dustings. Now I find myself stripping the sheets from Walter's mattress while Mallory boxes up the curios occupying his closet. Long gone are the clothes and garbage that littered the floor, the glass bongs and pipes... the crusty socks. All that remains is the taxidermied bedroom of my departed brother.

But no longer.

Mallory brought up the idea a couple months ago as we spent our usual Christmas Night together in the darkness, enjoying a tree strung with hundreds of multi-colored LED lights. Sparsely decorated, each year it is a testament to our new life together, one that left behind our former misfortunes to begin anew. Even keepsake and heirloom ornaments from our previous lives were boxed and moved with reverence to the basement.

This is our life now. A new beginning. And as Mallory had so perfectly put it, it was time to make the rest of the house ours.

Coming from any other woman I'd have thought the idea selfish, but not from Mallory. She'd barely known Walt, yet his death rocked us both. At his and Mom's joint funeral, an idea so horrible that I wonder to this day why we'd agreed to it, I'd caught her crying along with me, our hands interlocked throughout.

I'd been thinking about repurposing Walt's room for years, but even as Mallory suggested it and I agreed, it felt like abandoning the last living piece of my brother. That room where he'd spent his life was an extension of his soul. To gut it felt like a violation, as if we were gutting Walter himself. It wasn't until the day after Valentine's Day, after a night of the most invigorating and restorative love Mallory and I had ever made, that I decided it was time. Time to focus on the life I had ahead of me with my wife. That room was a ghost haunting our house, and it was time for its exorcism.

"He really had a thing for lesbian porn," Mallory chuckles, drawing my attention from the mattress I'm about to lift. She looks to me with a smile that touches her glistening eyes. "Vintage stuff."

Mallory looks so cute in heart-spackled lounge pants and my red Phi Beta Kappa hoodie. Her hair, which she's grown out, is pulled back into a ponytail that swings like a pendulum across her back. I bite back against the laughter that wants to emerge, watching her struggle to determine where each oversized VHS belongs, in the *keep* boxes or the trash.

"So my brother was, what? Something of a pornography hipster?"

We laugh through the grief that always accumulates in this room, and soon we're back at work, sponging the last reminders of my brother's suicide from our lives. I insist to myself that it won't be long before I'm able to pass the door without pausing to think of him.

I grip the mattress, wrestling against its awkward bulk for a moment before peeling it off the box spring. I'm not aware of my grunting and groaning until Mallory asks if I need help. I tell her I'm fine as I flop the mattress on its side and drag it toward the door. I'm nearly out when my struggle suddenly eases. I gaze back to see Mallory there, helping me drive it out. We guide it into the hallway and toward the basement door at the edge of the kitchen. Like myriad other artifacts from our former lives, the possessions of my late brother will find their own crypt below, filed away, never truly forgotten.

We reach the basement door. I stop and meet my wife's gaze as she lifts a strand of hair over an ear. "I'll go first. Just guide it down behind me," I say.

Mallory shakes her head. A mischievous smile builds on her face. "I've got a better idea." She nods toward the door, "Open it up."

I comply, curious where she's going with this. Gripping the knob, I open the door to the basement's musted exhale. Decades of flooding have rendered the place something of a cave. The gravel floor and stone foundation add to the effect.

I leap out of the way as Mallory heaves herself into the mattress, driving it through the doorway. It catches on the first couple stairs, folding back before lurching forward, driven the rest of the way under its own weight. Turning back to Mallory, I feel my eyebrows lift. My hands come to rest upon my hips.

She smiles and puckers her lips at me. "I'm not about to risk losing my husband to a mattress. You're a lot of things, baby, but a muscle-man isn't one of them."

My mouth cracks as I make with my feeble retort, but I've got nothing, so I just nod slowly. She's got me there.

Mallory wordlessly closes the gap between us and lays her arms on my shoulders, hands out over my back. I draw her closer, my arms circling her, pawing at the *shapely* parts of her. Our lips lock and hot energy builds in my lower regions. I flex myself against her thigh, making her aware of what she's conjured.

"We've got work to do, mister," Mallory says with a smirk.

We part without further escalation.

"So we do," I agree, turning back to the basement. Peering into the darkness, I source out the mattress in the low light, crumpled against the wall at the base of the stairs. "Probably not a good idea to do that with the box spring."

Hours later, we're on the floor in Walt's empty room, drinking Guinness from the can and marveling at all we'd accomplished. The sun has set, painting the room in shades of warm twilight.

"I guess the next step is to get some new furniture," I suggest. Mallory's arm threads the space between the wall and the small of my back. My fingers fan out in her hair.

"And you wanted a big screen TV, right?" She leans in and kisses me on the cheek.

"One of the new nanite ones. I'm trying to decide where to hang it. I think it would be best to get the furniture arranged first. Just to be—"

I start as the door suddenly creaks. A similar energy runs through Mallory, now quivering as she collects herself. Gazing across the empty room, which seems so much larger now, we watch as Mouf pokes his head through the slit in the door, revealing a box in the hallway we'd neglected to lug into the basement. I feel Mallory relax against me, and my nerves calm as well.

"You little jerk," I sigh, drawing little more than a passing glance from the cat, who squeezes with difficulty through the doorway. He lets out a melodramatic yawn and stretches his front paws before strutting toward us. It's Mallory he's after. Little traitor chose her over me.

"There's Mommy's handsome boy," Mallory says in her squeaky cat voice. Mouf's eyes open and close sluggishly as he saunters over to her. His admiring gaze is broken by several impromptu stops to inspect his surroundings with that dubious look all cats have mastered. It's like he's come to inspect our work.

I reach out and scratch him on the rump, short of his elevated tail. His ears press flat to his head, eyes widening. He halts in place, licking voraciously at the air. It's the dumbest thing I've ever seen.

"Leave him alone!" Mallory cries, feigning concern. She wriggles her arm out from me and gathers fat boy in her arms. "He's just a *baby*."

"Sure," I say, taking hold of her beer and relocating it before her foot catches it. With that I upend my own, draining the rest as suddenly and without warning Mouf just loses his mind in Mallory's arms, head snapping around erratically, casting hissing, unfocused ire about the room.

"Mouf," Mallory says, alarmed. "Mouf—*ow*!" She shrieks as he bites through the fabric of her hoodie and arches back in her arms, swatting at her face. Mallory fumbles with the cat a moment before tossing him into the center of the room where he lands with the rigid posture of a corpse, back arched to its zenith, eyes continuing to dart.

I feel Mallory's eyes on me, searching for explanation, but I'm unable to pry my gaze from the cat. The growling devolves jarringly into a series of what I can only describe as low, mewling chants. His voice assumes the character of a cantankerous old woman slinging cruel words at trespassing children.

We watch, thunderstruck, as he rears up on his haunches before releasing a long, menacing growl. His head seems earless. His pupils are fully-dilated diamonds which suddenly lock onto and trace an unseen object across the front of the room.

"What's wrong with him?" Mallory asks, voice trembling.

"I... I don't know," I answer, watching Mouf's head track its invisible target toward the stained-glass lamp. "Maybe he's seeing a—"

My mouth clamps shut as Mouf lets loose a screeching howl unlike anything I've ever heard from an animal, let alone a cat. He's still screaming as he bolts out of the room, colliding with the closed door across the hall before skittering into the kitchen.

We're left dumfounded, each struggling to isolate some clue in what we'd just seen to explain Mouf. He's always been the most unconcerned cat. A mouse could run across his paws and he couldn't be bothered to give chase. This behavior is not only a first, it leaves us paralyzed, gaping at the cracked doorway in the mottled light.

I start to crack a joke, to break the silence more than anything, but I cut myself off as an intense dread kindles behind my ribs, rendering my breathing shallow. I lower my beer carefully to the carpet. Glancing at Mallory, I see she's affected similarly.

"Do you... *feel* that?" I ask, shaking my head. There's no denying the sudden presence here, drilling into us with vague designs that whisper of violent deconstruction.

"I, I think I'm going to be sick." Mallory is on all fours, then on her feet. She dashes across the room, unable to find solid traction in her sudden rush out. I'm right behind her, toppled beer cans now offering up Guinness to the carpet. I don't care about the mess. I have to get out of this room.

Unlike Mallory, I succeed in tripping over my feet and kiss the floor not once, but *twice* before reaching the hallway. There, I simply halt in place, equal parts puzzled and disturbed.

Painted light from the stained-glass lamp in Walter's room casts mottled colors upon walls once slathered in band posters and pinups, gone but for their tack marks.

My gaze settles upon the box we'd neglected, now resting at my feet with a label in Mallory's longhand reading: "Walter Nightstand."

I'd missed a lot as she'd packed things up. There are no doubt boxes in the basement at this very moment containing treasures never beheld by these eyes, and suddenly I'm left feeling like there's something else here I've yet to decode.

Crouching so that my thighs flank the box, I strip the packing tape and unfold the lid. It's almost as though the contents of the box are erased around the orange cylinders nested in the middle of it all. I lift one of them, shaking the prescription bottle. I'm shocked to hear and feel it rattle with a full complement of pills.

I pluck another from the box.

Same.

The last of them is also full. Unused.

Had Walter been... sober his final months? Maybe not *sober* in the academic sense, but was it possible he hadn't been rolling on Adderall up until the moment he took his own life?

Rotating the bottle still in my hand, I verify the date as May 2019. The others are June and July of that same year.

Had nearly every observation I'd made of Walter in the final months of his life been baseless? Had I judged him so harshly... so *needlessly*?

What was really going on with him back then?

Displaced air comes like an exhale from Walter's former bedroom... with no apparent source. The lingering dread I'd felt in that room diminishes as I drop the prescription bottle back in its box with a heavy mind. Before me is a room both dead and alive in its own right. It commands its own presence. It draws breath.

I shake my head as the sound of the toilet flushing reaches my ears. All at once the idea of Walter's ghost still occupying the room is as ludicrous as trying to find meaning in his suicide. I'd spent too many nights in that room staring up at the ceiling, grasping at the margins of this world, hoping Walter might speak.

Whatever this is, whatever now breathes on the other side of this threshold… it isn't my brother.

I glance up as Mallory exits the bathroom, running a towel across her mouth. She walks slowly toward me, leaving the bathroom light on and the door open. Her face is a case study in bewilderment.

"You don't think…" I start, but even though the words are there, they sound so preposterous I can't bring myself to finish.

"Don't go there," she says in a quivering but stern voice. "I'll have nightmares for weeks."

"No," I say, shaking my head. "There's just no way."

We don't venture back in, not that night anyway.

are you coming with me

THE DEN, I muse, a shawl of sorrow falling over me. *I remember it now. What we'd done. How we'd felt.*

Kelly listens with the bland detachment of a parent listening to her child recite the same story to no end. Beneath it all is a smile which periodically teases up her lips.

We're streaking like a pair of shooting stars through the black reaches of space. We face each another as if passengers on some invisible train barreling through the cosmos. A part of me knows there are faster, even *instantaneous* ways to get where we're headed, but that same part of me insists Kelly is taking her time intentionally. Though she seems to have given in to my wishes, now taking me to Earth, she's obviously stalling.

We told ourselves it was a bad batch of Guinness, I say. *Never drank the stuff again. But it was Walt. He was upset because we were clearing out his room.*

That kind of emotional resonance is borderline mythical, Kelly returns. *You hear the occasional story of people seeing a ghost or sensing an unseen presence that inspires the most crippling dread. More often than not it's fabricated by mortals bored of their existence... but we have confirmed cases on this side.* Kelly rotates away as a distant planet grows along our trajectory. She points at the red orb, now recognizable as Mars. *There are human beings there now,* she says.

Still clinging to my past life, I can't help a mild awe spreading over me at the sight of human structures nestled in the cratered hollows of the desert planet. It's impressive, but its novelty would hit harder with someone who hadn't seen humanity reach Mars during his lifetime. My eyes widen as the makings of man begin to deconstruct themselves as if hastily re-wound in time. In an instant I'm able to touch the margins of time, and suddenly I'm willing the clock forward, gaping at the marred face of Planet Mars as settlements of concentric circles joined by snaking lengths of umbilicus build themselves into larger structures. Only now I push time beyond the date of my death, completely arrested by the sight of humanity's sprawl and the eventual terraforming that would build an atmosphere and edge out desert hardpan with windswept grass.

The red planet is suddenly green, suddenly a world with its own lessons to impart.

You're definitely progressing well if you've learned how to warp time. Shedding our linear perception of it is among the hardest tasks we face on this side. Well done, Mark. She glances at the settlements below, now flanked by bodies of shimmering water and glowing like a terrestrial starfield.

And suddenly I'm done marveling at the makings of humanity and I'm grounded in what lay ahead. *If Walt is capable of reaching out to us on that side... he may not be completely lost,* I say.

Kelly swivels back with a face of hardened stone. *You mustn't get your hopes up... not until you see him. Then... you'll know.*

I get that you're trying to prepare me for some existential trauma, and I don't care if I sound naïve or unenlightened or whatever. This is my soulmate. You're all my soulmates. I'd never give up on any of you.

She shakes her head, *I don't think you're naïve. It's because I care so much that I don't want to see you put through this. Not yet. You've only just arrived. To have a part of you carved out and consumed... you need more time.*

You said there were others we would need.

We're going there now. You knew Shannon and Eric in our former life. There are two others you won't know immediately, though once you touch them you'll have known their souls for eons.

A part of me agrees with her, though on the whole I'm lost. She seems to sense this in a way I can feel flowing off her. Slowly, her gossamer form rotates back to our destination, now growing before us. I drift up beside her. Hands find each other, and once again that warming sensation passes between us, clearing my soul's emotional slate as Earth gains clarity in stark greens and blues. The planet grows until it is all we see.

I'd seen movies in my past life that showed space shuttles reentering Earth's atmosphere. The grating friction as they exited the vacuum of space always had them awash in chaotic flame. I brace for such an experience, shielding my face with the hand not currently holding Kelly's.

She lifts her free hand, and it finds a home on my cheek. *You've nothing to fear,* she informs me as the black of space is siphoned away beneath burgeoning baby blue. *We're on an entirely different plane. Their physics don't apply to us.* Her soul grins as wisps of cloud sweep beneath and then suddenly above us. Rising quickly toward us now is the world I know, its clock wound back to the year of my death.

All at once, we're no longer hurtling through space but plummeting toward Earth.

My stomach coils as the ground rushes up faster to meet us. Once again Kelly assures me that I have nothing to fear. She's so calm, it's like she isn't even here, like the experience is no more stimulating than waiting for her car to be serviced. Though I acknowledge this, it doesn't comfort me in the least as we streak like falling stars toward the hurried bustle below.

I'm certain I'm about to die again, atomized on I-95's southbound reach into New Hampshire.

Everything is okay. We are not governed by the physical laws of the mortals. Do you feel wind on your face? Do you smell anything in the air?

I don't, but I know I could if I wanted. I feel nothing presently but panic as autonomous cars chauffer the pampered denizens of Earth at speeds in excess of 100 M.P.H. toward errands of little cosmic consequence. Boats carve tapering pennants of wake along the hurried Piscataqua River. Insectile dots scurry in and out of buildings.

I recognize the Kittery Outlets and the three bridges that span the Piscataqua between Maine and New Hampshire. Butted up to the river's edge are the enormous structures of the Portsmouth Naval Shipyard where once a man named Eric Wells had completed his life's lesson in saving the lives of three souls. Souls whose chain apparently wove into ours during Shannon's waning days.

Blanketing it all is a fresh accumulation of snow from the nastiest Nor'easter I'd experienced since childhood. Fifty inches in two days.

This snow was falling at the moment of my death. It had, in fact, *caused* my death.

I brace myself as we hurtle toward the skeletal pegboard of hibernating trees below, into the woods off US-1. Shielding my eyes, I'm unable to banish a lifelong attention to my own mortality, and Kelly offers nothing in new assurances. She knows my adherence to the old world, to my mortal life, will pass in time. So do I, not that it helps now. And so I wait, eyes closed against a world rising swiftly to meet us.

We've arrived, Kelly says softly, a current of sadness rippling her voice.

Confused, I lower my arm to find myself facing the cottage I'd shared with Mallory, now quiet and forlorn. A drift of snow as high as the roofline leans into the siding like a wave frozen mid-break. Banks of snow from the plow form a range of white peaks along the periphery of the driveway. I'm reminded of the elaborate foxholes Walt and I would dig there as children before we were suddenly banned for life from such things.

My gaze falls to the ground, where I'm standing barefoot atop five feet of packed snow. Lifting a foot, I find not the slightest indentation, nor do I feel the bite of arctic air on bare skin. I'm naked as the day I was born, standing in the middle of a sun-kissed winter wonderland, and I don't feel even the slightest discomfort.

You see now? Kelly asks.

I nod, still mostly lost in myself as the nature of *everything* continues building in me. Swiveling back to the cottage, I take a few steps toward the front door before halting and rotating back to Kelly. *How long have I...*

Been dead? she asks.

I nod.

One week.

Have I been in space that whole time?

Space? She cocks her head playfully.

I'm not sure what you want—

You've been in the bosom of God. Her soul brightens in a way that imparts cooling comfort. *It'll come back to you.*

I turn back to the cottage, recalling suddenly what's brought us here. *Walt's inside?*

Where he's been since he took his life, she answers darkly.

My gaze lifts to leafless branches fidgeting in a wind I cannot feel. I take another step toward the cottage, then I stop again. Kelly isn't following me.

Are you coming with me? I ask, feeling suddenly like a chick about to be kicked out of the nest for its first flight.

We have to wait for the others.

I can sense her apprehension here more than ever. It conjures memories of me forcing her to attend horror movies in college. She'd go to the most exotic lengths to prove she wasn't afraid, but would produce the most elaborate excuses to bail out in the final hour. These memories feel so contrived now, nearly as intangible as the idea of a naked man occupying a snowdrift with zero sense of the cold on his skin.

Because I have no skin.

How long will they be?

Not long now.

Not long at all, comes a voice simultaneously alien and familiar. I swivel right, gaze sweeping over the thin form of a girl sauntering gracefully down the snowdrift. Auburn curls hang in tight kinks over her shoulders and chest, contrasting with the whiteness all around her. *Are you certain it's a good idea to be bringing him here so soon?*

There are very strong emotions here, Kelly answers. She comes up beside me so we're abreast as we receive the newcomer. *They were brothers in life.*

He is a brother to all of us, the woman sighs. She stops a few feet from me and looks me up and down appraisingly, her soul smiling despite her obvious frustration. *Mark. Welcome home.* She lifts her hands and places them on my shoulders, and we exchange all the warmth our souls have to offer one another. Kelly draws closer, arms enfolding us and igniting a bonfire that I feel at the core of me.

And in this moment I know who this woman is. My wife from two lives past.

Jennifer, I say, eyes closed against the worry that they'll vent my emotions for all to read.

It's nice to see you again, Mark, Jennifer says softly.

You knew me as Ryan. I breathe deeply, still prone to such things despite my evolving consciousness. *Have you been on this side the whole time?*

I'm overdue to return. I was waiting for... well. Her soul darkens. It slices through both me and Kelly. *I was waiting for Walter to return.*

I'm sorry, Jennifer. It's all I can say.

Thank you, Jennifer says. After a few moments her warmth rebuilds along with that of others as new arms enfold us. I need not look up to see whose they are. Suddenly Shannon and Eric are joined with us, their energy flowing through the chain. I feel whole in a way I'd never experienced in life.

We are but individual pieces joined as one. And so together we remain, for centuries as far as I can tell, the wind swirling snow around us that winks in the shafts of sunlight pressing through the branches above.

Are there others? I ask, feeling as though my subconscious posed the question. I'm so deeply ensconced in the others that I barely realize it's me talking.

Seven on this side, three on the other side, Kelly answers.

I open my eyes, counting the faces pressed together around me, finding only five. With Walter inside, that still left one.

Carter is always the last to join. He doesn't like coming here, Shannon says, her sadness like the black, swollen tufts of a storm head building over us. *He takes Walter's situation worse than any of us.*

The two of them bonded in almost every life. Always drawn toward one another, Jennifer reveals, soul darkening in kind. With it, the rest of us wilt like flowers beneath autumn's first frost. *When Walter returned for his final life before Transcendence, Carter wanted to go with him, but Walter insisted on doing it alone, convinced his final lesson was just for him.*

The fissure in my soul vibrates painfully with this revelation. I feel it in the others as well.

He believes Walter's suicide was his fault. Because he wasn't there. Kelly's voice is heavy with emotion.

I can't help trying to stretch my soul to glance back over my past lives. I'm left certain of a single constant, that Elora and I had come together in almost every life just as Carter and Walter had. I'm not certain if Mallory and I have ever been romantically involved prior to our last life, but now that I understand how Walter's suicide altered the intended progressions of our lives, slivers of my time with Mallory begin to make more sense. What feelings I had left for her when I'd died remain with me, as do my secrets, though the imperceptible passage of time on this side has rendered them artificial now.

Are we really going to subject ourselves to this again? comes a grumbling voice that can only be Carter's. It's as abrasive as it is resentful, as if a sound itself could somehow wear a scar. I look to the snaking driveway and the treeline blotting out the main road. From between a pair of leafless oak trees emerges a slender, toned man with dirty-brown hair. His face is a sharp pennant, chin tapering to a pronounced divot.

Mark has returned to the fold, Shannon says. Our formation separates, contact is broken, and with it goes nearly all of the warmth.

Carter emerges from the trees and stalks toward us. His eyes run coldly over me. This attitude, his lack of warmth, is a drastic departure from the afterlife I've come to know, from the people I've reunited with here. As he sidles past me, I'm relieved that he doesn't reach out and touch me. I don't want any part of him on or in my soul. Our eyes meet for the briefest of moments before I redirect mine submissively to the snowy ground.

Have a little respect, please, Shannon growls as Carter edges through the group. He ignores her, walking to the lip of the porch. His back to us, he lowers his hands to the splintered railing and leans forward, peering into the darkness cast by the snow-dusted overhang.

We all stand waiting, watching, as Carter does... whatever it is he's doing. Centering himself, I suspect, but I can't be certain. Of my soulmates, his is a soul I feel incapable of understanding. Not through any form of divine intuition.

His name is familiar to me though. Familiar in a way I can't place.

Let's get this over with, Carter says at last, shoulders slumping in resignation. *Let's have Mark's spirit crushed and return to our purposeless existence.*

Carter—

Let's just get it over with! he barks, interrupting Jennifer with a voice so powerful it seems to rattle the framework of existence. I'm left feeling more repulsed than before. To see such a... *human* exchange between my soulmates feels unnatural. My soul ripples against it as I watch Carter ascend the porch steps. The others follow silently, each glancing backward to confirm I'm with them. Though I remain watching a moment, unsure if I've made the right decision in pushing to be brought here, eventually my feet set me moving toward the cottage.

As I reach the snow-caked front steps, a sense of deja-vu fuzzes through me. I've only been away from this place a week, I know this, yet my limited understanding of time on this side leaves me feeling like I've been away for both years and hours. It's unsettling, like vertigo born of a memory. I force myself along, trying to clear my thoughts.

This will feel a little strange, Kelly warns as I reach the closed front door. Carter and Eric have disappeared while I was distracted. Shannon, Kelly, and Jennifer remain with me on the porch. Shannon glances over her shoulder at Kelly, nodding before returning her attention to me. Her soul smiles as she extends her hand *through* the door, then, without a word, slips through the barrier and into the house.

Whoa, I gasp, calling up movies I'd seen depicting ghosts passing through walls as though they were porous. Apparently there is some truth in mortal fiction.

Try not to think about it, Jennifer says. *These barriers can be very real to us if we want them to be, but it's all in how we allow ourselves to interact with them.* She slips past Kelly toward the edge of the porch. Her eyes on mine, she leans back against the railing, allowing it to support her, and I swear for a second I see it shift against her weight. *Everything here is as real or artificial as we want it to be.* Now she steps away from the railing, lowering her hand *through* it. She lifts it up and down through the rotted, snow-glazed wood a few more times. *You're in control,* she says, pivoting back to the house, walking across the porch, and vanishing inside.

I look to Kelly, who gestures toward the threshold. *You first.*

Drawing a deep breath of nothing, I step reluctantly toward the door and lift a hand toward it. The Welcome sign Mallory and I had hung there with birds perched upon each letter rattles in the wind.

I touch a firm, plainly physical door.

You're still rooted in that side of existence… its corporeal limitations. Think about how we arrived here, falling through the atmosphere. We touched down without a scratch because the laws of their world don't apply to us. She steps closer, a hand falling gently on my shoulder. Her warmth probes my soul to its bottommost depths. I'm so lost in it that her free hand pressing mine against the door draws me suddenly back to the task at hand. With a thin, roguish smile, she pushes her hand *through* mine and *through* the door.

I don't know if it's my contact with her or a burst of divine understanding, but my hand follows hers through the wood, swallowed up to my forearm. I have little time to react as she guides me through, eyes closed. When I open them I'm in the mud room and subject to the curious, assessing looks of the others, watching my progress like parents witnessing a toddler's first steps. My hands move instinctively to my chest as two familiar presences tickle the margins of my soul. The weaker of the two is most definitely Mallory. Her sorrow is raw and palpable, it trembles my soul. The stronger of the two, well that nearly drives me to my knees under a sudden, oppressive agony exploding in me.

Walter.

I'm caught by multiple hands. The energy from my soulmates is like a lighthouse burning valiantly into the night, granting me strength as it heals. The darkness of Walt's madness is already bleeding through our collective warmth. Gazing up at my soulmates, I'm greeted by faces contorted with every imaginable expression of grief.

Kelly leans down, *You don't have to do this now. It can wait.* I can tell a large part of her wants me to call it off.

I shake my head. *No. I need to see him.*

Kelly looks to the others, then back to me. Her face is hard and cold. *Okay. Let's do it then.*

We walk daisy-chained down the hallway and into the kitchen. The lights are all out. The dishes are washed and drying in the rack beside the sink. Scattered among vases of lily and rose arrangements are condolence cards that no doubt bear my name.

I swivel away, further unsettled by the presence of artifacts corroborating my death. And then I see her.

Mallory, I gasp, forgetting everything and breaking the chain as I make for the living room. The immediate weight of Walter's insanity collapses upon me, driving me back to my knees after only a pair of steps. My gaze stays on Mallory as I'm buoyed on the pain.

Moments later I feel the hands of my soulmates fall upon me once more, and the agony shrinks against their warmth.

I'm panting, and a part of me is embarrassed by it since I have no lungs with which to draw breath, but I'm unable to control it. Just as I'm unable to control my gaze anchoring itself on Mallory, asleep in the recliner, as I ride out the rest of the dark. Her hair is a frizzy mess of silvered chestnut drifting over her chest and shoulders. Crumpled tissues garnish the floor around her. Her cheeks are flushed, swollen from the tears.

I died… unexpectedly, I muse.

It was an accident, Shannon says from behind me. She continues as I'm aided to my feet. *You were crushed by a roof that collapsed under all this snow.*

I'm having difficulty remembering it.

It'll come in time.

What reason would I have had to leave her like this? To check out when I did? There has to be a reason, right? There has *to be.*

There's no way to know just yet. You were set on new trajectories the moment Walter killed himself. Perhaps even sooner…

I step hesitantly toward Mallory, moving with deliberation so the others stay with me. It's not long before I halt, evaluating the pain I've left her in with a roiling stomach. *That's two husbands she lost before their time. Hers is a world of suffering. It breaks my heart.*

Her world was never supposed to be yours to share, Kelly says softly.

For a moment I worry that Mallory might do something drastic, kill herself like Walt had, but then I remember just what kind of woman she is, always stronger than me.

Most are. I'm a coward.

She'll be okay, Eric speaks from behind us. *We've been looking in on her.*

I find that difficult to believe. It's obvious they go out of their way to avoid this place. A part of me understands why, but it's not enough to keep a seed of contempt from planting itself in me. But I say nothing. I still have much to learn.

It's difficult for me to do, but somehow I'm able to turn away from Mallory and back toward the others, now spaced across the living room and strung by hand in a spiritual lifeline. In the archway at the head of them is Carter, who says nothing. He simply gazes at me with those cold, piercing eyes. For a moment I sense resentment in him, I'm certain of it, but the moment doesn't last long enough for me to be certain.

Sensing our time with Mallory reaching its close, Carter swivels without a word and starts us down the hallway toward Walt's bedroom-turned-den. What I at first mistake for the dull, muffled sound of the television behind Walter's closed door quickly assumes the frantic yet recognizable cadence of my brother's screaming voice. The words are unintelligible, but I don't require substance to feel each syllable stab into me like an eight-inch switchblade. As Carter reaches the door and pauses there, I realize with crippling certainty that I'm listening to the inane prattling of a mind out-of-sync with its own existence.

Are you certain you want this? Carter asks, seeming to seek the same *out* Kelly originally sought. When I shake my head, he does the same, his shoulders drooping. *Like you understand well enough to make the right decision anyway.* His voice deepens, *But you'll understand soon. By the end of it you'll be begging us—*

That's enough, Kelly snaps, her disgust with Carter rocking the chain.

Carter shakes his head, saying nothing, vanishing through the door with a slackened expression of defeat. The others are shunted in like a train vanishing into a tunnel. I am the last one in line. Every step I take toward the door is like gasoline on the fires of dread in me, but I press on. I must see my brother.

After decades suffering, swept along in the wake of his suicide, I need this right now. Yet as I'm tugged through the doorway I find myself drifting elsewhere...

It's been years since we gutted Walt's room, moved in our separate recliners, and mounted a ninety-inch nanite display television. The events of that first night with Mouf, when we'd fled the room under a veil of confusion and dread, seemed a one-shot occurrence. We've nearly forgotten it entirely, having installed carbon monoxide detectors throughout the house to warn against what we blamed on seeping vapors from the basement. Maybe a bad batch of Guinness.

On nights where my mind is preoccupied with thoughts of my brother, when I struggle desperately for the calm of sleep, I sometimes slip quietly out of bed and venture into his bedroom where I sit alone in the darkness. I whisper aloud to myself, to Walt, imploring him to materialize and assure me he's okay, that he's found the peace in death that had eluded him in life.

But he never answers. The feelings felt that night two years ago haven't returned. I'm just a depressed lunatic, sitting alone in my dead brother's room, talking to myself.

"Mark?"

The door creaks, snapping me out of a dreamlike half-in-half-out state. I'm cross-legged on the floor beneath the window, chin touching my chest as I doze. Peering up, I see Mallory's silhouette animated in the darkness as she steps into the room.

"Down here," I answer, breathing shallowly.

She says nothing as she seeks me out in the darkness. With careful deliberation she rounds the recliners and baby-steps closer. With her hand running along the windowsill, she settles beside me, head coming to rest on my shoulder.

"It's been a while since I've found you in here," she whispers, her voice still crackly with sleep. She nuzzles against me, her hand seeking mine out in the black. Our fingers interlace.

"Some days it hits me worse than others," I sigh, threading my arm between the small of her back and the wall. The other finds and grips her thigh gently. "Not sure I'll ever get over it. I was such a judgmental ass to him while he was alive. Not much of a brother." I breathe deeply, feeling her rise and fall with my swelling chest. "I should have seen the signs. I should have—"

"Shhhh," Mallory coos, a hand running up my chest and to my cheek. She guides me toward her and we kiss. "We've been through this. There's nothing you could have done. It's going on eight years now. You need to let go before this consumes you."

Strong words from someone I know still thinks of that night; someone equally impacted, and probably struggling with equal frustration to understand it. But I don't say this to her. I'd never say this to her. Instead, I continue to feel bad for myself.

"He wanted to buy a gun. That was my red flag, but I ignored it. I ignored it because..." I stop with Elora's name perched on my tongue. Hers is a name I've never uttered around Mallory. It's not that I'm hiding anything, I haven't spoken to Elora since North Conway, now eight years behind me. There's just never been a reason to bring her up. Like Walter, though, I think about her every day.

"Baby, maybe it's..." she trails off, obviously rethinking what she was about to say. Anxiety flexes against my ribs for I know exactly where she was going. It's something I've considered for a few years now.

"Maybe it's time I get some professional help?" I ask, feeling her hand tighten over mine.

"It isn't a sign of weakness to admit you have a problem. Your heart is too big. You care too much to let go. I've tried to be here for you, I've wanted to be the one to help you manage the pain you carry... but I don't think I have everything you need." She nuzzles some more and lifts my hand, planting kisses along my knuckles.

"I'm not sure there's anything anyone can do."

We remain there for some time, digesting it all. There's really nowhere else for the conversation to go. I'm broken, she knows it, I know it. We came together eight years ago in the aftermath of the greatest tragedies of our lives, and now here we are, still struggling to fill the holes in us. A part of me wonders if we've just been in shock all these years, that things might suddenly erode between us as they had between me and Kelly.

Kelly. Now there's someone I haven't thought about in a while. After the divorce was finalized and a sizable chunk of my income allotted to her, we sold the house and she moved north to Twisted Oak, Maine. When I'd seen her on that final court date she looked unwoven, haggard, her formerly trim and athletic body now wiry and gaunt. I think she was drunk then, too. She looked like a person who'd been cannibalizing herself, allowing her vices to seize control in ways they couldn't when I'd been around.

Despite everything she'd put me through, I couldn't help feeling bad for her.

"I have to get back to bed. Got an early shift tomorrow." Mallory pumps my hand a couple times before kissing me once more on the cheek.

"Goodnight," I say, finding her lips in the dark. The spark that was there between us in the early years is long gone, but she's still the best friend I've ever had. We connect on a different level that still feels odd considering the circumstances around how we met. "Thanks for sitting with me."

"You have anything going on tomorrow?"

Tomorrow. Saturday. "No, probably just going to read and putter around the house."

"Something tells me you'll be sleeping most of the day."

I grin, "You're probably right."

"Well, that's okay." Her smile touches her voice in a way that reinforces just how fortunate I am to have someone so genuine in my life.

"You're the hardest working man I've ever known. And you carry a great burden with you. You deserve a lazy day."

"Thanks, baby."

"Goodnight."

"Goodnight." I watch her cross the room, walking unguarded against objects in the dark. She steps into the hallway where I hear Mouf propositioning her with a lazy mew, as if saying, *get back to bed with me*. Mallory mumbles unintelligibly at the cat, the bedroom door closes, and I'm left alone once more in my brother's room.

"Oh, Walt," I whisper. "What have you done to me?"

now you will understand

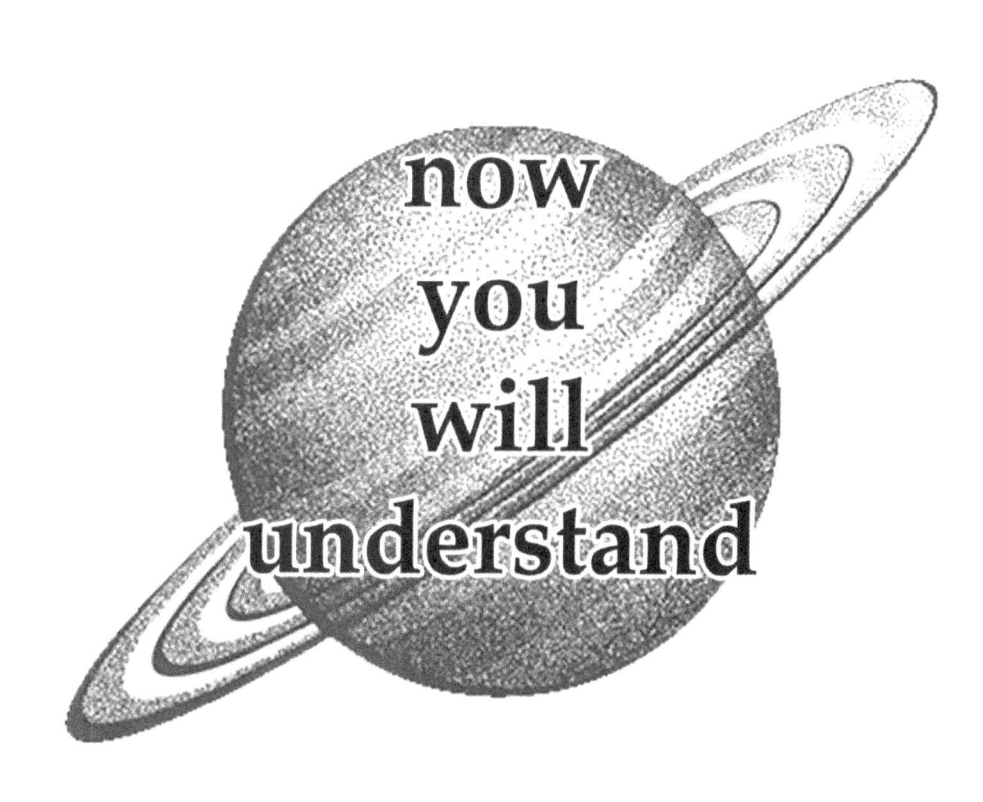

THE SENSATION SMACKS like a buffeting wind as I pass through the door, nearly driving me back with its raw, chaotic power. I'm anchored to Kelly, and our eyes meet, hers teeming with near-electric distress, mine no doubt flaring with wild panic.

I gaze past her at the others, still strung hand-in-hand in an arching formation. A barrier against what lay at the front of the room.

Walter. I can feel him. The emotions that ravage him are the turbulent bluster of a hurricane. The roar of his soul hits me like a speeding car, opening microfractures along the periphery of the rift he's carved in me.

Kelly, I—

Focus on us! Kelly roars through the din. *Draw from us or you'll lose yourself in this place!*

I'm in over my head. I realize this now. How very stupid, how very *mortal* it was for me to have insisted they bring me here. I clearly should have adhered to their warnings. As wave after wave of violent thought crashes upon me, threaded with the fraying tatters of my brother's lost soul, I feel the fissure in me widen.

I—gah! I gasp, collapsing to my knees. Squinting against a fresh squall of insane energy that trembles every part of me, I see Jennifer leading Shannon toward me, and she takes my other hand.

Any better? Shannon asks, leaning over me. I look up, watching her as she watches me, inspecting her as she inspects me. I see the same unease I'd observed in Kelly, but nothing that suggests we'll suffer permanent damage here. The chaos is lessened now that both of my hands are held.

I nod, swallowing hard and heaving myself to my feet. With a hand in each of mine, I move toward the gap opened by Jennifer's backtracking. Driving myself forward, I brace against the tear still opening in my soul, doing my best to draw from my soulmates and harden myself.

Walter! I cry into the swirling maelstrom. At the front of the room is my brother, huddled in the corner and clawing furiously at the floor and wall like a feral animal ferreting prey. He's exactly as I remember him, blonde curls, thin frame, but he also has an aged, *broken* character to him. He is completely nude, crouched on the balls of his feet as he works at the wall where his bed one sat.

Even if he hears you it won't matter, Carter informs me. I make no point to look at him, to validate what he's said. I don't acknowledge I've even heard him at all. Instead I press brazenly closer to Walter, stepping up to the rightmost recliner where I'd spent most of my nights reading.

Walt! It's me, Mark! I'm shouting into a storm, but for a moment Walter pauses with a rigid air of cognition, his hands lifting away from the wall. I swallow hard, preparing for the worst.

In an instant Walter splits into two identical copies of himself. One resumes scratching at the wall while the other whirls jerkily toward me, head snapping around, eyes sweeping the room before finding me again. They burn with a madness I swear I can *taste*.

Recoiling a few steps, I'm nearly stultified by the madness spilling from his gaze. Glancing back to the other Walter, still busy in the corner while leashed to his counterpart on some translucent, spiritual tether, my attention returns to his doppelganger, eyes flitting up and down me, seeming barely aware of even himself.

He only recognizes a part of you, Carter informs me. This time I turn to look at him, noting how closely he's watching this carbon copy of the man he'd loved across countless lives. The desolation built upon his face has a presence of its own. His heartbreak inks through the chain like black dye in water. *Not much of what you say will make sense to him.*

I rotate back to my brother, thoroughly alarmed as his body suddenly tenses, fingers curling into fists that pound absent-mindedly at his sides. He stands watching me with the eyes of a wild dog poised to eviscerate.

He takes a couple shuffling steps toward me, seeming momentarily unsure of his ability to walk.

Will he hurt me? I ask of the group.

You have no body, Carter answers.

Will he attack me?

Almost certainly.

I swallow hard, wanting to run, but I'm frozen in place. I can feel the others's pain as our emotions pool. They feel what I feel, yet they won't let me retreat. I'm being made to face the situation I'd demanded, and as the chaos of Walter's fragmented soul divides the very air before me, I feel my hope flee.

Walter. Walt, I—I... My stuttering speech seems only to add to his confusion. His eyes narrow at me, overflowing with hatred over tightly pursed lips. The other continues to dig at the wall behind him.

Please, Walt. Don't you recognize me? It's—

Mark! He cries out, rushing at me, clawing fitfully at the air. His gaping mouth reminds me of an animal poised to feed. A violent, insatiable hunger exists in him.

I try to push backward, but I'm held in place.

Please! I cry, pushing back against the others, fumbling at the hands clutching me. *What are you—let me go!*

You came here to understand, Carter's voice speaks softly, somehow finding its way through the din. *Now you will understand.*

I clench my eyes shut as Walt springs suddenly. His soul passes through me, blackening all of me. Lurching forward, eyes snapping open, I'm stripped of all feeling, all emotion, save for the suffering and confusion my brother has imparted. Nothing else exists.

Gah! I shriek as he passes through me again, falling to the floor in a clawing dive. His body lurches and writhes unnaturally in his scramble to pick himself back up. I swallow back on what feels like impending vomit, something a more ancient part of me likens to carving off a piece of my soul and leaving it here on the floor.

Walter rolls over, face twisted. His glaring eyes source me out in furious confusion, finding me as he heaves himself onto all fours and then his feet. My gaze follows, seeing in him the frustration that's plagued him since the blade of a razor passed over his flesh. His nostrils flare, lips curl, and his mouth drops open as Walter lets loose a scream that shakes every part of me. He finds words within the unintelligible drawl washing us in his madness.

You took it! You took it all! All my stuff! My work! How dare you?!
Walt... I... I didn't realize you—

His teeth gnashing, Walter springs at me again, passing through my soul and leaving me with the understanding that another pass will be the end of today's lesson, one way or another. The rift in me broadens, then begins to mend itself in the same space of microseconds.

Please, I gasp, searching for Kelly and finding a face doused in pity but unflinching in its charge to keep me here.

It's for your own good, Shannon says as Walter passes through me once more, reopening the fissure like an earthquake sundering desert hardpan. Shannon's bracing hand tightens around my arm. *Look*, she says, directing my attention to the unanchored piece of Walter now struggling up from the floor, sweeping the room with manic eyes. *He's already lost us. It's almost over.*

I watch him, trying to draw from my soulmates's warmth and apply it like a Band-Aid to the cuts Walt has left in me. Their souls flex toward me, flowing with love, and my gaze stays on my late brother, now blurring in a cyclonic frenzy. He releases a horrible, soul-shaking scream.

My soulmates tremble beside me as Walt's insanity swells, working to consume us all. I'm unable to tear my gaze from this warped version of him, which suddenly goes still. A tremor works itself through his body, then one of his arms snaps sickeningly back toward the Walt still clawing at the floor. Were his soul a construct of blood and bone, the arm would have snapped clean at the shoulder. It's followed by a similar gravitational seizing of the other arm, and his body is reeled jarringly backward.

Its force reminds me of a black hole, its gravity absolute and inescapable. And like light casually siphoned from a dying star, Walter is drawn screaming back toward his counterpart.

It's almost over, Shannon repeats, seeming for herself as much as anyone.

I tip forward, energy waning, attention seized by the merging pieces of my brother. *Is it over?* I ask, pleading. *Can we be done with this, please?* I clench my eyes shut, unable to look on any longer.

Yes, Kelly responds.

And all at once the storm ceases. I open my eyes to find myself on my back, gazing up into the emerald flutter of a great oak tree. The sun peeks through the beating foliage, and I blink against the light, struggling in the sudden quiet to banish the storm still winding down in me.

It's okay. Kelly's voice is easy, soothing. Her hand presses to my chest, warming my soul and mending the damage left by Walt.

It's just the two of us, I cannot feel the others. I'm also mildly aware of a sizable gap in space and time, a tickling sensation that tells me it's been years since we were in that room.

Leaning forward, I angle my head for a look around, my gaze eventually sharpening on an aged scar cut diagonally across the trunk of this tree. Cut just at the height of a Suburu Forester bumper, I'll add.

This was where Kelly had died.

I lose consciousness.

What feels like my eyes fluttering open is, I know, really just my soul emerging from sleep. Above me is the same tree, its branches still waving in the sunlight as a warm, westering wind carries leaves clattering across the sunbaked pavement at my feet. I struggle to sit up, to prop myself against the tree as my soul continues to stitch itself together.

Kelly.

I'm here, Kelly whispers, feeling my thoughts. Gentle hands grip me by the shoulder and arm, easing me back. I come to see her there, kneeling beside me, soul smiling.

How long...?

Time is relative.

Yes. Relatively vague perhaps.

The others? I ask.

Elsewhere... and everywhere, she whispers, smiling harder. *Distance is—*

Relative as well, I interrupt. *It's coming back to me in spurts.*

That's perfectly normal. I'm sure a lot more of this is starting to make sense to you now.

I gaze beyond her at a wending road, one I used every day on the way home from work. The trees are alive with the season, green and verdant. Above, not a single cloud dares cross the midday sun.

Looking back to Kelly, her blonde hair framing her face, my soul smiles, and I say, *A lot more than before, but there's still a lot to come.* Images of Walter's odd mitosis, of him attempting to tear me apart in the den, spring to mind. I can't help shivering at the recent memory as my soul momentarily darkens. *And some things I know I've never dealt with before.*

It gets easier. The next time you go to him he's likely to be more receptive to you, but don't let that give you false hope. He's still given to moments of violent confusion. He may try to attack you again. Her voice gathers weight as she speaks, not with loss of hope or courage, but with naked sincerity, with the insistence that I adhere to her every word. *It is absolutely critical that you never visit him alone. Not ever.*

Why? I ask, though I'm certain I already know the answer.

Because his madness might spread to you. You've no doubt felt it, that tearing in your soul. If you were to go to him alone, without the rest of us to bolster you... well, that tear could divide you... just like him.

What have you tried so far? To, you know, bring him out of it.

Kelly says, *Words alone won't do it. We can only make him aware of his state on a lower level, and it doesn't last beyond each visit. More direct actions were taken after you switched his room over to a den. He was so violent and confused that day that the others attempted to heal him through direct contact. It tore through our chain like a current of electricity... they barely made it out.*

We felt him that day, I add, *Mallory and I.*

As you've said, but that just... it's almost impossible. She searches my soul for understanding.

We both had to run out of that room. She vomited, I nearly passed out.

You truly believe you were able to feel him that strongly on your side? She seems almost to believe me.

Oh, yes. We never felt it like that again. Afterward I'd spent many sleepless nights in that room, trying to evoke him. It all makes sense now.

Kelly chews this over a moment. I can feel her soul thumbing back through the pages of her own vast existence. *You speak the truth, I can feel it in you, but this type of transference... I'm trying to think of how I might define it on this side. Think of it in terms of how some mortals view faith healing – difficult, if not impossible, to substantiate.*

Could it mean that there's hope for him? That our bond is stronger than anything we've seen yet on this side?

Her eyes close. I feel her soul palpitate as she opens herself to the penetrating whisper of God. *Only God knows*, she sighs.

I try to mimic her a moment, but end up feeling silly and stupid in short order. When I open my eyes Kelly is grinning.

You'll get it in time.

So I've been told... about many things.

Kelly's gaze lifts to the tree shading us.

You recognized this place before you lost consciousness. I felt it in you. She doesn't seem the least bit put off revisiting the site of her death. To my knowledge, it's she who brought us here.

Yes, I nod, angling my head for a better look at the trunk. The healed scarring where her bumper had struck the tree is like a pair of pursed wooden lips. It's still recognizable to those of us who remember what happened here, but for uninitiated passersby it's easily overlooked as an overachieving knot.

You were the last living person I saw in that life, Kelly says, smiling. *You sat with me, comforted me as I transitioned. I know that we hated each then – the excesses of human emotion, how pitiable – but I remember being glad you were with me.*

I thought you were already gone by the time I got there. I'm recalling more now. I feel my soul reaching across time to the final moments we'd shared here. *Your death reignited the pain I'd felt before Mom and Walt's deaths. I thought that Mallory purged it, and for a while I think she did, but even though my life skewed off course with Walt's suicide, it seems I was still on Earth to learn of pain... of suffering.*

Through cosmic intuition you grew closer to those who remained after Walter.

My mind shifts to Elora and the love that's seen us through every life. I think of Mallory, how I'd wronged her, how I've carried the secrets I'd kept from her to my grave.

Don't get too hung up on the events of your last life, Kelly says. *If you took anything meaningful from it, those lessons are with you even if they aren't obvious now. It is here you will come to understand them. Your dealings with others, mistakes you've made... secrets you've kept... none of them matter. Not then, not now.*

But I can't help myself dialing the world back, returning to the moment when things went bad again. Thanksgiving night, ten years after Kelly and I signed our divorce papers, my ex-wife showed up at my house uninvited for the final time.

I see tail lights through the trees ahead, a car off the road, headlamps askew as they wash undulating waves of newly fallen snow. That sinking feeling in my stomach intensifies and that all familiar weight settles on my chest. My knuckles grow white upon the steering wheel and my foot falls heavily upon the accelerator.

She did it. She actually did it.

"My God, Mark. We shouldn't have let her drive out of there," Mallory says, her voice deep and watery. She leans forward in the passenger seat, elbows on her knees, hands together, fingers laced up as though praying.

Swallowing hard, I unbutton the collar of my violet dress shirt, feeling strangely overdressed for what awaits. I apply the brakes, feeling the pedal shudder, wheels skidding over a patch of black ice. Pumping the brakes as all New Englanders have mastered prior to dropping out of the womb, I coast to a slow stop on the shoulder of the road, my headlights holding the dusted chrome of a black Forester.

I throw the car into Park and hit my hazards. Mallory is already dialing 9-1-1 in the passenger seat. Unbuckling my seatbelt, I step out onto snow-crusted gravel and advance up the shoulder toward the slanted wreck. The cold bites at my face, and I realize I've forgotten my jacket in the rush out the door. Such is the case when your ex-wife calls from the road to inform you she's about to end her life and it's all your fault. Minutes earlier she'd shown up on our doorstep as we ate pumpkin pie in the den. She was stinking drunk and disheveled, a wraith plucked straight out of a horror movie. In a torrent of curse-laden slurs, she informed me that I've ruined her life, and it's somehow my fault that she has no one with whom to spend Thanksgiving.

In my mind I can see how she reached this point, sitting alone at home under constant siege from her own bullying mind. I should have helped her. I should have tried to get her into a program long ago, but such things are difficult when your interactions are only ever heated and you never really see each other to begin with. Would she have listened to me? What kind of impact could I have expected to make with a one-man intervention?

Through snow deep as my knees, I slog my way urgently toward the car. Judging by the erratic treads in the snow, she seems to have swerved after losing control rather than deliberately hitting the tree. Her front tires are cut all the way to the left and will turn no more. She'd probably lost control on the same patch of black ice I'd encountered in the road.

I don't spend time pondering this as I'm suddenly peering into the driver's side window, hand already gripping the doorhandle. I haul the door open to the shattered form of a woman I'd fallen for at a UNH frat party. She's crushed against the steering wheel, blood oozing from her nose and puddling on the dash. Her hands grip the wheel with that rigid posture of lost control. Glazed eyes are engaged in a pensive study of the alcohol nips strewn about the floor.

"Kelly!" I gasp, pushing myself as far into the car as I can. In the light cast by my headlamps I see the spider's web of cracks in the windshield from where her head smashed into it. My logical side tells me not to move her, but I just can't leave her like this. I slip my hand beneath her chin before easing her back against the seat, every part of her feeling sickly disassembled beneath her skin.

"Don't move her!" Mallory cries, rushing through the snow after me. It's too late. I've already propped her back against the headrest, my cheeks wet with tears that catch winter's insufferable bite. Kelly's wide, lifeless eyes stare into mine. Her face is streaked with blood from the impact wound at her widow's peak, currently spilling fresh runners of blood down her nose and cheeks.

My jaw trembles as if I'm freezing to death. The rest of my body quickly follows suit. I'm vaguely aware of my feet carrying me backward, away from the car. Kelly's eyes stay with me as I retreat, face blank, expressionless.

Dead.

Something catches on my heel. My arms flail for something to take hold of, but there's nothing, and I fall backward into the snow in a plume of powder that eddies in the light cast by my headlamps. It settles quickly, nibbling at my face and hands, slipping into my shirt and biting at my skin.

I push myself up, hands already numbing from the snow. My attention drifts back to the car where Mallory is hunched over Kelly, hands working frantically toward some hopeless end.

We've been here before, and I know this story well.

The wind blasts through the trees, buffeting us in a mist of snow that tosses Kelly's hair before glazed, lifeless eyes. In the distance I hear the first siren crying out, followed by the long blare of a firetruck horn. Too many times in this life have I been forced to endure these scenarios. As I kneel in the snow, tears icing on my cheeks, I can't help giving in and breaking down entirely to the cold; to the death of a woman I once thought I'd loved; to the cruel world that bore me.

I need to draw strength from something before I'm crushed by it all. I look to Mallory, still engaged with Kelly, but there is nothing there, no real love anymore. Just companionship.

Reaching into the deepest part of me, I try to seize upon something, *anything* that might grant me the will to endure, to continue on with this wholly unfulfilling life.

All that wants to come as I sit there, grappling with *everything*, is Elora's face.

he'd
do
the
same
for
any
of
us

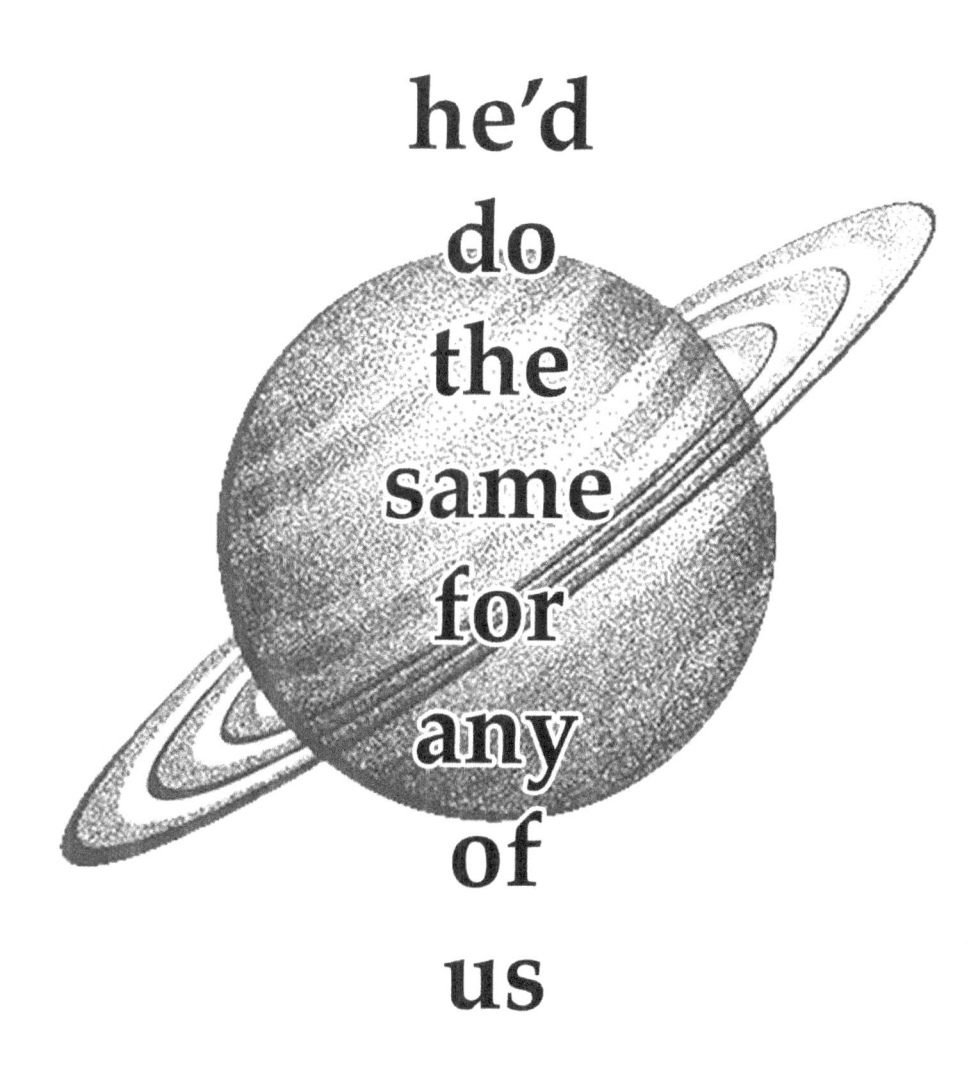

YOU WEREN'T A suicide, I say, a part of me still returning from that snowy roadside. I realize I'm pacing the shoulder and wonder how long I've been gone, assuming I was ever truly gone at all.

I lost control of the car when I called you. The road was icy, I was drunk. She speaks dryly, as if none of this matters, and in a way it doesn't.

I try to imagine what my group of souls would be reduced to under two suicides. *I think you might have corrected my course, or, well, at least pointed me back,* I say. *There was no altering things already set in motion, but you certainly brought me to a fork in the proverbial road.*

Kelly glides toward the tree, saying nothing, hand tracing the lips of the scar she'd left there.

For someone so set against venturing into the past, you certainly seem sentimental about this place. I walk toward her, halting as she swivels back to face me.

We are far from perfect, even on this side, she says. *We're taught to adhere to certain principles, certain rules as we approach Transcendence, but only God is perfect, Mark. Even the oldest of us struggle sometimes letting go.*

I close the gap between us and take her hands. Warmth blossoms between us, and for a moment we enjoy it in silence before once more I'm compelled deep inside me to continue plodding against the current. *Have you considered that these principles and rules are what's holding us back from saving Walt? Why can't we try thinking outside the box? If we're destined to stew here for all time with no hope of going back or returning to God, I see no reason why we shouldn't give everything we've got to save Walt.*

Her face flashes curiosity. Have I reached her on some level?

What exactly are you suggesting? she asks.

I'm not sure just yet. I know that the answer is out there somewhere, perhaps buried in my last life. I just need to find it.

She turns back to the tree, speaking reverently to the scar she'd left there. *I can't promise you the others will be willing to make this kind of sacrifice. I'm not even sure if I can do it, Mark. But if you can come up with something plausible... something worth the risk of losing ourselves along with him... I'll help you.*

I'll find something. I won't spend the rest of eternity stuck here while he toils away in my damned den. I'd rather join him and be done with it than wander the cosmos for eternity with my guilt.

She turns back to me, inspired. For the first time since I've arrived here I feel as if I'm finally making a real contribution.

I know he'd do the same for any of us, I say.

He would, she agrees. *You still have much to learn, Mark, but I'm with you on this. Do whatever soul searching you must, leaf through the pages of your past life, but know this – the longer you stay on this side, the more trivial that life will seem. If you think the answers are there, you must find them quickly.*

I understand.

You've recovered enough from the experience with Walter. I'll leave you to your thoughts. Remember: there are no boundaries for you here. You can be wherever and whenever you want. It's as simple as willing yourself there. She offers an impish grin, no doubt amused as she reads the apprehension in me. *Try not to overthink it.*

Thank you, I return. A part of me is embarrassed I'd even take *this long* to come around.

You're welcome. She closes the gap between us and draws me into her. I feel her warmth once more, and she feels mine, until all at once she's gone and I'm all alone, nude, pacing the road shoulder... thinking about Elora...

"We are Staple You Shut, and we're here to rock you *stupid*!" Elora can't contain the laughter that explodes from her. Heads sprout over high-backed booths throughout the diner. Staff at the bar and cash register gaze at us along with line cooks who've paused to peer through the serving window, taken momentarily by the larger-than-life personality of the woman across the table. A woman so splendidly oblivious to all of it.

I'm instantly, hopelessly enamored. A decade since I've seen her, and all it took was a first glance and five minutes of Elora being Elora. Much has changed in her over the years, as I suspect is also true about me. Her black hair is now salted. Her gym-crazy days seem behind her. Gone is the lean musculature I remember, swapped for healthy curves she wears so well.

She's as beautiful as ever.

Elora's laughter diminishes and she draws a long, recovering breath, a smile frozen on her face. "It's been so long, Mark. Gosh. With the way things ended that night..." her face darkens, its smile scrubbed away by memories of North Conway. She glances away, down into the steaming murk of her coffee. "I didn't think you'd ever speak to me again."

"I've wanted to at different times. I made such an idiot of myself that night." I watch as her gaze lifts back, the flicker of an emerging smile dancing in her eyes. "I was drunk. I had just broken up with..." it hurts to think of Kelly so soon after her death. She hasn't even been in the ground a month, and I still struggle with the idea that she's gone. Mallory has been despondent and distant. She doesn't seem to understand why. We barely talk about it.

I take a deep breath, my nose filling with the pervasive aromas of buttered pancakes, fried eggs, and coffee. A surge of electricity flares in my chest as Elora's hand enters my field of vision, reaching forward and finding mine.

"I'm sorry about Kelly," she says, drawing my attention back.

"Thank you." I'm unsure how else to respond.

"And you don't have to apologize for that night. You can't fault yourself for following your feelings." Her hand tightens on mine, her gaze hardens. "God knows I should have."

I'm thunderstruck. My first impulse is to pull my hand away. This isn't right. This *can't* be right. After all these years, after everything I've been through in my pursuit of this woman, failing to catch her and starting a life with Mallory... is Elora telling me she has feelings for me? Was this all it took after ten years? A drunken text as I cried over my phone in Walt's room? A breakfast date at a crappy diner outside Saugus, Massachusetts?

She senses something in me and withdraws her hand. Taking up her coffee, she sips uncomfortably, hand trembling to the point where the cup nearly spills over, before setting it back down. I'm relieved as our waitress approaches the table, coffee pot in-hand. Her kindness is forced, her smile fake; this woman has either been working here long enough to have had her spirits broken by it, or she's between jobs, not trying so hard to make this one work.

"Are we ready to order?" she asks, appraising us with a twinkle in her eye that says, *you'd better not be taking up one of my tables for coffee.*

Elora's attention is already on her. "I'm just fine with the coffee, thank you." She smiles up at the woman, creases marking her face in places they hadn't before. It's not until Elora looks back to me that I realize the waitress is waiting for me to answer as well.

"Um, I'm all set, thanks."

The waitress's smile falters in a telling way. She tosses fleeting glances at her other, more important tables before returning her gaze to us. "Well, if you change your mind just flag me down." And with that she's off tending her other patrons.

With our uncomfortable moment sufficiently interrupted, Elora and I return to the standard *catching up* stuff. "So is Staple You Shut still touring New England?" I ask, confident I already know the answer.

A mournful look assembles on her face, but she recovers quickly, forcing a smile. "I was the only thing holding that band together. We were already struggling when we played that show in North Conway. It just wasn't meant to be. We wanted to write and record original material, but the only shows we could book were cover jobs. As an artist there's nothing more strangling than being forced to regurgitate someone else's material over and over. We broke up a month or so after you saw us. I'm not sure what changed in me, but I just couldn't do it anymore..." She takes a moment, then, "It's like I lost something suddenly."

"I'm sorry to hear that."

"Thanks." She turns to the window, composing herself as cars speed autonomously by outside. It isn't long before she turns back to me, her smile rematerializing. "How are things with you? Still doing I-T?"

"Yep," I nod, trying to remember the last time I'd put in a full day. "I partnered with a co-worker a while back and we started our own company. I never thought I had what it takes to run *anything*, but after Mom and Walt..." I swallow hard, unsure why after all these years I have to fight back against crippling despair at the thought of them. Elora waits patiently as I pull myself together, almost seeming to catch some of my sorrow. "I just needed a change."

"Seems we both went through a major change at that time. It's interesting how we can be separated by so much space, yet still experience parallels."

"I've never known you to be so philosophical."

She lifts her coffee with an impish wink, "When you trade metal music for a tedious desk job you tend to get lost in your head a lot."

"Can't say I'm not guilty as well. Seems all I do is overanalyze."

There's a pause. We sip our coffee. Then our gazes meet once more, and I see in her eyes something that reminds me of the girl I parked with once upon a time at Ogunquit Beach. A girl I loved obsessively for years, then dumped unceremoniously before starting college.

"What made you reach out, Mark? After ten years... what changed?" Her confusion is partially eclipsed by a glimmer of hope in her eyes. I see myself mirrored in her, that desperate need to bare her soul and hear from me the words I'd longed for so long to hear from her.

That I love her and I want to be with her.

Truth told, I'm not sure what made me reach out to her. I was drunk and frustrated, sitting in my brother's room trying to channel him. My mind kept going back to the accident with Kelly, and how Elora's face wouldn't leave my mind even as the cops and firemen and paramedics arrived. It just felt right, after all the years, to finally make contact again and see where it went.

Elora studies my hands patiently. Hers inch forward.

"I'm not sure. It just felt like something I had to do," I say.

"After the way things ended in North Conway... I didn't think you'd ever speak to me again. Those texts I sent you. I've gone back and forth on it all these years, cursing myself." She sips air and exhales in a long sigh. "Lost in my head, sitting behind a desk. It's like penance – I'm forced to look back over every mistake I've ever made."

She's being overly dramatic, but I know why and I forgive it. She's exactly where I was ten years ago, dealing with loss and regret, struggling to grasp something she's lost.

Me. Elora finally wants me.

"Life's just a slow, painful march to the grave. I've given up searching for any meaning in it. It's all just a lesson in torture," I sigh.

"Are you not happy?" she asks, eyes glimmering.

I think on this a moment. I haven't considered the question since Mom and Walt's passing. It's as if I've settled for this life and the pain it's wrought. I know nothing else.

"No," I answer truthfully. "No, I'm not happy."

"Can you remember a time when you were?" She turns to gaze out the window again. Suddenly the mixed chatter of the other diners fuzzes out, and it's just the two of us here.

"I think so. Are you okay?"

Her chest swells against a long, thoughtful breath. I make note of every finer point in her body language, every nuance in her expression. The corners of her lips droop for just a moment, a fraction of a second, before she reigns them back in. Then she looks to me, face stony in its neutrality.

"I don't know."

"You can talk to me about it. About anything."

Her bottom lip quivers. She's losing the battle. I can tell she doesn't want to speak, that it will further agitate the emotions working to overpower her. But she does speak, and I know why.

She wants help. Just as I want help.

"I've wasted my life. I'm married to a man who doesn't love me, but won't divorce me because he's afraid of how it will look – how it will reflect on him as a *man*. I've lost all creative and artistic expression. It feels like I'm... *withering*..." her voice deepens with this last word. For a moment it looks like she's going to continue, but she leaves it, working visibly to impose control on herself.

I gradually reach across the table and take her hand. Our fingers lace. My first thought is to suggest she seek professional help as Mallory had suggested with me, but Elora is a smart woman. She's undoubtedly thought of that. This isn't what she needs to hear. What she needs is someone to patch the holes in her.

Our eyes meet as she blinks, releasing a lone tear down her cheek. It trundles down her chin and falls onto my hand.

"We've got a lot of history, Mark," she says at last, gripping me tightly. "We've both made mistakes, both hurt one another, but there's still time for us. We don't need to suffer alone anymore. We can help each other. *Fix* each other."

She lifts my hand to her face, pressing it to her cheek. I'm ravaged by an odd cocktail of anxiety and exhilaration. Decades of emotions now repressed have suddenly had the dust blown off of them, emerging from the darkness to toy with my morality.

Of course I think of Mallory. What would become of her if I left her for Elora? After ten years was I capable of doing that to her, of robbing her of a husband for the second time?

"I made the biggest mistake of my life when I broke things off with you before college," I say, zoning out on the table, mind racing. "You were the first girl who ever took an interest in me. You built me up from an awkward nerd with no self-confidence to slightly less awkward nerd with *too much* self-confidence."

She chuckles. I love making her laugh.

"I lost it all somewhere in my twenties," I sigh. "I became a neurotic mess – I'm *still* a neurotic mess. I realized I'd never stopped loving you, but it was too late."

"It's not too late now," she says, kissing my hand, lighting a fire in my chest... and certain places south of the belt.

"But it is," I sigh. "I murdered a man ten years ago. It was an accident, but it was still murder. I stole a person from this earth, from his *wife*. That woman is now *my* wife. I'd never be able to leave her. No matter how unhappy I may become with her, I can *never* hurt her like that."

I don't say that it had been Elora's text that distracted me from the road when I'd struck Nathan Kelson, but it's a thought I've considered these long years just the same. My world of hurt was founded with a single outgoing text from the love of my life.

Elora's lips droop into a frown she's powerless to banish. Sunlight winks in the tears welling in her eyes.

My chest shudders, the fire in me is squelched, I too am about to lose it. "I'm sorry. You have no idea how much I'd like to be with you. I still love you, I don't think I ever stopped, but I can't be the partner you need me to be. I can only offer you my friendship."

"True parallels," she says, working visibly to keep from stammering. "We've switched places, you and I. I'm where you were ten years ago, and you're where I was, leashed in artificial loyalty to another person." She blinks, tears now spilling in earnest down her cheeks. "I understand, Mark. I'm sorry for putting you in this position. It's just, when you texted me, after all this time... I thought... I..."

She thought we might have another chance. Just as I had thought when she coaxed me up to North Conway that we might have another chance. I remember what became of me that night, how self-destructive I'd been.

Having learned of the darkness eating away at Elora, I can't leave her like this. I don't need another death in my life. Another death on my conscience.

I pull her hand toward me and lift it as she did mine. She doesn't resist, allowing me to lead this part of her where I will. Resting my forehead against it, I can smell her flowery perfume and I can almost feel the current of pain running beneath her flesh.

I am not a bold man. I don't take chances, and I don't blurt things out off the top of my head without thinking them through, especially matters with these emotional stakes. But for some reason my mind bypasses its firewall, and I ask the question I know I'm meant to ask her.

"Do you want to get out of here? Go somewhere we can talk... in private?"

Our eyes meet, the sliver of a smile briefly flashing across her face. She blinks away more tears. "I'd like that a lot."

let's
do
guilt
trip
from
the
top

ELORA.

How is she doing now? Has she heard of my death?

She must have. We'd planned to spend a night together in Portland the week after I... checked out.

Suddenly my obsession with Walt is edged out by concern for Elora. Her condition improved immensely over the years of our ongoing affair, and a part of me fears she'll slip back toward the darkness we'd overcome together. Though we stayed with our spouses for our own hollow reasons, we lived for each other, always counting the days until we'd be together again. This took the form of many "business trips" for both of us. The best were the weeklong excursions where we could exist openly as man and wife; those destinations where we could be the people we were in our souls and not the downtrodden owners of our mutual, hollow existences.

My soul warms at the thought of her, but the concern remains. I step away from the tree, tracing its scar once more before willing myself into the air. It's much simpler than I'd anticipated, though I'm still hit with a spike of anxiety as the earth falls hastily away.

I stretch my consciousness out across the world, feeling for Elora as that tickle runs along the margins of my soul. And suddenly I know time is winding forward rapidly as I streak across the changing Earth. My soul touches Elora's as below the woodland gives way to the concrete sprawl of the Kittery Outlets and Southern New England beyond.

Elora is in Brookline, Massachusetts.

I gasp and grope at the open air as I'm flung southward over the Piscataqua River and the Portsmouth skyline, narrowly missing the pointed steeple of a church in the heart of the city. The landscape then tapers off to tangles of trees, dotted sparsely by grassy estuaries and marshland. I work to calm myself, assured that I'm being driven by my own will.

I hold the control here.

My soul calms after a minute or so, and I'm left revisiting that day in the diner. It plays through my mind like an in-flight movie, only this time with my personal commentary. Elora lost her art right after Walter's suicide. It makes more sense now that I understand the degree to which his death impacted us, how deep a rift he'd left. Each of us was stolen away from the lessons we'd sought to learn, and in our desperation, our lack of understanding, we came together.

Had I reached out to her because I sensed she might be losing her grip? Had I helped her avoid suicide?

For all I know, if Walter hadn't killed himself, Elora and I might have ended up marrying as we had in the majority of our lives. Mallory would have gone off and continued her life, detached in the way Tim more or less was. Fate is a force stronger than gravity, existence bends with it. Events like Walter's suicide aren't part of the plan, and they poison the chain forever.

Memories of time spent with Elora will not help me rescue Walter, but I need to check on her before I do anything else. I need to know that the love of *all* my lives is holding together without me.

The woodsy terrain below surrenders more and more to the urban overdevelopment of Massachusetts. Cars are packed more tightly together, people rushing busily along with their pointless errands. The prevalence of red, white, and blue colors leaves me thinking the date on their side is close to July 4th. I can't help chuckling. I was certain I'd see the collapse of the United States of America in my lifetime.

Sprouting ahead on the horizon is the Boston City skyline, skyscrapers sawing at the sky like jagged teeth. The ever-encroaching ocean has erased much of the former development along the coastal plane. There exists no greater example of the destructive power of humanity than the effects of global warming.

When this world dies, will all of its lessons go with it?

I'm falling now, passing over the reconstructed Tobin Bridge toward Brookline. Boats tread wake in the harbor beneath me as I streak forward over rooftops toward a sinking sun. I'm drawn away and into Brookline, the street widening beneath me until threaded by a commuter rail rising out of the city's bowels. Two story storefronts, music venues, and restaurants flank either side of the street.

I always liked Brookline. Elora and I spent a lot of time here. It was just far enough to go unnoticed and live for a weekend as true partners. I'm unsurprised that she's come here. Whether she's just visiting or has moved to this place remains to be determined.

My soul is drawn down to the sidewalk, shooting over the heads of oblivious pedestrians. I can't help bending my knees and pulling my legs up as if my feet might clock someone in the head. Bodies pass beneath me in a seamless blur until all at once I'm no longer moving forward, instead descending unhurriedly to the concrete. As my feet touch down, I realize I'm standing in front of a club that Elora and I visited often during our nine years together.

The Dandy.

As my eyes sweep the marquee above, I feel my soul warm and smile out at the world. *Tonight: The Pullout Method, featuring Staple You Shut.*

I walk toward the closed venue doors, swallowed up in shadow beneath an overhang. Posters for upcoming acts plaster the walls. I couldn't care less. Pushing forward, I pause before the door, lifting my hand and holding it palm-out.

You can do this, I tell myself, and doing my best to make myself *ethereal,* I push my hand through the door. Just as quickly, I extract it, confirming nothing was lost. Kelly's voice seems to whisper from the back of my mind, reminding me that the physical laws of the corporeal world don't apply to us.

Nodding to myself, I push my hand forward again and walk through the door. Just as I had entering the cottage back home, I close my eyes as my face passes through the padded entryway. When I open them again, I'm standing in a dark hallway with autographed band posters behind plexiglass. I can't help smiling and shaking my head at a shot of The Smashing Pumpkins with silvered scribbles haloing the head of each band member. They're all gothic, it must have been during the Adore tour.

I start toward the poster for a closer look, now reminded of the song that was playing the moment I punched the clock on my life, when the thumping of a bass drum thuds down the hallway. Rotating toward the sound, I follow it into an auditorium where a gaggle of aging rockers stand fussing over their instruments, doused in mottled stage light.

"All right, guys, let's do Guilt Trip from the top – Terri, can you turn my mike up?" comes a woman's voice I know well. My soul warms at the sound of it.

Elora.

I round the sound board where a petite punk-rocker scowls down at buttons and slides through a face-full of metal. She's dressed in tight black clothing, studded leather belt, pink spiked hair. She nods toward the stage in response to a request from the bass guitarist as I pass by.

Elora is framed by two metal columns that bulge at the ends as if pressed upon by the roof. Her hair is midnight black again, cropped above her shoulders and parted in a zig zag pattern. She's nibbling on a guitar pic as she adjusts her mike, legs splayed, guitar riding her midriff. It's difficult to believe she's almost fifty. She looks as though she's shed fifteen years since I last saw her. As has been a constant in her life, she is stunningly gorgeous, dressed in a short skirt with ripped fishnets and a t-shirt reading *STFU*.

Elora plucks the pick from her teeth and oscillates toward her bandmates. I recognize a couple of them, though the last time I saw them there was more hair, and the areas of their bodies that were once trim have apparently been permitted to sprawl. She smiles and turns back to the mike. "One, two, three—"

The auditorium explodes with syrupy metal guitar. The pace is slow at first, all drums and bass as it builds. Elora's head bobs along with the beat, hair stranding across her face as she plays. For a moment she seems lost in her finger work, then all at once presses her lips to the mike and launches into curse-laden song.

I shake my head as she steps back and loses herself in a minute-long solo before returning to the mike. When the song ends she turns and high-fives her bandmates, then they move onto another before ending their sound check. At this point I'm standing just beneath Elora like a rabid fan staking out his place at the stage hours before the opening act.

"All right," Elora says to the girl at the sound board. "We're good. Let's grab dinner." She unslings her guitar and walks it to a rectangular case near the drum kit. I levitate onto the stage, following her.

As Elora unsnaps the latches on her guitar case, I note that she's not wearing her wedding band anymore. Perhaps she finally found what she needed to kick her husband to the curb. I crouch beside her, wanting nothing more than to reach out and touch her, but something tells me it won't give me what I think I need.

Elora lowers her guitar into its custom-fitted mold then pauses and unclips something from the padded inner lining. As she brings it close, I feel my heart flex toward her. It's a photograph of the two of us, a selfie I took in a hammock while we visited the Bahamas. Behind us is a sun setting between twisting palms. I remember that week very well as one of the precious times we were permitted to exist as Mr. and Mrs. Wells.

The rightful Mr. and Mrs. Wells.

Sadness seeps from Elora's soul. It bites like cold air at skin I don't have, but I don't despair. This is different. I know that she's okay, that she's moved on to a new chapter in life. Sadness is something we all manage to carry longer than we rightfully should. It's how we learn to rise each morning and face the world, to advance in spite of our pain's weight, that helps us endure.

I step around the guitar case, settling on my knees facing her. She breathes thoughtfully, chest swelling, hand pressed to her heart as if bracing against something unseen. I watch her as she rides her emotions until a voice calls from backstage.

"Elora, you coming?"

Elora emerges gracefully from herself, glancing around to make sure nobody has seen her. "Yeah, gimme a sec," she calls back, eyes falling once more to the photograph in her hand. Elora lifts an index finger, kisses it, then presses it to my lined face. "Forever," she whispers, clipping the photograph back inside the case and snapping it closed. With that she's back on her feet, striding offstage.

She's okay. Somehow, despite the rift Walt tore through our chain, she's found her way in the aftermath of my death. The band is back together, she's writing music and expressing herself, and it's clear that she's finally removed herself from her loveless marriage.

I'm free to continue perusing the past, but there's one thing I need to do first. My body slowly levitates off the stage and up toward the ceiling. I pass through the roof and into dwindling twilight with eyes open. Moments later my body is flung suddenly northward, back toward home.

Back toward Mallory.

I pull into the driveway of the cottage, my Georgiecoil sedan trundling autonomously over unmitigated potholes I once faulted Walter for not tending. Its all-electric motor runs on a whisper, over which you can hear the grinding gravel. The car rocks gently on its suspension, lacking the force to wake a baby, but strangely it's enough to shake my suitcase to the floor behind me.

Unlike the vacations I take with Mallory once a year, this suitcase contains no souvenirs from my trip. My souvenirs are the memories Elora and I now share of Cozumel, Mexico, a week of passion that I've sold to my wife as a weeklong network build for a startup in San Francisco. I even took pictures inside the wiring closet and server room of a local client so I could send photographic updates.

I'm a scoundrel.

"Greetings, sir," my digital assistant Isla speaks up, preempting the music pumping from the stereo system. "You asked me to remind you to pick up flowers for Mallory."

My fists slam down on the steering wheel, shifting the car into manual pilot mode, its self-guidance systems relenting to me. Seeing as I have ten feet left to drive, I suck it up and maneuver my own car for the first time in at least half a decade.

"Thanks, Isla," I grumble at the digital voice. The jet caught some kind of crazy tailwind on the flight back, resulting in an early arrival. My reminder is too late.

Guiding my car into the rotary, I coast to a slow stop and reach for the park icon on the main computer console. The console occupies most of the dash, scrolling statistics including speed, mileage, and electrical consumption. It sadly doesn't take out the trash.

The nanite display flutters in a series of aquatic ripples before Isla's soft voice bids me goodbye and the whispering engine cycles down. I'm reminded of the days when I still had the RAV4. Back then it required an RF fob in the car for it to run. Now everything is coded to my fingerprint.

For a moment I just sit there in my car, listening to its clicks and sighs, debating whether I should just pull back out and go to the florist over the state line in Portsmouth. I always bring Mallory flowers when I return from "business trips." In the end I decide not to. I can always surprise her with flowers tomorrow.

I take more time in the car, sorting through the mixed feelings of guilt and bliss as I relive the highlights of my trip with Elora. Snorkeling in an ocean of bathwater, dining on the beach beneath palm-thatched umbrellas, and of course making love whenever the impulse struck.

I draw a long breath and lean back against the headrest. Closing my eyes, I can't help a smile building at the memory of a stingray brushing Elora's leg while snorkeling. It was the first time I'd ever heard a scream underwater. That self-identified "weak swimmer" was treading water toward shore with the prowess of an Olympic athlete.

I breathe deeply again. As I exhale, I utter our private term of endearment, our own way of saying *I love you*. "Forever."

A knock at the window startles me out of my mind. My eyes flutter like I've just woken from a deep sleep, and my gaze shifts to the figure peering in at me, every inch of her face committed to the smile she's beaming my way.

Mallory. She's dressed in her gardening clothes, a matching set of gray sweats crusted with dirt. Mud-slimed gloves adjust a navy-blue baseball cap.

I return the smile and reach for the door handle. She steps away from the car as I unbuckle my seatbelt and grunt my way out of the contoured seat.

"You're early." She's already advancing with open arms, but reconsiders, taking note of the filth on her. I move into her arms just the same, drawing her in tightly and pressing my lips to hers.

"Oh, you're going to be *filthy*," she says, shaking her head as we part.

"I don't care." And I don't.

She peels the gloves from her hands and tosses them in the grass. It's a mild spring day, the air threaded with lilac and pine. A westering sun melts over the trees in striking hues of gold and violet.

Pushing her hair back over her ears, Mallory asks, "Did you catch a different flight?"

I shake my head, rounding the Georgiecoil, headed for the rear passenger door. "No. We caught some kind of tailwind. I've always heard of things like that happening, never experienced it." I extract my suitcase from the backseat, leaning down to hoist it up from the floor and going rigid as a current of pain spreads down my back. A reward for growing older.

"Well that's great!" she exclaims, genuinely happy to see me and blissfully oblivious to the secrets I keep. I'm a fantastic actor, deceiving her all these years, going to extravagant lengths not simply to tell her that I still love her, but to *show* her. I suppose a part of me still feels those feelings, I certainly don't resent her place in my life, but the fires that burned in me for her have cooled to embers in the aftermath of Kelly's accident.

"I was hoping we might go out for dinner," Mallory says, gaze clinging to me as I round on her. "There's a new place in Newington, very eclectic, I'm told. They make all their own bread."

Shifting my suitcase into the other hand, I fish my backpack out of a snarl of CAT8 Ethernet cable on the passenger floor and sling it over my shoulder. "Sounds great."

"Says the guy who's been eating at awesome West Coast restaurants all week." She tosses me a playful smile, her usual mischief. She trusts me implicitly, and it stabs at my heart.

"I've been sticking mostly to Chinese," I lie, so convincingly it stabs harder. "It'll be nice to have something bread-y." I start toward the house as Mallory catches me gently by the arm. She inches up on her tip toes and kisses my cheek. Imparted in the gesture is all the love she still feels for me, all the love that exists between us.

"It's good to have you home. It's so lonely here without you." She settles back and fixes an adoring gaze on me. I smile back, a veil over the guilt dividing me. But it's not enough to keep me from living this double life. I'm getting what I need out of it, and Mallory is getting what she needs. Perhaps one day my secrets will see the light of day with her, but for now this is how it must play out.

"It's good to be back, baby," I say, leaning down and kissing her. The gesture stirs no emotion in me save for the remorse I still carry for her first husband.

Nathan Kelson. His ghost will be with me forever.

I pull back, shrugging my shoulder to adjust the straps of my backpack. "Let's go get ready for dinner."

pork
fat
melts
in
your
mouth

MALLORY.

Bits and pieces of our life together wash over me like waves pummeling a sodden shore. Everything I kept from her, all of it taken with me to the grave. After more than seventeen years of marriage, forty-nine years on the earth, and two days away from my 50th birthday, I died in an accident and took with me the hurtful secrets of my dual lives. Knowing now how trivial such things are, or at least *beginning* to know, the part of me still adhering to that existence is relieved Mallory never found out. She loved me so unconditionally, the man who'd murdered her husband and failed to love her back in the ways she'd deserved.

Time is moving faster. That tickle runs along the edges of me. The sun is down by the time I shoot across the Piscataqua River and back into Maine. I can't help wondering if Elora and Staple You Shut are already into their first set at The Dandy or if the gig was now somehow years ago.

I'd been afraid of heights in my life as Mark Wells. I hid it from everyone, especially my frequent travel partner, Elora. It's become obvious that I'm growing more accustomed to my untethered existence as a world of lights streaks beneath me in the darkness like some Earthbound starfield. There are few boundaries on this side of things. It's an amazing feeling, more liberating than any sensation I've ever experienced, but I worry soon it'll become as commonplace for me as it seems to my soulmates. What a shame to lose such wonder.

The world is rising toward me suddenly, startling me as my body races toward the dark profile of the Kittery Outlets. Working to collect myself, I watch as the outlets vanish behind the shadowed flutter of leaf-choked branches. There are no landmarks here to indicate where, exactly, I'll be touching down. Yet I know the cottage is there. I know my soul has willed itself back to Mallory.

All at once I pass through shadow and substance, into the light of my kitchen. My bare feet touch down on the tiled floor and I fall in a hurry to my knees under the penetrating chaos of Walter rooms away. It's not as bad as it was when I first came here, but it's enough to leave me thinking of the warnings I'd received from the others about coming alone. I've been empowered and hardened by knowledge since then, but it's not enough to entirely dull the dry rending of my soul.

Turning to peer down the hallway toward Walt's old bedroom, I force myself to my feet, unwilling to take a single step in that direction.

Every room seems lit, every lamp and ceiling fixture burning with warm LED light. But Mallory is nowhere to be found. Gazing once more down the hallway, I turn away as Walter's consciousness seems to flex toward me. I do my best to weather it, but I know I can't stay here long.

My feet carry me toward the living room. I pause where the linoleum meets the carpeting, sweeping the room for signs of Mallory. I see only an empty living room, pristine in its spotless absence of character, unchanged over the long years. Now that I'm no longer around to clutter the place, I imagine Mallory has an easier time keeping up with cleaning. Mouf has been dead for years, ending the days of fur tumbleweeds and tufts of fuzz gathered in every corner. Searching my limited understanding of existence, I look for information about the souls of animals. I turn up nothing. The subject feels so inconsequential, in fact, that I fear the nothingness I've found is, in fact, my answer. But I've no way of knowing for certain.

Only God knows.

A rumble in the basement draws me back to my charge here. Backstepping, I turn toward the basement door, hanging slightly ajar off the kitchen. It is farther into the hallway than I'd care to probe, and I spend a moment grappling with throwing caution to the wind and subjecting myself to more of Walt. Then my ever-evolving soul reminds me that there are no boundaries here. I don't have to take a single step down that hallway.

My soul smiles as my attention settles on my feet. I will myself downward through the floor, watching as my extremities disappear into the mat tiles.

Mallory and I had the basement finished a few years earlier, replacing the rock floor and stone walls with a poured foundation and sheetrock. It was more out of necessity than a need for additional space. The foundation had been crumbling and was in dire need of reinforcement. Such undertakings were almost impossible in Mom's day. The project was completed in a week.

Boxes line the unadorned sheetrock, spaced along the wall with no clear order. They cast sharp shadows under the track lighting. A few boxes stand open with their contents arrayed upon the floor. Pictures, keepsakes, travel souvenirs. Mallory is nowhere to be seen, but I can feel her soul here.

I swivel toward the open closet door, yet another storage space, positioned beside a bathroom we've never used. As if on cue, she steps out of the dark closet hugging a cardboard box marked "Walt's Room." My soul shudders at the sight of it. She's dressed in sweats with a purple bandana barely containing wisps of silver and chestnut. She looks healthy, busy. This lifts my spirits, though I wonder if a part of it is my soul mending itself, now at safer distance from Walter.

Mallory grunts, setting the box down with others she's apparently lugged out. A chirping comes from the kangaroo-style pouch at her midriff, and she thrusts her hand inside, fishing out a paper-thin sliver of metal, non-conductive substrate, and light emitting diodes.

Her phone.

A smile spreads across her face as she prods the touchscreen, tapping out what I believe to be a message before shaking her head at its glowing face and returning it to the pouch. Moments later the thudding of the front door carries downward.

Is she seeing someone already? Such things don't concern the untethered soul, or so I try telling myself as a jealous current of possession slithers though me.

The floorboards begin to creak under the slow approach of Mallory's mystery guest, making their way through the mudroom toward the kitchen. Mallory pauses over the box she's brought out and cants her head upward with an expression that at least tells me this visitor is expected.

"You okay up there?" she yells, her voice spiked with a mischief I know well.

"Never better, young lady!" comes the booming voice of Tim Massi. A familiar warmth fans out across my soul, further bolstering me against the permeating madness of Walter's swan song. That slow-moving figure above is my 73-year-old former business partner. The idea that they might be romantically involved abandons me, and I'm left feeling only gratitude. I know Tim Massi. More so now that I can look back through memories of what he was on this side. He's here to check on her. He's probably been checking on her every day since I passed.

Mallory fluffs down her sweatshirt and climbs the stairs. I follow, rising reluctantly through the floor to the intensity of Walter's energy washing over me once more. With Tim's presence it's easier to tolerate than before. I nearly pass *through* him as I rise into the kitchen, seeing first his worn leather boots, then jeans sizes too large under a buffalo plaid flannel. A baseball cap rests atop his head, its brim fraying freely.

The basement door opens and Mallory steps into the room, immediately approaching and hugging Tim. "You're late."

They separate and he steps back from her with a teetering lean that's worried me for years. "Well it's not like you're ready for a night on the town or anything."

"Just lost in all the sorting. The memories." She seems to go elsewhere a moment before refocusing on Tim, angling herself toward the opposite hallway. Walt's hallway. "I'll go throw on some street clothes. Where are we going tonight?"

"I was thinking that sausage bar downtown."

She shakes her head and rolls her eyes with flair. "It's always pork and beer with you. I'm surprised that body of yours is still holding up! I still have no idea how you stay so skinny."

"Just good genes," he chuckles. "And pork fat melts in your mouth. It's delicious." Nowhere in him is that air of responsibility she'd once observed in her friends after her husband's death. Tim isn't here to grasp at pieces of me, he's here for *her*.

Or, more appropriately, they are here for each other.

Mallory disappears down the hallway into the bedroom, leaving Tim alone with the ghost of his former partner. I rotate slowly to face him, half expecting him to acknowledge me there somehow. The energy flowing from his soul is so potent it's a wonder he doesn't also feel me. He pivots toward the living room, looking over the artifacts of my existence with Mallory, most of them holdovers from the family I'd lost.

I step closer to him, so close I might smell him were we on the same plane of existence. My soul shudders as the warmth spreads between us, and a tremor of energy ripples out from Walter's room. It's as if my late brother can sense the extra presence and it's adding to his confusion. I try to keep my soul focused on Tim as I sift back through the times we've shared. Reaching out, I lay my hand on his shoulder, certain of a flickering resonance now striking through him.

Tim's gaze is suddenly static, locked with mine.

Can he sense me?

Tim could already have a foot in the grave for all I know. Something tells me that we have a way of knowing when our soulmates will join us. Such power I have yet to understand, let alone channel, but my instincts tell me Tim has some life yet to live.

Tim shakes his head and draws a long breath. His face washes neutral, and the rigidity leaves him. I think back to moments in my life when I'd suddenly felt shaky or *off*, when a chill would run through me for no apparent reason. Could that have been one of my soulmates reaching out to me? I thought such resonance was mythic.

It's not a good idea to come here on your own, a voice startles me from behind.

I whirl around to Carter's stone-chiseled face. Turning for a last look at Tim, I watch him shuffle toward the kitchen table, draw out a chair, and fall into it with a look of euphoric relief.

My gaze returns to Carter.

There's so much you have yet to learn about this place, Mark. You must be careful.

Do you come here a lot? I ask, biting back against sudden, black resentment. I *know* Carter. I *love* Carter. But the side of me still clinging to my former existence insists he's nothing but a miserable wretch. A hindrance more than anything.

He studies me pensively, eyebrows lifted. His silence speaks volumes, reinforcing his lack of patience with me. On a certain level I get it. It's like trying to teach long division to a dog. What I can't seem to get beyond is how obliging the others are compared to him, then I remind myself that Carter's lost more than any of us.

I'm sorry if I—

I'm trying to spare you more pain, Mark. This isn't some mortal impulse to impose domination over you. It's me looking out for the chain. We can't lose another.

"Okay," Mallory's voice drifts down the hallway. I welcome it, turning away from Carter, turning my back on the darkness he's brought into my home. Tim labors to his feet as Mallory steps into the room wearing jeans and a red cardigan. "We ready?"

"I was ready for a beer at eight this morning, young lady," Tim chuckles.

"Only *one*," Mallory chides, wagging a finger at him. "It's a wonder your liver hasn't packed its bags and moved out."

They are so natural together.

Tim starts to launch a comeback, but I'm torn away from the conversation as Carter steps in front of me, blocking them out. *You need not concern yourself with them,* Carter says. *Their existence is a movie for us to watch, its lessons are lost on all but the actors.*

I try to peer over his shoulder as Mallory and Tim exit, but Carter insinuates himself between us. My hands make fists. Fury blazes in me, firewalled only by the understanding that I shouldn't pick fights with people I'm bound to for all eternity.

I get that you've lost a lot, Carter, we all have, I say. *That's why I'm trying to bring him back, to make us whole again. I'd think that you of all people would want to help me.*

You haven't been here long enough to understand how hopeless the situation is. There are few cases where these things have been turned around. We don't have doctors or medicines for this kind of thing. This is one of two ultimate ends we face – we either Transcend and go to God, or we wallow in the madness of our failure to reach Him. Walter failed, now we must live with him.

I refuse to just live *with him.*

Carter's face hardens, his soul tenses, and all of the sudden I feel actual anger wafting off him. *And I refuse to lose any of us to him!* he growls.

Pausing to peer imploringly into his eyes, I say, *Then help me.*

Be gone! Leave this place now! he cries, his face stretching frighteningly out of proportion, jaw lengthening like a snake's about to slip its hinges.

It feels so very... *Walter.*

I stagger backward and away from him, soul reeling against the fear he's driven into me. His hands press to his face, seeming to guide it back to normal form as the fury in his soul quiets. What's left is an expression of the blackest despondence, of the most reluctantly accepted defeat.

And suddenly I know that he's already tried to help Walter... and nearly driven himself mad in the process. Parts of Walter have clearly overwritten segments of Carter's soul, corrupting him.

Carter. I'm—

Just go, he sighs. His pathetic, almost infantile gaze meets with mine, eyes imploring. *Please.*

Without a word I will myself up and away, off-world and beyond the reaches of the solar system. Unlike my initial trip to Earth with Kelly, I'm left suspended in the black vacuum of deep space in an instant, alone save for the drawling voice of God so simultaneously everywhere and nowhere.

I think of Mallory and Tim as I allow my soul to slumber. In my absence they've bonded and formed a friendship. Elora has found strength in her music. Somehow, we'd *all* saved each other in the aftermath of the worst tragedy we could possibly suffer. Together our souls endured.

No earthly errands remain for me. I'm free to continue sorting through the memories of my former existence, and I will do so in defiance of the consequences I've observed in Carter.

I refuse to give up on Walter.

I sleep, thinking of the box Mallory was carrying.

I stagger down the basement stairs, customarily drunk. The last time I looked at my watch it was 11:37 P.M. I'd spent at least an hour after that swaddled in the darkness of Walter's room. It was there the idea to venture downstairs to look through his former belongings occurred to me. Perhaps I'd find something to rouse his soul from its quiet hibernation.

Here I am, seventeen years after his death, a week away from my 50th birthday, and I'd not once thought to go through the items we'd packed away.

Only I had, many times, each another reminder of the coward I am.

My foot misses the last step, and I flail out for a few frantic seconds before stabilizing myself. The glass of Macallan 30 I've been nursing shatters on the floor. Grumbling, I step carefully over to the light switch, spilled scotch seeping into my sock, and throw it. The glare of the track lighting winks in the shards garnishing the floor, thirty-year-old scotch swelling like a pet stain in the carpet.

Mallory is going to kill me.

I stumble into the bathroom as quickly as my booze-tampered faculties will permit and shuck one of the black hand towels nobody uses from its hanger. I make my way back out to the spill and, wincing to my knees, begin to dab at the spot. The idea to wring the scotch back into the glass briefly enters and exits my inebriated mind.

When I finish (dropping the hand towel indiscriminately over the smaller shards I tell myself I'll get to tomorrow), my gaze finds its way to the closet at the back of the room. The closet where we'd moved the boxes of Walt's stuff after the basement was refinished. I'm compelled in a meandering shuffle toward the door, halting with my hand inches from the handle.

Do I really want to do this? I've gone almost twenty years without disturbing Walter's things, the den conversion excluded. What might I hope to mine from the boxes in this closet? These artifacts are sentimental only to a dead man, their secrets lost with him.

My hand inches closer, closing over the handle. I open the door, and the smell of paint and cardboard wafts out. Stepping into the dark, I lift the top box in a large stack of five. Mallory had packed this one judging by the loping scrawl I barely decipher as *Walt's Room*.

As though struck suddenly by lightning, I'm transported back in time in my mind to the day we'd cleared out the room. To the day I'd found his Adderall supply from the final three months of his life intact, blowing up everything I'd ever known about my brother.

Chewing at my bottom lip, I'm once again possessed by second thoughts about unearthing Walter's life. But again I manage to shrug it off, feeling somehow obligated not only to do this, but to do it now. Taking the box in a bear hug, I lug it out and settle on my knees outside the doorway, lowering the box with the same care I'd apply to a crate of nitroglycerin. Inside is an eclectic cornucopia of things *Walter*. Extracting a rolled poster, I unfurl it to the exaggerated neon and felt trim of a marijuana leaf. Typical stoner décor. I set it aside and extract other posters, laying them with the first.

And then I see the notebooks. Over a dozen of them in every shape, size, and color imaginable. Decidedly and characteristically hodgepodge, this is the exact form Walter's final project in life *would* take; the chronicle of his spiritual and metaphysical meltdown during Mom's final days. I'd completely forgotten it. He'd been so protective… I'd just put it out of my mind. Had I discovered these notebooks instead of Mallory, I might have read them long ago.

Each of the nylon coversheets holds the same title, distinguished from one another only by a single Roman numeral beneath Walter's chicken scratch. It reads: *In the Arms of Saturn*.

I remove the notebooks one at a time, handling them with the same care I'd show a 16th century bible. I begin to arrange them on the floor, hoping none are missing. After a minute I have twelve notebooks arrayed around me, enumerated II to XII. The last one in the box is marked with a single I, its cardboard cover adorned with the York Hospital name and logo. That was where it had started, the day of Mom's seizure and forced admittance to the ER.

It's personal. Walt's voice seems to echo along the decades as I fondle the first volume in his apparent oeuvre. I slip my a finger beneath the cover, pinching it between my finger and my thumb. I'm holding in my hands a misplaced door into Walter's soul, his last thoughts before he took his own life. Do I dare invade his privacy like this?

Sucking at the stale basement air, my scotch buzz is suddenly chased by a shiver rolling through me. In an instant I'm sobered, and I lower the book warily toward the others.

No. This is Walter's. He didn't want me to read it.

Turning as I rise to my feet, I walk toward the site of my spill and snatch up the towel from the floor. With a glance back at the stacked notebooks, I leave them to keep their secrets and climb to the kitchen, resolved to sleep it off and return the volumes to the closet tomorrow. The house is dark and still, disturbed only by the faint, whispering whir of the refrigerator motor and the glow of the climate control panel.

I walk to the kitchen sink, realizing that I've still got glass to pick up downstairs. For a moment I consider grabbing a beer from the fridge, but I decide against it. Something tells me I'm going to have a difficult time recovering my buzz now. Instead, I pour a glass of water from the tap and drink as though I've been nursing a dry throat for decades. I pour another and upend it in similar fashion. After my third, I turn back to the basement door, still ajar, casting a shaft of cold light across the hallway tiles.

In an instant I'm moving back across the kitchen. I throw the door open and descend the stairs two at a time. Rushing over to the collection of Walt's manuscripts, I pluck the first one up from the floor and throw it open before can I lose my nerve.

In The Arms of Saturn

I used to have this dream when I was a kid. Almost every night I'd wake up crying for my mother. In the dream I was running through the woods, chased by some animal. Through the trees there was this light, a pale, yellow glow that seemed to throb like it was alive. I'd eventually break into this field, still chased by the animal, and there at its center...

The planet Saturn. I know this because I've had this dream.

I close the notebook, suddenly unable to draw a satisfying breath. Settling against the wall, I slide to the floor, reading on, discovering in Walt's bafflingly well-crafted syntax that he'd dreamed of the same bear, of the same esoteric siren call from Saturn.

This revelation sets a tremble running through me. I read further, finding a hidden talent in Walter that, had it been nurtured, could have landed him among the authors of the world. His prose is unimpeachable, the eloquence of his voice... otherworldly. I read on, delving deeper into the mind of my lost brother. Time passes in an instant, and before long soft light starts to trickle through the basement windows.

I'm not going to work today. I may do nothing else at all until I've read every page.

The depth of Walter's world view, of life as we know it, makes me question the person I'd known him to be. I'd expect such things from a philosophy major, not a lay-about who'd never been bothered to strike out on his own, whose very existence revolved around smoking pot, popping Adderall, and drinking beer.

But he was more than that, wasn't he? The Adderall had proven that. He'd been obsessively focused on his journals, but this energy had come from some unseen force, not the pills I'd flushed more than a decade ago.

Walter had been so mixed up... so lost.

But not all of that was his fault, was it, Mom? My mind drifts only briefly to the night she'd emerged from her condition long enough to share her secrets with me. What she hadn't come out and made clear was that she'd kept Walter home in order to stay relevant.

I don't linger long there, for here before me, reaching deep into the darkness of our existence, is a multi-volume tome around which an entire religion could be crafted. Walter writes of soul-bonding, of sharing multiple lives with a cadre of interlocked cosmic explorers. Sometimes you're a man, sometimes you're a woman. Sometimes you're someone's child, sometimes you're their wife or husband or bitterest enemy. Sometimes you're still so rooted in your prior life you can't help feeling like a prisoner in your own body, like your very *gender* is wrong. Just... wrong.

Walt goes on, building an intricate mythology that is so plausible I find myself wishing it were the true way of things.

I don't emerge from the basement that day. Even as Mallory discovers and eventually joins me reading, I cannot tear myself away. By the time the daylight starts to wither, and I find myself suddenly tempted by the sultry voice of sleep, I've already burned through six of the notebooks. Mallory is coming up close behind me, equally engaged. As I turn the last page on notebook VI, I close it with a deliberate reverence and set it by Mallory's pile. She looks up from the volume in her lap. Our gazes meet.

"I had no idea," I whisper, startled by my voice after sitting silent for so long. "My brother was a brilliant and insightful man. All I ever saw were the addictions, the laziness."

"People often go to deep places when they know they're about to die," Mallory whispers back, glancing at the notebook in her lap then folding it back and setting it down. "I see it in the hospital all the time. It's as though they know they're about to... *transcend* or something, like something is speaking to them from the other side."

That word, *transcend*. It falls on me with overwhelming gravity.

I draw a long breath, extracting the subtext from Mallory's statement despite the other items trying to occupy my mind. "He knew he was going to do this. Of course he did. Even before he found out about Mom he was talking about buying a gun. There were other hints, too. I didn't notice them because I was too consumed with my own problems."

Mallory eases a stack of notebooks aside and scoots over to me, wrapping her arms around my waist and resting her head on my shoulder. "It's been almost twenty years, Mark. I'd tell you to let go, but I know you never will. That's okay, I know how important he was to you, but you can't blame yourself for what happened to him. That's on Walt, not you. All these books he's written, this system of beliefs he's crafted, they go to show exactly what was going on with him. He wanted to hit the reset button on his life. He wasn't happy. He wanted to start again."

For some reason I think of the day our snow fort collapsed…

She's right, of course. Mallory's always been good at reading between the lines. I suppose it's because she's seen people at their most desperate lows in the hospital. She's stared in the face of despondency countless times, probed the bottommost depths of love and loss.

For a moment I remember love for her.

I want to read further, but my arid eyes will no longer cooperate. Not an ounce of food or water has passed my lips all day, and I don't care. I'm not hungry, just tired, both mentally and physically exhausted. Easing Mallory off of me, I plant a kiss on her head then one on her lips. She smiles up at me, still blissfully enamored and ignorant to my second life after the long years.

I smile back convincingly and say, "I've gotta go to bed."

"I'm right behind you," she says. "You want dinner first?"

I shake my head. "No. I'm actually feeling kind of sick." I'm not, but it's not all a lie. The emotions stirred by Walter's words, combined with the guilt of my one-sided marriage has me feeling off kilter. A part of me hopes I'll have it sorted out after a night of unbroken sleep, but I can't help approaching it realistically. I'll likely end up waking in the early morning hours and returning to the basement to continue reading.

i
think
i
know
how
to
save
him

I EXPLODE INTO consciousness, soul reeling against the sudden revelation that has shaken it. Walter's books, *In the Arms of Saturn*, they have to be it! All I have to do is—

A tremor rocks me, shaking my very being with the force of an unexpected shockwave. Far off in the reaches of blackest space, God's voice whispers unintelligibly. I can feel the others, they can feel me. We understand, together, that another of us has passed on Earth.

I know immediately that it's Tim. Had my instincts on how long he'd had to live been off during that last visit, or had the years hastened their march during my slumber?

How long have I been out? How long have I slept in this place, alone with God?

I have only to think of myself suspended above the rings of Saturn, and in an instant I'm there. Before me the golden face of our governing planet smiles upon me, its atmosphere roiling with proto-antediluvian wrath. Beneath my bare feet are the floating bands that hug the planet, the larger of its rocks delineated in pocks and pits in the radiating sunlight.

Tim. Where are you?

I feel him, I sense his confusion.

My soul rockets downward along the planet's rings. As the debris field sharpens, a figure takes form ahead. His back is arched, his limbs drawn behind him. His chest is heaved toward the planet as if offering his heart to it. He looks as though he's sleeping, cradled in the ether, watched over by twinkling stars at unfathomable distance and tempestuous storms from the planet's surface.

I come within feet of my former manager-turned-business-partner and stop. He's younger than I'd ever known him in life, though that thin body he's always had (despite the copious amounts of beer he drank) is the same. His balding head, always concealed with that terrible combover, has sprouted a thick jungle of almond hair, flowing over his ears and obscuring his face. The creases I'd known in his skin are no longer there, nor are the liver spots and other mortal age marks.

Like me, he's been restored to pristine condition, wherever he was in the prime of his life. Now here I am, the first to greet him and explain the situation. I don't question it, but I can't help feeling underqualified.

It's good to see you again, Tim, I whisper, trying my best not to startle him. Studying him closely, I draw nearer as his eyes slowly open. I can't help my soul smiling upon him. I'm overjoyed as his smiles back.

Mark, he says, gaze drifting over my shoulder to the massive planet. He beholds it as a child would Santa Claus after waiting up in the darkness on Christmas Eve. Without warning his glee is suddenly and willfully reigned in, his face draining of emotion.

He understands he's been here before. Many times. I can't help wondering why I wasn't so quick.

I reach for his body and pause before making contact. Even without touch, the warmth spreading between us is like a bonfire. It chains through the group in a way we both sense. We're bolstered further against Walter's madness with Tim's sudden arrival.

I touch him, the fire between us suddenly burning harder. As I had with Shannon, at one time only a simpering voice, Tim and I remain like this for some time, basking in each other, sharing all of ourselves. When we finally separate after minutes, hours, maybe days, it's against the stabbing throb of Walter's insanity millions of miles away.

Tim lurches forward, clutching at his chest like he's having a heart attack. *Gah,* he gasps. *Walter. What am I—gah, what's going on?*

Come back to me, I urge, pulling him close. In an instant the arms of the others encircle us, our souls flaring together against Walter. Eric,

Shannon, Kelly, and Jennifer silently announce their presence as every shred of comfort they have to offer diffuses with mine into Tim. We feel his soul calm, buoyed on the love and strength of his soulmates. In turn, his energy flows back into us, stoking the fire and hardening the group.

For all I know we remain like this for years, floating above Saturn's iconic rings. I'm able to glean from Tim that I'd been asleep in the deepest reaches of space for six years while the living pressed on with their lives. My mind moves to my final days when I'd been reading Walt's journals, and for a moment I feel myself returning there and have to reground myself.

All in good time. Tim must be cared for first.

He was a suicide, Tim says at last, leaving me flummoxed as to why I'm still struggling to acclimate here and he seems to already be in-the-know.

He couldn't handle the strain of Transcendence, Shannon explains, her voice soft and distant, burdened with the sorrow we all carry. *His final lesson. He was to return to God.*

We're all silent a moment as we listen to God's voice, reaching out to us from the edges of eternity. It washes us, penetrates us, but it offers nothing in the way of comfort or condolence. This is the way of the universe, the cost some of us pay for our existence. These things are decompiling with greater haste in me, but I'm still not close to Tim's apparent level of enlightenment… and this feels suddenly by design.

I think for a moment about Mallory. Now that Tim is gone will she be okay? Feeling out for her, I stretch my consciousness through the ether to where I feel her on Earth. It's as though I'm there with her while simultaneously held above Saturn's rings.

Mallory is okay. She's been expecting Tim to go for some time.

Reaching out next to Elora, I find her still living the life she'd always wanted, writing and recording metal music. The rest of me is drawn back to the group. Elora and Mallory are all that remain of us on Earth, and though they seem to be doing okay, I worry that with so few of us there they might succumb to the same dark impulses as Walter.

I think I know how to save him, I say, expecting my words to be met with laughter. In an instant I sense reluctance rippling through the group. Only Tim and Kelly seem willing to acquiesce.

How? Shannon asks, drawing me out of my head as for a moment I glance back over my final days with Walt's journals.

He was writing a book up until you passed, I explain. *Volumes of existential postulations. Some of it was snippets of his life that led him to these revelations, but most of it was a spot-on description of existence as we know it. Everything. The way we bond here and return to life together. He described it all.*

I feel their collective interest pique.

This was his obsession, I continue. *I think he was crossing the plane somehow, communing with God, but he couldn't handle it. It was what he was working on up until the moment he took his life. I think that if we bring it up with him, remind him of it, he might be receptive.*

The group is silent, and for the briefest space of time even God's voice seems to quiet. We float together, cradled in space, sharing every thought, feeling, and emotion. My sincerity and confidence is imparted to them and I feel it reverberating back on me. For the first time since I transitioned, they're starting to see me as more than some child playing at adult games.

When do we try it? Kelly asks, at last breaking the silence and stepping up for me as she'd said she would.

I need more time, I answer, feeling relief among my soulmates. *I have to reach back to the last days of my life, remember what I'd read in those notebooks. There's got to be a line, a passage that will resonate with him. Something I can use to ground him and calm his madness.*

We'll have issues with Carter, Eric sighs, reminding us that he's the only one of us not present, excluding Walter.

We'll cross that bridge when we get to it, I return. At the mentioning of Carter's name I'm struck suddenly, thinking I've missed something, but I'm not left pondering it for long as the woman who'd been my mother speaks up.

Take the time you need, Mark, Shannon whispers, her hand coming to rest on my shoulder. *When you're ready, you know how to find us.*

She's giving me more credit than I deserve, but a part of my soul assures me I'll know how to gather them when the time arrives. The question is, will I need them? Will I *want* them with me?

In a flash I'm hurtled back toward Earth as recollections of my former life play out. Like a spotlight cutting through the darkness of Walter's mania, I'm certain his salvation rests somewhere in those notes.

As if he'd left them like breadcrumbs for me to follow.

I'm retiring," Tim says, letting himself into my office. I snap out of my reading, hunched over notebook IX as windows scroll diagnostic data on four translucent monitors before me.

Tim hobbles in behind the feeds, dressed in his usual flannel and blue jeans. His combover is a shadow of its former glory, just a few wisps of white traversing an otherwise scorched dome. A beaming, mischievous smile creases every inch of his face as he stops, listing slightly before finding his equilibrium.

I worry more and more about that lately.

"Retiring?" I ask, certain I've misheard him.

He oscillates around to peer back into the shop through my office window. There, a half-dozen workbenches sit littered with ongoing projects. Server chassis, PCI cards, ATX cases, and a whole host of antiquated tech we reverently refer to as *legacy* stand testament to our company's ongoing success.

"Getting too old for this stuff," he says, turning back to me, still smiling.

"You were too old for this stuff ten years ago," I chuckle. "What's changed?" I glance at the diagnostics streaking across my extended displays, saving a few to our cloud servers to revisit later.

"New perspective. I can't have much time left. Don't want to spend my last days getting yelled at by end-users."

"What are you going to do?" A part of me thinks he's pulling my leg. He's so often full of it. But there's something about him today, some twinkle in his eye that makes me believe there will be no surprise twist at the end of this conversation.

"Fish, read, play my guitar. The usual, brotha'."

He's serious.

Though he's completely blindsided me, I'm shocked my friend *anxiety* doesn't pay a visit. In its own way this news is a relief. I mean, it's not like he can lift server cases or get around very well in general anymore. Still, to lose someone you've known and worked with so closely for the better part of thirty years. It's rough.

"Whe—when is your last day?" I'm surprised to hear myself stutter. Perhaps I'm not taking this as well as I think. Could I be in shock?

"I'm thinking a month or so. But I'm getting the final prep work done this week – meeting with my lawyer to go over a few things. Oh, that reminds me, I need you to take care of that Stone Lock software update at Twisted Oak Public Library on Friday morning if you don't mind. I've got a meeting that morning."

"No problem." I study him carefully, still not convinced he isn't going to throw in some joke revealing he's been kidding the whole time, but he doesn't.

"Thanks, brotha."

"Sure."

He starts to turn and walk out, then pauses and looks back at me over his shoulder. "You okay? You look a little... I dunno... *squirrely*."

"Far as I know, I'm fine." I supplement the statement with a shrug and watch with mounting confusion as he turns back and approaches my desk. Gazing past my monitors, he comes in for a good look at the notebook open before me. His gaze shifts to the others beside it.

"Writing?"

I shake my head, seeing no reason not to share. "Reading. These were... well, I guess they were journals. Written by my brother before he killed himself."

He leans on the desk, lowering his face for a closer look. He cocks his head as he reads, looking like a dog struggling to work out unfamiliar commands from its master. He straightens. "All these years and you've just *now* decided to read them?"

I'm unsure if I've misread him, but he seems exasperated, almost like he's offended I'm just now getting to my brother's notebooks. I quickly dismiss it as paranoia. Why would Tim care about my brother's journals?

"Mallory boxed them up when we first cleared out his room. I'd forgotten about them until I found them the other night. I've been reading nonstop since." Appraising him as he leans in for another look, I'm left wondering what has him so interested. To my knowledge, he'd never met Walt. "Are you okay?"

He snaps back up, looking as though he's just woken from a dream. At the very least, he's been lost in thought. His eyes lock with mine, and an uncomfortable silence settles. It's odd. I've known this man for decades, been through all kinds of stress and drama with him. Outside of Mallory and Elora, he's the only person in the world with whom I'm this close. Yet in this moment, our eyes locked, we're like strangers struggling to read each other.

"I'm fine," he says at last, standing upright and backing away a few steps. "Think maybe I'm coming down with a cold or something."

It's a cover, but I'm glad to at least have something flimsy to pin it on. I play along, "You never got your flu shot this year, did you?"

Tim shrugs, "Meant to. Guess I just forgot." He considers the notebook again a moment before his gaze returns to me. "Be careful. Might be things in there you don't want to see."

"Thanks, Tim." I'm vaguely aware of my hand settling protectively upon the notebook, just as Walter's once had.

He nods, shuffling out my door and onto the shop floor. I watch him continue to one of the workbenches where he returns to a diagnostic.

My gaze lands hard on Walt's notebook, then shifts momentarily to the reports scrolling before me, the work I should be paying attention to instead of reading.

Without another thought I tell myself I'll get to the reports later. I'm back in Walter's work in an instant, unaware that I'd just shared my final conversation with Tim on this side.

"So, according to Walt, you could have been my *mother* in your last life," Mallory reflects in a low and dreamy voice. She's seated across the kitchen table, quietly reading and catching up quickly, equally engrossed. She's still dressed in her pink scrubs, having arrived home from work only an hour ago. They're usually the first things she sheds as she enters the house.

"That's messed up," I say, glancing up from the last of Walter's notebooks. I'm about three quarters through it, and it's beginning to show signs of wrapping up. Instead of detailing the afterlife and the meaning of it all, Walter has shifted into talk of his own mortality. It's harder to read than the rest, but I'm forcing myself to the end. Through these notebooks I've gained a knowledge of my late brother's inner workings unlike anything I thought I knew.

The house is quiet with the exception of the winter wind swirling snow and whistling along the eaves outside. It figures the night before Tim needs me to cover for him at a library four towns north there's a Nor'easter blanketing the area with snow and ice. It doesn't matter how old I get or how much driving experience I garner in the snow, it'll always make me nervous, and it's even worse when the car is in self-pilot mode.

I foresee a night of heavy drinking tomorrow, assuming I don't just call it a day after I'm done in Twisted Oak. Trying not to think about it, I return to my reading.

> *...It was a mistake coming here this time. I don't quite understand what I was trying to accomplish, but I do know I've failed miserably. I'm incapable of connecting with anyone outside of Mark, and even then I feel like I'm a burden on him. Why it took me this long to realize it, I don't know, but I'm tired of being something that everyone must take care of. I'm ready to return to the other side, to let the universe decide where I'll end up*

next. I'll go when Mom goes, return with her. That way Mark can have a life of his own without me as a drag on it. I hope he's able to find peace and realizes that the things plaguing him lately aren't his fault. The universe cuts the path we follow in this life. It's all pre-determined. Every decision we make, every bit of happiness and pain we feel, are just steps along that path. And they deliver us all to the same final destination when we've finally found what we came here for.

Death. Transcendence...

It's not until droplets begin to patter Walter's untidy longhand that I realize I'm crying. His suicide was partly my fault. I knew I'd heard his door close the night Mom spoke to me in the dark. He'd heard everything, and I can't help feeling as though this pushed him the remaining steps toward the edge.

I lean back in my chair, wiping tears, and in this moment the world seems smaller. As I lower my hands back to the pages of Walter's journal, I note the gooseflesh studding my skin. I shiver as a rush of energy spreads through me, noting as I recover that I've gathered Mallory's gaze.

"What is it?" she asks, poised as she so often is to provide comfort.

"It's nothing," I croak, flipping through the remaining pages. Nineteen to go.

Mallory rises and circles the table, tugging her chair along. She settles beside me, hands pressed to my cheeks. Guiding my face upward, our eyes meet, hers full of adoration and concern, mine no doubt bloodshot and swollen from tears born of insight.

"Are you getting what you need out of these books?" she asks, running a hand over the stubble on my head. She draws me close and kisses me first on the tip of my nose, then on my lips. Her forehead pressed to mine, her arms enfold me.

"I don't know," I weep, chest heaving as my emotions run unchecked. Teeming within me is an orgy of pain and relief. Relief from the enlightenment I've found in my brother's final work. Pain from the understanding that he'd realized he was a burden.

It all converges in me at once, the decades of pain and remorse, the knowledge of why my brother did what he did, the understanding that I truly am a coward.

"Are you okay—"

I push my lips into hers, silencing her with my kiss. My hands rise to her cheeks, guiding her closer. My tongue meets with hers. She's breathing heavily, pressed against me, kissing back with a raw desire that soon sees her climbing onto my lap. Her body writhes against mine, grinds into mine with a passion unfelt for over a decade.

She moans as my hands run the contours of her, greedily cupping at her breasts, groping with the unfocused longing of a teenager, wanting her more than ever. My heart thuds against my purple dress shirt. I need this.

We need this.

My fingers slip under her scrubs, groping ravenously at her flesh. I'm kissing and biting my way down her neck before my hands find the coordination to strip the shirt off her body. She moans as I unsnap her bra.

"Yes," she whispers, "Oh, Mark, yes."

I'm suckling at her nipple, her chest heaving. There's no way we're making it into the bedroom, I want her here and now. Teasing at its twin with deft fingers, I suckle at her until I can wait no longer. Without a word I lift and deliver her gently to the floor. There I shuck off the rest of her clothes and kiss my way down her belly. Pushing her legs up, I move between them, tasting her. She's gripping my head, pulling me closer, trying to smother me in her as my tongue inspects every slick fold of flesh there.

Her body shudders as she climaxes, crying out at the ceiling above, her thunder reverberating through the house.

I'm on top of her, my lips on hers as she recovers. My hand moves down to the place where we're made to meet, and I guide myself gently in. Her face lights up in ecstasy, eyes wide, mouth frozen in a pout. My hand finds hers as I move slowly in and out, urged along by hot breath on my neck.

"Yes, God, *yes*," she whispers, her voice growing louder and more persistent with every thrust. Faster, I feel a brimming explosion. Her panting intensifies. She's right along with me until all at once we climax together. Her arms fall over me, gripping me with palpable possession as I collapse atop her.

We stay like this a few minutes, breathing in sync, then I roll off and curl up beside her, hand draped across her midriff. Eventually she rolls toward me, the ghost of a smile playing at the corners of her lips.

"What was that all about?" There's clear gratitude in her voice.

I'm unsure how to answer. Elora's face flashes through my mind in a way that disturbs me as I take in the innocent face of my wife of nearly twenty years. "I... I don't know." Her face blurs. A panic wells in me.

I close my eyes, her hands already on my cheeks, where they so often go when she senses I need her. She scoots closer and pulls my head to her chest, my tears falling on her bare skin.

"It's okay," she whispers, somehow drawing me in tighter. "I've got you. I've got you."

i
need
to
see
those
last
pages

AHEAD OF ME the moon takes form, its pale, pocked face fitted with circular settlements built into the larger craters. Access tunnels reach between them, winking here and there with white strobing light. Farther out on the dusted plain are a dozen Helium-3 harvesters. They look like those circular robot vacuums people were so crazy about in my thirties, only much larger.

I couldn't care less about the moon. The emotions stirred in me at revisiting my final night with Mallory are complex and difficult to decode. I try not to dwell on them, to move on to my completion of Walt's books, but the nagging compulsion to understand that night is too powerful to resist.

Then suddenly it clicks. Mallory and I sensed on a deeper level that we were soon to part ways.

I died hours later, killed in an accident that would have taken Tim had I not covered for him. Even now, as Planet Earth swells before me, I can't help marveling at God's master plan. It's easy for a mortal to misinterpret a thing like my death, to leaf back through the pages of time and question why. Did Tim blame himself for what happened to me? Or did he, on some level, understand that it was always meant to be that way? That I was destined to die in that accident and he was destined to follow years later?

My mind is whirring. I need to return to that night when I'd sat over Walt's final volume in the waning hours of my life. I need to see those last pages.

I wake in the dark stillness of my bedroom. Mallory's nude body is spooned up to mine, her arm draped across my chest, hot breath on my shoulder.

Glancing toward my bedstand, I squint against the soft glare of the alarm clock. 2:13 A.M.

I wriggle carefully out of Mallory's embrace and kiss her forehead. It's a hollow gesture, devoid of any real emotion, but it feels right just the same. For a moment I'm visited by the ghost of my former self, a man who'd believed he loved her, later to discover that those emotions were simply masked guilt. I don't regret getting with Mallory. We've always been great for each other, with hardly an argument, but that doesn't change the fact that I belong to another.

I belong to Elora.

I slide carefully out of bed without waking her. Stealing across the carpet in the darkness, I feel my way toward the door and step into the hallway, advancing into the dull kitchen light. The notebooks are where we'd left them on the table, mine still open on the page I'd been reading.

Stopping before the table, I turn to the fridge, realizing that I haven't had any beers or whiskey tonight. It's not like me to unwind without booze. Maybe this is the start of a new life.

I flip on the overhead kitchen lights, squinting against the glare as I shuffle to the table, sit, and open the notebook I'd been reading.

Okay Walter, I think, gazing down at the hand-scrawled text. Let's see how this wraps.

The remaining pages are much like the one I'd been reading earlier. Walt goes on to explain that he'll harden himself on the other side in preparation for his final return to Earth, that he understands he's been reincarnated countless times and that it's time for him to Transcend. Nowhere does he invoke me directly, which leaves me believing he truly didn't intend for me to read this, that he wrote it to ground himself and nothing more.

It's not until I reach the final page that I realize I'm wrong. It's only half a page, with a salutation reading: *Brother*. The sight of it leaves me breathless.

>*Brother,*
>
>*I told you this was personal, but you've obviously decided to read it anyway. No worries. Where I am now I'm sure I don't care.*
>
>*I'm sorry that I had to leave you in the way I did, but my purpose here had run its course. I wasn't about to make myself your problem. It's not like I was ever really cut out for this world anyway. I should have heeded the call of Saturn when I was younger and taken the out, but I stayed in the game to take care of Mom. That was my purpose. Now it's ended, and so must I end.*
>
>*I love and wish you all the best in this life. I hope you find your answers quickly so we can be together again.*

On that note, I'll leave you with this last thought: Life is but a lesson learned. We take that lesson back with us to God, but the lesson itself is not what molds and defines us. We are who we are because of the souls we journey with. Our chain of souls. They are all that matters, and in time we will all Transcend and be together within God.

Goodbye, Mark.

I set the notebook down and sit back in my chair, blood pounding in my ears as the world takes liquid form. The final page in my brother's existential journey feels like his voice reaching to me across the margins of existence. This is a side of Walter I never knew existed, something he kept so perfectly concealed I'd swear his journals were written by someone else entirely. Had he been channeling some force from the other side? Had something been speaking for, or even *through* him?

I think back to the day of the snow fort collapse. He'd said, "Carter saved me."

Perhaps one day I'll know the answer. For now I have to get ready for work in Twisted Oak.

and
i
will
do
it
alone

OF ALL WALT'S wisdom, not once in those volumes did he consider the consequences of suicide. Such was his failure in grasping that final lesson, but the failure wasn't entirely his to own. Someone had found a way to commune with him through the ether.

But who? Who'd been responsible for driving him off the rails?

It's impossible not to conjure Walter's eight-year-old face as he'd recovered in the aftermath of the snow fort collapse, and suddenly I realize what I've missed up until now.

'Carter saved me,' he'd said.

Carter had done a lot more than that, I think.

I fall fearlessly through Earth's atmosphere, and as the scenery lightens from black to baby blue around stringy wisps of cloud, I know where I'm headed.

I know what I must do. I'll save Walter or go insane trying.

I know now that I've found the only possible item from his former existence that might resonate with him.

And I will do it alone.

Beneath me the landscape takes shape. Lush, verdant forests are an emerald green with summer, arresting in their beauty. The bustle of mortal men and women, their trivial comings and goings, is reminiscent of scurrying insects.

The Piscataqua River snakes its way inland, spanned by its three bridges connecting Maine and New Hampshire. Ahead are the outlets, and beyond, the cottage where Walter's soul awaits.

I close my eyes, my earthbound soul streaking across the sky like a star. This is it. This is where I make my last stand, my final attempt to save the man who was my brother. Here I'll either be successful and extract him from his madness, or I'll fail and join him forever.

As the cottage sharpens through the trees, I prepare to surrender to my fate. There's just one area of the past worth a look first.

I've never liked Twisted Oak, a coastal community only by technicality which stands apart from the rest of Maine in its dark and grisly history. Founded by Irish settlers in the days of colonization, it was the site of what local legend refers to as the Rysher Family Curse. The story tells of a gunsmith named Timothy Rysher who came to America with his wife and seven children, all of whom died in various accidents over a five-year period. It's said that Rysher went mad and grew reclusive, supposedly spending the bulk of his time working on some great masterwork of a weapon. Folks claim he disappeared with it into a sprawling patch of woodland called the Farmer's Pasture and has been haunting it since. Those who truly believe the legend tell tales of voices whispering in the trees.

"You've received a text from Elora, sir," Isla speaks through my car speakers. Her animated avatar smiles up at me from the dashboard-spanning display. Blonde hair, epicanthic eyes, teeth white as the currently-driven snow.

"Read it," I say, taking a deep breath as my Georgiecoil crosses a bridge into Twisted Oak. To my right a channel flows into an unseen but reliably angry ocean. Gray clouds choke the sky. Visibility is nonexistent. I'm alone on the road. Most people have resolved sensibly to wait out the storm indoors, but not me. I.T. takes no days off. Rain, sleet, and snow... all that bull.

"It says, *Miss you already. Think you might get out for a night this weekend?* Would you like to respond, sir?"

"Respond. *Try to stop me.* Send."

"I've sent your message, sir. Will there be anything else?"

"No."

Isla's face disappears, and my attention finds its way back to the falling snow. I hate driving in conditions like this and barely trust the car to do a better job as it bores autonomously through the storm. As I wait for Elora to answer my text, my mind slips back to Walter's journals. There's so much in there to process, all of it so complex and intricate that I feel another read-through may be in order. Who would have thought my late brother, the addict and lay-about, would be capable of creating something so structured and eloquent? It makes me miss conversations we'd never had.

"You've received a text from Elora, sir."

"Read it."

"It says, *The usual place then? I'll be counting the minutes. Forever, my love.* Would you like to respond, sir?"

"Respond. *As will I. Forever.* Send."

"I've sent your message, sir. Will there be anything else?"

"When's this snow supposed to let up?"

"Checking local forecasts. Precipitation should taper off close to 11 A-M. Total accumulation over three feet with a separate system coming in around 2 P-M. This is expected to bring another two feet. Can I be of further service to you?"

I shake my head at the avatar. "No."

Three feet. Then two more. I can remember only a single other winter that had been this bad, but weather worldwide has been intensifying for the better part of a decade now. It's amazing the road crews have been able to keep the roads as clear as they are.

Fifteen minutes later I arrive at Twisted Oak Public Library, its glassed façade and palatial turrets reflecting the winter drab on itself. I switch the car to manual and guide it toward the front door, drawing as close to the building as possible, the nose of my sedan inching out over an entryway yet to be shoveled.

I power down the car, doubting the library will be open today. I expect to be finished before the first of them can arrive anyway.

Bracing against the coming cold, I sling my messenger bag over my shoulder and step out into the driving ice and snow. I trudge quickly through the drifts, around my car, and toward the front of the building. Fiddling in my pocket, I fumble out my phone and launch my digital keyring app as I step beneath a glass awning. As with every storm that hits New England, I find myself wondering briefly why I don't just move to Florida.

It takes me a moment thumbing through my keys. Fortunately I don't lose the handheld in the snow as my numbing fingers prod at it. Locating the correct RFID, I mash it with my thumb and hold the phone up to the automatic door. A burst of tropical air buffets me, and I hurry inside, stomping my booted feet to rid them of excess snow.

The floorplan is open with a welcome area like a glass cathedral. Posters advertising community goings-on plaster the walls and columns. An empty circulation desk sits at the center of the room, littered with books. Beside it is an unchanging table showcasing the works of local author and short-lived celebrity, Kirk Matthews.

I proceed across the foyer and into the server room at the far side of the building, beyond stacks of books and digital media. Here the glass ceilings surrender to the pitted gray of drop tiles. Above, a tin roof slopes toward a snow-drifted courtyard where a bust of Timothy Rysher stands buried up to his nose in powder.

As I reach the server room I produce my Bluetooth earbuds from my bag. "Isla, shuffle my entire music collection."

"Shuffling music collection," Isla's soft voice returns through the earbuds. Seconds later I'm listening to the soft rock of The Antlers, calming my nerves after the ride in. I locate the server room RF key in my phone and let myself in. Racks of blinking switches, routers, and leaf (formerly *blade*) servers are bolted to the floor beneath runners of horizontal Ethernet cabling patched to jacks throughout the building. At the end of the narrow space is a desk and access terminal.

"Let's get this over with," I say, barely able to hear my own voice over the music in my ears. I approach the terminal and sit. Dialing into the Stone Lock server, I launch the control console and initiate the software update. Different libraries use different flavors of this same product, used to protect public access terminals from viruses by effectively restoring them to the same base image after each logout. This helps when patrons who don't appreciate the finer points of internet pornography sit down at a computer formerly used by Twisted Oak's depraved and don't want to inadvertently stray into said person's browser history.

The 62GB download completes in seconds and I'm directed to reboot the server. It shuts down and comes back up minutes later. By now *You Were The Last High* by The Dandy Warhols has me tapping my fingers on the desk, ready to move out into the library and initiate the Stone Lock update on the client computers. I launch the control console on the server and verify that the clients are ready to receive the update. This complete, I push it across the network and venture out to watch its progress.

I walk the dark and quiet library with a spring in my step, almost dancing along with the music. Moments like this, when I tend my work alone and without distraction, are the ones I love the most. Just me and my music. It almost makes me forget I'm working.

Passing through the foyer and into the public computer wing, I'm pleased to see progress bars ticking away on each of the eight computers spaced along the wall, most already at 50%. Excellent. I should be out of here within a half hour if things keep going this way.

Smiling to myself, I turn and walk away, down the darkened halls of the library, thinking that I should probably get back into a running routine again. These thoughts don't linger long as snippets from Walter's journals once again find their way into my mind.

The universe cuts the path we follow in this life. It's all pre-determined. Every decision we make, every bit of happiness and pain we feel, are just steps along that path. And they deliver us all to one final destination when we've finally found what we came here for.

Death. Transcendence...

It's all pre-determined, and there's a certain comfort in that. I can't help smiling to myself, amused that after almost fifty years on this rock I've never subscribed to a system of spirituality. Now the hand-scrawled journals of my late brother have pushed me closer to faith than I've ever been. For the first time in my life I'm staring into the black void of death and considering the possibility that there might be some light in there.

I pause as *The Last High* ends and a song I haven't heard in almost two decades starts to play. *Set the Ray to Jerry* by The Smashing Pumpkins. I'm drawn instantly back in time to that weekend in North Conway when Elora and I came so close to something. Our fight, my drunk driving, smoking, my one night stand that random woman. It was all part of the plan, right? All part of the universe's grand design?

I breathe deeply, closing my eyes and feeling every part of me *settle* into the beauty of this song. I think of Elora. My beloved Elora, who I was never destined to possess and who would always own my heart.

I'm startled out of my silent reflection as the world suddenly begins to tremble around me. My eyes open in time to see the ceiling tiles buckle under the snow.

I've found what I came here for. I'm ready to go home.

i'll
spend
my
sanity
giving
him
all
of
it

NEVER HAVE I been more certain of something I must do. It isn't coincidence that I finished Walter's journals mere hours before my death. It isn't coincidence that I *found faith* in his words hours before my death. I'd learned what I needed to draw my brother's soul out of his insanity in place of the lesson in pain and suffering I'd originally sought.

My soul passes through the roof of the cottage and into the living room. It's so effortless now; I'm evolving, my consciousness toeing the margins of enlightenment.

And I am hardened.

I start into the kitchen, already feeling Walt's insanity breaking upon me. I pause as a familiar presence tugs at my soul. Turning slowly, I find Mallory asleep on the couch, a book open on her chest. Her face is six years older, still beautiful despite the newer creases there. Her chestnut hair is almost entirely gray now.

She looks a lot like Mom the night I'd returned here to live.

Before I realize what's happening, I'm kneeling beside her as if offering confession. I reach for her but recall what had happened when I'd tried the same with Tim. The last thing I want is to startle her from sleep, especially given how turbulent things are certain to become in this place.

We shared a strange adventure, I whisper. *If all goes well, I should be able to spare you the pain we've experienced on this side.* But it had already seeped onto their side, hadn't it? It had brought us together in life and bolstered us when the fabric of our shared existence began to fray. I can feel the turmoil churning out of Walter's soul, groping for me like a famished creature desperate for sustenance.

I'll spare you this pain, I whisper. *I promise.*

Mallory stirs. I'm relieved as she goes still again, eyes remaining closed.

Moving to my feet, I turn and stride across the living room, into the kitchen. As expected, another familiar presence announces itself, the only true opposition I'll find in my charge. I walk undeterred, my resolve stronger than the will of God.

I turn the corner to find Carter standing in the hallway before Walter's bedroom door, his hand pressed against the wood. Though his back is to me, I know he feels me here. I pause in a square of dusk light, peering through the darkness at his naked body, waiting for the inevitable conflict.

I was alone with him in there for all of sixty seconds before my soul started to deteriorate, Carter whispers, not looking back. *And I've been on this side now for almost a century. My soul was as full and acclimated as it was going to get, yet I still failed him and lost parts of myself in the process.* He turns slowly, gaze sweeping up and down me. In his eyes I see not the contempt and frustration I expect, but instead a crippling defeat. Paralyzing, even. *I've tried to sway you from this course of action, make you understand that there is nothing you can do to help him. But you're determined to lose yourself with him, and I can't stand sentinel here forever.*

Carter takes a few slow, deliberate steps toward me, halting at the edge of shadow. *There's just one thing I need to know: What makes you think you'll be able to reach him, Mark? What can* you *do that I couldn't?*

He's my brother, I answer. *And haven't you already done enough?*

Carter ignores my question, but I feel understanding in him. Despite this, he growls back at me, *Your mind is still tied to that world. He is not your brother, he is your soulmate. As I am your soulmate.*

He is both of those things. I went back to that existence alongside him to learn of pain and loss. In not watching out for him I got a lot more than I bargained for. I departed that world only after I found what I needed to save him. After decades dealing with his death, I found what I needed to repair his fragmented mind.

And what is that?

His writings. Existential and spiritual postulations that showed an intimate knowledge of things on this side, of how the universe – God – is structured. The very day I finished reading his last volume I died in a random accident, drawn to this side so I could use my knowledge to save him.

Carter says nothing, his gaze moving to the floor. Suddenly I sense he's ready to spill the secret I'd already been circling, something he's kept hidden from the rest of us, somehow concealed behind the parts of Walter imprinted on him. I feel the rift in my soul widen as Walter's consciousness seems to reach through the walls, feeling us out.

Why did you do it? I ask. How did you do it?

Our bond is stronger than any other, Carter says, his voice weighted with regret. *I was supposed to go back with him this final time, to be with him as I've ALWAYS been with him. But he wouldn't allow it. He wanted to go alone. I didn't understand... I still don't understand.*

But why did you —

I wanted to help him. To aid him along, so he could be done with it and I could follow him, live my last life and return to God as well. It was a huge mistake. I overwhelmed him. By the time I realized what I'd done... how far I'd gone even in saving his life that day in the snow... it was too late. Then Shannon started to deteriorate, and he scrambled to assimilate all he'd learned. He never even knew what was happening to him. Suicide is the only force that can remove us from the path originally laid out. I pushed him off the path, Mark. It's all my fault.

Then when he transitioned you tried to help him, I say. *Tried to make him whole again.*

Carter nods with a rapid, manic insistence that shows the madness he carries. *First I tried, then we all tried. There is no drawing him out.*

I will draw him out, I say, stepping forward and laying my hand on his shoulder. With the contact comes all of his pain and suffering, the guilt he's concealed from the others. I feel my soul ripple as it passes through me.

Carter gazes up, his eyes cold and hopeless. I do my best to push some of my warmth into him. I'm relieved to see him nod slowly.

I'm coming with you, he says.

I shake my head. *I have to do this alone. It has to be me.*

He searches my soul, probing deeply. After a moment his hand rises to my chest and our eyes meet once more. *I'm regretful we didn't spend more of our lives together, Mark. I feel we could have learned a lot from each other.*

We'll have that opportunity.

I certainly hope so, he says, driving into me all the warmth and strength his broken soul can assemble. Then, without another word, he vanishes to parts unknown, leaving me alone at the edge of Walter's aura.

There's no sense in delaying. It's time for me to do what I came to do.

I advance slowly down the hallway, feeling Walter's presence grow with every step, throbbing like a beating heart, reaching out with every metronomic pulse to devour the consciousness of others. He has no grasp of space or time, no self-awareness save for the insatiable need to finish his work, to complete his lesson. A lesson he no longer understands.

Stopping at the door, I lift my hand and press it against the wood as Carter had. This contact alone is enough to singe the edges of my soul. I'm without the bolstering power of my soulmates, and though I'm stronger than I was when I'd appeared here, I can't help already feeling my consciousness slipping away.

This must be done quickly. I don't have time to delay or second guess myself.

I push through the door and into the howling chaos of Walter's bedroom. The voice of God is dulled by Walter's screaming soul in a way I hadn't noticed before. I feel suddenly empty without it, and I gasp, backtracking toward the door as the fissure in my soul widens. My back makes contact with the wood, and I will go no farther. There is no escape, my soul won't allow me to back down.

Shielding my eyes from the churning storm, I push forward into the madness, my soul fraying with every step. My gaze settles upon my brother, still crouched in the corner and clawing at the walls. I try to dredge up the more important and impactful passages from his journals as I press forward, but it's as if my mind has been bleached.

Walter! I cry, gasping as his cleft attention settles upon me. It stabs at me like a switchblade, and I fall to my knees, catching myself as my hands hit the floor. It's all I can do to stay on all fours, let alone rise back to my feet.

Walter! I cry out again, anticipating a repeat of his mitosis from the last time I dared share this space with him. He knows I'm here, he can feel me, but his behavior is different. For a moment he stops scratching at the wall and scuttles back to consider his lack of progress in tearing through the sheetrock; not a scratch despite his decades of feverish work. I'm foolish enough to hope he'll turn and face me, I need his full attention for this, but my heart sinks as I watch his body twitch, writhing violently before returning to work on the wall.

I must go to him.

You... wrote... me a... letter! I scream into the swirling din, now crawling toward him like a dog. *You... said... we were... who we... are on both... sides... because... because of the souls we... travel with!* The pain spreads with every inch I draw closer, but I feel recognition in him. A part of me is getting through.

I force myself onward, advancing through the chaos as the world itself begins to grow formless around me. Walter's soul is the only stationary object. My destination. My destiny.

Soon it will be all I know.

I... read your... book!

I'm nearly driven to the floor in shock as Walter splits suddenly as he had before. Of the two Walters before me, the original continues to scratch away in the corner while the new one positions himself rigidly in my path, leering at me with brandished claws. I do my best to compose myself and continue forward, avoiding eye contact with feral Walt.

You thought that... ugh... your lesson was... complete. You killed yourself... grr... argh... you've crossed over... in... pieces. You need to—

Feral Walt charges suddenly, claws slashing wildly at the air. His eyes blaze with an electric fury unlike anything I've known, and I brace myself for what I know is coming.

He dives through me, slashing wildly but unable to make contact. But in a way he does. The fissure in my soul widens, a hollow ringing is all I can hear. The world continues to spin, further shedding its form, and I feel as though I'm going to lose consciousness. But then my gaze settles on Walter in the corner once more. Somehow I'm able to keep myself moving toward him, now just five feet away. Every inch feels like a mile, my soul flaking apart with every miniscule advancement.

Gah! I fall on my chest as feral Walt passes back through me. Eyes snapping open, I watch as he launches back to his feet, prepared to lunge again. Using all the energy I can muster, I roll out of the way, avoiding him as he lands tumbling on the floor. I'm able to will myself back onto all fours, pushing ever closer to Walt as his doppelganger recovers behind me.

I... have... it... all. Everything... you've been... looking for. I'm two feet away, close enough to touch him, but that's not all I intend to do. As the swell of his madness continues to erase my soul, eating me inside and out, I feel myself slip further away. Yet the closer I draw to him, the more I pick up a weak voice drowned out in the chaos. I push toward the voice, toward the remains of the brother I'd known.

I love... you... Walter, I whisper, wrapping my arms tightly around him and attempting to still him. The sounds of feral Walt screeching behind me pierces the swirling chaos as the Walter I'd just unanchored squirms in my arms. With the last of my soul's warmth I transmit my memories to this piece of Walter. I give him everything, simultaneously drinking in the venom that has poisoned his soul. I gasp as feral Walt is sucked back, passing through me in the process, and for a moment I feel my grip waning and struggle to keep hold.

The room I'm in feels... unfamiliar. There are parts of it I recognize, but only through the haze of memory. I'm aware that my consciousness is being corrupted, that I'll soon lose myself here.

Your book... everything you put into... In the Arms of... Saturn... it's all true. You've crossed over... but... you're... sick. Come back to us... Walt... come... back... to me.

Walter's soul shudders in my arms, erupting with black power as I do my best to impart every word I can remember from his book. I'll stay with him forever if I have to. I'll spend my sanity giving him all of it.

And so it seems destined. Already I feel like a stranger to myself.

Am I home in my den? What's Walter doing in my house when... didn't he die almost twenty years ago?

I fall backward, plummeting into darkness and hauling Walter with me, our souls screaming together into oblivion.

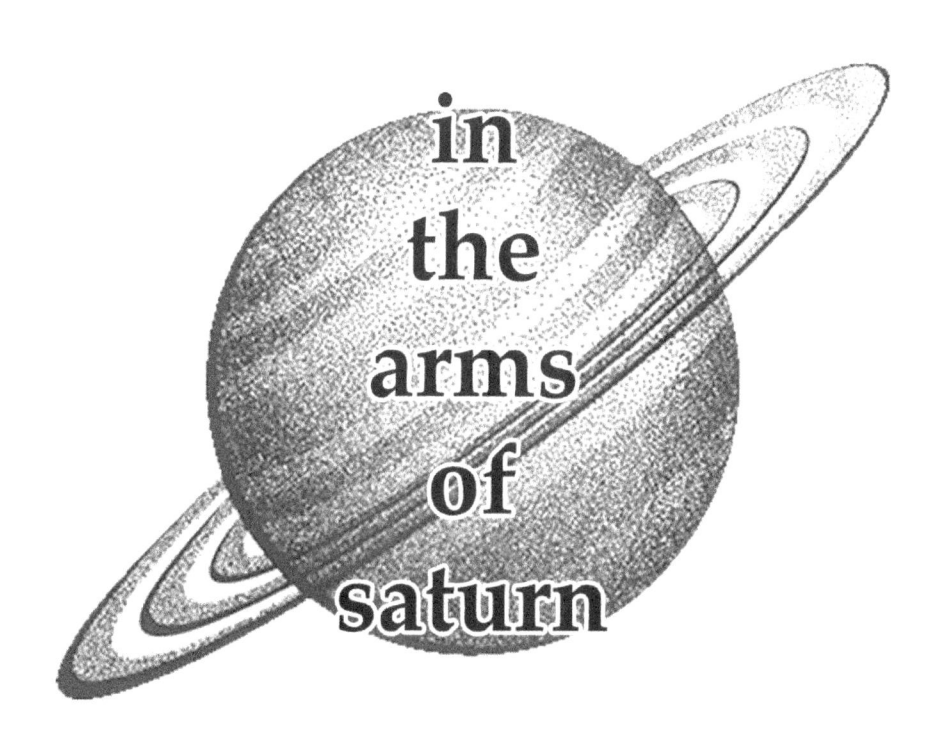

in the arms of saturn

I WAKE FEELING ancient, as though I've been asleep for eons. Before me lay a field of floating rocks and debris, celestial bodies in ceaseless motion, stretching for thousands of miles into the distance and blending in an arresting band of gilded stardust.

I've been here before.

I flail out as my soul rockets upward then across the rings of Saturn. Billowing, lemon-colored clouds churn in the atmosphere before me. Its chaotic whirl reminds me of something recent.

My soul stops at a distance where the bands hugging the planet cannot be discerned for the space rocks comprising them. Stars twinkle in the far reaches of the universe. Sol burns brightly at the center of the solar system.

Hi there, stranger, comes a voice like a sweet melody lulling me back toward sleep. I rotate to find Elora floating before me, looking exactly as she had the night I'd met her at Mrs. Miles's. Slim, athletic, with midnight black hair drifting languidly in the vacuum.

I will myself toward her and we are once more in each other's embrace. Our combined warmth is a bonfire I could tend for eternity.

How long? I ask, not entirely certain what I'm getting at. I close my eyes, pressing my cheek to hers. The attachment we'd shared in our previous life has yet to fade completely. I suspect she hasn't been here long.

Time is ours to conduct, she informs me, though I can feel in her the same lack of understanding I'd suffered to a degree. Too much time asleep, consumed with saving—

Walter. Where's Walter? I push away from her, as much as it pains me to do so, and glance around, expecting him to appear out of the void, but he doesn't come. Clutching at my chest, I reach out across the universe, searching for my brother, prepared to feel that familiar fissure spread.

But it doesn't. The fissure is no longer there.

I turn back to Elora, her soul smiling at me, and I understand suddenly that this goes well beyond her relief to see me awake. She's elated. The break in our chain is healed.

It all comes rushing back, the transition, my confrontation with Walter, my resolve to save his soul.

The last thing I remember is losing consciousness, still holding onto him in his room. I struggle to piece it together, but it seems so… artificial now.

A hand settles on my shoulder. Kelly.

I thought we were going to face him together, Kelly says, her soul grinning. I feel her relief at seeing me conscious and sane.

I had to do it on my own. I had to get to him unfiltered. Again I peer around, searching for my brother, again I work to flex my consciousness across the universe, but Walter isn't anywhere, fragmented or otherwise.

Where is Walter? I ask again.

He is everywhere, Carter speaks from behind me. He slowly drifts around the group, coming face to face with me. Gone is the contemptuous man who'd tried to stop me. What drifts over is a soul mended and at peace, shining like the sun. Every bit of damage has been repaired, every hole filled, every crack patched.

Carter beckons me into a tight embrace. His warmth flows through the chain.

Thank you, Mark, Carter whispers. *Thank you for saving him.*

If I saved him, why isn't he here?

He's returned to God, Shannon says, drifting out of the ether. *He's become one with the universe and allowed another soul to be born.* Shannon joins the contact, and all at once I feel the others here, too, all of us now on this side.

For a moment I'm distracted from the shared euphoria of our contact and struck by an aching sadness at not having said goodbye to Walter.

Even the serenity of knowing my soulmates are all assembled here with me fails to siphon off the loss.

Don't fret, Mark, Jennifer urges. *He is all around us. He is part of God.*

I close my eyes, drinking in the universe around me. My sorrow undiminished, I struggle to pick out a piece of Walter in God's chattering voice.

We'll all be with him in time, Kelly whispers.

When it's our time, Carter says.

I think on this a moment. My soul is relatively young compared with Walt's, but a part of me can remember traveling the highways toward Alexandria on horseback. I see myself walking the ramparts of Jerusalem when it was young. I feel the lives I've claimed by sword and musket and Browning Automatic Rifle.

I've seen centuries of life.

But I've never been one to belabor a good thing; I've never been given to staying very long in one place, and I know I've got what I need to complete this final lesson. That is to say, the keys to my success rest with the souls to which I'm bound.

When it's our time, I whisper. I open my eyes, seeking Elora out in the group, gaze already on me. She knows. After all the lives we've shared, all the times we've died and returned and found each other again, she knows what I intend to do.

We'll all come with you, Mark, Carter says, drifting toward me and laying a hand on my shoulder. I turn to him with a shining soul.

I know you wanted to go back with Walt, to help him through, I say. *I'll not make the same mistake he did. Join me if you wish, but there is only one of you I absolutely need with me.*

All eyes fall on Elora as she drifts over. Warmth floods the chain and for a moment we remain together, basking in it.

I think I'll pop up eventually as one of your children, Kelly says after some time. She hovers against the face of Saturn. I reach out and take her hand, the warmth of our souls exchanged. Elora floats off, giving us time together.

Kelly smiles, *We'll always have U-N-H, huh?*

We will. Thank you for everything, I say, drifting backward and releasing her hand as Mallory floats toward me next.

As Kelly goes, she tosses me a wink. *You're talking like you'll never see me again. You'll be changing my diapers in no time.*

Mallory chuckles as she floats past Kelly, closing the rest of the gap between the two of us.

I don't know if we've ever shared a life before, Mallory whispers, wrapping her arms around me. Mine encircle the small of her back. *I know it wasn't everything it should have been, but it definitely wasn't bad.*

No, I agree, resting my head against hers. Our eyes meet, inches apart. *I'm glad we had each other. If it weren't for you I would have lost myself after Walt's death. Perhaps taken my own life.*

Then we were good for each other after all. Her soul smiles, its fire burning into me.

We were.

Mallory and I drift apart only enough for the others to crowd back in. We come together, arm in arm, soul to soul, and bask in the strength of the chain for the last time. When we're done, I open my eyes to find Elora before me. Even on this side, when things like love are rendered inconsequential, the bond we share is unwavering.

The others release us, and Elora and I drift toward the planet. They stay watching us a moment before vanishing into the ether, silently wishing us luck. There is no sadness, no sorrow, no loss or regret. There is only joy, only love.

We'll all be together in the next life anyway.

I take Elora's hands and draw her to me.

Walter didn't want Carter to come back with him. He wanted to make it through on his own. I don't want that. I can't do it without you.

I'll be with you every step of the way, Elora says, her love flowing into me like a steady river draining into the ocean. *You can help me, too.*

You don't have to do this just for me. I—

No, we've had our time, millennia together on both sides, she says. *I'm ready to go back with you one last time, one last stop on the road to God... to Walter. It's time to Transcend.* She rests her head on my chest, and I lay mine upon hers. We float together in silence, motes of stardust against the tempestuous face of Mother Saturn.

In our final moments on this side we reach out together to Walter, letting him know we'll be with him soon. Time is relative anyway.

The break in our chain is repaired and our group is free to move along as it always has. As it always will. And speaking for all of us, I'm pretty excited to meet the new member of our group, already born on Earth… perhaps Mars.

Our mutual attention stays fixed upon Saturn as we commit to our decision.

Forever, I whisper to her.

Forever, she whispers back.

Here we come, Walt.

Acknowledgements

There are always too many people to thank, but I'm going to give this a shot and apologize if I miss anyone. Five years is a long time.

Sam Dunbar was the first editor this book had. Saturn has taken vastly different form since you read it half a decade ago, Sam. That's not to say your contributions aren't still in there.

To the people who read Saturn for content feedback, this book wouldn't be whole without you. Thank you so much Abby Bozeman, Ginny Estes, Kristen Gustavsen, Erin Sullivan, Melanie Tromblee, Vickie Wacek, Lindsay Warner, and Terri Yankus.

To my daughter Evy: baby, you were the only force capable of drawing me out of this edit. You kept me from overworking, and in-turn from overthinking everything. I'll never think about this book without hearing your tiny voice barking orders for me to dance for your pleasure or join you on the floor to color. As always, I love you with all I've got.

In the Arms of Saturn really forced me to consider all sides of life and loss, but nothing could prepare me for the loss of the greatest mentor I've ever had in 2019. Brenda Lewis was my Language Arts and homeroom teacher in 7th and 8th grade Junior High, and I can't overemphasize the role she played in my life. She was the last of the old-schoolers at York who taught grammar through diagraming sentences, which is a tragedy in itself. Brenda will always be the greatest contributing factor to my art because she took an interest in me. She saw that I enjoyed reading and encouraged me to read like my life depended on it, eventually discovering that my love for great stories and the artful arrangement of words went beyond just reading. She saw in me a force that could *create,* and she nurtured it aggressively. One of my life's greatest regrets is not having reconnected with her before she left us.

She and I were kindred. And for the record, she did *not* eat chalk.

Big thanks go as always to those who've contributed to this book without realizing it. Good or bad, these are the people who've left their marks on me and in doing so left their marks on my book. In no particular order: Sheila Yorke, Lisa & Michael Yorke, Amy Wheeler, Raney Tromblee, Morgan Tromblee, Erin Marquis, Kay Eden, Ryan & Josie Wilford, Carter, Isla, and Georgie Wilford, Cecelia and Melanie Sullivan, Tim Sullivan, Zachary & Melanie Strout, Gary Rooney, Lorri Gagnon, Cindy Chase, Jim Smith, Annette Goldberg, Dina Wilford, Cedric Wilford, Liz Widmer, Shawn & Jill Cola, Dylan & Asher Wilford, the Cummings family, the folks at Area Home Care, Jock and Bly at Two Son's, and everyone at Red Door Title.

Oh, and Stephen King. Can't forget the Master.

-MW
(February – December, 2015)
(August – November, 2020)

Bands Discovered During This Edit

Balance and Composure
Circa Survive
Citizen
Cults
Dead Poet Society
DIIV
DVSR
Good Tiger
High Wire
Hopesfall
Lift After Youth
Moon Fever
Norma Jean
Nothing
Paerish
Saosin
Secondhand Sound
Teenage Wrist
The Blue Stones
The Story So Far
Turnover
VUKOVI
Wallflower
Wilmette

About the Author

Michael Wilford lives in Ogunquit, Maine with his daughter Evy, dog Spock, and cat Commander Black. He enjoys reading, collecting vinyl, sourcing out exotic teas, and clearing his head with long walks.

Michael is the author of three books under the pen name Earl Yorke. *In the Arms of Saturn* is his debut novel… as himself.

For more info and free stories, please visit:

theothermichaelwilford.com
earlyorke.com